REPORT
OF LONELINESS

by
Augustin Buzura

Translated from the Romanian by

Ramona Mitrică, Mike Phillips and Mihai Rîşnoveanu

PROFUSION GOLD

Profusion, London 2016

PROFUSION GOLD SERIES
Stelian Ţurlea - *Greuceanu – Novel with a Policeman* (novel)
Liviu Antonesei - *The Innocent and Collateral Victims of a Bloody War with Russia* (short stories)
Augustin Buzura - *Report on the State of Loneliness* (novel)

Series Editor: Mike Phillips
Published by Profusion International Creative Consultancy
mail@profusion.org.uk • www.profusion.org.uk

Report on the State of Loneliness by Augustin Buzura
Published originally in Romanian as
Raport despre starea singurătăţii
Polirom, 2009

Cover and typesetting by SGS Creative. Cover photo by Laura Lazăr

ISBN-13: 978-0956867643; ISBN-10: 0956867642

Augustin Buzura

REPORT ON THE STATE
OF LONELINESS

Introduction

Augustin Buzura was born on the 22nd September 1938, in Berința, Maramureș County, Romania, and studied General Medicine in Cluj, specialising in psychiatry. In 1963 he published his debut collection of stories *Capul Bunei Speranțe* (Cape of Good Hope) in Bucharest, and in the following year he gave up practising as a doctor and joined *Tribuna* magazine as an editorial assistant. Since then he has established a huge body of work starting with another collection of stories in 1967, *De ce zboară vulturul?* (Why Does the Eagle Fly?), and followed by several novels confronting government censorship, *Absenții* (The Absentees, 1970), *Fețele tăcerii* (The Faces of Silence, 1974), *Orgolii* (Pride, 1977), *Vocile nopții* (Voices of the Night, 1980), *Refugii* (Refuges, 1984) and *Drumul cenușii* (The Road of Ashes, 1988).

These novels cemented Buzura's fame, as a major dissident figure both in Romania and abroad. At the same time he was subject to official suspicion and harassment, which took considerable ingenuity to survive. As each new book approached publication, for instance, he had to undergo strict revisions and lengthy interviews with his censors. On the other hand, uncensored samizdat copies of the forthcoming publication circulated freely around the universities.

The end of the dictatorship in 1989 offered new opportunities. Buzura joined the inter-European Gulliver cultural seminar which also included Gunter Grass and

Vaclav Havel, and became a hugely influential essayist and literary journalist. In this role he toured a number of international venues, culminating in a huge festival and exhibition, mounted with the Smithsonian, in Washington DC. During this period he wrote for almost all the literary magazines published in Romania, as well as being the founder of several publications established under the aegis of the Romanian Cultural Foundation, an organisation he led as president until 2003. At that point he became the President of the renamed Romanian Cultural Institute until January 2005. In the same year, he re-launched the magazine *Cultura* (Culture), which he leads as editor-in-chief and editorialist.

1999 saw the publication of *Recviem pentru nebuni şi bestii* (Requiem for fools and beasts, 1999), a novel of Romania in transition out of the regime. Now free of the traditional constraints, Buzura took the opportunity to launch a stinging satire against political corruption and moral decay. In a recent interview he summarised the views which informed the novel.

Unfortunately, only people whose days are not numbered can live in Romania, and we are all at the mercy of the Almighty. Numerous, too, are the sufferings of culture. And when we talk about culture, politicians do everything in their power to reform it, which means to minimise it. Obviously, all this happens with the support of prominent intellectuals. You cannot have great expectations from a people who are not physically, morally and intellectually healthy. The hungry cannot defend democracy and freedom. Romania is a humiliated country, and three quarters of its inhabitants are reduced to the condition of being subhuman. Our great national problems have become what do we eat today, what will we wear from day to day, how will we pay our bills.

Buzura's latest novel, *Raport asupra singurătății* (Report on the State of Loneliness, 2009), explores the Romanian landscape over more than 70 years, subtly locating the history of a myriad of individuals and events within their broader European context. The novel purports to be the diary of Dr Cassian, an aging and retired professional, who has withdrawn from his life in the city, next to his son, and fled to a cabin in the mountains. Once there, he encounters the daughter of a former love, and inspired by her presence, he reflects on his former life, which stretches through the tragedies of the 2nd World War, the brutalities and absurdity of the Romanian dictatorship, and concludes with the corruption and moral complexities of its aftermath.

Report elaborates on the themes Buzura tackles in previous novels, and extends them into a bewildering and uneasy terrain, where Death is a hostile and unpredictable character, waiting around every corner, and also the inevitable conclusion of every narrative. Simultaneously, Dr Cassian's contemplation of the natural world and its wonders offers a spiritual logic to the tragic march of life into oblivion, and this spirituality furnishes the antidote to despair.

Here, absolutely everything has importance: small, red ants about whom I don't know how they manage to sneak in under the window or through various cracks which are impossible to cover, and the fine, brown dust that settles step by step on everything I don't touch, and the abundant, untameable grass that throbs from between the wooden beams of the cabin or among the stones of the foundations, and the small or violent clouds, and the mist that appears and disappears especially early in the morning. Then, the pine trees and the birds, diurnal or nocturnal, the sun, the stars and everything that I feel but only see with the eyes of the mind. I have the strange feeling I depend on them and that, in their turn, each one belongs to me, becoming an essential component of my being. The light and shadows are changing unceasingly, the same for the taste and temperature of the air. It is a continual, liberating movement, which integrates me and helps me, at the same time as them, to become equally heaven and earth, to pulsate together with the universe, to feel accomplished and, for a moment, immortal, invincible, stronger than the death I ignore although, in any moment, it can annul my senses and the illusion that I have managed to surpass my limits. As so many times before, the soul which has escaped control is looking for something outside words, it knocks with fury and despair on a massive gate that refuses to open. I am here and I am there, especially there, still undefeated. I have the certitude that beyond the gate lay the salvation, the miracle, the un-fated mystery of the words; that something which attracts me and repels me with equal strength, the source of despair and nostalgia. I wish with all my might to stay there forever, in the same place: a beggar at the gates of eternity... Me – who?

This is a framework rooted in the spirit of Orthodox theology, where the elements of Life and Death in an individual's experience are opposed and at the same time united. The narrator's diary, therefore, ranges through a century of history in Central Europe, recording the turmoil visited on individuals in the region, while painstakingly placing them inside the context of their times.

Ironically, one element of the writing which stands out is Buzura's wry humour. His description of a Ceauşescu outing in the country has a deadpan tone which recalls the flavour of his confrontations with the censors of the dictatorship.

The hunt was a great success, said the first secretary, but each person who was engaged in organising it had an opinion which they confessed later on, in a whisper, to their families and close friends. The village midwife, whose husband was the chief of the Militia station, told me that once the Comrade had left, many arrests were made, since not everything worked as it should have. The people responsible for the pheasants had gotten dead drunk and, instead of the birds, they threw from the ditches, into the crosshairs of the Comrade's gun, a load of rabbits – something which had the effect of confusing him. Of course, he had noticed himself that something was not right, but since the animals jumped two or three metres away from the ditch straight into the gun sights, he did not hold back from shooting vigorously towards the bush from which the rabbits were flying. The pheasants, also located in the same ditches, had started running to the valley, as the guards had forgotten the direction in which they had to be thrown. The Comrade heard the noises made by the birds, but he did not understand why none of them came into the crosshairs of his gun, while instead of the noises characteristic of the hunt, people had started singing – a gesture which was interpreted to him as an expression of the great joy of having him in their midst, after preparing to receive him for such a long time. The hunt was almost compromised because of the wild boars and bears which, since they were given everything necessary in their cages, had become lazy and no longer wanted to leave them. Even more, since they had waited for the presidential bullet for a long time, they had grown accustomed to people and gave no sign that the agitation of the beaters scared them very much.

Report marks a concluding moment in Buzura's great series of novels about the Central European social and political landscape. He explores, without reserve, over more than 70 years, its clashes of nationalisms, its cruelty and militaristic savagery, its loves and romantic fantasies, its peasant transformations, its desperate longing for European significance, and much, much more. All this is seen through the eyes of individuals, naïve and sophisticated, ignorant and learned, spiritually pure and downright evil. In the end, Buzura delivers his own credo.

I am leaving, but one thing is repugnant to me: the pity of others. On the other hand, Mr Executioner, things have been and will always be the way you wanted, I know this. I am ready, but until that time, until that moment, you have no power over me. You cannot stop me from rebelling, from loving and detesting, from believing stubbornly that, by dying, I will discover something which I never managed to discover while I was alive.

Mike Phillips

Everything is hard,
Time and walking.
Starting is hard,
And so is stopping.
Dust, spirit
Even the air on your shoulders
Is hard
But the hardest and the worst
Will be the end of the road.
(Lucian Blaga – *The little she-cricket*)

I arrived all right. Full stop. *I have everything I need for a while.* Full stop. *I love you very much.* Full stop. *That's precisely why I left.* Full stop. *Don't look for me. I'll come on my own.* Full stop. *Dr Cassian Robert.*

This would have been, more or less, the content of a telegram, if I'd had somewhere from which to send one; and everything I wrote is true, except for the story of my return. I didn't leave with that intention and, as long as I am lucid and in command, *I won't return home.* At least this is what I believe at this moment. Unfortunately, having arrived here, at the spot where I intended, in the mountains, at my chalet about whose existence my family has no idea, I don't feel happy, as I had hoped, because a strange feeling of anxiety and loneliness overwhelms me. I left because I couldn't stand anymore the humiliation of being taken care of, understood, and tolerated with all my infirmities. My family's unnatural benevolence was damaging me. I had hoped that, liberated from the pity and protection of my own (family), my body would muster up all its strength or... but I can't yet name

11

the feeling that I fear. Senile meandering, my son Dan, accustomed to seeing everything through the psychiatrist's lens, would call it, because he hasn't yet reached the point of having such fears, or maybe his fears are not *yet* so intense. *Not yet*. Theoretically, he still has enough time before he discovers that everything hurts, that this kind of pain can't even be alleviated. At least this is what I imagine. This pain is the pain of not being able to resign yourself, of being incapable of accepting your weaknesses, of experiencing the defeat of not knowing what you will be when you no longer exist.

I close my eyes and it's as if I see the time that has been given to me. I lived my whole life together with Dan, a life ruled by haste, duty, misery, theft – because, in fact, I had to steal what in a normal world would have been my right – and unfortunately we never had the time to talk. I had hoped that later on it would be better, that we would be more relaxed... but it wasn't to be. Now that all this is behind us, I still find myself compelled to search for answers to some of the thousands of questions tormenting me. It would be, otherwise, as if I hadn't lived at all. Convinced that I should always have them in sight, I told myself that I should get these answers down on paper. Unfortunately, though, in those times when I stubbornly believed that writing was the best solution for me, the only serious one, I had no clue that I was in for torture.

So now I cannot run, delay or lie anymore, I cannot use any more excuses: *I must write*. Of course I do not know what will happen. But do we know for real the true course of past events? What is worth remembering and what not?

But this is not a question that I should ask myself yet. I will write in any case. It is an order of my whole being, of everything I am, a decision that can't be contested or doubted. That feeling of pointlessness, so far hiding behind every gesture, has left me as well, so there is no going back. Now, when time, too patient with me so far, could stop at any point, with no warning, I will write what I believe and feel. Therefore, just the desk, the paper, the pen, the heavy silence of the surrounding mountains, and my poor being, left to fight its fears, the absurdity and the isolation. This is another kind of loneliness, completely different from the one for which I had been searching obstinately; a loneliness or a brutal beauty reminding me every second about death.

I still haven't necessarily figured out what I shall be writing about and, especially, for whom. My experiences have transformed themselves into emotions, into a habit of being and of thinking. I know well that I don't have enough words for them and, after all, who would be interested? I loved, I hated, I won, but mainly I lost, like any other human being. The world of today forces me into unusual events and requires a different kind of sensibility from me.

Finally, I feel with all my being that everything is pointless, but I encourage myself that now at least I am living my own pointlessness. Here there are no others: just the clouds, the unending darkness, the wild beasts and the wind.

Of course, this need to write is not new – I have tried many times to pin myself down to the desk – but in the past I could still postpone it. I would always find new reasons to postpone writing and absolutely all of them were plausible. Sometimes I didn't like the pens and the ink. I needed a certain black – strong, even violent. The blue seemed too mild for the intense emotions of the moment; and, when I had found the black I dreamed of, the paper of the copybooks seemed too thin or too yellowish. Speaking about yellow – I never liked it. When, finally, I had everything I had imagined, I would sit down at the desk and, at the first attempt, I looked idiotically solemn, as if entering a role that didn't suit me. As I expected, that ended in another postponement. At other times, I felt exasperatingly hungry – a pathological hunger, unbearable, which could not be satisfied in any way. When I was running out of all these thin pretexts, Nature itself came in to help: too hot, too cold, very humid, before the rain, after the rain. This time, though, only a catastrophe might be able to save me, a thunderbolt, a war, a meteorite fallen especially for me, or *her – the one* I can't get used to, *the one* I run away from all the time, ineffectually, because I sense *her* everywhere, especially during the night, when lucidity no longer helps me, and I become a fragile construction, dominated by terrors and darkness, another being – *something else* or *somebody else* – who everything is against.

Sometimes, out of the blue, or triggered by a dream I cannot remember, a dreadful state of panic invades me. Everything seems to end in that very moment and, confused, I don't know what to do anymore; to run, to take a pill, to have a drink or to freeze, hoping that *She, The Inevitable*, could give me one more chance, a delay, not to discover answers, but to continue torturing myself with questions.

Of course, I know that everything is just a devastating road to death. Worlds disappear, stars, universes die, and many times – thinking that it would help – I would try to imagine all these amazing catastrophes. They would always remain at a distance from me, though. No emotions came with them, and they would impress me less than contemplating my own old and desiccated hands, like dry soil heavy with clay, on which drought had left endless ditches and brown stains. In fact, it is more and more clear to me that death, like a desert, advances from outside towards the inside, and, soon after, it joins with the opposite other, the older and more and more aggressive death expanding out of my soul.

The terrestrial death is a spiritual death, a Greek savant says, and the true death is a celestial rebirth. This wretched body is only a prison, an absurd struggle conducted while we search and wait for the light. I am, therefore, just on this side of liberation but I am afraid. I don't want, I am not able to want, I don't feel strong or intelligent enough to want, precisely what I've been desiring most of all: light, liberation from every constraint. I believe, but I am afraid of what I believe. I wait, and I am awfully afraid. Terrible state: between animal and angel. You try to run from one, and you are afraid of the other. Here, between heaven and earth, between night and light. God, what use is everything I know to me, if I am so terrified?

I write feverishly everything that passes through my mind, not knowing why I do it, or where this unrestrained impulse comes from. I write, although it is clear to me that I cannot stop the desert advancing rapidly, irreversibly. Oddly enough, as the number of the words written on the paper increases, I delude myself that I am less lonely and not so afraid. I still *am*. Still alive. If this is what I feel I am, it is what I involuntarily put into each word. I am alive, I am conscious, meaning that I know what I am and what I have been, and if, against all the odds, I should reach the point when I had nothing more to say, I would still write, thousands and thousands of times: *I am alive!* And this especially during the night, when the dimensions of all the monsters, inside and outside of me, are expanding, and when Death – a suffocating presence – shows me the real measure of my being. On rare occasions, I have the sensation that I can spot a light: a kind of answer to a complicated question which I cannot yet express. I live it, but I can't manage yet to formulate it, and this interior pain, the mix of panic and hope, of faith and doubt, fades away. I buoy myself up with the thought that if I can't express it, at least I have the chance to feel it, and in the end I realize that the only things left for me – meaning: for me *also* – are questions without an answer …and Death.

I close my eyes for a second. I have treated tens of thousands of people, I have stolen another few thousands from Death. So I've been always meeting her, especially in the mountains, but, even if, to my left and right, the bullets were taking lives, I wasn't afraid. I behaved as if the danger had nothing to do with me. I didn't feel that it was about me. And for many years it wasn't. She ignored me, more than she did others, so that I should be resigned, serene, understanding that *the time has come*, that there is no salvation. But I am not peaceful. I haven't had enough of life – as ridiculous as it is – with all its limitations and shortcomings. Sometimes I want to fall on my knees to ask for the sentence to be postponed, and, in fact, there is no doubt in my mind that this is why I write.

Little by little, with infinite patience, with no noise, and without my family knowing it, I built myself a hut – here on the top of the mountain, in the neighbourhood of the old Meteo Station. It was abandoned many years before by the Institute, but not by the person who serviced it from the moment of its establishment, the meteorologist Gheorghe Toma.

He and his daughter, Mara, became, in reality, the masters of the mountain and a kind of archive of the place. During my long periods of absence, the hut was in their care, especially Mara's. She often stayed overnight as well, not because it would have been too difficult for her to return to the Station, but because she liked to stay here, among the books, and spend her vacation quietly - as she used to say jokingly, in those days when she was allowing more than two phrases to come out of her mouth.

I had insisted on building my hut far from the world and far from the tourist routes, near the only peak, over which three alpinists had apparently managed to climb, long ago. Their accounts, when they came back, or to put it more accurately, their scared silence, along with their refusal to give details, only managed to amplify the mystery of this steep slope, baptized *The Margin of Life* by those who tried to confront it. On some maps, under the number marking its height – 1903 metres – its real name is noted – *The Saint's Stone*. The legend says that, long ago, when Saint Peter left the Paradise Gate and came to earth, disguised as a sick, old beggar, to test people's goodness and faith, he made a first stop here on this peak. That means that only one step separates Paradise from this mountain top; that is if, against all the odds, one should manage to conquer its obstacles. Others believe the mountain top is also the entry gate to a parallel world, or even to Shambhala.[1] For most though, this peak remains only a mysterious story, preserved in people's memory because of some real tragedies. In time, the myth of Saint Peter has been replaced by occurrences with devils, extraterrestrial creatures, flying saucers and little green men.

---

1 The birth place of Kalki, the final incarnation of Vishnu who will usher in a new Golden Age, Shambhala gradually came to be seen as a Buddhist Pure Land, a fabulous kingdom whose reality is visionary or spiritual as much as physical or geographic.

That is why the Saint's Stone, or *The Margin of Life*, as it has been called lately, became such a terrifying story that no one dares to brave it. Its height no longer provokes any alpinist. The most it can do, maybe, is make an amateur smile.

My attempts, in fact two lamentable failures, convinced me that *The Margin of Life* was difficult, or, perhaps, even impossible to conquer. To me, at least, it seemed like a live being, huge and merciless, who reacts against you from the first moment. Strange winds, violent enough to provoke avalanches of stone, hot air waves, as if you were on the slope of an active volcano, frozen watches, unusable batteries and compasses, monsters given shape by smoke and fog, deceiving lights. Then the terrible sensation of being rejected, along with the resulting panic, forces you to run, to find yourself as far as possible from this almost indescribable nightmare. What is strange is that you don't have the time to think – to stop and see what happens after you have made the first step... and the second; or time to assess how the rock reacts after you have fixed several pitons into it. Instead, you suddenly enter a nightmare which swallows you and dictates your movements. In the end you are left with nothing concrete. You find it impossible to describe with any precision what drove you away. Time disappears, so does the ability to control yourself, and it takes a long time to gain relief from the horror, as well as from your feeling of being liberated when you walk away from the slope. The moment you enter the space you become different, you no longer belong to yourself, you become a slave of inertia, of fear, and of all the stories about the mountain, which once again come alive in your mind and subdue your will. Later on I realised that I had walked, without willing it, in the shoes of those who had spoken to me about the mountain or who had previously failed to make the climb.

In other words I started my climb prepared to lose, rather than to win. I started to build my cabin here, near the peak, only when I discovered, or to put it better, when I felt, that I was left with only enough time for impossible projects, I desired to see it all the time, day and night, during all the seasons that I would still be granted. I intended to feel it, to smell it, to explore all its changes, convinced that one day I would make a new attempt, in spite of my age and in spite of how much more I had found about the mountain. Of course, this peak is not my only failure; and not even the most painful one, if I compare it with everything back there in my past. I should file it under the label 'failures without importance', because it's the most insignificant failure from what is called life. *My life.* I want to climb *The Margin of Life* specifically because, at my age, the attempt seems even more impossible than logic allows one to accept. But I persevere in thinking that, in the end, I will finally get one victory. Because life cannot be repeated. In any case, I can be found somewhere on the way, or even there, up there, where I shall remain in waiting until a saint arrives. Any one of them. Maybe he will liberate me from a few obsessions. Why so many failures? Why so much loneliness? And especially why, in our part of the world, is it our fate to live in pain, fear and humiliation?

I don't really have anyone with whom to exchange words. A long time ago, aware that all words had been emptied of meaning, falsified, or altered, I resorted to just nodding, answering with words of one syllable or limiting myself to gestures. This was not rebellious, nor infantile, but a defence reaction against the wave of lies which had begun to cover everything like a tide coming in. Here I can talk to myself, I can tell lies or fundamental truths, I can laugh or cry. It doesn't matter, nobody listens to me. Everything around me, the thick beech forest nearby, the grass, the birds, the wild animals, the sky and, sometimes, the clouds speak another language, which I try my best to understand. For my own language I am left with writing, a rather difficult matter, to which I sincerely regret committing myself, because I don't know, or maybe there aren't any useful words to describe what I would like to tell you. That is why, instead of freeing myself, as I had hoped, I find myself burdened, with each phrase, by an increasing dissatisfaction. By the way, this last sentence made me laugh. What would I do if I weren't writing?

Here, where time flows differently, where days and nights seem endless, I feel as if I'm on foreign ground, which is often like being in an unknown country which I will never leave – a rough country, merciless and sublime, whose customs I am forced to learn if I really want to live. A country which I have passed through thousands and thousands of times, but which I started to know only after I had settled in it, that is, after I had abandoned *the other* life.

My family remained at home or, to be more precise, in the city, because only Dan Robert, my son, could be at home, together with Claudia, his naughty and capricious girlfriend, as unpredictable as she is beautiful. If they'd buried the hatchet, that is. Radu Robert, my grandson, and his fiancée Laura Tomescu, live in a modest block in the opposite part of the city. Poor but independent, as they wished.

I left – or, to use a more accurate term, I ran – from home, although it would have been sensible to remain somewhere close by a hospital, given the fact that at my age all infirmities show their fangs. But, I repeat, it was impossible not to. I could no longer stand their pity and goodwill. They agreed with me even in the most eccentric of situations, events which I often created in order to check the accuracy of my view. No one contradicted me, all of them showed me an understanding which was more humiliating than the illness itself. I was not their equal anymore, but an obstacle. I belonged to a world that had vanished together with my few friends, but I wasn't ready for death. I wasn't calling for her even in the moments of desperate loneliness. I still dared to put together projects, I still wanted to fight, in spite of the other inside me, watching everything with an irony that was infinite. You want to do this only now? Only now have you got the will to fight? When your time is behind you? Don't you think that death forgot you! She doesn't forget anyone. She only laughs at those who once dared to confront her. She is waiting to be begged, wished, courted. She wants to humiliate you in every way possible.

Of course I belong to the past, a past in which I didn't fit, a past I detested with my whole being. Unfortunately it was my fate to live in a world where I was forced to steal, as I said before, my peace, love, and food. I even had to steal in order to defend my right to work. As a consequence, it would be logical for me to wish for a world of absolute certainties, instead of the one with which I never bonded. Logic would dictate my getting used to the thought that there is no forgiveness, no postponing, no miracles. On the other hand, in spite of rationality, and in spite of the feeling that she, Death, or the future world, or the next phase of our travel towards something else, is close, I still feel a terrible revolt in each and every cell of my whole body, a

21

violent insurrection against everything that reason tells me will happen. And this is where the madness begins. In spite of all the signs of decline, of age, of how very few joys are reserved for me, I can't limit myself to what it is permitted. I feel the need to live normally, as if I didn't know my age, my strengths, or how many steps are left to me. I am writing and shouting: *I am not afraid of death, I am not afraid, I am not afraid,* writing and shouting, but, as I hear my voice, it is more and more clear to me that I am lying. I am afraid, a terrible fear that cannot be metamorphosed into courage, or not even into indifference. In fact, it is not indifference that I wish for, but the strength to look everything in the face, openly, no matter how hard it would be to endure, in the hope that I would manage to understand something about the destiny through which I lived.

For the time being I have no other solution than to split my day into small matters, that is, as much as possible, getting to know and making peace, with everything that surrounds me, even these humiliating white pages. But there are also the nights which, in the foreseeable future, don't promise peace. Sometimes I am tense, listening to the wind, to the noise of logs on the fire, and I expect to hear voices, incomprehensible calls or, even more bizarrely, cries for help. And, the more I focus, the more the feeling of anticipation increases, and my imagination invents monsters, enemies from which only the daylight saves me. In the few moments when I manage to fall asleep, I am haunted only by dreams that I wouldn't have been pleased to confront even in my youth. The anxieties and fears which torture me during the day become some of the most unexpected images during the night. I travel through unknown spaces, weird, with no trace of life, tormented desert landscapes, charged with the feeling of unpredictable, terrible danger. I collapse into deep wells, tight, with no prospect of escaping, and I cross fragile little bridges, improvised over huge and agitated waters; but, in particular, I fall into these deep, nasty holes. In dreams I fall, an endless fall into nausea and suffocating night, which seems concrete and material, even though, in reality, I have tested my forces, during my whole life, against the heights of the most stubborn mountains.

I have no doubt that the cruel terror of these collapses, and of the living darkness, are concessions made to me by the final night, whose real name I shall try, as much as possible, to avoid. Or they signify worlds, spaces in which *I have been* once, in who knows what existence. *Someone* wishes to open my carapace towards other worlds, to assure me that this world, the one in which I am now, is the most beautiful of all. Here, between earth and sky, between death and life, I must discover the courage to live, as if I didn't know that I have no time left.

It would be absurd to fill in the days I have left with death, a topic that tires me terribly. I left home specifically because the care of my family, and their humiliating concessions reminded me of this sad and inevitable sunset, which, no matter how much I want to, I still don't have the strength to accept. Here, I have the certainty that I have gained more time; that it flows differently, slowly, sleepy, indifferently, adapting itself to my rhythms. Only *Her* perfidious shadow disturbs its calm.

The truth is that, once I arrived here – permanently relocated? – my first surprise was in connection with time. Had I entered somehow into another dimension, whose characteristic seemed to be its slowness? Paradoxically, time had become very generous with me, and my senses, up till then tired, numb, had suffered an unexpected transformation. They were now more and more alive. Although I had been here a thousand times before and had arranged with my own hand each object around the place, I had the certainty that only now was I discovering them as they were in reality, and, more than that, only here did I find myself facing the most disturbing of all questions: have I really come for good? Of course my decision was not a spontaneous one – the fruit of fury, of momentary unhappiness. It wasn't, either, a consequence of the need for novelty, for something else. Instead it was a conclusion towards which I had been pushed by every event, small or big, by the gestures of those surrounding me, seen or presumed, by the whole atmosphere in which I was living; and not least by the fact that I couldn't stand myself the way I was, a kind of a small flame, which could have been extinguished by the most insignificant puff of wind, a flicker that everyone was trying to protect, not because they believed in its usefulness, but from a natural and Christian pity.

I have gone to the mountains, I wrote in a note for them, which I am not too convinced they found – *do not worry, I am feeling well and I have all I need*. This was followed by a couple of words of love, which I knew would not calm or conciliate them.

'Where should I look for him?', Dan would ask himself, very irritated. 'In the end, some policeman will bring him home, since no one can get lost in this country, in spite of the general confusion. Old age and its problems!' – he will conclude afterwards, and, in fact, this could be a small element of the truth. The smallest one, though. In reality, all I know is that it hurts, that I am frightened and that I don't understand much. I always had the impression that I am a precise thinker, that I do nothing by chance, but, analysing the facts *afterwards*, I discover that something was missing from my calculations, that I had made a terrible mistake when I tried to cast myself in the role of fate.

This confusion, with all its recent nuances, began to terrorise me immediately after I was left alone in the cottage. The owner of the donkey who transported all I needed, Vasile Dogaru, was a former woodsman, who had also remained in the area after retirement. He took the money hastily, brought me the usual fresh water, looked around with attention to make sure that everything was in order, and explained to me his reason for being in a hurry – the wolves and the bears which are more numerous than ever. Then, before departing, he said, more to himself than otherwise: 'This is not a cottage for an old and lonely man. How would he manage? What would he do here, in the back of beyond with no help? I'll have to come by all the time. Probably we won't die at the same time and one of us will have to dig the grave for the other. Maybe he fell out with his son, with his grandchildren, with the world, maybe this is why he was in a hurry to come to the mountains where...'

Where what? I didn't have an answer so I preferred to leave him with the impression that I hadn't heard. I followed him though, until he disappeared beyond the rocks to the right of the cottage. There it was, I said to myself, a man who has managed to save himself. When I met him, he was a drunkard without rival. He turned a blind eye to those stealing wood, and they paid him, sometimes with money, but invariably with alcohol. 'I drink because I am afraid of being caught. And I don't need so much *țuică*,[2] I have to get rid of it somehow.' His wife, a drunkard too, on the same

2 Brandy

scale, also had an unassailable explanation: 'I drink because of Vasile, since I can't stand seeing him drunk all the time.'

I met him again after a while, a rather long while it's true. His wife had been killed by a tree, which was knocked down by a storm that appeared out of nowhere, and his memory of those times seemed to have been obscured by alcohol. 'Since the democracy everyone steals as much as possible, so who is to fear a poor woodsman! I have to pay them not to kill me. Now I steal along with them, since the pension is not enough even for bread.' A couple of goats and the donkey helped him survive. We'd known each other for a long time but our conversations were reduced mainly to the weather, wild animals and the donkey's stubbornness.

I didn't like his sudden departure. I was indeed left alone, terribly alone. Is this actually what I wanted? This was one question of whose answer I was no longer all that sure. The anxiety, which gradually took control of me, didn't diminish, not even when I tried specifically to take the essential arguments into consideration. This was what I had wished for, the running away, or, speaking euphemistically, the departure from home. It was not a spontaneous gesture, the result of a passing rage, but a decision made after long deliberation. I wanted to give my son the freedom to clarify his relationship, so curious, with Claudia, who he didn't have the courage to marry, but who he didn't have the strength to leave either, content with this childish display of a strange relationship. Dan often seemed determined to convince his friends that, in fact, it wasn't he who needed a real woman to awaken all his senses, but it was I, the old, helpless, fastidious man who couldn't deny himself some support, even discreet supervision. Unfortunately I didn't tell him what I thought either, or how things looked from my side. Although it was my duty to do so, I limited myself to leaving them with the impression that I had come round to believing exactly what they wanted me to believe, although I was conscious that the charade couldn't last for too long.

Claudia didn't seem the right woman for Dan, or for an extremely busy man. She was beautiful, but also very emotionally unstable. She seemed to be hiding something, to be haunted by an unpleasant memory, by a deed of which she was ashamed. Unaccustomed to meditate over her own errors, she gave everyone the impression that someone else was to blame. Other people had dragged her into various difficulties: her, the weak woman, helpless, always taken by surprise. For the time being, her beauty was a cover for her shortcomings, and acted as a substitute for her real personality. Consequently, Dan was ready to forgive all her errors, which, even I, without wanting to, discovered easily. Her main preoccupation was her own body, looking good, maintaining her physical condition, her tan, and her current relationship, a relationship that saved her from financial problems, and, of course, conferred respectability. This meant that she didn't get involved anyhow and with anyone, but that she was permanently focused on searching for another man, an even better one. She didn't seem to make love out of passion, but because sex was good for one's health, the current man being nothing much more than a substitute for the one who was to come next, the one for whom she had to search. When the issue was about her health, morals and feelings didn't matter. I think she is the kind of woman who you must maintain in a state of uncertainty, if you want to keep her close to you. The moment she is confident that she controls the situation, she disappears, determined to find yet another victim.

I don't know how she appeared in our house, I mean in Dan's house, because I had moved in with him only at the moment when the flu, pneumonia and other complications had brought me very near to my end. At the beginning she treated me like a senile old man, or a child, and then, after I recovered, she did all she could in order to win my affection or at least my trust. As a result I had become the sole judge of the little quarrels between her and Dan. During my illness, which was long and weird, she wasted a lot of time preparing all kinds of teas and soups for me, and, when the pills didn't help me, changing my compresses. But, after I had recovered, the gratitude I expressed to her didn't save me from her coldness. The incompatibility between us couldn't be camouflaged by conventional words and gestures. Possibly, on the other hand, I might have been wrong, or, rather, I might be unfair to her, since my emotions and understanding yield no access to those of other generations. So far, I am sure that her cold beauty is the only incontestable matter. I didn't try, neither did I want too much to penetrate beyond what was visible on the surface. I should have done it, probably, not so much in order to warn Dan, but because I should have been curious to know her, before the event, as a possible member of the family. It's hard to believe that Dan didn't see certain defects for himself; but maybe he is content merely with her oh so well made body.

Strange! Their souls slip through my fingers and escape, although memory brings them so close that I can imagine each detail of their appearance, or their clothes. For example, it is only now that the bright red of Claudia's dresses irritates me.

I don't know why, but I always postponed the actual

meetings, meaning that I didn't make time for them, although I can't remember doing anything noteworthy instead: and all this starts to hurt only when it is too late, when you discover how short the distance is between birth and death. As a matter of fact, I am certain that I haven't yet done anything right, that everything has just started, that astonishment and suffering will disturb my last days or months, when I'll discover what I should have known, what I should have lived to find out, were it not for the fact that life or history or whatever it was, had violently imposed its own point of view.

For whose sins have I paid?

A ray of light remained stubbornly on the paper in front of me, and, suddenly, I noticed the blackness of the pen, alive, strong; essential for expressing equally strong feelings, which, only now I am writing, I realise that I miss. Then the light suddenly disappeared, dispelled by a peal of thunder; everything went dark, and, in the next instant, I had the strange feeling that I had appeared along with the thunder from the world behind the night. I have never before felt anything like it. A mixed feeling: energy and confusion, at the same time, and, on top of that, curiosity and hope. For a fraction of a second, I seemed to slide into a space forbidden to words, to reason: a bizarre incongruity of the senses. The objects inside this space, illuminated by an unnatural light, changed simultaneously with me, so I was certain that they wanted to confess to me their connection, unsuspected before then, with the sky.

I am trying to write, I must write, but words don't help me.

I see the words in vain. I feel them, they even crowd together in front of me, solid bricks which can no longer build anything. They were like me. In fact, all of them have become what they shouldn't be: pseudonyms of deceit and death. I wrote them down, **hope, life, light, beauty**, *but, this time, they can no longer deceive me. They are, also – banal doppelgangers of death, only revealing their meaning when nothing can be reversed. I shout, saddened by this truth, but it is much too late. Who would believe me? Who would hear me? My friends are no more, and their silence deafens me. I pause for a moment in confusion: does anyone still have true friends? I pray. With desperation. But what is left to ask for, when the time from now on is measured in seconds? And why would I continue to live, why would the Master of Time be generous with me, if up to now all I have done is to be silent, to be afraid and to steal tiny pleasures? I've always begged you, God, for anything my lust and weakness urged me to, and I never gave you anything in return. I cursed you, often passionately, but I didn't do the same to those who tore me down and humiliated me. And why would you forgive me when I've never asked you for forgiveness until today? Sometimes I used the light and the power you gave me against you. And, right now, I have no time left for good deeds, nor for as many prayers as you deserve. I am left with the most terrible punishment of all: understanding that I could be a human being, and understanding that I have probably become one only now, in the moment when I don't exist anymore! Only tears can replace my poor words. Tears – all I have left, apart from that faint and hesitant light which is still deceiving me.*

Gradually, the silence transformed into panic. Clouds hovered brutally, lower and lower, and lightning, repeated, violent, gave me the sensation that I was in the middle of a sphere of fire. I had no doubt I was writing the last words, which would disappear with me in the fire that was about to embrace us. Everything was feverishness, panic and waiting. Finally, I felt that death wished to show me her last visage: the true one. The waiting had destroyed my understanding of what I am, death or life, hallucination or dream.

From all I experienced, from that whole tension, what remained alive was only *curiosity*, although the word might not be the appropriate one. I had become unimaginably light, or it may simply be that I was no longer the self I had known.

A powerful stroke of lightning, blinding, threw me into a completely different world, which I easily managed to comprehend. I had become, incredibly, the clouds which menacingly enclosed the cabin. I was part of the living light of the lightning. I was the fir trees burdened by the rain. I was the chain of mountains that I could admire from somewhere above, but not very high above, as if I was over a scale model. I was also the foaming water wandering between the stones, before becoming bigger and bigger streams, and the birds resting in their nests, and all the wild animals, and the people whose biographies were part of my being.

I was myself, and themselves, and the world comprised into a huge mind, perhaps the eternity scattered throughout everything I had encountered. I knew all the past and future events too. I was absolutely not interested in anything *any more*, because I had the answers to every question already shouted in desperation. This time, although I hadn't asked the questions, their answers had been offered to me, naturally and simply. I was spirit and this seemed to be the *certainty*, the end of my search.

I returned from I don't where and why. The strokes of lightning didn't stop, they seemed to be huge magnesium stripes burning noisily. Light and darkness were alternating quickly, but now nothing mattered anymore. Embraced by a strange silence and peace, I was imperceptibly sliding into a different age, a very distant one, in which waiting and hope gained new powers. A stunning sun, reflected by tens of pools, took command of the field, after the unconstrained rain had covered everything in a dirty grey, vanquished gradually by the green of the healthy plants and by the speed of the floating clouds. This was, in fact, the moment I was waiting for. Those rain drops, became smaller and smaller, fewer and fewer. Immediately, the sunlight, liberated from the oppression of the clouds, and now more powerful, everything wrapped up in a thin vapour, became at first hardly perceptible, and then, very near. It was our long awaited salvation, the rainbow. Had we managed to drag ourselves, on our elbows and knees, up to the point where the rainbow took shape, that is, up to one of its ends, a wish would have been granted to us.

There were three of us, the names of the others have been erased from my memory. I only remember we were so young that we didn't even know precisely the number of cattle we were watching over or what they looked like. On this occasion, time once more fulfilled its duty, so that only the memory of the watch and the emotion of waiting were still left intact, and, of course, the fact that I was so tense I had forgotten the prayer which should have been said while crawling towards the rainbow. Oh, God, good God, I was saying, and in my mind was the image of a big dark bird, which day after day, until the autumn rains started, calmly hovered above us in the height of the skies. I didn't know the bird's name, although it scoured my dreams for many nights, so much so that not only had I reached the point where I wanted to be a bird myself, but I also wanted to ask the rainbow to grant my wish.

Fear, tension, sometimes anxiety, and more than all those put together, the worry that my wish could truly be granted, were succeeding each other, in turns, rapidly. Beyond them, there was another being inside me, about whose existence I only became aware a long time afterwards; after, that is, I had gathered the strength to look at this experience with my eyes open. This being inside me, was so happy to touch the warm wet grass, and to hear the rippling of the water collected in the tracks left by the cattle and the horses, that, from time to time, the grovelling of my body truly seemed like an ascension. Oh, God, my God, I kept repeating between the tears, once I had discovered that, in reality, in spite of the distances we had covered and in spite of our weakness, the rainbow was further and further away, on top of a distant hill, which we didn't have the strength to climb any further. Thus, defeated, we were retreating, encouraging ourselves with the thought that the next bout of rain and sun would give birth to a more good-hearted and more gracious rainbow, and with the thought that if we had mastered the prayer and we hadn't doubted his power, then the dream, the change, would have been possible. During all those summer nights, the wounds on my elbows and knees brought to my sleep that bird with no name, who I envied for her freedom and the chance to see beings and places from far away; things which I was convinced that I, as a human, would never get to know.

Over the years, the image of the bird faded, but what remained inside me was the light that followed the rain, refreshing, heavy with hope, a kind of promise waiting for its fulfilment. This was a light which could still warm me up even now, here where I have come to defend myself, simultaneously, from life and death. Nevertheless, I realize that my biggest enemy is not death, but the fear of death. That is because, for the time being, I have neither the strength to replace her with life, nor to look at her directly. An agony inside, the continuous need to run away and shout, sometimes chokes me and makes me freeze, while I look around desperately, as if the fear of death was a real person about to take shape in the next few seconds.

I know very well that my defeats are more numerous than my victories, and returning home would be the last of many failures.

Around lunchtime, an unexpected event, which I would have overlooked on another occasion, disturbed me profoundly: Mara's visit. I have no doubt, that her appearance meant that the Gods were stretching out a helping hand, to save me from the ridiculous state into which I had fallen so rapidly. Fear had propelled me into a nightmare, so evil and manipulative, that it started as a peaceful dream, so as to make even more overwhelming the terror which was due to follow.

In any case, I had no respect for myself. The opposite was true, because, here on the mountain, I had become exactly what I despised most: an incoherent, capricious man, tortured by moods, which, once upon a time, I would have had under control, in much more difficult conditions. For a couple of seconds even my young woman visitor seemed to be a hallucination. Her shadow in the window persisted stubbornly however, and then the noise of the key in the door brought me completely back to reality.

Mara was not surprised to find me here. She rushed to kiss me and then, embarrassed, resumed looking at the key in her hand.

"I came to dust the place, because, look, even here, behind the devil's back, I don't know where it all comes from... And, what do I find, the door open... I didn't imagine I would find you here... this is not the weather to come to the mountains," she remarked in the most natural tone.

God, I don't know how to be happy. I don't know how to pray. I don't know how to curse. I don't know how to cry. I don't know how to say what I feel. I don't know how to say what I don't know. I have become something unstructured, incomplete, something which can't communicate. I am nothing more than a pain which doesn't know how to express itself, to groan, to shout.

She is stunningly beautiful, but I am not capable of saying this, and, in addition, I can't see exactly where I'm located on the short and absurd ladder of life. Unlike me, she has the advantage of time *ahead of her, and of her youth, which humiliates me. What good are experience, culture, diplomas, which certify, in front of I don't know who, that I was somebody, when I feel my hands to be dry, cold, and my face hollow. On top of all that is my body, the one I am, meaning the framework which can hardly contain a rebellious soul, already annoyed because of the fragility of the structure hosting it, and always terrified by the provisional character of the worn out construction I feel myself to be? In Mara's presence, I am and I am not. Or, more exactly: I am something I shouldn't be. In any case, I feel that I have lost my wisdom, and can't find my way towards her. Amen.*

It happened by chance that, in those days, I was at the fully working Meteorological Station, when her mother went into labour two months earlier than expected. It was her luck and my joy to be there just when she needed a doctor.

Teodora was a beautiful woman, of impressive physical strength; she took care of the Station and of the domestic animals. "It's not too good to get too attached to them, she used to say to me, because they become, without you noticing, part of the family and then you don't find the strength to sacrifice them, when pushed by hunger or isolation. And what can one do here? Note down the temperature at precise hours, the humidity, prepare the food, listen to the radio and, when one feels like it, make love... But what about the long winter nights?" she used to ask provocatively. "I believe that even my own Gheorghe got bored with the same menu. As far as I am concerned, I am not even going to mention it!"

"And do you think I might be able to save you from boredom?", I used to ask, while she was dying with laughter:

"Who would risk addressing such bewilderment? Try and see how much time you have left. Because this husband of mine, in order to escape that obligation will pour some kids into me and quiet me down."

Her invitation, so direct, cut out any trace of daring in me. She had her own way of provoking me, but, the moment I took my heart in my mouth and answered her in a way that was equally direct, she would back down, scared. To my delight, of course, as I wasn't prepared to cheat on a friend. Her game, though, never ceased and, probably, if I were more determined, we would have gone past the stage of allusions, allusions which, with the time passing, became banal and brought us to a full stop.

Teodora was, nevertheless, a woman you couldn't forget, who would pop up in your thoughts when you least expected it. Now, when a confession would be of no importance, I admit that many times I went to that forgotten-by-God Station determined to get the hell away from any principles, but on the actual date, as I went, our love scenes were already played out in my imagination. I left and I returned with her in my mind, but in Teodora's presence any trace of courage would simply vanish. If she had made the first step, like all the women in this world, I would never have left her. Unfortunately, time and circumstances always took me to other roads, therefore when I met her again up there, at the Station, she was just 6 months pregnant.

"If I get out of this alive, that's it, I won't let you escape anymore. You keep popping up, more and more often, in my dreams, in my thoughts, and I don't like that. I have no choice, I have to get this done with you. No matter what."

This time she was serious and, in my turn, I assured her that on my own part I wished for nothing else. She became convinced of that as I started to visit her more and more often, and, of course, as I started to take care of her, in the name of the narrative which, finally, was about to take shape. Maybe the inner connection established between us, beyond words, brought me to the Station on the very day that she happened to give birth. "That's it, from now on the waiting is over, you have no way out," she told me, strangely enough, just as she was about to give birth. "You'll pay a lot for this, including for the time wasted before I even met you!"

In spite of my obsession that I might encounter some complications, Teodora gave birth easily. "Now that you have seen me like that, as I wouldn't have wanted you to see me, I am afraid you will run away again, but I swear I will find you anywhere!", she threatened me.

Certainly, both parents wished for a boy, but, in the end, Mara's charm and good health convinced them they had nothing to regret. The girl was growing up normally, endured the harsh weather very well, and also life among the rather numerous animals, from their courtyard – a little Noah's Ark isolated by a high fence, strong, able to stop the wild animals' attacks during the winters, which were more and more long and unfriendly. Teodora didn't keep her word, instead she poured out all her affection over this child. But between us a kind of complicit understanding was established, as if the promised struggle had already taken place. Nevertheless we spoke openly about the outburst of forces that had happened in our minds and this gave us a pleasant calm, solidarity, in the name of what could have been. It was, of course, a temporary armistice during which both parties forgot, now and then, what they had promised each other, without either of them achieving what they wanted.

Mara left the Station only during school time when she lived with some relatives, then at boarding school, which she didn't like. As a consequence her parents would see her appearing at home all of a sudden. But unsatisfied by the tiny perimeter within which her parents lived, her curiosity would push her to explore the surroundings, and to stay late far from home, to her mother's desperation, but not to the father's, the meteorologist: "Bad people, thieves and villains don't waste their time in the mountains. They have nothing to gain here. Wild animals attack people only rarely, during the winter... She knows by herself how to stay away from the chasms..."

Unfortunately that odd, telepathic connection between me and Teodora lasted only while our affection ran hot. Lack of courage, over severe moral precepts, the fact that we couldn't ignore for one moment the opinion of others, fear of complications and various worries of this kind brought us to a miserable deadlock. We kept postponing our meetings, and when they were inevitable, we tried not to keep them to just the two of us, even if the painful longing for one another was reaching a paroxysm. That is why, our cowardice or, if you want, our exacerbated lucidity punished us. Every time she accompanied me through the forest, apparently to show me the shortest route, we kissed each other like mad, as if I was going to go to war, or to climb up Everest or never see each other again. We never took the next step however. Maybe this was also because, subconsciously, a phrase was stuck in my mind, a phrase she had said a long time before, playfully, during the period of our equivocal jokes: "Oh, God, how much I would love us to have a child together," and I, the coward, the rascal, was terrified of that child.

Time, as was normal, abandoned his former generosity. We were not to enjoy having each other in any way, and, in the end, exactly what she wanted most – the child – brought about her death. In reality we were both scared of the child and the changes it would have brought into our life. This thought tortured me for a long time and stopped me from doing what, in reality, we both wanted.

Teodora died unexpectedly because of septicaemia, following a failed attempt at an abortion. She had resorted to a bad midwife in those years when abortion was forbidden. I could have done anything to help her, risk prison even, and, of course, divorce. But Teodora didn't tell me about her condition, although, as I remembered later, we had met at least twice during that period. Sometimes I missed her terribly and then I was tortured by remorse because of her death, and my guilty nature made me judge myself too harshly. I was sure that her soul was hovering somewhere above the fir tree forests, above the clearing where the Station was, above my house, in order to remind me that we abandoned each other so brutally to pain and loneliness, that we let each other be too easily led by prejudices. At other times I told myself that her pregnancy could have been the result of a random relationship and her decision to lose it could have had some justification, only to be ashamed of my thoughts afterwards.

For her husband, Gheorghe Toma, the meteorologist, the blow was terrible. He kept doing his job as a mechanic, in complete silence. As far as Teodora is concerned, nobody knows if she was buried with a priest or if he, in the madness and the desperation that overcame him, just put her in the ground with no one's help. Later on, another family was appointed in Teodora's position, and they stayed there until the closing of the Station. Gheorghe Toma never made friends with the newcomers in spite of all the time they spent together. They remained strangers and nothing more. They made sacrifices, endured, counted their money and dreamt only of leaving the Station.

After their departure, Gheorghe and Mara continued to live in the building. They had nowhere to go and no one with whom to leave the animals. Who would feed the pack of dogs, some of them abandoned by the shepherds because they had gone wild. The dogs had allowed the wolves to steal a couple of sheep, and these had left part of the prey in recompense. Besides, he thought it would be unfair to abandon Teodora there, although the woodmen and shepherds, who still went that way now and then, spread the rumour that, in reality, the grave was empty, that the meteorologist's woman had run away with a fellow who used to go hunting in that area. Some thought that the bloke could only be "Mister Paul," a professor from Bucharest, good looking man, who didn't "forgive" either the woodmen's wives or the carters' wives he met by chance. Everyone found it strange that, after Teodora's disappearance, Mister Paul didn't show up there anymore. For my part, I didn't believe a word of such a story; even if she might have been able to leave her husband, it would have been impossible for Teodora to do the same to her daughter, Mara, over whom she kept pouring out her huge reserves of affection. And, apart from everything else, who could get lost in a country in which almost every person was followed, checked, kept, directly or indirectly, under observation? Little by little, time took care of Toma's painful wound as well: but, while he got back his desire to speak, he started to lose his sight and none of the doctors I approached gave him any hope. Strangely, he didn't seem interested to find out if this illness would ever heal, or further, about what new disaster awaited him. Every time we met he continued to initiate me into the secrets of meteorology and of the wild animals' behaviour: "You wander a lot in the mountains and it is good for you to know what can happen."

He always asked me to describe the sky for him: colour, clouds, their size, their distance to the horizon, from what cardinal point they had appeared, if they seemed fixed or if they were moving etc.

"In a maximum of three hours the storm will erupt," he used to say when I discovered, at the end of the horizon, one tiny little grey cloud or another, staining the blue immensity of the sky. "You have time to get home or, if not, you can sleep here, of course if Mara would like that as well."

She would agree but she would request that, in exchange for the food, I should help her to milk the cows, to gather the goats, the hens, and to do everything that was necessary in order to welcome the night in peace. In reality she wanted us to remain on our own for a longer time, so that I could answer her questions, especially those regarding her future, when she would eventually lose her dad.

"What will I do? We haven't kept in touch with our relatives, we have lived as if the whole Universe was made of us and God only. Will you help me, old man? You are the one who brought me into this world, aren't you a little bit responsible for my future as well?"

She borrowed the form of address from her father and she found it normal to speak to me with "you"[3] to consider me equal, and I have to admit this treatment pleased me a lot.

Now that I helped you come out in this world, I'll have to help you get married as well, to assist you when you give birth and then to take care of your pension as well. I can't promise anything past that, but I shall try..."

I suggested I could find her a job in the city, even at the hospital where I worked, but she used to come over, check everything doubtfully, observe the reactions of the people around, and then, only when it was just the two of us, she would mention the events which would justify her return to the Station. "You must come here while it is not too late," I used to threaten her. "What will you do if your father dies? Or me?"

I had asked Toma the same question, but he seemed to have had the answer already prepared, for a long time: "Take her with you. She is a smart girl, with lyceum studies, she

---

3   The familiar and informal "you" – first person singular

is strong, she could work in a factory, in a shop, she is not fastidious. There is nothing here for her to do."

"This means that you would like to abandon the mountain yourself..."

"Yes, that would be an idea," he hesitated. "But where house, where food, where? Better here in a chasm than in an old people's home. I came to the Station for the money. The job was well paid and, I must admit, I liked that. I was thinking of putting together a sum of money and then leaving. Two jobs as geography teachers wouldn't have been impossible to find. Teodora was so beautiful that I was jealous even of the ray of the sun caressing her face. I would have had her covered, like the Muslims. Just us, the fir trees, the wind, the rain, the snow and God Almighty, to whose care we entrusted ourselves. That's what I wanted. But, I don't know, I assessed my resources badly. Teodora was more of a woman than I had imagined, and loneliness was not my best adviser. I was not good enough for her, unfortunately! I am not sure if she cheated on me, I don't think so though, but I am aware that I offered her too little, and that my love only, excessive as it was maybe, was not enough for her. She had a dissatisfaction always nagging at her, which she never expressed, but I could sense it. Anyway, things rushed towards the most unexpected finale. I didn't have her, the money, or the job. And, here we are, nothing can be changed".

That is how, because of the endless hesitations, mine and theirs as well, we had reached a dead end. I kept telling myself that I couldn't change their life by force, if they didn't believe that was necessary, and they were deadly afraid of the idea of something new. Therefore everything remained frozen. Here, in the mountains, I was obliged to come less and less often, until I took the decision to build this cabin which, in the end, remained in Mara's care.

Who would have imagined then that, instead of taking them down to the city, I would be the one taking refuge up in the mountains? I hadn't been to the cabin for almost a year, so I hadn't seen Mara for almost a year either. So, in the first moment when I woke up from my confusion, I had the certitude that I was in front of Teodora – the same overflowing health, the same beauty: rich lips, red, strong nose, black eyes, unusually wide, deepened in their sockets, and the pain hidden in them made me think that my unexpected appearance, meaning what was left after that long and bizarre illness I had suffered from, had disappointed her. It was only her eyes which gave away this disappointment and surprise, because she didn't manage to impose on them what she had forbidden to her words.

"In fact, I came to take some books," Mara justified herself. "I don't know if you happen to have some books of prayers. I feel the need to pray but I can't find words. I can't. I fail," she said, embarrassed by my silence and bewilderment. I should have warned her that my reactions are much too slow, that I am in a phase of deplorable confusion.

"God also understands what you don't express in words necessarily," trying to comfort her. "But where did this need come from? Do you really want to pray?"

A foolish question, and, of course, my uncalled-for curiosity annoyed her.

"Yes, I do want to pray to God for the devil to take me sooner!"

"This is going to happen anyway – very soon to me, and sometime later to you. Concretely: can I help you with anything?" I offered immediately and she burst into a laugh:

"I haven't thought of help. We'll talk tomorrow, now I have to go back, to give water to the animals. I didn't think I would find you here. Someone should give you a belting to stop you neglecting yourself, old man, you seem – how shall I put it to make myself understood – like a desperate man!"

"Yes, I admit, no one looks too well at my age," I defended myself, somewhat embarrassed. "And how is your old man?" I asked next, and she answered after a long hesitation:

"He is gone... the only good thing that happened to him after mum died."

"So you are all on your own?", I insisted and she seemed very upset by the pointless question:

"And how was I beforehand? I was left with the animals, an entire menagerie, and the dogs, and then your books!"

"And how did the old man die?" I tried to keep the conversation going, but she kissed me hurriedly:

"Have to run, have no choice. If you remain here for a couple of days, we'll talk..."

"I am not leaving anymore," I assured her. "I feel like saying as with marriages: *till death do us part!*"

She disappeared like a storm, without telling me when she was going to be back, but after she left, instead of sadness, agitation, curiosity, I was hungry. Waiting for the morning to come, I felt the way I used to before a decisive meeting. Some other time, in a similar situation, I would have shaved, taken a shower, changed my clothes, put some after shave on, meaning I would have tried hard to recreate my inner comfort, a feel good mood. This time I simply ate with desperation. The woman's face had thrown me into another age. Look into the mirror, you idiot, I felt like telling myself in that second, but I couldn't tell what was hurting me more: the thought that Mara might not return or losing

45

Teodora. Here, where I could have, possibly saved her from death. Only late at night, when I looked around carefully, I noticed Mara's absence, which was the most painful and humiliating fact possible. I felt myself to be a man to whom everything was forbidden, even a banal and consolatory caress, and just at that moment I started to write.

Oh, Lord, the long night has arrived and my questions are not waiting for answers anymore, because from what I used to be there is only sand and pain left. Stay with me a bit more, you absurd miracle, while fear envelops me, as hope used to do. Don't go away just yet, I beg you, please, have mercy, woman, understand that my kingdom with a single phantom will only exist during the time you are here. Don't leave me right now, when even my words run away, those words that whisper to me that I am the one who won't exist anymore! Oh, Lord, I admit my defeat now. I am afraid to die, although I know that in eternity unimaginable beauties are waiting for me, rivers of milk and honey. Yes, I am afraid to die, the same way that I was afraid to live. Is it that difficult to appreciate how many fears and nightmares were born out of pain? Stay for a while, even **after** *the eternal cold embraces me and when the soul escapes towards I don't know where. Let me look at you from above, with no sadness and no fear, from the sky of naive and fearful people. Help me lie to the One who will judge me, if I should be worthy of it, and help me tell him that I was not always alone, that here in the Country of Delays, où tout est pris à la légère, in the most difficult moment you remained next to me, you beautiful being, in silence. I implore you, stay a little bit more even after I don't exist. Give me the courage to ask the Great and Endless One: why is that the* East *should be a synonym for* fear, hunger *and* want? *Why is that I had to be born here, in*

*the East, where all the pains and the fears of the world gathered,
where everything has to be stolen: love, food, peace, life. Woman,
put your hand on my head and I shall believe that death has lost
her way, that finally time for love has also been granted to us.
Don't leave me just yet, my forgiveness, my light! Let me believe
that night hasn't yet come, and that I am not where I am. Amen.*

I have to admit that the existence of that Other Cassian,
the lucid being from inside me, who mercilessly judges not
only my actions, but also my most hidden thoughts, gives
me pleasure, even if his verdicts haunt me for a long time,
forcing me to be cautious, which, is frequently not to my
advantage. I was always afraid of being ridiculous, afraid of
that moment when I might lose my grasp of my limitations,
afraid of starting to believe that I am something other than
I am, bigger or smaller, better or worse, afraid of judging
myself or others at a superficial level, in accordance with my
first impulse. It is true that in the past I would find myself
either crying, or with my voice trembling, impossible to
control, when I discovered a good deed, a significant phrase,
a generous gesture, and a sports triumph or any other type
of victory. It happened even when I listened to the national
Anthem. The Other Cassian was rather indulgent with
such reactions, especially when they were not in public,
considering them almost natural for someone involved in
the destiny of their community.

One thought, however, in front of which lucidity was
helpless, had been haunting me obstinately since I had
reached the cabin. If, one particular day, a major inconvenience
connected with my age, should put me in a situation of
not being able to move any more, of being paralysed by a
heart attack or something of the kind, what would I do on

my own, without being able to communicate, without the chance of being helped properly? It is probable that such a speculation would have forbidden or, at least, postponed my plan of retiring for good to the cabin. Unfortunately, these questions came to my mind only after I came here, where I am not left with much choice: either return, to forestall the possible accident, or, fat chance, convincing Mara to end what illness started, and thus get her used to the idea that she should, out of pity and understanding, use my gun which was always at hand. Of course it was not good to let myself be overcome by such obsessions, especially that nothing of what I was, none of my organs, not even a dream, seemed to foretell any of these situations or even the ultimate collapse.

In the end it was difficult for me to reflect openly on my meeting with Mara the previous day. It had been so brief and so intense, but, this morning the prolonged waiting for her, placed me in a state bordering on the ridiculous. In reality, I didn't know how she was, what had happened to her since I saw her last, what traces were left in her heart by the death of her father, how she coped with loneliness or if she was indeed lonely. I even composed in my mind a psychic portrait similar to Teodora's, so that, as a consequence, I found myself waiting for the person to whom I had assigned a couple of human qualities, which I needed myself. Towards noon, when she appeared accompanied by two big dogs, shepherd dogs, I was tired and agitated: my will and lucidity proving themselves weaker than the painful sentiment of waiting.

"I'll leave a dog with you for company," she said with no introduction, as if she were leaving in the very next second. "The other one I need because there is a bear hovering around. It hasn't attacked anyone so far, but there is no guarantee I couldn't be the first. Look, I brought you some milk, cheese, fresh water and, because you look rather poorly, next week I'll kill a pig as well."

I didn't know what to say. I had enough food. Hunger was not my enemy at that moment, but an unbearable emotion, which was almost making me cry. I was following her movements carefully and I have no doubt Mara was doing the same with me, because we both wanted to get past the embarrassing moments and uncertainties of the beginning. What will the next move be? What will she ask for? What should I ask for? The questions were, of course, equally ridiculous and useless: age, experience, my power over her, all told me we must enter a more conventional situation, but, before I could find the right tone, she took it ahead of me:

" How long are you going to stay? Just checking if it's worth killing the pig."

"I don't know," I answered in all honesty. "As much as I can. Until the end, probably..."

"The end of the week? Of the year? Of the summer? You promise one thing, I believe it, but then one day you remember something else and disappear. Then perhaps months or even years go by. I come and take care of your cabin, hoping that one day I will find you here."

"And hasn't it happened just like that?". I tried to joke about it.

"Yes, but after how long? I was lucky with your library here, but then the risk is that I would become a clever woman."

"I had made up my mind to remain here until the end of life, but, when I made this decision, I had forgotten to put into balance all the unpleasant parts connected to age!"   "What unpleasant parts do you have? You practiced mountain climbing. I also heard some time ago from my father that women liked you, and, if you weren't so bony, you could deceive one. You are not how you imagine you are. How strange is that," she exclaimed after a break in which she measured me with her eyes from top to toe, "you have someone to run from, I have no one to run to."

"We'll have time to talk about these pains as well," I interrupted her, convinced that it was too early for me to tell her about my reasons for running away from home. "Tell me, how did your father die? Rather early."

"I think he only made two decisions in his life: to come here, to the Station, and to get married, although I am convinced that even in these situations he was discreetly guided by my mother. He didn't want anything other than money and exclusivity over my mother. I can talk, for sure, about the money. He put aside some, especially after he sold everything he had in the countryside, but, as you know, he didn't do much with that money. He kept postponing everything, even buying a house in town and looking for a job. He was only competent enough to communicate the compulsory data to the Centre and to start up projects. After mother's death, he lost himself, just like that. He would go into town to buy flowers but he would forget why he went, he would come to my high school, bring me a horn-shaped roll, a cake, promise he would wait for me after classes, and then he would appear only two or three weeks later. He didn't complain, or explain himself, he seemed tormented by something secret, an important thought, an interest which was well above our tiny concerns. The closing of the Station sped up his death, I believe. He couldn't find reasons to exist anymore, he would wander across the mountains, collecting medicinal plants and blackberries and strawberries, but he wouldn't sell them to anyone, so that they faded in front of our eyes. He had developed a real passion for animals, and especially for the chickens. He named each of them, he paid them exaggerated attention, so, the poor chickens, no question, became family and, of course, started to take advantage of that status. They climbed up on his shoulders, and jumped on his head, filling the house with a horrible smell. Then followed the dogs. Occasionally, when a few friends or lost tourists looked for him, he would reconnect to reality, but, immediately after their departure, silence and alienation would take possession of him again.

An educated man in his youth, father had abandoned his books without many regrets. He had liberated himself from one more obligation, that of reading, and of being informed even about what was new in his profession. With me, but now only with me, he started to communicate more just after he lost his sight. At that point he got obsessed by the radio. He listened to the news religiously, commenting on it in a loud voice, and everything happening in the world became a reason for him not to leave the mountain. In his opinion, I was a being who would easily survive from what the mountain was offering: wild fruit, medicinal plants, game, fresh air, unpolluted water. It would have been useless to contradict him, nothing would have changed. After he had lost his sight, as I said, we would spend some more time together, but, in time, he learned how to walk on his own to my mother's tomb, where he would remain for ages. I never found out what he was telling her, but I could sometimes see him gesticulating with too much energy. Accompanied by a shepherd's dog, he would go away from the cabin, but he would return home guided by the same animal, as soon as he heard my signal to return. In any case, he gave the impression that he had resigned himself to his fate, and that the loss of sight didn't change him seriously. It's true, he was eating less and less, in spite of my insistence, he was speaking more and more to himself, and not only at my mother's tomb, but nothing at all seemed to announce his death, which was something I didn't want to think of for anything in the world. In front of me, everything was confusing, and worrying. I wasn't concerned about the food, but about the loneliness, the nights and the winters that were to come. The day he died I was not at the Station. I had gone to town to buy bread, oil and other items. On my way back I had stopped at Dogaru's. He insisted that I should remain there for the night because there were two carnivorous bears around who might have attacked his donkeys. Early in the morning, I started to walk home, feeling unusually upset. I found my father in bed, reclining against the wall, with the chickens resting on his knees, and his shoulders. In fact, the dogs had welcomed me at some distance from the house, extremely agitated, and I had already understood that something was not in order. The radio was going on and on and on, announcing typhoons and earthquakes somewhere in Japan.

I buried father in a Christian way as it happened that a monk passed by around that time, looking for medicinal plants. He was a friend of Dogaru and of the shepherds from the shelters around us. We did the burial in a hurry because a terrible storm had appeared from nowhere, uprooting trees, and rolling stones. If we hadn't hurried to fill in the grave with earth, the wind would probably have taken the coffin as well. One of my father's clouds, from a far end of the sky maybe, one of those little clouds one wouldn't normally notice, but which could create at any time unsuspected catastrophes at any time, felt obliged to say good bye, in its own way. In any case, I will never forget the night that followed. I don't know why, but even today, it is difficult for me to describe it. There are no words! I was petrified with fear. I cried. I felt like going crazy. I even thought of my father's gun which had been unused for a long time. I was on my own on top of a mountain, with no job, no qualifications, no friends, with relatives almost unknown to me, and tortured by a strong feeling of uncertainty. Everything was working against me, even my own memory which continuously invented monsters and catastrophes."

Mara's voice became more and more faded. Had she got tired, or was she, perhaps, afraid that the echo could trigger the avalanche of horrors following her? This being how things were, I thought the moment was not right for continuing our discussion, and any words of encouragement would have been completely out of place. What could I have said to her? Don't worry, I came to save you! Or, you will remain with me as long as I live. But how long would I live? What guarantee could she get? Besides, she had told me that I looked rather bony, a correct observation, which I couldn't interpret in my favour no matter how hard I tried. The only realistic solution didn't satisfy me for the moment: to move her to the city, where an unskilled position could be easily found, and even a husband for such a beautiful woman. In other words, that would have implied my return home, not to Dan's, but to my house in the city, which I had left during my absurd illness. And the mountain? The renunciation had a name.

So here was the chance to get out of trouble in an

honourable way, since I had left home in a hurry, not taking into account all the possibilities. No matter what my justifications were, what I did was called, in Dan's vision, senile vagabondage. Therefore, if he should find me home all of a sudden, he would leave me in peace after a couple of pathetic phrases of greeting. That fact, however, won't change my feeling of being dead among the living. Of course, I had never told him about my obsession with climbing the Margin of Life. Doing it now would have been absurd, and would have only confirmed his diagnosis. No doubt saving Mara was more important than my ambition, but nothing was urging me to hurry, as long as it seemed that the problems of adaptation were now more or less sorted. Of course, there was another solution: to send Dan a letter with my proposals for Mara's future. With the request that my son should read it in Mara's presence after I died. The thought that Dan would help her – it would be my last wish after all! – restored a little of my trust in the possibility of remaining in the mountains for some more time.

Mara was very disturbed by the recollection of her father and, to calm herself down, she had started to tidy up the house, to change the location of objects, to clear up my rucksack packed with pills – brought *"for all contingencies"* – books, tins and other similar useful nothings. I was following her movements with attention as I hadn't yet got used to her presence, and to the unexpected chance of having her company.

"You came exactly when I had planned everything differently for the little future I had left," I told her in my mind. "Will you stay, will you not, will you come back, will you not? I can ask you, that's not hard, but I don't know how sincere your answer could be, because, in reality, a whole life lies between us. Meaning the life I had already lived."

Saying this, I felt that I was sliding, or, to put it better, that I was getting effortlessly, even passionately, lost in my own past, where I was encountering a few close friends. I was happy to meet them but after a while I found myself saying: "God, but he is dead!" and, suddenly, the night would invade my whole being. Not to be. Never. For ever. For always. Now I don't pass easily anymore over a feeling about whose gravity and depth I hadn't been conscious. I understand, finally, what *not to be* means, and, strangely, it is Mara herself who makes me remember it.

"May I know what are you thinking about?" I asked eventually, angry with my errors and with her hard work, in fact, with her efforts to disguise her agitation. "Have you thought about it, do you know what you want? For me things are clear: I want at any price to climb that mountain, so I wish for days as sunny as possible, and, if possible, for fewer back pains. I wish, especially, for this exasperating feeling of loneliness to stop torturing me. But what would you like to do if a golden fish granted you three wishes?"

"To die. To die. And die again," came her prompt answer. "At least that is what I wished for until this morning. Now, I feel like I'd like to postpone that a bit, I mean I am not so sure anymore, but no other idea crosses my mind either! I agree, there were days when it felt good to be here, at the end of the world, times when I could think of nothing at all, when I was not too scared of tomorrow, but there were months, even years, when I could see nothing ahead and didn't know what to do or what to wait for. If you were me, what would you ask the golden fish for?"

"Don't you think it's too easy to answer with a question?", I scolded her jokingly. "Well then, look what I'd ask him for

- Mister, what do you think will happen to me? But, until the golden fish makes up his mind and gives me an answer, I wouldn't mind hearing your view on this. I can't promise I'll agree with you, or that I'll take your advice. Or better still, don't tell me now. We can't sort everything out in one day. I find it hard to believe that you'll stay here until the end of your days, but I wouldn't want, either, to hear that you are leaving too soon."

I couldn't tell her that it was precisely she who had shaken my decision to stay, but I asked whether she knew anything about the Margin of Life. Before she answered though, she burst into a laugh: "Dad told me about your obsession. I observed the mountain myself during every season, but I haven't discovered anything new. Legends and rumours are, anyway, stronger than those who want to conquer it. No one dares to come near this mountain. As far as I am concerned, I don't think it hides any mystery. Dad said that, in the best scenario, the stories could be about a magnetic deviation created by an iron deposit. What's extraordinary is that he didn't think that UFOs were out of the question; not even angels. But St Peter had no reason to search for people who did neither good, nor wrong. Here, after the war, during the collectivization, they were serious battles between those who ran into the mountains and the Securitate people hunting for them. Maybe the souls haven't found their rest yet. They are probably still fighting up until now. If you would like to know the place better, I will try to help you. I mean that I could be your golden fish ready to grant you one wish, and if we both perish, no loss! You have lived your life, and I don't see why I should live mine anymore. I know it's not the same, but the conclusion is somewhere around here. So I'll come with you. That way I can have a purpose in life. At least for a couple of days."

Her unexpected proposal almost made me lose my balance. I was convinced that it might be my last trip – in all possible meanings – the last ascension. As the Other Cassian would say, my endeavour – a ridiculous one, – to surpass my limits, but, of course, Mara shouldn't have to take the same risk. Each person has to fight his own war with life, but you have to be aware of that and try to leave the most indelible traces on your way towards death. Sometimes, these traces can taste like victory. If you give yourself some leeway, of course.

"But there is no hurry". I tried to postpone the discussion. "I'll have to train and to search the ground with more care. I am not afraid, so far, except about my own strength. I am now just recovering after a malady which I didn't understand too well myself, even though I am a medic. I had fever, I was dozing off, rambling, living as if I were inside a nightmare, a more gentle nightmare than usual. I was travelling through unknown spaces, then again and again through multiple others. I was crawling thorough unfamiliar territories or flying above them with the same amount of difficulty, everything was effort, confusing, seeking, anxiety. A world in sepia. Let me tell you one more thing. I am under the impression that in reality my soul was wandering somewhere else, and had abandoned me at that moment. But neither heaven, nor hell would admit me. It seems that I have to wait longer."

As I observed the wish being expressed on her face, I realised we had entered a mine field again, one for which Mara was in no way prepared. I knew that she had been acquainted with pain from early on, and that she had experienced fears, which may or may not have had a name. I knew also that she had felt loneliness, and a lack of perspective, but youth gave all these feelings calmer tints. In any case she had an ally – time. As far as I was concerned though, time and experience were imposing other rules, a totally different way of seeing things. They were ordering me to hurry up, but the legitimate fear of ridicule forced me to hide from her what I felt and thought, limiting myself to watching her reactions, and carefully exploring the size of her universe. Then, before assigning her a role in my project, I remembered her wish – which I hadn't taken seriously at the time although she had uttered it without hesitation: "To die. To die. And die again" – as if death had been her concern for a long time, and, of course, would have remained her only solution after she had eliminated all the others, one by one.

"You are much too hardworking for the first day," I told her jokingly, surprised by the focus with which she was removing specks of dust from the books. "Are you hurrying to get somewhere? Do you have some obligation?"

"Of course I have. Towards the animals, since there are two things I manage to do well: feed them and cry. If you come with me and help a bit, we'll return quickly and I'll stay here over night. You are my only neighbour. There won't be no one around to gossip about us..."

"Unfortunately I am too old for any neighbour to suspect me or to gossip about something like that," I answered in a rather dull fashion.

She burst into laughter: "A man who is able to climb to the top of a mountain can be suspected of anything," she answered, smiling significantly. "You are surprised by such remark, aren't you? All of a sudden I felt like playing around a bit, making foolish comments. I hope you don't mind. After so much silence, sometimes I am under the impression that I forgot to laugh, to speak. Don't be surprised by my manners, but, if at some point, you would like to tell me something nice I wouldn't mind, you know. I'd ask you though, not to encourage me without a reason. And don't look at me when you say something, since your words might impress me. Tears come to my eyes at any sign of affection."

"I wouldn't be surprised," I admitted. "Only I don't understand what kind of tears those are: laughing or crying?"

All of a sudden, I remembered my nephew Radu, a great specialist in computers, a *hacker*, for whom I foresee some handcuffs on his wrists soon, if he doesn't calm down. He usually managed to walk the line between seriousness and mockery, and for a while he started to make fun of me. In his mind, the world divides between *them* and *the rest of the world*, meaning between *young* and *old people*, between the *expired* and *the valid ones*, between *losers* and *winners*.

"I am not interested in honour, morality, this intellectual salad," he keeps telling me. "I want money. That's all. The rest is just words! All that is done by the winners is good, right, moral, true."

He believes that we, *the expired ones*, his father's generation and mine, spoiled the world by being cowardly, fearful and opportunist, by giving free rein to communism, misery, darkness, and, as a consequence, they – *the valid ones* – have now to suffer because of us. He got his wife, or the woman he is living with – whatever - through the internet. For a month, evening after evening, he had made electronic dates with every suitor but for the time being he is contented with Laura.

"As far as your idea of staying here over night," my nephew Radu would ask slyly, "are you into collecting antiques?"

"I only lived in town for a little while, but I did notice

that everyone there is running after vintage stuff. Collecting antiques. That way I would finally be in fashion," was Mara's cunning reply.

Her answer put me in the situation of not being able to find a suitable reply, but, as she didn't seem interested in continuing the discussion either, we found ourselves laughing with delight, apparently contented, as if we had found a convenient solution for both of us. Inside myself, sooner than I expected, I had gotten over a threshold and regained my inner peace, entirely thanks to her. What now? It was clear to me that Mara had to be saved. From her gestures, her face expression and the movement of her lips, I could guess her indecision. To leave straight away to see to her animals or to tell me something she thought I must find out with no delay. To ask me to save her from the secluded place we were in or to postpone what she thought I should know about her. Unfortunately, once more I had acted like a medic without experience, but with time in hand. I was waiting for her to tell me more clearly what she wanted, although the return to town – mine and hers – seemed to be out of question. I closed my eyes and all of a sudden I felt the terrible snows which were going to come, the killing wind, the loneliness, the hunger and the aggression of the wild animals, even the autumn, with its exasperating fogs and rains, and all the shortcomings I had neglected before moving into the cabin. If we remained here though, it was clear that I would be more dependent on Mara than her on me. In any case, the subject had to be analysed with patience and over some time. I didn't think Mara was ready, either, for a very open discussion about her situation.

After some hesitation, she suddenly communicated to me her decision to go on her own: "I would gain some time, because the road is not easy as you know. I'll take the dog with me as well since you have nothing to feed him with. We need to organise ourselves first and then."

Her sudden departure annoyed me: it was clear something had made her unhappy. She probably expected me to react in a different way, to offer her a solution, to seem more interested in her future. Unfortunately, without a specific reason, I didn't have the strength to hold her back anymore, although her tempestuous reaction left a trace of doubt and sadness I tried for some time after to wipe out of my mind. I thought that life in this place imposed different rules on her. She didn't live too much among people and, moreover, there was the natural embarrassment, and probably a different sense of time. For her, time was not so overwhelming, she spoke about it and about death with ease. Of course, Mara lived around death, but, in spite of that, she didn't know what death was – the end was for *the others* only, and in the end, I felt like laughing. In my lifetime, Mara wouldn't understand that, for me, the phrases see you later, see you tomorrow, or see you soon, have a different connotation, being associated at one and the same time with sadness and hope. How could I have made her understand that *tomorrow* is not exactly *really tomorrow* for both of us? This was my suffering which, of course, Mara couldn't have felt in depth.

Anyway, she left, followed by my tormenting questions and worries, leaving behind her, as I was to discover later on, a desperate need for life, even if I was guessing at the fragility of that *tomorrow*. Her presence, the fact that I was not alone here in the mountains, away from any human dwelling, made me experience a feeling unknown until then: rebirth, a deep tension, a return from a long agony, which turned my whole being upside down, a feeling which, in the first moment, scared me. "It is death," I thought, "the peace, the reconciliation, the happy moments which precede the end sometimes!"

All of a sudden, I remembered the faces, turned unexpectedly serene, of so many suffering people who died in my arms or whose illnesses had humiliated me by making me admit my powerlessness. Everything seemed to have come together in order to unpredictably disturb my awakening to life. Then I remembered the numerous dreams in which I was flying, in which I was something else. Those images, made out of pain and fear, never left me. I was floating with ease above some ancient cities, a long time asleep in history – Nineveh, Athens, Babylon, Syracuse – or above endless spaces, hot, terrorized by a deadly sun which had dried out any trace of life. I was feeling, with all my being, a scorching wind throwing hot waves of sand in my face, wrapping me up in a merciless and suffocating corset, without slowing down my flight. I was inside a hostile world, unknown but somehow also known, in spaces which did not touch, nor brutally reject me, since I felt as if, to some extent, they belonged to me. I was flying and, many times, also struggling to escape from among a crowd of creatures, strong, aggressive and hairy, human beings and monkeys at the same time; creatures which seemed, in daylight, characters from some bad science-fiction stories. There were also unbearable nights when these creatures followed me persistently, in other spaces, where all known and unknown beings, imagined, extinct, seemed to be massed together. Sometimes I confronted them with open arms, most times. However, I would wake up wet with sweat. No matter what the circumstances or the efforts were, these nightmares – usually popping up in the calmest days – became a permanent threat. They were warning me that nothing could be complete, beautiful, final, that there is always something which disturbs the clearest waters, for reasons that we cannot know.

Mara didn't appear, as she had promised, in a few hours; she didn't come the second day either, or the third one, so that the tormented waiting for her took on unsuspected dimensions. Each noise coming from the direction in which she had left – a rustle of leaves, the birds' quarrelling, the agitation of the wild animals, the excessive strength of the wind, the rolling of a pebble, would become, for a second, hope and joy, followed by, with the same rapidity, pain and worry. I was weak, afraid, or maybe had Mara become, without me noticing, the creature to whom I was tied, with all my senses? Perhaps it was both one and the other, and there was also the revolt of the man I used to be, the man whom time hadn't managed to bury completely in the memory. In spite of the evidence, I persisted in not admitting that everything was going towards loss, towards defeat, towards extinction.

Bizarre condition: to get to the stage where you defend yourself from the aggression of your own feelings, where you try and be different from what you feel – *to look* different, meaning *to look like, not to be*. Nobody stops me here, nobody forbids me from doing anything, there is no one in front of whom I could be ridiculous or important, I have no one to conquer or to influence. In this space, I make my own rules, I say what I want, I do as much as I have the strength to do. I don't see why I should continue to play a part written by others, why I should remain a dull, colourless creature, armoured with flat, harmless replies, or why I would veil or hide what I feel and what I believe? On the other hand, if

I think about it properly, I have no doubt that in order to make a change, in order to be how I think I should have been, I would need a much longer time than the one that is going to be granted to me, if any will be still granted to me before my natural disappearance. I have kept in my memory, for tens of years, the world's misery, and the pains and fears of my friends and my patients, let alone my own worries and losses, along with the fear and the aggression of fellow humans, which always put me in the situation of defending myself. It wasn't difficult, therefore, for me to discover the roots of my own behaviour, the caution and lack of trust with which I face everything, good and bad, the important and the unimportant events. It is clear to me that now, at the embarrassing age of wisdom, I will find it difficult to say things as they are, things that follow the same logic, or things of which I have no reason to boast. I say nothing, I listen and search where I have to. I understand, and go further. In fact, why would wisdom be any good to me, when time and my own body have become my own fiercest adversaries: when, after all that had been, all the feelings remaining to me are named disappointment, disgust and weakness? What if, by some absurd chance, rummaging through the events that chased me here to the mountain, I found an answer to an old question: could it have been any different? Given the circumstances, any answer apart from *no* would be ridiculous. This is how it was, this is what was possible, no matter how much I am now terrorised by unhappiness.

Mara: a human being whom, strictly speaking, I don't know, and in whose promises I cannot trust. We met rarely, superficially, and each time, after the first niceties you say to any acquaintance or to anyone you meet by chance, I ignored her. The memory of her parents can't be a strong enough connection, and neither can be the loneliness she lives in. In spite of all this, I am waiting for her, bizarrely, like a saviour. If she doesn't come back I will have to find her! This would clear up one more mystery: why did she change her mind, why didn't she want me to accompany her? Why did she leave suddenly as if she had an important obligation towards someone? The animals could have waited a bit. In any case, in all our discussions, the most convincing part was her will to escape this secluded place. Her fear of change was also intense. I have met thousands of people who wanted to give up a vice, or themselves, or various sins which imposed great humiliations on them. They talked a lot about their will, but, in reality, they would not move a finger to free themselves, either because they wouldn't try hard enough, or because they didn't really want to do it. Leaving all that aside, the fact that I became so close to Mara, who hadn't even been part of my project, seems to me rather ridiculous. If she came back, that would be good, but if she didn't, I would have to limit myself to what I had planned before I came here to the cabin, to the Saint's Stone. This seemed the reasonable way to look at things. On the other hand, the emotions desire, decide, and impose something else: she is absolutely essential to me. She is part of a plan for salvation, apparently put together by the lucid part of myself, which takes into consideration both soul and years. Horrible word: *years!*

Today. I wanted to start the day and the page by writing: *this is finally a day in which I felt good, meaning more calm*, but in the end I changed my mind, and I came nearer the truth. *Today I am resigned.* In the very moment I wrote the words

65

down, or to put it better, I drew them down – the way I used to do in high school, at the written tests, when I didn't know the subject – that was the moment I felt a strange need to laugh at these hesitations. Sure, I needed some time to return to this copybook which was destined, no doubt, for the rains or for the fire.

Last evening I put a blanket on my back and, with the gun in my hand, in case it was needed to scare the bears Dogaru told me about, I remained for a couple of hours out on the veranda. I wanted to observe the Saint's Stone, the surroundings, and especially the sky with its stars so big and so restless, the clouds of meteorites disturbing its dark blue from time to time; the dark blue in which I felt I was losing myself, gradually, overcome by a strange drunkenness of the sky. There I was, living, with intensity, a pleasant wandering, serene over the vastness which offered itself generously to me. All around the night birds were making their presence known, but their short, strong shrieks did not inhibit my diving into the dark blue, and neither did the noises made by the huge and incomprehensible avalanches coming from the Stone which had so much obsessed me. I was, finally, light, almost immaterial and, without necessarily planning it, I was seeing the white traces, milky, the lights lost within the vastness of galaxies and universes long gone or which were struggling to be born. I was convinced that what I was seeing through that sieve of dark blue was eternity, which for a couple of moments I had the privilege to meet. In any case I was not heading towards death, but towards life. The mental and biological indicators had changed their direction, their flow. I, quite simply, existed; and I had received a sign, a wave of hope, a certainty, thanks to the very kindness of that Spirit who destroys and creates universes, stirs up galaxies in order for them to die or to be re-born.

Therefore when I wrote *today*, I didn't mean to pin myself to time, meaning that I wasn't thinking whether it was Monday, Tuesday or Saturday, 10 or 20 June or December. Instead, I was thinking of that profound pulsation, which had convinced me that a secret was whispered to me, that I had witnessed a miracle. At the same time, coming back to reality, I realised that there is no salvation for this horrible and sad individual: for me, the one that I am. I close my eyes and realise that all the things I know, the past - as much as it is left in my memory – my past and that of those who entrusted theirs to me – the books, the characters, the prisoners of my own anxiety, the savants, the heroes and the stupid ones who accompanied me during the Time, the stars – alive or departed – the boundless spaces which humiliate any intelligence, that which created me and taught me to enquire and to feel - all these make up *today*, and the feeling that covers them cunningly, which is *vanity*. I wrote the Ecclesiarch's word several times, in big letters, then I split it into syllables, horizontally and vertically, I wrote it calligraphically, slowly, with a lot of patience, as if I was facing a great discovery, but after a while I had to repeat what I had known for a long time: that *I am as long as I am*, and nothing more. There is no salvation, returning, forgiveness, I repeated to myself obsessively, and, while I was following the contour of each letter, the bizarre geography drawn by the word, my resignation was significantly growing. It was ridiculous to expect something else, to have hopes, when, in reality, everything is moving towards loss, towards oblivion. While I was analysing myself, however, I was discovering insignificant bits of a more complicated feeling, of which vanity was a part. I was facing, no doubt, an unusual situation. I was seeing the sky again, that very sky of mine, with happiness, but also with that secret nostalgia which overwhelms you when, after a long while, you return to your place of birth. So, beyond that incomprehensible mix of feelings, I realised that I was facing another step, towards *something else*, towards a stage that refuses description, a feeling which was coming from somewhere in the vastness of the worlds surrounding us. I was night, and day, stars and galaxies. I was everything that my imagination and my strange need for eternity could comprehend.

Also *today*, Mara appeared. I was not waiting for her anymore, and I was comforting myself with the thought that there were too many things between us, and so the joy of the reunion was somehow concealed behind the shadow of vanity. In fact she also avoided any sentimental overflow, she just smiled casually, then turned her back to me and, with some caution, made an effort to align on a shelf a big number of bottles, jars and bags of dry herbs. That was her way of waiting for my reactions which, of course, were late in coming. In the end, annoyed by waiting too long she turned back to me:

"I guess you didn't miss me if you didn't greet me with questions like where have you been and what have you been doing? Why did you promise something and then do something else?"

"What matters is that you arrived in the end," I answered happily, putting an end to those long and confusing moments of waiting. "I did think, of course, about some unpleasant event, especially since you had mentioned an aggressive bear. But, as I didn't believe that was the only ferocious bear in the neighbourhood, I didn't make further assumptions, and limited myself to waiting. After all you could have had certain obligations. I was here a long time ago, as you know, and I don't know you that well."

"That's a pity" she whispered. "But you could try, you still have plenty to discover. Anyway after the first day in which I had lots of reasons not to come, I started to wait for you myself. I was thinking that you might want to see the graves of my parents or, simply, that you might need me in some way. You know the way, you walked it many times, so we couldn't have passed by each other. That's what I thought, but the more I waited and told myself in vain that you were going to appear, the more you were not coming."

Her confession, so sincere, touched me more than it should have: "My regret is immense, I didn't think of that, but maybe that was also because you did specify even the number of hours you were going to be away."

"It is true, but when I saw the graves I imagined that you might take me by surprise. You were closer to them than you were to me. I don't blame you, you'll come some other time," she concluded, and she didn't let me answer, as she probably knew I didn't have an answer, and, after she sat herself next to me, she continued with more and more confidence: "I had just reached home, and there came Dogaru. He had been to the city and brought me, as usual, bread, salt, sugar and salami, but also a bottle of cognac which, of course, I don't need. I pay for it and he drinks it. This became a habit. It is my obligation. Unfortunately he got drunk, sooner than on other occasions, and he started to remember his wife, his wasted youth, my father, my mother, merely to end up telling me about his fears, about loneliness and his fear of death. It's a nightmare on this mountain: all its inhabitants fear death, only I fear life! Then he asked me to allow him place his head on my leg and I felt pity towards him since

69

every person needs a bit of tenderness. In reality it was a kind of begging, so I allowed him. I'll hold him for a little while and then send him to bed, I said to myself, because he didn't seem able to walk home. In that state his balance was playing him tricks. Unfortunately he didn't stop there and his hands started to wander where it was improper, and so we quarrelled, I slapped him a couple of times, he cried, but didn't stop. He had slept at the station several times before but never did something like that, and then he remained on the bed where I had pushed him but he continued to swear at me and curse. Well, I didn't know that side of him, a very ugly one; he had made other attempts before, more timidly, but I had ignored him. After he left, I thought everything through once again, as it was an unusual event, and, of course, I had to agree with him."

"You shouldn't let this trouble you. He's grown wild since he started to drink. Did he apologise at least?" I enquired, for the sake of keeping the dialogue going.

"Oh, no, he didn't seem to remember anything. He kissed me on the forehead in a fatherly manner, as usual, then we talked about the weather for a bit, whether it's getting warmer or not, then he took his donkey and he was gone. After that, though, I thought of his very dirty accusations, which I don't want to tell you about. I cried a lot, and when I finally calmed myself down, so that the day should be really black, the monk who buried my father appeared. Our story is a bit more complicated, and every time I think about it, I shiver with fear, but also with pleasure. Understand it how you want. In any case, Dogaru said that he knew some things from the priest, details that concerned only the two of us, meaning the monk and myself, and that is why apparently he wanted to try his luck as well. So the monk arrived at a very special moment. Instead of greeting him, I seized a stick that I always keep nearby and kept hitting him. I believe he must be still hurting. He didn't ask for explanations, he must have thought I had gone mad, so he ran away and didn't come back. After I was left on my own, I cried like crazy and felt like taking my life. In fact what is the meaning of my life? Do I just leave to get food for some animals? Do I just live to defend myself from some bastards? Do I live here for the sake of two graves? Often, during the night, I cry and think of the nearest abyss, of father's gun, still unused. In the morning though, I observe the fog rising towards the top of the mountains, I notice the dew, the birds, the forest full of life and then I run from here, from the mountains, and death doesn't seem to me so urgent anymore. This is why I was late."

"I couldn't even imagine this," I said, trying to apologise indirectly. "It is clear that we know each other rather little, we are not a team yet, as they say in sports. I notice though that there is nowhere you can be on your own."

"When I see a human being," she says in a sad voice, "instead of being happy, I start to panic, to prepare my defence. Lately I've been thinking seriously of going to a monastery, but I don't know any prayers and couldn't find any in your books either. Don't you pray?" she enquired.

"Unfortunately not as much as I should, and not loudly. At my age, if you haven't managed to know the One From Above, you have lived in vain. I regret a lot of things, but I am not ready to talk about this yet."

Lord, I close my eyes and try to find the way known only by the soul, but no word can help me anymore, they are all signs of disappointment and death. They became what they shouldn't be:

71

lies. I can't manage anymore to believe in hope, light, justice and beauty, while they are, no doubt, agreeable pseudonyms of death. I should pray and I finally do but I don't know what to ask for anymore. And why would I be heard? I, the one who, in the saddest moment of passing through this life, kept silent or lied in the name of the truth, hope and justice? Lord, if I die without succeeding in making you believe what I say, at least look at my tears, now when no word helps me anymore. Forgive me for existing without having existed.

Buddha in Benares:
Monks, suffering, as a noble truth, is this: birth is suffering, aging is suffering, sickness is suffering, death is suffering; association with the loathed is suffering, dissociation from the loved is suffering, not to get what one wants is suffering.

Redemption... *the noble eightfold path, that is to say: right view, right intention; right speech, right action, right livelihood, right concentration, right effort, right meditation.*

My table is full of books and truths, discovered or understood too late. During my youth I always took refuge at the periphery of the events. The great causes were outside me so I suffered for all kind of small causes. They shadowed my horizon, they prevented me from seeing what I see now, when, unfortunately, it is too late. I had the bad luck of encountering only mediocre saints playing the parts of the great saints. It may be that only those could be seen. Late discoveries, and the future is all I cannot be anymore. It is a permanent loss which I can feel through all my nerves, and with suffering. Mara became suffering, as well, or a synthesis of all that is forbidden, inaccessible to me, a symbol of my life forever faded. Unrest, inconsistency and false targets, or, punishment for all the matters I didn't manage to understand or to discover at the right time. I follow her with my eyes continuously. She wants to comfort me, she does her best to make me feel good. Inside her, probably even without knowing it, she plays the part of the daughter or even of the wife. I think she expects me to praise her for how useful she became to me.

She prepares light soups for me, teas, feeds me with plenty of honey. She even intends to give me massages, as if my physical rehabilitation would depend on time. (A stupid thought: it is the end of spring and people usually die in spring or in autumn. She can't possibly be aware of such truths but she might be sensing them. After all, how much of us is from the present, and how much is what we inherit, what our ancestors left us from beyond any words, understanding and logic?). A massage would be good, but I'll have to cover her eyes. If I can't stand myself the way I am now, why should she make such an effort? Yes, this is the solution: with her eyes covered! She tried to free herself from her dirty stories and so she entrusted them to me with a disarming ease. Now she is waiting for my verdict, and especially for my forgiveness, but I don't see how it might help her. She insists that I should see her, indirectly saying that the verdict should come sooner rather than later. One plausible hypothesis is not out of the question: she is finally pleased that she managed to free herself from some tormenting memories. If only I could get rid of this stupid gravity. If I could escape playing the part of the medic who is used to listening, and focus on interpreting the gestures and what hides beyond the words, things would be simpler. Unfortunately I can't figure out what inhibits me, why I don't have the strength to let myself contaminated by her naturalness. I've always hidden what I think, what I feel, what is right for me. I stayed in the shadow of others, I was in the service of others, I ignored myself, and here, now, I find this mask, this part profoundly ridiculous, now when the play has ended, when life, the crumb of life left, forces me to reclaim my own expression. I feel as if I'm in a children's game. She is the mother, I – the son, who lets himself be fed, taken care of, spoilt. Mara walks around in front of my eyes. She is carefree, I can't hear her steps, it seems as if she's floating, although she is not frail, on the contrary. I try hard not to stare at her, and especially to keep my hands still so that I don't make any improper gestures. Not necessarily from a male impulse, although *the being I used to be*, and especially that *impulse*, hadn't completely died. I was yet to discover her inner structure, what she was hiding beyond the words, if she was indeed hiding anything. I was yet to discover, as well, how to steal a bit of energy from her. She confessed the story of her monk to me, of their sin to be more precise, without many hesitations in her voice, as if she was talking about someone else or as if she was recounting a story heard from someone else. I would have thought it was someone else's story, if I hadn't seen her tears.

I'm trying to reconstruct the story out of Mara's confession, and the deeper I dive into it, the more I experience it: it interests me, it hurts, it haunts me so much that it becomes mine too.

Thus Father Serafim was brought to the Station by Dogaru, who had known him for a long time, the same way he knew the very few good people and the numerous bad ones, the weird ones, cursed by fate, or the ones who were simply lost in the area. Fear and booze transformed Dogaru into a useful information point used by everybody, without exception. Mara was to find sometime later that the monk's appearance, right when she needed the most help, hadn't been by chance. At that time, after the funeral, lost, confused, she didn't notice when the monk disappeared. She didn't ask herself why he didn't wait for the rain to stop either. In any case, he had re-entered, unnoticed, the night from which he emerged, while she kept running absurdly to the graves and to the stables, where she had actually slept during the first nights. The last image of her father, his distorted figure, as if he had seen something terrible in the moment of his *departure*, haunted her constantly, so she had to get used to the house again, little by little, and especially her own room where anxiety and uncertainty persisted. Her father's figure became, paradoxically, the symbol of loneliness and lack of perspective. He was not anymore the gentle and harmless being who used to foresee, with serenity, the storms and the sunny days. He was now the one who sentenced her to loneliness and fear, the one who left her there without protection and hope. If it weren't for the pity and the care for those innocent animals, who usually greeted her with joy, she probably would have gone mad before long, but the cow, the sheep and especially the dogs made her days a bit more bearable, as if they were taking over part of her grief, diminishing the shock of the nights when darkness filled her room with monstrous and threatening apparitions.

The monk reappeared at the Station in such a moment of confusion, when night was trying hard, as usual, to squeeze those horrible creatures into her soul, and if she hadn't recognised his unmistakable baritone voice, which had helped her father cross to *the other side*, she would have probably left him to the mercy of the dogs who were very agitated. Finally, she was not alone anymore, and the ecclesiastic should have given her more peace and security, but it was not to be that way. She fed him, she prepared hot water for him to wash himself. They talked about the people they knew in that part of the world. She prepared his bed in the nearby building where the former meteorologists used to live, but a feeling of tension and rejection gave her no peace, although Mara thought that would be her normal reaction to any stranger. She was happy, though, with the thought that she would have the opportunity to organise a religious memorial service for her father, before blessing the rooms from which her father's soul refused to leave.

Strangely, in the moment she put her head on the pillow, her anxiety calmed down and, for the first time, she didn't feel the need to look through the corners for the embodiment of her fears, so for the first time since her father's departure she managed to get some sleep. On top of that, the wild animals had avoided the cabin or maybe she had fallen in such a deep sleep that she only heard the dogs barking in the morning, and even those barks were short, idle, a sign of small quarrels between themselves. The monk's presence brought her now, after a long time, a total relaxation of the senses, which she had given up hoping for; so, little by little, Mara found herself regretting that she had greeted the monk with distrust and caution. Looking for some excuses, as she had no doubt that the monk had noticed her cold attitude, Mara lingered in bed, planning to start the day in a different way. She could still not think of the way to reach out for the monk's understanding and forgiveness. She knew from her father, and especially from Dogaru, that you must confess to the priests all burdens you have on your soul, what you think, what sins you committed, by your thoughts and by your deeds, after which you might receive your punishment: prayers you repeat tens of times, fasting periods and so on, and only after that comes forgiveness. Because their duty is to understand and to forgive. In fact, Mara's beliefs about sin and forgiveness were very simple, a kind of a banal barter with the Creator, I give you this, you give me that, and we go on from there. This is exactly how she thought when the gratitude she felt, following the first quiet night after her father's death, made her commit to action. She decided to express her gratitude towards the monk by inviting him to a very good meal, especially since such a gesture meant for her domestic reconciliation, family, peace.

Unfortunately the day didn't continue as it had started, but once again the anguish and fears returned, a sign that her first instinct, that strange feeling she had, was warning her of the danger and shouldn't have been ignored. The screech of the door coming from the former meteorologists' house along with the racket of the dogs made her go near the window, and what she saw made her instinctively cover her eyes as soon as she could. Naked, with a bucket of water in one hand and a towel in the other, Father Serafim paused for a bit in front of the door as if he was all on his own in that wilderness, and then, after he'd made sure of the dogs' complicity, he took a few steps, and facing the window behind which he thought someone was probably watching him, he poured the bucket straight on the top of his head. He wasn't in a hurry go back or even to dry himself. Instead he was gently caressing his black hair and his long beard, while, strangely enough, he was carefully observing the sky as if he was waiting to see a sign appearing on that huge screen, or even to catch a glimpse of the saint of the neighbouring mountain himself. In the end, thinking that he had been ignored, he returned to the house. After a time in which the fear and waiting in Mara's soul had given up any defence, he came out dressed up in his usual priestly robes. This time he was leaning forward a bit, eyes fixed the ground, as the clerical clothes required, maybe also because sinful demons express themselves with some difficulty in full daylight. The hairy, athletic man from a little while ago, cut out of a bodybuilding manual, the male who had exhibited his manhood shamelessly, in the hope of being seen, seemed to belong to another world, another reality about which Mara had often thought. Even during the time when her father was still alive, she had been pushed by numerous dreams about the taste of brutal, desperate love, and she had intended to find out more about it. She was equally afraid and interested, all the more because she hadn't yet managed to imagine how her first love story would happen. She hadn't yet imagined her first sin, and of course she had no image of how *the first one who... meaning her first man* would look like, and especially, she had no idea of how life would be *after*. While her father kept losing his strength and his eyesight, her need of someone able to protect her increased, her tortured feelings towards that yet unknown man ceased to be love, as before, but fear of future. Father Serafim's presence, though, interested her, in spite of its uneasy aspects and in spite of the caution with which she met his every gesture and word. In the end, she invited him into the house, since, in any case, the monk seemed determined not to leave the entrance step on which he had seated himself. Although she had a vague presentiment, somewhere between welcome and rejection, Mara started to prepare his breakfast, as she had imagined, long time ago, that she would welcome her destined one, her *man*. The fact that she could also eat something different, and escape, even in this way, the exasperating daily habit, started to please her. She laid the table cloth carefully, set the cutlery, brought a couple of wild flowers and, failing a suitable jar, she put them in a plastic cup. When the omelette, tea and cheese were ready she remembered that her mother used to light a candle before inviting the guests to take their seats at the table. Unfortunately the bread was missing as Dogaru had neglected her for many days. Nevertheless she didn't feel she would need to apologise. The monk hadn't announced his visit, he hadn't promised he would return, he came out of the blue so it was clearly understood she would offer him whatever she had available, not what she would have liked to offer him. Anyhow, Mara made great efforts to hide her awkwardness as she hadn't prepared the meal just for the monk, but also to prove herself that, if needed, she could be different, that she hadn't gone completely wild, as she usually reproached herself. She had made all the preparations in silence, focused and happy that she didn't lose her temper and didn't forget anything, and, when Father Serafim blessed the meal in a solemn voice, she burst into tears. A crack had appeared in the mind, a path towards a domestic universe had suddenly appeared, and she was somewhat surprised to experience that. They exchanged no words until the final prayer of thanks, and then the monk took out his tobacco box and, with confident gestures he rolled himself a cigarette.

"I have this sin as well but, for the time being, I don't want to make you an accomplice," he assured her while leaving the room. "Living in this wilderness one acquires certain habits which, without noticing, start taking possession of you. One is obliged to kill one's loneliness somehow."

Mara felt like laughing at his excuse, and although she would have liked to ask him for details regarding his bad habits acquired in the loneliness of the mountain, in order to compare them with hers, she suddenly remembered her parents' graves and thought of a religious service in the memory of her father, whose soul was still not letting go of the house and of her.

In reality everyone fears death, but too few think with acuity about that moment, and even fewer realise that they could be the victims themselves, the next in line. Her father had not been an exception.

"What brings you here, Father," Mara asked eventually. "I am surprised that Uncle Dogaru didn't send me any oil as I have none left."

"This time I didn't look for him, as he had started to drink a lot and I am weak, sinful and inclined to catch vices. For the moment I am not ready to fight all temptations placed by the Devil in my way."

"Then why did you become a monk?" Mara asked in complete candour.

"I thought that the religious robe and the holiness of the church would defend me from sinning, but that is not how it works. I fight strongly with myself, with this miserable inclination towards sin. I've chosen the most difficult path: that of redemption, of destroying who I am. I am like a lost sheep and, like the Psalmist, I assure The One Who Holds us in His Power that I haven't forgotten his commands. I repent tremendously each sin of thinking or acting, and as much as possible, I compensate by living in this wilderness. I trust, more and more every day, that I have started walking the path to atonement which is long and full of temptations."

"Running from people? This doesn't look like a sign of a great power to me..."

"Avoiding them, as we have to live our lives, and I have found my own way of living. This centres on the medicinal plants, mistletoe, speedwell, sweet woodruff, juniper.[4] I am now looking for low-growing juniper, more scientifically, *Juniperus nana*. I have a lot of patients for whom I prepare teas and ointments, but mostly I sell the plants to the old pharmacists who know how to use them: *Succus juniperi inspissatus, Spiritus juniperi, Spisitus angelicae compositus*. To know where it grows, when it blossoms, when it should be picked, as well as how to prepare it: artemisia absinthium, meaning the grass-of-the-virgins, Lord's-wood, good mugwort, black mugwort, green mugwort, low-growing mugwort.[5] Doesn't this sound nice? You need to know precisely that this month, for example, you need to pick albăstrele, amăreală, angelica, arnica, barba-popii, chimenul, cicoare, cimbrişor de câmp, coada-şoricelului, coada-calului, coada-racului, colăceii-babei (Malva sylvestris), creţişoară, cornişorul, hasmaţuiul, iarba-şarpelui, limba-mielului, lichenul cerbului, măghiranul, mama-pădurii, muşeţelul regal, măceşul, măcrişul, patlagina, odoleanul, rozmarinul, trei-fraţi-pătaţi, stugurele ursului, unguraşul, valeriana, and many others."[6]

---

4 In Romanian – vâsc, ventrilică, vinariţă, ienupăr

5 Wormwood, southernwood

6 Bluebottles, bachelor's buttons, milkwort, priest's-beard, meadowsweet, caraway, fennel, chicory, shepherd's thyme, mousetail, yarrow, horsetail, silverweed, crayfishtail, old woman's knotted breads, lady's mantle, the little-horn, Lycopodium, clubmoss, cow parsley, *Echium vulgare*, Viper's Bugloss or Blueweed, lambtongue, star flower, *Borago officinalis* or *Echium amoenum*, *Asplenium scolopendrium*, hart's-tongue fern, marjoram, common toothwort, royal camomile, rosehip, sorrel, fleawort, all-heal, rosemary, heartsease, bearberry, white horehound, valerian)

"But in order to collect medicinal plants you don't need to become a monk," Mara interrupted him, glad that she had found the question necessary to continue the dialogue, and glad that she could give the monk the impression that she was interested in what he was saying. The names of the plants enunciated with great importance in Romanian, and many more that she couldn't manage to memorise, in Latin, made her believe that he wanted to convince her of the seriousness of his occupation, and in the end this agglomeration of names sounded like a rationalisation, so her question, almost accidentally uttered, seemed to be the beginning of a conversation Mara needed. Father Serafim had come out of the blue, performed the funeral service, left during the storm as if pushed from behind, or as if summoned by an important duty that could not be delayed. As a result she knew almost nothing about him, and, if she thought about it carefully, she wasn't even sure if the person in front of her was one and the same as the one who had helped her father to cross to the world of righteous, according to custom. She behaved as if he was the one, although the memory of her tears and the terrible fear of those times forced her to maintain a sharp vigilance.

"It is a question with two answers," the monk said. "The first one is that I felt very weak and I needed protection, peace, a quiet life. It was not faith, or if you like the search of certainty, that brought me to the monastery, but it was the fear of the real life, of confrontation. But the most correct answer would be: I don't know. I followed the first thought that crossed my mind, I wasn't aware of the harshness of the place towards which I was heading, the hardships and the suffering that hide behind a commonplace word: *submission*. I had no idea about how hard the path towards Him is. As in many times when there is a need for running away or isolation, you must not exclude one big danger: woman. I did my studies with not much enthusiasm. Nature equipped me a lot of qualities, but only with a drop of each. And so I studied for one year at the Conservatoire, two years at the Polytechnic, and then another two years at the Medicine, followed, of course, by almost two years long compulsory army service. At the end of each new attempt I realised that wasn't what I had been looking for and, before I could open my eyes, I would find myself failing the school year. The woman who completely reduced my life to dust appeared during my medical studies – let's call them that! She was tall, well built, with dark eyes like the tar of Hell, like the bottom of an abyss, or like countryside wells, deep and dark. Big bosom, powerful, rebellious like yours, my daughter – in one word, a creature more beautiful than anyone I had met before. God forgive me for the sinful thought and the careless turn of phrase, but, against my will, I turned my head around after her in the street and the woman did exactly the same thing in the same second, so, instinctively, we stopped and analysed each other with unrestrained joy and curiosity. Then I went near her, naturally, and, after a short hesitation, I kissed her; and she was so taken by surprise by my gesture that she didn't even step aside, or show the slightest restraint, except that after a while she whispered, somehow frightened, that she was married, but, in spite of that she agreed to meet me. She then confessed to me, in all sincerity, that she was on very good terms with her husband and she would have to classify this episode in the list of inexplicable encounters. She was convinced that in a previous life we must have been brother and sister, not lovers, as I firmly believed. Moreover, from the first moment, she assured me that she had no intention of leaving her husband so she suggested we shouldn't see each other anymore. Preoccupied, up to borders of obsession, with her face and body traits, I didn't find out her name, her profession, or even who her husband was.

From the coffee shop where we had met she jumped straight into a taxi passing in front of us, so that it was impossible for me to guess which part of the city she was living in. This gesture left no room for nuance, it was clear that I had disappointed her. I had got so excited and the victory was so unexpected, that I had let myself be overwhelmed by euphoria, and didn't succeed in matching the high level of the moment! During the following days I kept asking myself what I should have said or done so that the woman would grant me the chance of a new rendezvous, but nothing seemed appropriate, no idea gave me any hope, and her abrupt departure, her running away – to put it in other words, only increased my unhappiness. For weeks in a row I didn't go to classes or training, but remained in the street, in the area where I had met her, hoping that she would still pass by. I was determined not to give up because, after all, she belonged to me by a will or by a superior order, and this fact was threatening to become a disease without name and without cure. In the end I figured out that I was waiting in vain and, besides, I wasn't completely certain anymore that I would recognise her, so I resolved, in a stupid, childish way, not to save what could have been still saved from my classes, but to find myself another woman. That is the truth: you fulfil yourself through a woman. She is, in reality, the aim of all our explorations, the most irrepressible secret need, the end of the road. One woman, one love, one blind desire for unity. This is what I believed then."

"And today?" Mara asked, intrigued to hear such words particularly from the mouth of a monk.

"Love without lust remains, but its object is different. A higher one, the highest, the only one that protects you. Temptations, of course, don't disappear, they can't possibly disappear as long as the earth, of which we are conceived, is alive, and has the divine breath; but I discovered what is most important and I acquired the weapons to help me in this terrible confrontation."

"Are weapons enough?" Mara asked amused by the seriousness with which the monk was trying to defend himself. "Is their master, I wonder, ready to handle them? Does he have the necessary power and ability?"

"Satan tests our strength and always, always lays all possible traps for us. Sometimes we win, sometimes we lose, and our judgement and punishment await us in heaven. That is where we will have to answer. The success itself is abstinence. Saint Basil the Great considered that abstinence implies destroying guilt, alienating oneself from passions, eradicating time, and even the most wicked senses and desires of our nature. Abstinence is the beginning of clerical life!"

"Could that be our only redemption?" Mara wondered disappointed.

"Redemption for myself and for those who choose this path. Of course, without desires, without interests, without senses, people cease to exist. But I chose my path knowing that it is the hardest. No one forced me."

Mara was not happy with his answers but she was pleased she had someone to talk with, that she didn't forget all the words, as she often did, when her moments of fear used to end with an exasperating weeping and with the thought of running away, of abandoning the mountain at any price. She persisted in believing that, one day, a miracle, a force, an unusual event would open a horizon for her, would give her a chance to get rid of those moments: *anywhere, but not here!*

Mara, of course, is still dreaming about her chances. As far as the former student, Sever Moraru, the future monk, was concerned, things had taken an unexpected turn. The woman he had encountered, the woman from a previous life, was late in making her appearance, but in compensation, as he had wished for, a multitude of women appeared! There was no discrimination, no passion. There were simply as many as possible, all guilty of having the same sex with *him*. Some were his colleagues, numerous sterile ones who were gravitating around the gynaecology clinic, worried that they would have to go on their own to some unknown clinic, far from any city. Some were older wives, neglected by their tired or bored husbands, generous not only with pleasures but with their purses as well. Others were old maids or immature young ones, unripe but eager for sensations, and all of them could find consolation with the one who didn't get tired of waiting, exploring, delving deeper into a permanent night of the senses.

His movements were stereotypical, always kissing the same places, every time looking for the shortest road, because, at the beginning, all of them had a tormenting appetite, and it was only after a couple of dates that his movements would diversify, but not too much, because it was not love which pushed him in the woman's arms. It was hate or an attempt to temper his aggressiveness. During the few occasions when he stayed on his own in the damp and well-used hostel room, when, as rarely happened, he didn't have any appointments, he was invaded, as if by memories from a forgotten existence, by the fragrances of the women he'd had, the good and bad perfumes, especially the good ones, yielding the smack of perspiration, mixed with the flavour of soaps and creams.

He could feel their lips, some of them very fine, delicate, often in contrast with the muscles of the creatures. He could even hear their moans and puerile phrases, pathetic, sincere, referring to eternity.

In fact, he had few memories about the faces and names of those women. Instead, he remembered more about the spaces where he had met them, the elegant hotels, with sophisticated furniture and showers, but he remembered, in particular, the one-star rooms, without a shower, with basins which even the water seemed to avoid. Sometimes, putting together all the women's gestures with the strange memory of the senses, he recomposed that Same One, continually surprised by how impossible the way towards her had seemed to be, while the path to the others had been so simple and so unexpectedly banal. He remembered also, somewhat embarrassed, the anger of one of those women, when she wanted to hold on to him for longer than he had intended:

"After all, you are nothing but a provider of services, and, if you do your job properly, you will be paid and then recommended to another!"

Of course, he lost out on his studies but not on the hope that, in the end, his patience would be repaid. And, one day, that's exactly what happened.

At a film premiere he spotted her on another man's arm, probably the husband she had, in fact, told him about. He wasn't on his own either, as he was accompanying a freshly divorced woman who, pleased with his services, had promised him a long trip to a hot and far way country. He wouldn't have wanted to miss that opportunity if *She* herself had not appeared, the one most dreamed of and most sought after, the reason for all his failures. As expected, he only watched bits of the movie since he hardly took his eyes away from the back of her head, and, at the end, he did everything possible to free himself from the clutches of his generous companion, so as to be able to follow The One.

This time luck didn't desert him. He found the block of flats she lived in, then more easily, discovered her floor and flat number. For the first time, he finally had the certainty and belief that, before attempting any dialogue, he would try and find out as much as possible about her.

Now, the need for her didn't seem so tormenting anymore, it had taken numerous small steps, but, since he now knew where she lived, he could prepare, gradually and thoroughly, the great encounter and the much awaited revenge. That is how he started to prey on her again, especially since this time, school was not an issue anymore.

One fine morning, with the neighbours' help, he discovered that the man she had kissed so affectionately, before he got into the car, was her husband, Claudiu Barbu. He was a long distance pilot, a profession which kept him far from the country and his wife for long periods of time.

She, Madalina Barbu, or Madame Madeleine as the women in the neighbourhood called her, owned a small import-export trade company, with a couple of employees who bought and sold all kind of exotic products from somewhere in Asia brought in mainly by her husband's female colleagues.

When, in addition, he had managed to find out the pilot's flight schedule, the future Father Serafim started to imagine the moment of meeting up with her and all the possible scenarios. At her house or in the street? What would he say to her? What would be his opening phrase? And what if Madeleine did not recognise him and called the police?

He was not ruling out, either, the possibility that she might have been busy with someone else during those days. Beautiful but faithful – that was yet another possibility which he also had to consider. In the end, he abandoned himself to the inspiration of the moment.

Burning with eagerness and wearing his best clothes, he went to her house after, of course, he had witnessed the usual departure scene from a distance. More than that, he had waited for one more hour in the street, in case the man might have forgotten something and came back. Then, with an excitement hard to contain, he knocked at the woman's door. She had opened it with no hesitation and with a simply familiar air.

"You? But how did you find me? This is not possible, it's beyond any imagination. And what a nerve! Go away immediately. If my husband returns he will shoot you. Haven't you thought about that?"

"I believe that's exactly what I want," he answered. "Because, anyway, I am like a dead man since the moment you ran away. Everything that followed was just continual loss and seeking."

"Let's get out of the house as soon as possible," she urged him. "The company employees might turn up and this would be very dangerous!"

Her gestures though, he noticed with surprise, did not match the panic in her words, and he reacted accordingly. He locked the door and, entangled in a long kiss, more out of the need not to hear her words than out of passion or desperation, he pushed her towards the bed. Surprisingly, she didn't put up any resistance. She didn't reject him either when he undressed her, nor when he left her for a couple of seconds in order to take off his own coat and trousers.

Their unrestrained lust and haste matched the frustration of their long waiting. They seemed to be blind, deaf, manoeuvred by another person, from outside, another person who they couldn't oppose or whose decisions they couldn't even comment on. An amazing explosion followed, in which everything was consumed before it had begun. For a couple of moments they were lost, as if someone had suddenly torn off the surface of their existence, resulting in a deafening lightning, blindness, a fusion above their power of understanding. Then followed a reassuring amazement – which lasted as long as the time that was necessary to see each other and find each other again, accompanied by the sensation that, before this, they had actually been two spirits coming from different spaces, in order to give birth to the two bodies which had once been a single structure. A violent fight had just taken place, and their individual desires, which were to vanish and to dissipate into the void, had encountered each other, after which followed shyness and fear.

"Swear to me that we will never speak about what has just happened, that we will never do it ever again," she insisted, trying to sort out what she could from the torn clothes. "Please, go, leave me alone if you really want us to see each other again. I need time, I need to understand what has happened."

Repelled by the panic in the woman's voice, he hurried out of the room. In a way, he was happy to be out of the danger, of which he only now became conscious, and he refused to think about the meeting with the woman who had brought with her his failure and his madness. Was it worth it? He had known tens of women but none of them had stirred up such a passion in him, none had ever taken him beyond what he could feel and understand.

No matter how hard he tried, it was impossible to find the words which could correctly define his emotions. They had received new, unique nuances. Chance had not only offered him a certain woman, but an entire world, a space which had been forbidden to him before; and the first impulse that came into his mind was to stop. Not a step further, not another attempt. All his senses commanded him to lose himself in this experience, to live it through as if it were the last; but in the rare moments of lucidity he was looking for a middle way, a comforting solution. This liaison could have a future, he told himself, only if she was the one to search him out, only if she was the one who took the next step.

The monk was so marked by the intensity and the effects of this meeting, that Mara, as she confessed to me, was under the impression that it had just taken place, moments before, or that, in reality, it was a simple invention intended to impress through the force and the complexity of his feelings. Unfortunately there was a yawning gap between the logic and the actions of the future Father Serafim. Although he had planned it, he was not able to wait for too long, and, being blindly propelled by that unrestrained need of her, he grabbed the phone. A very hasty: "I'll come in an hour to that coffee place!" convinced him that he had called in the most inappropriate moment, that in reality she was not alone, as he had hoped.

"Don't follow me anymore, don't call me anymore," were her requests, repeated with desperation. "Even if, against all reason, I should be the one you have been always searching for, even if we should be truly made to be together, I am a married woman and I have no intention of getting a divorce. Unfortunately, you appeared too late and I'm terrified by what happens between us. We must not see each other anymore."

In the end, in spite of her pleadings, they did meet in his studio, after the future monk had explained in great detail how much he had lost because of her. He thought that she would give in to rational arguments, rather than instinctively accepting his proposition, partly because she wanted to get rid of the guilt which accompanied her natural feelings. As a result he didn't exclude the possibility of repeating the event, as logic dictated. Instead, he chose the opposite course.

Without any words or explanations, another emotional discharge followed. She was not in a hurry anymore, didn't reproach him with anything, she seemed to live intently each gesture, move, breath. They fell asleep, then, for a couple of minutes, in his narrow hospital bed, which he had bought very cheaply from the storekeeper of a clinic.

He suggested they meet again, same place, in a week's time, and, persuaded by his insistence, the woman gave in. So, for a while, their relationship became normal from a certain point of view. They were dying and reviving together, and he was firmly convinced that they were both living their lives only in thoughts of their next appointment.

The madness that overcame him took him even further from his university studies, and, because he had to make a living, he took a job as a driver for a network of chemist's shops. He got this thanks to one of his occasional lovers. He supplied the shops with medicines, collected medicinal plants from several harvesters in his little van, and, each week, he also had to prove his gratitude towards the one who had given him this means of making a living, and given him a relative security.

He was doing his duty, with his senses directed towards, and only towards Madeleine, along with the spiritual ascension and the misery of supporting each other. His senses assured him that all would be well, but the reality was a brutal contradiction. Sooner than he had expected, the woman suggested that they should separate forever.

The episode, the tragedy, or whatever it was, happened in his little room, on a day when the pilot had been sent to China. The woman, Lina – as he had baptised her because the name Madeleine gave him the impression of distance, coldness – came to their appointment in a completely different mental state than the one he was used to. If previously everything seemed to be implied, known, the sensuality and the lust pushing away any words, now she started to talk without sense. She talked about the weather, the neighbours, shops, girlfriends whose names he had never heard before, as if she wanted to introduce him to her real world. Although he liked enormously to listen to her and to learn all the tones of her voice, unknown until then, since they had mostly whispered before, this time he felt that something was not in order. That melancholy visibly spread out over what they were and what they told each other. The sounds gradually lost their meaning, and became murky. Nothing connected with the present anymore. Nothing connected with what they were themselves in those moments. They came to that place not to experience what they had eagerly waited for an entire endless week, but to meet with a painful past, and, in particular, with brutal reality.

For the first time, their love became more lucid, leaving space for caresses and, also, for words. Beyond the natural eagerness of belonging to each other, of merging together until their individual selves disappeared, there now arose the need to stick closely together, and the need to extend endlessly what was not only happiness anymore, but what had become the anticipation of fear and disaster – the end of their journey.

The simple fact that she was clinging onto him, not willing to leave any tiny space in between their two bodies, confirmed to him that he wasn't wrong and that his senses were warning him about a real danger. Sometime later, when sweat and exhaustion managed to separate them eventually, Lina took his face into her palms and watched him for a long time, determined to prepare him for a critical and painful moment:

"And here comes the end of it. We were mad, irresponsible, in fact, I don't even know how this could happen. In any case, we need to stop here by any means. I can't continue, I am weak and afraid. I have nothing with which to reproach my husband. Rationally, nothing justifies my behaviour. Once I get home, all the joy I have here becomes guilt, remorse and fear. You must understand that I can't take this anymore. It is not so much the fear, although that is reasonably significant as well, but the disgust. In the morning I sleep with you, in the evening with him. I can't control my tears anymore, and the shame. If I get a divorce, you realize that I'll lose everything. My shops belong to Claudiu, in reality. Without him, if I had to work as a teacher, on a salary smaller than the monthly tips of a taxi driver, no matter how much I love you, I couldn't survive. You, in fact, have nothing at all. No skills, no job, and a very uncertain future on which we couldn't count. You know that well. The poverty awaiting us would destroy our love, in time, and we would get to hate each other in the end. No matter how painful the separation might be, and it hurts me terribly, it is better if it takes place now, rather than later, when we would be forced into it by the circumstances."

The future Father Serafim didn't contradict her, any explanations would have been useless; his love and his crazy need of her died violently the very moment she brought his real situation into discussion. Logically, he shouldn't have been upset, but thankful to destiny that he had been offered the chance to experience such feelings and moments, as he never had before. Unfortunately, in a couple of moments, everything collapsed: Madeleine, his Lina, had become a stranger from whom he felt only that he had to part as soon as possible. He still had the strength though to assure her that all would be as she wished, and he also had the strength to refuse her last kiss, before departure. Their love had become history, and the monument he had erected to her with so much faith, the losses and damages he had suffered in the process were already visible. If she hadn't spoken, hadn't explained herself, his fall wouldn't have been so brutal; but he had to experience that miracle in order to discover that in reality, without those moments, he was lonely and defeated.

"In a city like ours, all you can do is three things: watch TV, make politics or sleep with the wives of those who make politics." This was the conclusion drawn by the student Sever Moraru. Then, since he didn't have any strength left for another woman anyway, or for any unfulfilled obligations, he stopped at a bar where the drivers used to go. After a couple of glasses of whisky, he went to a taxi rank where, after long negotiations, explaining that he had made an important bet, he booked three cars. In the first one he placed his shoes, in the second one, his coat, and in the third one he climbed in himself. That's what he had done, as well, when, after several attempts, he had passed the anatomy exam – the first in the series of very difficult exams, baptised "The Donkeys' Footbridge"[7] by the students. Thinking about everything that had happened to him before then, this exam was the first true victory he could remember.

For the next couple of days he didn't go out of the house, although he wasn't feeling unwell. He was afraid he might bump into her, Madeleine, this time by pure chance. He was determined to somehow get used to the thought that, after the moment of separation, Lina would exist for him only as a painful memory, and that her absence would bring his fall to an end.

"Why should I love her to distraction, why should I sacrifice my hours and days for her, why should I dedicate all my thoughts and energy to her, when the level her brain has achieved is nowhere near that of her beauty? She is not capable of love, of suffering, or, at least, of empathy. She seems incapable of losing the little she has at home for the richness that true love could offer her."

He tried to fool himself with such thoughts, but he knew very well that, before her, no one and nothing had given him that total joy, the light and strength that raised him above words. At the same time, no one had thrown him so easily into a place where humiliation and defeat had the bitterest taste, and, all of a sudden, while he was trying to stop an inappropriate and useless tear, the monk remembered *Job*'s words, which Mara recited, giving me the opportunity to

---

7 Or the Donkey's Stairs – referring to a series of events or things placed in ascending or descending order

recollect a beautiful chapter from the Bible:

"I loathe my life; I will give free utterance to my complaint; I will speak in the bitterness of my soul. I will say to God, do not condemn me; let me know why you contend against me. Does it seem good to you to oppress, to despise the work of your hands and favour the designs of the wicked? Have you eyes of flesh? Do you see as man sees? Are your days as the days of man, or your years as a man's years, that you seek out my iniquity and search for my sin, although you know that I am not guilty, and there is none to deliver out of your hand? Your hands fashioned and made me, and now you have destroyed me altogether. Remember that you have made me out of clay; and will you return me to the dust?" [8]

When she got to *"the land of gloom like thick darkness, like deep shadow without any order, where light is as thick as night,"* Mara said that the monk's tears, which sprang from the night of his sins, and from the unrest of his body, proved that Madeleine was more powerful than his will.

I breathe in, powerfully and noisily, the fresh air which makes me slightly dizzy. Beyond the glass of the window, there was blue sky, deep, bright, without clouds and shadows, only the wind blowing roughly and with a meaningless fury. A couple of leaves, brought from nowhere, touch the glass hastily, only to get lost afterwards in the anonymity which I sometimes feel bringing all my being, to the brink of tears. A couple of leaves, a couple of insignificant lives, more untold pain. Ridiculous, involuntary sadness. I find myself identifying with everything that dies in agony. Behind me, only failures or unfinished matters, and infinite pity. I have tried to live normally in abnormal times, but it seemed to be too hard for me. Beyond my powers. Then, as time went

---

8   Job 10, 1:9 and 21:22, English Standard Version (ESV)

by, I didn't know anymore what was normal and what was abnormal, and then, pity imposed itself, dominant and sometimes devastating. Pity for others, but not for myself. I forgot myself. I ignored myself. I abandoned myself. I acted as if I was on automatic pilot. I became, mostly, the suffering of others. I identified myself to confusion with the people I met. Now I am what I used to be, a medic, a medic only, and I have no time for anything else. The little left for me must be dedicated to impossible matters only. In reality: "I don't hate people, but I am afraid of them." Strindberg.

Between my flickering life and my death, which is taking an increasingly distinct shape, Mara intervenes. She gives me, without knowing it, moments of calm and confidence. Perhaps out of pity, perhaps out of the ridiculous need to help her, in fact I don't know myself exactly why, I took upon myself her grief again, as well as Father Serafim's. I am *them*, in the same way in which I got to be the dying leaves, the meteors burning out during the nights of August, the trees set on fire by lightning, and the light of the long burnt out stars. I am all there is of pain and revolt, but also of the happiness of being, in one single moment, the eye which can see, the soul which can feel death and immortality, the sublime and the ridiculous, the creation and our current existence, the magnificent and the absurd, governing us at the same time. Tears come quickly, easily, from eyes tired of search and restlessness. I can be, therefore, the monk terrorized by his wish to be angel and devil at the same time, but I can also be the human being liberated of all constraints. To be more precise: I will give it another try. So...

Before assuming the saintly status of a monk, meaning before he took the oath of obedience, poverty and chastity,

Father Serafim was known under the name of Sever Moraru; and, not long after his separation from Madeleine, he was called into the army, which made him very happy. Finally he was really going to escape from the memory of her face, which followed him obsessively. He wished passionately to be sent to a unit of parachutists or to a mountain corps, where the physical effort and the risk would test his own endurance – in other words, prepare him, especially from the physical point of view, for the Foreign Legion, where he hoped he would forever bury his inadequacy and his desires. To his regret though, he only became a poor infantry man in a unit near the city from which he wasn't meant to escape. Since he had some medical training, he was sent to the infirmary, after his compulsory induction. From that point he escorted his sick comrades to surgeries in the city – in rows of four, marching and singing in rhythm.

Our officer knows the whole score
He teaches us that and much, much more,
How to master the weapon and hold it steady,
When the next war comes we'll be ready.[9]

Now, the military uniform protected him even more, giving him a kind of confidence bordering on aggression. To his surprise he felt more and more attracted by the city and the pleasures he could rarely afford, in the little free time available. All of a sudden he could notice many things which were unknown to him while a civilian. He discovered true architectural marvels, buildings which had survived the earthquakes, and also plenty of beautiful women, and he lived with a feeling that it was only now that he could attempt

---

9   In Romanian there are rhymes; also strong Moldavian pronunciations: Ofițeru știi multi, / Și ne-nvață și pe noi, / Cum să țânem arma-n mână / Și să fim pi ia stăpână / Contra unui noi război.

any enterprise he wished. He didn't fear anymore that he might meet Madeleine, although he didn't exclude such a possibility altogether; but now, finally, under the cover of the military uniform, he would manage to pass indifferently by her, or, late at night, he would not find it as hard to watch her profile through the thin bedroom curtain. Life, however, has its own strange occurrences. On a Sunday like any other, going out to the city more out of boredom than anything else, the thing he wanted and didn't want at the same time happened. He discovered Madeleine's face in the window of an antique shop where, when they were together, they used to stop and admire the exhibits, especially the old clocks.

"God, but where have you disappeared to all this time?" she exclaimed with indignation, as if she didn't know how they separated. "I searched all the chemists' one by one, but, apart from the fact that all the old hags regretted you'd gone into the army, I couldn't find anything else. How are you, tell me quickly, where are you?"

The woman's voice changed everything in a few seconds only, so much so that he started to feel guilty for his absence. Without breathing, he recited the address of his unit and the phone number where he could be contacted sometimes. Strangely, time had condensed and together with it the tension between them also disappeared; the brutal words which separated them, the emptiness she left behind her, and, of course, the pain of believing in her with such intensity.

"But you know very well, it was you who didn't want us to see each other anymore," he still managed to say. "All I did was to respect your feelings, the wish you repeated so many times."

"Yes, I am not contradicting you. When I was with

you, I felt I was the luckiest woman, but, once back at home, reliving again the madness uniting us, I was terribly afraid and wished with all my heart not to see you again. Unfortunately, this pain, the refusal to see you did not last long, and I would find myself regretting the stupidity of having said such words to you, and I blamed you for taking them seriously. Anyway, this is not the first time I have worried and asked myself: what are you up to, how are you, why can't I do without you? It is enough to see you and, suddenly, I lose my mind, my dignity and I feel like I belong to you. I go now, but I will soon look for you at your unit," she assured him, leaving him bewildered right where she had found him, in front of the shop window.

She had gained the victory again, and he couldn't manage to diminish it, even by telling himself that, in fact, his feelings were about more than the need for her, for Madeleine herself. Instead, as for any true soldier, it was just about the banal and animal need of a woman. Any woman. Nothing, however, could contradict the evidence anymore. The old feelings, the unhealthy and uncontrolled love, burst out with the same energy as before, the very moment he found himself in front of her at the unit gate. She, very elegant, smelled of the *Chanel 5* which usually announced her presence. He couldn't suppress his admiration:

"Who invented such women? It is enough for you to look at me and... you know what I mean?"

Madeleine had brought him a great number of snacks, *sprays*, deodorants, pyjamas, *T-shirts*, as if – in this way, indirectly – she was preparing him for another separation, a longer one. The meeting at the gate had been consummated in silence, and it was only after she'd seen herself free of her bags that Madeleine whispered to him, full of emotion: "I obtained from your top commander one hour of freedom. I think it would be good not to waste it around here!"

"You got to him?" the future monk wondered, to which she burst out in a complicit peal of laughter:

"The colonel – isn't he a man subject to sin, too?"

Without staying any longer to chat, they went out into the street and, communicating to each other only with their eyes, they got lost nearby, in a field of maize, where they relived, with fury and despair, their reconciliation. On these occasions they were also celebrating the fact that he had abandoned the search for a potential avenue to the Foreign Legion, or to fighting, with a special forces unit, on some battlefield. The months of military service which he had left, were spent waiting for her in various motel rooms, modest and of precarious hygiene, rented by the hour. There, in a hurry, insatiable, they lost themselves in the same mute struggle, out of which they both came drained of strength and happy. Their relationship seemed to have entered the state of normality. They were not interested in the past or in the future, they almost did not talk to each other, they lived the moment frantically and with despair, aware that everything was against them and that, over and above all the obstacles, they belonged to each other. Sever Moraru unexpectedly had everything anyone could wish or dream of, beyond any position or fortune. He had a total love, an achievement, and the secrecy and passion with which they lived the little time stolen from military life, from the barracks, and from the husband, which all convinced him that nothing could rise above what was happening to him in those moments.

Madeleine lived the moments of complete fusion with such intensity that she could hardly stop her tears, even after tiredness put them back, one beside the other, under the sweat-drenched sheets. Encouraged by these states of her spirits, by the peacefulness and calm brought by the unhoped-for rediscovery of love, Sever felt that, finally, he could dare to think of the future. Of *their* future: meaning, the recommencement of university, marriage, and everything that would follow.

Unfortunately, one day, Lina stopped appearing for their habitual meetings. The hours of nightmares in which imagination brought to his mind only terrible diseases, serious car or family accidents, and even death provoked by the jealousy of the husband, made him trample over his promise not to call her on the phone. To his surprise, no one was there to answer at the other end of the line, not even during the latest hours of the night, until one day when the dispatch operator's robot brought to his attention the fact that the number which he had called with such despair was no longer allocated to a subscriber. Because it was impossible for him to stay at the level of absurd hypotheses and powerless anxiety, he took the decision to go looking for her at home, no matter what the risk might be.

He went dressed in the regular military uniform, under the pretext that he had been sent to see a certain officer, but the neighbours informed him that Mr Barbu, the pilot, to whose door he had run by mistake, had obtained a very good contract, for several years, with an important airline in Canada, and he had left the country together with his lady wife. Here was the unique hypothesis of which he had never thought, although, in the moments of lucidity, after their love was consummated with fury and passion, he had often been tried by the perfidious fear that everything was too beautiful to last. Now he no longer knew what to believe, the tension of the waiting and the passionate, illicit encounters had suddenly become a memory. He felt released of all that he had experienced, he only had a feeling of emptiness, of nothingness and of endless time, which he could no longer manage to fill, except with the a painful question: "How could she... ?"

The woman's running away from him, since it was running away, and he could not avoid the phrase, had paralysed him. The pain and the humiliation due to the fact that he had been wrong again, brought him back to reality, brutally, with his feet on the ground. He had lost the woman, but he was left, as in the olden days, with women in general, and his relationship with them was going to be, again, this time, without any spiritual participation. As such, he proposed to himself to be more lucid and no longer to attribute his own feelings and interpretations to creatures that nature had endowed only with hormones and cunning. The old ties and obligations, restarted with increased energy, had not managed to help him escape her memory, not even in the most intimate of moments. By comparison with her, other women seemed colourless, artificial, lacking, so that he made love with hatred, in order to take revenge. This disgust, this absurd nonsense in which he could see no sense, the human misery hidden under various names and masks, directed him on the road to the monastery. In any case, his motive was not his faith and love for God. The thought had taken root in his mind following a discussion with a monk he had met by chance, who begged for money for the painted decoration of the monastery. The feeling of being lost, above all else, had spurred him into trying this solution as well. He would abandon himself, not just to the will Heaven, but especially to that of an earthly master who, in the name of the Lord, was going, in the end, to provide his living and to guide him towards holiness. The mandatory rules – obedience, poverty and chastity – didn't seem to discourage him. Nobody ever died of that! He had talked to that particular monk of his great sadness – losing Madeleine –simply because he could no longer keep this pain only for himself, especially since he did not have steadfast friends, but only women interested in his virility. In those moments of grief, he would have confessed to anyone had the inclination to listen. To his surprise, he had been understood and commiserated with, sooner than he'd expected, because his counsellor had also gone through such a crisis, and the world he entered had offered him soothing and support.

"Lord," the future monk prayed, after the first weeks of apprenticeship, and of obedience, "what could I ask of you, how could I succeed, I wonder, to make myself heard and understood, when in reality I am not able to be myself. I can't reconcile myself to this anonymity either, I don't know any prayers and, above all else, I don't like the space and the people where I've found sanctuary. Lord, I have become powerless and I see all the faces of my insignificance, from all angles, from all positions, and the fact that others have suffered too, that I am just like those in whose proximity I live, cannot satisfy me. Help me, Lord, to find you, or chase me away from this world I can't comprehend. Take my mind or my moral clarity, so that I can't see and feel what I am and what I cannot be."

He had never confessed the subtext of his desires to his confessor, against whom he experienced a violent feeling of rejection. He had immediately admitted all his possible sins, even those he had not committed and had not crossed his mind, everything in order to escape the merciless eyes and the parental distance the confessor tried to impose on him. It was only in the numerous and secretive prayers to the Almighty that he admitted to his guilt, his suffering, and his need to find a direction.

Little by little, after a while, he had started to believe that his prayers were coming true. He learnt the holy mysteries. He worked in the fields – which drained him of strength. He ate a diet based on fish. He experienced everything else happening around him, such as the numerous nuances of obedience: and all these tempered his need to run away and the tendency to be different. After a while, he no longer wanted to be the same as people outside of the community. Instead, he wanted to discover in depth the secret of peacefulness and of bringing peacefulness to others; but his road was not easy at all, perhaps because he also lived in fear, ceaselessly looking around him, as if he were expecting only unpleasant surprises or dangers which had to be avoided. Friar Nifon, the man who had recommended him to the abbot, no longer showed him the friendship for which Sever Moraru had hoped, not that he avoided him either. It had not been too long since Nifon had lived through the torture of fitting in, the nuances of obedience, its great inconveniences. That is why his opinion was that the novice had to make the first step, since any advice that was too soon given, before being requested, could have contrary effects. With time, however, the novice started to believe he belonged to that community and it was at that moment that he learned from Brother Nifon that, even in his situation, he didn't have obligations alone, but also rights.

As the monk already hinted, there were some deeds that he didn't have to tell the confessor, things that appertain to the sinful nature of a man in his prime. One day every month, he could leave the monastery after he'd done all his duties, and, as with every occasion up to that moment, exactly at the point when he seemed to have been resigned to his fate, accepting and understanding the rules and rhythms of the monastery, the devil put on an appearance in the shape of a woman. Natalia Preda, one of the owners of the chain of pharmacies where he'd worked as a driver, was a creature whom he knew "all that was hers on the inside and out," as the pious church fathers would say. He owed his position there to her. She had made him generous gifts, and it had been with her that he had made the greatest expense of energy, because, of all the creatures whose beds he'd visited, she had been very, very hard to satisfy. Together with three foreigners, with whom she spoke in English, she had come to visit the monastery, and he – by the efforts of the abbot and of the evil one – had happened to be outdoors gathering hay, which had been freshly scythed, near the entrance.

"Sever Moraru?" she enquired, and, after a short hesitation, and without waiting for an answer, she started to kiss him with a passion that did not seem, not even from a great distance, like the relationship between a woman from the flock of the faithful and a pious confessor. When she realised she had reacted rather exaggeratedly, the woman hurried to mention a family relationship as a subject of discussion, after which she apologised and took him aside: "Did you go completely stupid? What are you looking for in this deserted place? I swear I wouldn't have been surprised if I saw you as an actor in porn films, or as the owner of one of the semi-clandestine brothels that have appeared everywhere, as if sprung from the earth, but here. Get these rags off as fast as you can and come with me! It's your luck that your beard and hair did not grow too much, I might have just missed you otherwise!"

Instead of "Stay back, Satan!" as the saying goes in that house of the Lord, he tried to explain to her his need of peace and reconciliation with himself, his resignation, the remorse for the sinful life he'd led up to that time, but especially the desire to care, in the years to come, for people's souls, since he had not been able to care for their bodies. Without willing it, there came to his mind all the advice of the saintly or pious church fathers, Pachomios, Athanasios, Orsisios, Theodore the Sanctified, St Basil the Great, Makarios from Alexandria, Ivan Cazian and all the others who made encouragements for the monastic life. The Blessed Makarios, for example, condemned relations with any woman. How could he forget these encouragements which his confessor reminded him of three times a week? The oil feeds the flame of the lamp; in the same way, talking to a woman ignites the fire of lustfulness. The woman's gaze: poisoned arrows that wound the soul to death. Defend yourself from talking to women, the same as you defend yourself from poison, if you want to stay pure. It is in them that the most annihilating poison is hidden. As the fire left to its own devices causes flames, in just the same way the remembrance of women left in the soul ignites lustfulness.

On the other hand, it was dangerous for the monk to hear anything about people who belonged to this world. Cleanliness of heart, silence of the mouth and sincere obedience were qualities that he lacked. His submission was a pretence, and he was ashamed of this infidelity. In comparison, the pious Theodore had showed the way by renouncing all worldly temptations, refusing even to see his own mother when she came to visit him. He was impenetrable, and St Basil the

Great was just as categorical when it came to restraining oneself, in fact, to mortifying the body.

"I don't know what I feel," he said to Natalia, with sorrow in his voice. "Not even my beard was that of a monk. All that I do, ever since I've known myself, is done with hesitation. Maybe that, in the end..."

"If you somehow believe that knob of yours, which is otherwise healthy and energetic, was given to you only and only to pee with, you are a moron and you deserve your fate! I would not be surprised to hear that you've changed your appearance, but giving up on sex – I can't believe it! Next week, or as soon as I can, I'll try to free you from these hypocrites, so that you won't get completely ruined, and if I can't manage it on my own, I will come with a decisive helper: your Canadian woman with whom I allowed you to cheat on me from time to time, because I, too, was making a concession to the husband every now and then!"

"Has Madeleine returned?" he asked involuntarily. "Did you know her?"

"You wretched pervert! See how your eyes sparkle? If I tell the hypocrites from here what you used to do to us, what a terrible output you had, they will kick you out as fast as you can blink. Not because they might be saintlier, but out of pure and worldly envy. One week today, at the latest, we will be ringing the end of your voluntary exile! I will be at this precise hour at the gate, where I expect you to present yourself with all your rags gathered!"

Madeleine's reappearance had thrown him again, with brutality, into the real world which he'd done everything he could to forget. After a long and tormenting hesitation, he took the decision not to abandon the monastery, but to look for her at any risk, so that he could have an explanation, like with two civilised people who once loved each other passionately, because her desertions, her silences and unexpected absences were unbearable. He wanted to learn what it was that brought her to him, why she came and why she ran away afterwards, and whether her feelings matched her desires and their trysts, in the moments of sinful action.

He seemed not yet to believe that he had been mistaken to such an extent, and, of course, he now needed words above all else. His friend, Brother Nifon, explained to him what he needed to do in order to receive the permission he was entitled to, and, on that particular morning, he followed the advice to the letter; however, to his surprise, the abbot didn't even want to hear about it. He simply did not allow it. With no explanation.

"In here, voting, half plus one, public opinion and so on, have no value. Our rule is obedience and will," the abbot, annoyed, explained to him.

"Most pious father, I am still entitled to a leave and, if you won't allow it, I will run away!" Brother Serafim replied just as categorically.

"If you run away, you will suffer the consequences," the abbot retorted, angered by the prospect of disobedience, and by the affront he had received.

Of course, the discussion had been much more tense, and the new denizen of the monastery had had too little time to learn from other people's experience a very delicate chapter of the local tradition. Given that, centuries in the past, one of the monastery's abbots had been received in the ranks of the saints, his rules had become laws for the followers, and total obedience was not open to discussion. As such, one could read, in the charter that listed punishments, that on the first serious breach the guilty one should receive "forty strokes bar one" with the whip, a fact that caused laughter in the person concerned. Who would do such a thing in this year, and this end of century at the end of the millennium?

Brother Serafim had already packed everything he needed a long time before, and in advance of the hour agreed with Natalia, he tried to get out, like any normal person, by using the main gate, but he was stopped. This was a sign that the abbot was not joking. He then returned to his cell and, without knowing that his superior was searching the surroundings of the monastery with binoculars, from the bell tower, he tried to get away by sneaking through the vineyard, on the road towards the less visible point of the fence to the street; but he was caught up from behind by the abbot's very fast car.

He was now aware that the first punishment in the rulebook was going to be applied to him. In the abbot's precinct, while he freed his back from his clothes, he warned the abbot and the monastery's watchman – a former officer converted to holy matters – that he was going to count the lashes. If they went over what the law provided, even with one caress, he was going to beat them up so hard that they wouldn't forget, not even in the life to come, what was going to happen to them.

"I did judo in the army, I feel obliged to warn you, and I would appreciate it if you should not neglect this detail."

The abbot had naturally not taken the threat seriously, and after the extra stroke, which had been knowingly given, he found himself smacked on the watchman's head, and then, at the same speed, on the walls of the room. Both the abbot and the watchman had to take so many kicks and fists, that, in order not to be become a laughing stock, they didn't dare to call for help, or to leave the room before rearranging their attire. Even more than this, they were afraid the scandal would reach at the ears of their superiors. In the meantime, our monk took the abbot's car, and, on seeing it, the gatekeeper opened the great gates in a hurry. From here, he jumped into Natalia's car. Natalia, horrified by the blood gushing from his back, and by the streaks left by the lashes, took refuge in the neighbouring oak woods, trying to administer first aid. They then went to the Clinic for Forensic Medicine in order to get an official report, which, as it happened, was unnecessary, and, from there, in order to give him the well-deserved and long waited for reward, they stopped in one of the flats which she kept reserved for her sinful activities.

"With this kind of certificate on your hands, you may even get to be a bishop," she assured him. "Who needs scandal in a world where it is only this kind of misadventure that is awaited and savoured by the public? You will get well and, if you don't recover from this holy foolishness, I will take you back myself! You will be received, and I have no doubts about it, with flowers and tears. You must be an idiot not to realise that, in this country, which is led by talk shows, polls, the opinions of soothsaying witches and newspaper editorials, a press article and a picture of your back would finish them all off. It's not the truth that matters, but what is written about it. If you accept me as your manager, I'll get you sanctified before you become completely senile!"

As expected, Brother Serafim's thoughts were not about leaving the monastery immediately, but on meeting Madeleine before she returned to Canada. Unfortunately, the wounds from the lashes hurt him terribly, so that he had to stay for a few days in the self-interested care of Natalia. With the photograph and the medical certificate in her hands, and without asking for his permission, she went to negotiate with the abbot.

"The rules you told me of," concluded Natalia after she listened attentively to the justifications, spoken with a well simulated calm. "Of course, in the monastery, like in the army, relationships are different and, in all fairness, democracy is not relevant here. I, too, know the holy church father's dictum: that God does not settle on somebody's shoulders a greater burden than that which the person can carry. In fact, there must be a clear hierarchy in all institutions, an order, we know that very well. But I am talking about beatings: you will have to convince the hundreds of thousands of readers of newspapers, and some other millions of TV viewers, that whipping was necessary. There will be an invasion of journalists waiting for you. They are, in their great majority, nasty and ignorant, and they are not interested in traditions, in the path to redemption, or the ancestral faith – but only in scandals. What's more, you will cause damage to the memory of the saint who had this unfortunate idea. I've read for myself there are monasteries where not even animals and birds of the female sex are admitted, and the road to the average monastery is paved with endless privations and torments. In exchange for the promise that you will not hurt him when he is out of the hospital, that you will allow him to come in and go out when he wishes, of course – with the discretion and due care – you should consider that you've bought my silence. You don't have to put it down in writing, only to swear on the Bible!"

The promise was extracted with difficulty, after violent word exchanges of the least elegant type. The abbot had never made any such promises and pledges, but the fear of what could happen to him was, in the end, a good counsel.

Of course, Natalia didn't expect to obtain the victory so soon, just as she had not thought of making an appeal for the support of the press, because, if there was an investigation, she would not have come out too well either, but the dialogue she'd just had cemented the conviction that, later on, after his wounds healed, the life of her friend, in the monastery, was not going to be easy at all. She had extracted or, to be more exact, she had stolen a favour, but not a change in the rules of that specific institution; as such, she was obliged to think of the next move, when the trump card of the medical certificate would not be in existence.

As for Friar Serafim, he was clear enough that, in reality, that had not been a victory for him, but for the woman, to whom he would have to always be grateful. In any case, he had become even more aware that whatever it was that had connected them up to that time could not be truly called love, and, from that point, it was not hard to suppose that, one day, Natalia's interest in him could get diluted or even disappear. In other words, he was repeating the same mistake. He was entrusting his fate to another woman, and risking other new and painful consequences. This, however, was not the feeling that terrorised him the most. His emotion was actually unexpected: sincere regret for what he had done. In turning him down, the abbot had probably put him to the test. It was a test of obedience and humility, one of the many necessary in order to enter that much sought- after community. This was a hypothesis about which he had not thought until then, just as he had avoided asking himself about who he truly was. He had, also, especially avoided asking himself this; why was it that he had never managed to pursue anything to the end, and since he had not managed to achieve anything, was his love story with Madeleine and that feeling of complete accomplishment, true? He felt he was waking up from a horrible dream, but his release from the nightmare, his waking up, were not accompanied by joy, as would have been natural. Instead, fear was all he felt. It seemed to him that it was too late for anything, and his most persistent thought was to run away from the town, even from the country, away from everything that he had once been.

One evening, talking to Natalia, he tried to steer the discussion towards the failures that followed him stubbornly, and his future in years to come, from the perspective that the monastery was not, as she had also maintained, a good solution in the long run, or for life. Unfortunately, the woman was not accustomed to this kind of discussion, especially in such a serious tone of voice, so that, miming comprehension, she tried looking for an answer in her usual style.

"I would think of the movies instead, even if I started out as a porn actor, since, and I can testify to this, you are well endowed for such a role. You have everything you need, even in excess, that's why that perverted woman of the pilot's wants you."

Understanding this was not the moment for a serious discussion, Serafim adopted her tone, but without too much pleasure:

"Since you can't avoid the subject, I would be tempted by a meeting with her. I promise it will be the last and that it will be about a discussion and only a discussion. What do you say?"

"I am thinking that, after all that has happened, I should understand you," she started in a voice which was disarmingly serious. "Why did that woman make you go

115

crazy? What has she got? Where does she surpass me? What does she do to you? You've slept with the both of us, you know us well. I've fulfilled all your whims, you've had the most impossible advantages with me, but, with all this, I still have to chase you even today."

"Well, it was not just for nothing. I think I am good at something, in the end, as you have noticed," trying to call a halt to a possible argument out of which he had no way of coming out a winner. "Otherwise you would not waste your time with me."

"She abandoned you any time she wanted to, she ran away without saying one word to you and yet she is still in the first place at the top of your preferences."

"I have nothing to explain," he said sincerely. "It just happens, purely and simply, she dominates me. I am not choosing her. It is as if somebody pushes me towards her from behind, dictates to me what to do, and masters my thoughts. I don't know what else I can add."

"Should I understand that you like nonsense, caprices, episodes of abandonment – if there are no other differences? You knew me before knowing her and, suddenly, you forgot I even existed, although I gave you a helping hand in the most difficult moments. Is she better in the bed? What does she say to you? How does she keep you on a leash? The things I could learn from her!"

To his anxiety, the discussion had slid towards an area where no one had the means to come out the winner, and which didn't make things any more clear either. Unfortunately – and this was an easily foreseen consequence of her questions – self-hatred accentuated his aggression, the need to punish himself, to furnish excuses for having chosen, without putting up a struggle, a life of the lowest level, lacking any control and perspective.

"I think I could reply with a question, which I hope you've asked yourself. It would be good if I was mistaken but, as far as I can see, you were not interested in any way in my soul, because I don't remember any talk about it ever coming up. Madeleine, it is clear to me, doesn't have a great interest in it either. When the husband ignores her, when she can no longer swallow her tears, she remembers me. Just like you, by the way. So, you have nothing to learn from her, you know absolutely everything. It's just that she is a chronic disease, a calamity I can't escape. Logic chooses you, the soul and the body chooses her. I can't understand more than this myself. On the other hand, scientists have noted that men are polygamous, by default, and probably this explains the need for both! At some point, when my hormones are fewer, both of you will abandon me."

"The soul has priority only when the actor ignores her, not her husband," Natalia emphasised, with the air that she had just made a great gaffe by unveiling a secret to him. "That little actor was tried by several women, but, as we know, up to this point only his soul rose to the height of Mădălina's expectations, because it's just you and the actor who satisfy her. Women are very complicated, but I am convinced that, for the moment, with the gift that you have, you did not have the time to concentrate on such a detail. Later on, when the time comes for you to feel the great power of gravity with certain parts of your body, you will discover how many other things passed you by in your playful life."

"And what do you think I should do?" he asked, knowingly ignoring the story of the actor, which had hurt him terribly. "Give me some advice, you're the person who's the closest to me. Neither you or she ever proposed anything else to me," he concluded, and, just as he expected, deeds took priority over the words.

On that occasion, the monk could only remember the amazingly white sheet, which Natalia had changed without him realising it, and upon which he had discovered her stretched out, waiting for him, anticipating the hatred and fury with which he had jumped on her. He didn't love her, that was clear, in his relationship with her, this feeling had always been completely missing, and now, more than ever, he was punishing himself by allowing her to knead senselessly the wounds, as yet unhealed, on his back. He detested himself, saying to himself in his thoughts the most hurtful and truthful words, and she, instead of the tears and prayers for mercy which the monk expected, was living that coupling with an intensity and joy only rarely encountered. Among her victorious moans, among grunts and thrusts, the monk heard a promise and prayer that made him attack her with even more hatred:

"I will never leave you. Kill me, do everything you want to me, as much as you want, but don't forget I need you, my love!"

"Don't you leave me, fuck your mother's mother," he replied in his thoughts, although aware that, without Natalia, he would be even less than he was at that moment, and that, in reality, she had no blame in this.

Later on – when he rested, without a trace of energy left, stretched on that insufferable sheet drenched in sweat and blood dripping from the wounds left by the abbot's whip – he discovered her face, which was lit up by a terrible joy, strengthening in him the feeling that he had lost this battle as well. Instead of seeing her lying stretched out, as he had wanted, so that he could put her in the situation where she would pray for him to stop, Natalia had simply annihilated him, leaving him only with his obsession for the woman who had just returned from Canada. He had loved that woman beyond all tears and words, but, just like Natalia, she had never made him understand that she loved him especially for his soul. This time, however, he was terribly interested by a new character, who had appeared so suddenly in his and Madeleine's lives: the actor. Apart from the woman's unexpected disappearances, the monk realised that, in reality, he knew next to nothing about this creature whom he believed belonged to him as a gift of destiny. He could not manage to remember any event, or even a reply coming from her. She was just the feeling of full and unique love, something that did not start during their lifetimes, and, in the same way, could not possibly end.

The meaning of Madeleine was also to do with her facial expressions. She shared with him a number of complicit gazes, which were warm and possessive, or – not infrequently – which foretold of the panic that overcame her after their prolonged moment of blind and total union was consummated. Up to the time when he was forced to recompose her from events and words, the monk had lived with the conviction that the woman belonged to him. He had believed, until then, that before the husband, parents, or anybody else, he was the only one with full rights over her, and because he never doubted this, he had never put the existence of another man in the discussion, with the exception of her legitimate husband.

Natalia had prepared this surprise for him over a long period, and, furthermore, she had wanted to make him understand that it was useless to create illusions since, in reality, he didn't mean much more to Madeleine either. When, after long persistence, he managed to learn the name of the actor – Ion Poenaru – the monk discovered that he knew a lot of facts about his competition, given that he was part of the minor celebrities of the town who were remarkable more for their political, rather than artistic, activity. Small, dark, and nasty – this was how a journalist had characterised him. A pit-bull with the face of a Pekingese, was the opinion of another, an individual who was always at the place where there was or was going to be a conflict, an eternal contrarian character who usually dominated by his voice and aggressiveness, not by ideas. For the rest, in the theatre, as an actor, he was generally bearing a tray on the stage, and his only line was "With pleasure!" if it happened that someone thanked him for the service.

He got to be known because of some events that took place before the Revolution, on the stage of the theatre where he was hired. Interpreting the role of a typesetter who was printing a communist newspaper in dark secrecy, he had confused the exclamation mark, without meaning to, with the question mark, so that, instead of rejoicing at the fact that *România liberă* – Free Romania – had been printed, he questioned involuntarily whether Romania was free. This change of accent – *România liberă – Free Romania?* – inspired the mirth of the entire auditorium, bringing him, at the same time, the people's admiration and the fury of the party activists, who saw in this event an attempt to undermine the social order. In different circumstances, he appeared on the stage wearing some thick, rudimentary, woollen gloves and, of course, a matching scarf. People burst into laughter, thinking that the actor was protesting, in his own way, or was being ironical, about the dramatic lack of heating in the auditoria and, naturally, in people's houses. In reality, his hands were covered by untreated eczema, and he had added the scarf only in order to match the gloves. After the Revolution, these incidents stood as the basis of his new biography. They exemplified the suffering he had to bear, being followed around by the Securitate, the fight against the communist regime and much more – all broadcast, of course, on every wavelength. All this naturally propelled him into the foreground of general interest, in a space in which the old heroes had to disappear, and there were no other heroes available.

The context was one in which politics were at a very primitive stage, a contest of yelling and swearing substituting for argument. There was a widespread feeling of guilt among people who had made compromises with the old regime, and – in particular – "had not fought." In addition there was the great shameless nerve of the actor, and all this had propelled him into the posture of a judge, someone to be courted and spoiled. In other words, Ion Poenaru dominated authoritatively the times of those who shouted the loudest. From here, from the TV screens or behind the microphones, the road to the beds of some local beauties had become very short.

Of course, the poor man had to satisfy his body as well, not just his soul, but the prey offered him was not easily disposable, and he took everything with the appetite and hurry lent by his immense shamelessness. Natalia related to the monk, with a luxury of details, what people said in town of the actor's relationship with Madeleine, and she also added details which forcefully nudged the vanity of a man. The true surprise, however, was that the story was not finished yet, on the contrary – it was said that it was not business calling her back to Romania periodically. Instead, it was love for the actor. As could be expected, Natalia's revelations had the effect of a boomerang on the monk. Beyond the pain of overwhelming defeat, however, which accentuated his irritating feeling of uselessness, the small amount of lucidity he had left urged him to take advantage of the situation in order to break with Madeleine, once and for all – a gesture with which he wanted to mark the start of his rehabilitation.

"I would like to see her one more time," he whispered to Natalia before she was about to leave. "There are still some words which I haven't yet told her."

"This woman is like a drug, she gives you an addiction, she doesn't let up. All who've gone through her bed think the same. After the first contact, the first intake, you are lost, it's impossible to forget her. I will not stop you seeing her, but I can't pretend forever that I don't see you wavering."

Despite Natalia's warning, as soon as he was left on his own, he ran to the telephone, determined to have the final discussion, but her warm voice, her joy, not faked at all, at hearing him, tempered his fury.

"Where are you?" she asked, and the monk told her the address, involuntarily, out of pure inertia. "I'll be there in a few minutes," she whispered, switching off the phone and leaving him in the most impossible situation. The desire to see her, and the fear that Natalia might return, dominated him in turns, without giving him the time to think of the different reactions possible in the two different situations. To his surprise, however, the woman appeared faster than he'd expected. Her eyes were full of tears, and the panic of not knowing where she was, as well as the joy at seeing him again, pushed her into his arms, as if out of the wish to hide in them and to ask for his protection.

"I thought I was never going to see you again," she

whispered and, instead of waiting for a reply, she covered his mouth with both her hands: "Don't chastise me, as I deserve, I've reproached myself for more things than you ever could. Love me so that I can understand that you forgive me!"

Once again, just as if hypnotised, he was not able to oppose her. Things happened just as they had every time. They were elevated above the misery of this world; above the pitiful and unworthy lives that they lived. When they were left without any energy in them, laying there one near the other, almost undressed, with their clothes crumpled, he wished for Natalia to turn up, so that he could break off for good with one of them, but especially with the one who was not the source of addiction. Once the woman started to get ready herself to leave, the monk's courage increased and he asked about the actor, and whether his own role was just to cover a lack on the actor's part, but, for a long time, her tears took the place of reply.

"Stupid man, do you think I ran away to Canada for another man? Do you have the impression that I enjoyed explaining to your wretched priests why was I looking for you with such energy? And if you have me, just like you want me, ready, submissive, lost, what need do you have for words? What else can I say?"

"And if things are as you say, what do you think will come of us?" he enquired, feeling defeated, and she hurried to give him an answer of which she seemed to have thought for a long time.

"Given that you wear those black monk clothes, have trust that the Lord on High will show us the way! Because it was Him who helped us meet!"

"Lord, don't dump our human miseries on His account!" he exclaimed, scared and also surprised that he had finally reacted like a rabid animal. In reality, they felt free from the obligation to lose themselves in useless demonstrations and contradictions. Mere words could not substitute for reality. Instead, they were rather harmful. They had become again what they had wanted to be, contenting themselves with staying in an embrace and looking into each other's eyes, unsatiated, trying to assure themselves by the means of their senses that everything was alright, that their relationship had proved its stability. The fears, the despair, the wait, the time and the distances that had separated them were the price of these moments.

"Who can understand him?!" Mara concluded, but she had not had yet the chance to discover that even the greatest love is composed of thousands of nothings, gestures, gazes, states of feeling, that will and reason are powerless, that everything which is beautiful, alive, truthful, and creates connection and attraction is above words and explanations. It is a secret, absurd world, accessible only to those who have gone through it and had the good luck to measure, with their own senses, the joy, the pain and the fear – inseparable, and exalted together beyond tears, a special world in which what is important and truthful is especially that which cannot be said. As such, we are mere marionettes in a game which is above our power to oppose and understand it, an absurd play in which all you do is to try and understand the intentions of the Great Puppeteer; and, at the same time, to rejoice at the fact that you are living this surprising joy.

Whether there's a fall or an elevation in time, I couldn't say. In any case, everything is *now*, in the immediate. Neither yesterday, nor tomorrow. Everything seems alive, unchanged, ageless. In the same way as back then, I can't say, not even today, what that white, static, ice-built world, that world in front of which I involuntarily find myself, wants to say to me. I try to concentrate, hoping that I would finally understand, or at least feel the reason for my sliding towards I don't know where. So, I want to familiarise myself with this dazzling space. I feel its dead light like a corset that is too tight, white but a white that veers to the bluish, a corset stopping both time and life. I am again in a world turned to stone in a state of obedience and waiting, with the suffocating frost, and the immense moon, near me, ruling, by means of its frozen and strange light, the gully, guarded by the mountains, and crossed by a river on whose side, in that landscape, the tiny, dark houses seemed unreal, a species of confused blots in a naïve drawing. The dead light, the lowering and trembling skies, and the dread inducing howls of the wolves, taken over by a strange madness – everything, more or less, foretells the complete loneliness which, at times, insinuates itself into the soul like an overwhelming pain.

On such a night I heard desperate knocks on the door: "Doctor, sir, the lady calls you, come quick, she's dying!" but the shouting didn't surprise me, because in that particular space, in the world of the woodcutters, it seemed that people were attracted to death, in some way, called by death, as if they had come to live here only in order to die. I didn't wait for prayers or explanations, I didn't take an interest in who the lady was, I got dressed immediately, took my medical kit and climbed in the sleigh pulled by two horses who were agitated by the wolves' howling. The old man driving the sleigh was talking continuously, more in order to encourage his beasts than anything else, so that I couldn't get anything new from him, but it was clear to me that in such weather, nobody called you for some insignificant suffering. I admit, also, that, despite the weather, back then the road felt like a release from the obsession that something unusual had to happen to me, that I would escape, even for one moment, from the conformity to which life itself condemned me in that valley, outside of time and frozen by the wolves' howls.

The moon also seemed unnatural to me, big, surrounded by an immense, luminous, restless halo that sucked me in together with the sleigh and horses and the old man, whom the cold and fear forced to huddle by my side, so much so that I had the sensation that all of us present would become soon enough just a little part of the sky and night that subjugated us. I was not afraid. Neither life nor death tired me in those moments. I felt possessed by a force which was above my will and understanding. I just travelled in order to travel, and my curiosity was attenuated. I felt that nothing could be bad and that was enough for me: everything was part of that call.

I couldn't say how long the trip was, and I can't remember either how I got into that room, or why I told that man to go away. I only know that I took out, in a hurry, the stethoscope, the blood pressure meter, the hypodermics and whatever else was in the bag, and only then did I notice the woman, the sick person, lying in a big bed made of pine wood, covered up to her chin by a woollen, shaggy, striped blanket. I didn't ask what was hurting, and I didn't manage to see her face until later on, because the uncertain light of the petrol lamp and the night's frost had blurred my eyesight and, inside of me, I was still continuing my run towards the high, dark skies which hadn't ceased to suck me in. Although nothing urged me to hurry, I undressed her with mechanical gestures. I moved the stethoscope over her chest and back and then, because I could not find the radial artery and the pulse on it, I fixed my hand under her breast, searching for the heart, but it was only at that moment that I realised my fingers were frozen, and that I would be forced to wait for a while before they thawed, and before I could feel anything.

"I knew you were going to come," I heard her kind voice, contented and grateful. "I never doubted for a moment that this would need to happen at some point," she added after a while, then I felt her hands resting on mine, which had continued to wait for the moment when it would feel the beating of the heart. I didn't reply immediately, although the voice sounded terribly familiar, but, before concentrating on her face, I did my best to identify her in my memory, and I remembered where I had heard that voice, contented and serene like the peacefulness of autumn, but it was impossible. It seemed as if the voice had existed in me since forever, like an intense, nameless joy, an inexplicable gift from the heavens, which I had just rediscovered. Then, almost involuntarily, I met her big, deep eyes, as dark as all the sins in the world, the high, calm forehead, the fleshy lips, incapable of mastering their trembling. It was at the same time that I perceived the beating of her heart, hurried, muffled, and as my senses helped me concentrate on her, memory was searching desperately somewhere in the past, in this life or maybe in others, for the circumstances in which we had belonged to each other. This was what I was convinced of, by everything I felt in those moments convinced me of, even the fact that she had pulled me closer to her in that tall bed with a hard mattress of wheat straw. Forgetting what I had been called for, I did not oppose it. I understood my place was there, so that our souls might gather energy together in order to face life, and to face the events that were going to separate us in a little while. In those moments, I no longer needed explanations, or facts. I needed nothing, except that the woman was near me, without a name, without words, without a past. I was living that life, our life of some other time, and if I closed my eyes in order to feel even more intensely the joy that visited me, behind my eyelids there flowed immense waves of green light, so that I had the impression that all the fields of this world were tumbling down on me. When peacefulness became whole, so much so that I was getting to the point where I couldn't stand it anymore, I would allow my hands to convince themselves on their own that everything was real, that she, that woman, existed and needed me, that the overwhelming happiness was true, and that the only thing which came to my mind was a prayer from which the call of death was missing, the need to die in that moment in order not to be forced to look for each other again, in other times and other lives.

I no longer remember, unfortunately, when and how I reached home. I was not able, either, despite the despair with which I looked for it, to find that house, neither did the face of the woman ever emerge from the multitude of people who needed me in the following months, nor did the cart-driver's face, but I was always grateful to that place, to that gully without a name, in between the mountains. I was always grateful, also, for the things I lived during that terrible winter night, when I discovered that I could feel something else besides fear, sorrow and humiliation, and that joy and contentment can be uplifting.

In the numerous moments of desperate guesswork, I often managed to feel again the emotions I had experienced in the grey room illuminated by the petrol lamp and by the face of the woman with deep, chasm-like eyes, and, as time passed, she called me with an increasing force to that strange world from where I came at some point, or to where I was going to travel. It is clear to me that we did not meet by chance, but where, when, why, and what the connection between us was, I had no way to learn. I had to be content with the light on the woman's face, never extinguished or far way, with her deceptive call and, of course, with the comfort that, in reality, we have been or will be more than we know or can suspect.

I loved you before I discovered I loved you. Now I know, you've been mine before the howling of the wolves, the moon, death and frosts brought me to you. Now, yet again, you are nowhere, you are only love. Love of everything. All the love. And this makes me believe that the person who came under the guise of a cart-driver, two horses and a sleigh, a nameless and body-less destiny, will come together again on other and other shadows, and, at the end of our wanderings through time, after we'll have known everything that needs to be known, you will be with me again. I remembered this precisely when I was almost about to forget, when the fact that I knew myself to be a prisoner in my own body hurt me. Now it's fine, that's why I pray to you, Lord, don't take away this illusion, too. Don't let me discover that there might exist something which is deeper than love. Don't take away my hope that I shall see her again!

Mara had learned from the monk, that, to Natalia's joy, Madeleine had left in her usual manner, without saying anything, without leaving him any hope, so that not even Natalia could manage to explain this behaviour to herself.

"She could also have found a stallion over there, beyond the ocean, even more than one, or as many as she needs to satisfy her. She could even have brought one over from here. For any rational person, couplings three different nations are too expensive!"

The monk had waited for her in vain, for several hours, and, because the phone had been unplugged, he had stalked her until close to dawn, under her windows, convinced that, at some point later on, he would see the much expected light. It was only the following day, when he was discovered by a neighbour on the stairs in front of her door, that he learnt with a tightened heart that Mrs Barbu, the pilot's wife, had left for Canada again. At that time, in those moments, he would have preferred to know that she was in bed, even with the little actor himself, or with anyone else– if only he could meet her again. That was not necessarily because he wanted her, a permanent feeling to which he had grown accustomed, but because he wished to separate from her in the way he believed was proper. Nothing had happened by chance: not their meeting, nor their separation, so he wanted an explanation. The time for honest confessions had come: words had finally become compulsory, even more so, as, in the hours of mad love, he had been visited by the thought of leaving for Canada. He wanted to convince himself in any way about the seriousness of her feelings. Knowing only too well that Natalia would not give him the necessary money for the plane, and that the only solution , procuring the money by himself, required time and patience, the monk strove to explain to Natalia that, by the time he took a definitive decision about his future, the monastery would be the best possibility. Aware that Natalia wouldn't be able to make do without him, and as he didn't have too much courage, he agreed to be accompanied to the abbot so that, together, they could present the conditions of his return, the most important being the picking of medicinal plants – in other words, the freedom to leave the monastery whenever he wanted or when the woman needed him. It was clear that Natalia's generosity had been equal to the expectations of the *'most pious'* abbot, whose responsibility it also was to find a justification, if needed, for the frequent disappearances of friar Serafim. He had returned defeated after following his supposed rival, the little actor, for two days, and he had convinced himself that Madeleine hadn't dropped in at his apartment, not even by mistake. For a sum which was not at all negligible, the caretaker had described with a luxury of detail the man who had visited the actor, since it seemed that men were his true passion. This being the case, Madeleine might have seemed even more quirky, were it not for the fact that all this confirmed a first impression:

"With me, she loves me sincerely, she feels my absence, but she doesn't want to separate from the husband for financial reasons. In her own way, she is trying to keep us both. She is an indecisive creature, so I know that I must find out what exactly can tip the balance. I feel the need to know her better and only then will I take a decision," the monk said to himself, although he knew well that he was not capable of renouncing the woman.

Madeleine was mingled in all his thoughts or dreams, and she continued to be a painful need which was beyond his power to control. It was also beyond his ability to understand this blind passion which stood behind all his failures, but, without her, his life would have been truly bland. The lonelier he got, the greater was the punishment demanded by the obligation of obedience, and the more alive the face and the remembrance of Madeleine's gestures became. In fact, everything reminded him of what had passed between them, even the moans coming from Natalia, who laughed and cried with joy in the car parked in the forest near the monastery, as she no longer had the patience to reach their little secret room. After she declared herself satisfied, Natalia took care to tell him, as if just by chance, what else was gossiped in town at the expense of his great love. Her frequent visit to the old country were, in fact, the consequence of the beatings she got from the pilot, because she hadn't managed to forget her bad habits in Canada, either. "After all," Natalia would say to him in conclusion, "what mysteries could a commonplace nymphomaniac hide?" The monk didn't take the things he heard seriously, although, without realising it, they built up in his soul like rust, so that her face, even when it sneaked in among the male and female saints to whom he was trying to pray, brought in a shadow, or even, beside it, a new feeling: hatred.

"What devils borrowed her face so that I can't have peace anywhere, not even in front of the holy altar? Can there be a greater punishment than this type of love? What power can such a creature hold so that she forces you to think of her every moment?"

In the end, he found himself facing a verdict that freed him from humiliation, waiting, love, jealousy and hatred: "Neither mine, or anyone else's!"

For a long time, he had lacked the courage to think in detail about what such a conclusion could be hiding, but, from the moment he had the strength to say it, he felt free, master of himself; and Natalia's stories and inventions, which had become more numerous, fell away, like water off a duck's back. Now he listened to them with greater detachment, allowing her to see in his serenity the effect she had waited for a long time, Madeleine's face becoming commonplace, her fall from the pedestal. The fact of having Natalia by his side, generous and never having had enough of sin, a matter in which she was more similar to Madeleine that she could ever admit, gave him relative peace. In any event, Natalia found the shortest way to the convenient solution, and the price she required, always the same, suited him, and, of course, was within his power.

"We all had some great failed or inaccessible love, at least one disturbing and unforgettable defeat. We all met at least once a mysterious man or woman who perturbed our memory, but we can't live endlessly only to lay flowers on their graves or believing in miracles," was her conclusion, which the monk never tried to contest or modify. This is how his life carried on, for a while, under the sign of the conventional and the predictable; and, since he was becoming more integrated into the monastery's schedule, he tried to concentrate on those he had ignored: his brothers, also hidden behind soutanes, beards, and routine habits.

What could it be that tied them to the monastery? Faith? Fear of the world? Poverty? What kept them together so much that they could no longer break away? How far does obedience go? Mara didn't know what to believe, she had no idea whether friar Serafim had passed the examinations necessary for being accepted into the restrained and severe world of the monks. As it happened, she managed to find the answer to one question she would have never asked by herself:

"Despite her experience and her well-developed instinct of self-preservation, Madeleine didn't suspect how dangerous love itself can be. In any case, I no longer have any doubts about it, she will remain forever mine and mine only," the monk had said after skipping over a multitude of events.

What was the road up to this point, in what way did Madeleine belong to him. Was she still alive? These remained as question marks because, when she asked them, the monk's eyes would suddenly turn red, while his face was enveloped by a strange grimace, as if he found himself facing a decisive struggle, betraying the effort of hiding an unintelligible cry of victory, and he suddenly became a different person.

Of everything I was fated to live through up to now, I am left only with loneliness. Loneliness alone. What would be its unit of measurement? In any case, I accept it, just as I accepted death and love, once upon a time. It is the connection between them, and the hour in which I find myself that is told, precisely, by this girl dressed in my shirt and pullover, a creature who is unaware of her femininity, who walks around me so that I feel her better than if she were glued to me. I follow her with my eyes, without wanting to, and I forget what I am, I ignore my age, my deficiencies, the dread of the approaching and inevitable road without return. I know that she is life, the expression of the loss of which I was not aware, the final pain, and the humiliation of being more fragile than the vegetation in front of the window, violently alive, but which will die, year by year, only in order to be reborn.

While she arranges various objects on the table, she recalls one of her little sins and she recounts it to me, with fear and respect, as if she found herself in front of the Almighty Judge. Was I entitled to give a verdict, too? I, who truly knew what sinning meant. I, who kept within me my own sorrows, fears, humiliations, sins and anxiety, as well as those of everyone known and unknown? It's not because I want this, but because I cannot separate myself from them in any way. But do I really have the right to condemn Destiny, Karma, or that Somebody who left her here, alone, except for some animals, forcing her to live and be aware of a hostile, brutal, and unjust world? I stop for a moment, perplexed: in fact, who can judge the One who judges us? In the end, everything is incomprehensible to me, even the thought that I have an opportunity, but I am not courageous enough to confess what exactly I was hiding under this word, how much hope and how much honesty. I am looking at her moving in front of me, and the feeling of guilt hinders me from following the contours of her body, her breasts, the strands of hair which, from time to time, cover her eyes without being able to stop a tear.

Camus: *"And, each time I read a story about the plague, from the depths of a heart poisoned by its own revolts and the violence of the others, a clear cry lifts itself, saying that, in fact, there are more things in people to admire, rather than to despise."*

I wrote this last phrase in big letters on the first page of this notebook, one of the many brought here to the mountain cabin, hoping that, by looking back, I would find arguments in favour of the fuller half of the glass. Yes, for mankind, in general, one can find sufficient arguments, but as far as what regards myself, I do have, for the time being, many hesitations.

Having had enough of cooking and putting things in order,

Mara suddenly sat down in front of me and looked at me with a daring of which I would not thought her capable:

"Old man, it's time you finish with lazing about. At some point you will have to stop pitying yourself, and, of course, you'll have to climb the mountain on your own legs! I have no wish to carry you around on my back, or to lecture you. Wasn't this why you came here?"

"The mountain," I replied feeling sad, "is my story, my wager and, as you know well enough, I won't go unprepared. For the moment, I am stalking it, I am trying to get used to the thought that this is my last chance. Don't forget that people my age have problems with climbing the stairs, but I have come here to try, no matter what happens"

"Are you thinking you can leave me here with the sheep, the pigs and these wild beasts? You are no longer on your own," she said, threatening me in all seriousness. "The mountain cannot be conquered on your own, wasn't this what was said to us? To me or to my father, I can't remember. In other words, should I stay here, should I wait for you with my heart in my mouth, not knowing where you might be? What if you meet with a saint who wants to take you with him? How will you let me know? Around here, people say that up there, on the summit, St Peter himself haunts the place, and I don't think there can be more pleasant individuals like you around this corner of the world. He is probably bored also with so many people who are correct, without sins and taste, with whom he's filled up Paradise. Of course, with you, we can't talk of an issue like death, but about a delay, and how much longer do you think I can wait for you? By the time you decide to tell me what you have in mind and before I invite you to eat, I think a massage wouldn't be bad for you," she concluded, pointing at the bed with her hand.

I could not understand what had happened to Mara, what had changed her, where this surprising detachment had come from, along with her contagious optimism which I was trying not to upset.

"It will be my pleasure," I replied, "but with a single condition: that I should blindfold your eyes. I don't want you to see me like this. Age inscribes its traces without mercy. It's natural, you will say, but it is precisely this naturalness that I can't bear. I am embarrassed by what is left of me. In any case, it is a non-negotiable condition."

It was clear I had not found the most appropriate tone. The barely controlled revolt and discontent in my voice forced her to sound the retreat for a few moments, only for her to come back:

"Frankly – you're not ugly, old man. You have a taut face and your hands are like any other man's. If I weren't embarrassed, I would say that you are still handsome, and even if you weren't, what importance does it have? Here, where the devil's mother lives, there's just us and the birds of the sky, we have no competition. I am, indisputably, the most beautiful, and you are, of course, the most handsome. We must stand as ourselves just as the Lord on High made us, and I want at any cost for you to live, to be strong, because I've had enough of so much loneliness."

"You are looking for your loneliness, but I don't think you have any idea how terribly it hurts."

With me, it was other people's pity that chased me away from home and I don't know whether it was true, but it seemed I felt it in her voce as well. Pity is the morality of the weak. Hegel *dixit*! As for loneliness... were I the one I used to be, what would I do? I asked myself this without

137

thinking of the consequences of the answer, since I was invaded with infinite brutality by her mother's face, her voice, her melancholy gaze, sometimes anxious but most often hesitant. Look, I was confused, powerless, humiliated by my own body, in front of Teodora's daughter, who is as beautiful as she was, but much more provocative, and I was tormented by a feeling which was impossible to confess, but which I couldn't deny or avoid. It will stay there, deep in the subconscious, where humiliations, betrayals, defeats, shameful deeds go and hide, but it will torment me ceaselessly because these states of feeling don't die, they reappear again and again, diminishing any joy.

I detested myself for my inability to take things as they are, to accept the evidence. Despite my age and experience, I didn't have the courage to say to myself, speaking with my entire mouth, that the things I felt were, ultimately, a vehement revolt by the life that wanted to express itself at any cost. Continuing to look at her strong breasts, agitated at the smallest movement, the contour of her loins, the gaze with which, for a second, she tested the wall of seriousness with which I had surrounded myself only to withdraw, resigned, I told myself in my head that I should not appeal to morals, in the moment when her mother, who knows from what world, was sending me a new challenge or – even more certainly – striving to take revenge for the hesitations of times past. Happiness, the true accomplishment, was suffocated by morals. Instead of being contented that I had resisted temptations, I felt, as time went by, the dimensions of my loss, since it wasn't because of too much happiness that she didn't come towards me. She knew she was entitled to it, and, because she could not find it at home, in her family, she was looking somewhere else for it, and I, instead of easing her suffering, only emphasised it even more. Many times, out of the blue, I was seized by a nameless and incendiary longing, pushed to the verge of illness. Confused, I would look in all directions, but especially heavenwards, because that intense burning was also accompanied by a light which flooded me. Sometimes I would pronounce her name and, strangely, my heartbeats grew faster, a sign that Teodora's soul was still floating above this area which was scrutinised assiduously by saints and sinners alike, perturbed by who knows what unaccomplished duty. I don't know if she was also looking for me, but, in any case, we would meet. From the night of my ignorance and confusion I would reply to her *I am present*, words that also carried in their subtext the forgiveness I always asked of her, even if, back then, I didn't feel guilty or, to be more exact, I was not aware of my guilt. Mara was in front of me and the feelings of the present didn't seem much too different. The needle of the scales pointed, although from other reasons, towards loss.

"I don't know what to do to convince you that it would be much better if I blindfolded your eyes," I said again, and she, surprised, but able to find counterarguments immediately, said after a short hesitation:

"As you wish, but it would be better to reach a compromise: I won't have my eyes blindfolded and I'll massage you only on your face and shoulders!"

Without waiting for an answer, she sat behind me, and took my glasses off. While I felt her rough, restless fingers travelling on my forehead, I forced myself not to think about her, to push her out of my mind, and to send down into my soul, as I had so many times in the rare moments of peacefulness, that green, calm light that came from nowhere in order to take away with it the sorrows from which I had never managed to run away.

"The saddest eater of noodle soup in the world has prepared for your dessert a surprise with honeycomb, pollen and other such products which will force you to look at life with more courage," she said in one breath, but I continued to circle around that dead point, in which desire, morals and impotence had united as if in order to increase the pain that was testing me. In reality, I didn't hurt anyone. I did not lust for another man's goods. I did not create illusions. I wasn't waiting for a miracle, and, ultimately, I felt the painful need to touch her, to feel her nearby, but without remorse or other contortions of the soul, and only if she wanted it too. Aiming for this, I called to my help all the memories, the women I'd had or desired, the sad story between me and her mother, and the scientific knowledge which had accompanied me here, high up in the mountains. I called, that is, on everything which could help me to get past inhibitions and remorse, such as my notes about interior exile, a work I'd started many years previously, (in the times when psychoanalysis was forbidden), and never taken to its correct conclusion because I was obsessed about not being sufficiently informed.

"*Why life can be buried for ten dollars*"
Personal ad mentioned by **Freud** in a letter to Maria Bonaparte.

Saint Thomas Aquinas says that *the setting up of a brothel by the monks of Perpignan is a meritorious work.*

Saint Augustine about the necessity of prostitutes: "*They are in the city the same as the cesspit in the palace. Suppress* *the cesspit and the palace will become infected."*

Norbert Elias: *"Civilisation equals the repression and mutilation of instincts."*

Jos Van Ussel – *Histoire de la répression sexuelle* – quoted by **Jaccard**: *"Up to the 16th Century, attitudes and lifestyles were in favour of sex. It was generally permitted for everyone to satisfy their sexual needs in order not to endanger their health. In some towns, the authorities actually opened houses of tolerance. Sensuality was felt, it was lived in a manner that is foreign to us nowadays. Caresses, embraces, kisses: nurses and parents masturbated their children in order to soothe them; the interdiction that hangs over the sexual relations between adults and adolescents did not exist; premarital sexual relations were institutionalised; the family and the servants slept naked in the same room; baths were taken in group, and, on the occasion of some solemn event, the most beautiful young woman in the town was exposed naked. Insofar as what regards young people, there was no need to inform them of things because they could see, feel, and learn what interested them while at the side of the adults. On the Isle of Elba, at the time when Napoleon was hosted there, it was not something unusual for seven people to sleep naked in the same bed, with no distinction of sex. It was a rare occurrence for somebody to keep their shirt on when going to bed; if they did, they would have been suspected of suffering from some infirmity, since, if they were healthy, why would they hide their body?"*

Marguerite of Navarre – *Heptameron, 1559*: *"Nightshirts for women are simple curiosities."*

Georg Groddeck: *"Disease is a creation, a work of art, sometimes the only one which the individual is capable of in his alienation. Hence, its pathetic character as a final instance, place and cry, constituted crazily, romantically: with the price of life."*

Georg Groddeck: *"running away from the human community, alienating and alienated."*

The massage did me very well. The closeness to her, the shrinking of distances, the normality of the touch seemed like an unhoped-for gain. Strange – when her fingers came to caress my lips involuntarily, I felt, for the first time since I was here, the liberation from fear and death, a liberation I owed to her and not to the heaven where I took refuge periodically, and, without wanting to, I realised I was crossing myself. This was a gesture which caused her to laugh:

"Who were you thinking of? What sin, what ugly thought were you chasing away from your mind? Did you confuse me with somebody else? I am not the Virgin Mary, not even a virgin, and life has walked over me as well."

It was difficult for me to reply to her, although she had opened up a delicate and interesting subject, behind which I deciphered not quite her need to give herself to somebody, but an attempt to take another step in my direction. Maybe even the step that I, for such a long time, had hesitated to take. As for my involuntary gesture, it has a simple explanation. I pray more and more often, not with the intention of reconciling myself with the Divine in some way, and not because of weakness or fear, but because is a painful need. A mode in which I can say to the Almighty that I feel him, that He is the result of my searching. In fact, all the great books talked only of this to me, but I had understood them very late. Now, I, too, have the certainty. I finally know. In a way, I was grateful to Mara as well for something I will never be able to explain to her.

"I want you to know that I am not waiting for an answer to this question in particular," Mara continued, "but I have another one which has disturbed me for a long time. Did you sleep with my mother?"

"Were you asking yourself whether you were my daughter?" I said, hurrying to welcome her question. "Would that be to your liking?"

"I am not playing this way," she said rebelliously, surprised by the dilemma in which my question had placed her, "I don't want you to avoid the answer."

"You would have to promise to tell me, in all sincerity, why you asked," I insisted, to which Mara hurried to nod her approval:

"If you will be very honest!"

"I promise, although you have no way of verifying it. The answer is simple: no. I did not sleep with her. But I am sorry I didn't do it."

"Since you regret it, I am trying to believe you," she agreed gladly. "However, did you love her?"

"Yes, very much."

"So, then?"

"I'd have to explain to you, and explain it to myself. The fear of complications, the obsessions of morality, the respect for your father. That's about that. In any case, I loved her so much that, if we had been strong enough to take that step, it is hard to imagine what would have happened. It would have been an explosion, a death, and a resurrection, I can't find the words, not even now. We would talk, but we never went beyond intention, beyond desire. She wasn't any more daring either. In the end, having postponed it forever, I wouldn't say we established a distance from each other, but, in any case, the temperature of our relationship decreased, patience and fear, step by step, came to possess us, and, unfortunately, time, without my realising it, passed. It was possible for it to happen, several times, in the forest, it was so close, but I felt her hesitation, or maybe that's what I imagined, that's what I wanted, and, as usual, we separated feeling ashamed. Often she seemed to hear footsteps. At other times she could have sworn that we were followed around by your father or that beasts of prey might be nearby. Most of the time, however, the whooshing of a bird was enough to release us from the obligation to graduate to the deed, and make us promise ourselves a future date, which, as you see, has not come. This is where I always lost: believing that I had the time, that circumstances would help us later on. The fact of sharing the blame does not free me from regrets, but have you thought I could be your father? You have to believe me, I would have had at least this much courage."

"Of course, I don't regret you are not my father, but I am not happy about it either. In any case, you were a permanent subject of discussion between my parents, and not some of the kinder ones too," Mara said, stressed it, "so I could imagine anything. When you were going to come by or were in the area, father went through real nervous crises. He reproached mother that she loved you, that she was a slut, that he had proofs about your liaison, otherwise you would have had nothing to seek out in this place, that he even saw you himself."

"I would have never suspected it, and Teodora never even

suggested that he was jealous, either. Her gestures were clear, certain, they didn't seem to hide anything, and she didn't avoid paying me attention. On the contrary. It would have never crossed my mind that, in reality, she provoked him, she defied him. Your father, in his turn, behaved admirably, he helped me with the building of the cabin and in no case did I feel his gaze following me, or, often, when I went above the limits with the *ţuica* brandy, he would never try to drop a hint."

"Because of these scandals, I had moments when I hated you, and I thought of telling you myself. When mother went to town, and she had to go pretty often, father was taken over by madness: he would look at the watch all the time, he would listen with concentration in the hope that he could decipher an unusual noise coming from the forest, he would climb up and down this wretched ridge several times, and when mother got home he would ask her to account in detail for every minute, for every delay and conversation she'd had, nothings from which he tried to deduce her possible sins. He would often call her into a room, or take me outside. I think they made love or maybe he especially wanted to deduce from her behaviour in those intimate moments whether she had cheated on him, whether she was reacting differently from the usual. I would tell myself many times that I couldn't run away from home, because, in the moments when she could not control her crying, mother repeated half a phrase to me, continuously. If it wasn't for you... but I never managed to learn the rest of it, the explanation. Perhaps she would have been even unhappier without me, or, on the contrary, she didn't leave him because of me, and she didn't assume the risk of doing what she felt she had to do. By running away, I would have given her a chance to follow me, to assume her liberty, or I could have made them feel their solidarity, my running away bringing them closer. But to where could I have run away? There was no one. I didn't really know any family relations very well, father had made us distant from everyone. He had a precious treasure, my mother, because of whom he'd isolated himself, and she had accepted this, being convinced they would not stay here, in the mountains, for very long. Maybe it was also because she loved him, I don't know. Here, alone, I would think of all the people I'd met, of what I knew or what had happened to me, and, for a while, I would not feel so abandoned when I rifled through my memory and invented questions. I thought about you quite a lot and, I have to confess, you came around here often, sometimes accompanied, sometimes on your own, but you never took me into consideration. I was just the cleaning girl. Back in those days, just like now, I would condemn you for forgetting my mother. If you really loved her, how could you forget her? After the death of my parents, I cared for your house out of inertia and because of the library. I would read everything that fell into my hands, even your medical stories about which I didn't understand a thing, and I was thinking that you would come on your own at some point, with better thoughts, or that a buyer would appear in order to take over the house. I waited for you, especially, because you were at our side in all the good and bad, and, I admit, I was thinking of the memory of your sins with my mother. It's good that at least now…"

Looking at her attentively, it seemed to me that she had put a great effort into talking to me and that she could barely contain her tears, and this is why I didn't insist that she continued. I avoided the questions I wanted to ask precisely at the time when I would have had the chance of receiving an answer to most of them. On the other hand, I could have given the impression that I was avoiding any engagement, then, because there's no doubt she felt the need for it, I could have taken her in my arms, and felt her very strong body, that is, the life with whose nostalgia I was living, but I very quickly chased away this miserable thought because it would have been merely an attempted theft. It would not have been too hard to guess her reactions, but fear made me leave the initiative to her, the fear of my intentions being misunderstood, and the fear that she might decipher my hidden thought, my desire to steal something from her warmth, disturbing the atmosphere of sincerity that had started to be established between us. In the end, I think I worked out her state of mind in those moments, as she, with a smile of gratitude, dismissed her memories and invited me to dinner.

"I'd like us to move around a little, if you want, or, for a start, try to sleep for an hour, and, later on, I would like to show you the surroundings. New trees have grown, others have died, many things changed since last time you've been here. Maybe you will come to see my parents. I loved them as they were, and I feel their absence. Sometimes I cry because of my longing for them, some other times, when I care for the flowers on the graves, I condemn them for going away without caring about me. What am I? I always ask myself this when I feel that I have forgotten all words, and in front of me, no matter how hard I'd try, I only see fear and death."

In order to temper her emotions, she gestured at the dining table again, and, when I discovered the clean plates, the steaming soup, the open honey jars, the *cașcaval* cheese and the curds beside the *mămăliga* corn meal mush placed on a wooden cutting board, I had a sensation of naturalness. I was *then* and *there* and, paradoxically, I felt good.

I am writing and, I admit, it starts to be to my liking, although I encounter, more and more frequently, the people who are no more, the dead... my dead people! Some of their lives were extinguished a long time ago, some have disappeared without a trace. The loves of long ago, those that enriched me, that lifted my soul above ugliness and misery, they are left only as luminous points in a memory, which, in its turn, is full of gaps. How could everything pass by so quickly? Stupid question. They just passed and that's that! In front of my eyes – a sort of film without sound in which I feel, at the same time, both an actor and a spectator. I search ceaselessly for something that could tell me more than I know and feel, a key, another angle, a sense, an explanation of the things that run through my mind. For the moment there's a single certainty: by writing I feel less afraid, maybe also because I have moved from another age where I would suffer the pains and fears more readily. I am starting to see with an eye of the mind, whose existence I never suspected, the manner in which words set like a construction, putting up a wall between me and death. I am writing, and I feel, bizarrely, how I release myself from death's domain. The papers in front of me are a space between me and non-being. Maybe a shout. Maybe something that forces me to look forward, as much as I am permitted.

Far away, above the trees, coming out of a bluish mist, is *that* mountain. The Margin of Life, a kind of flattened head on which the saints or extra-terrestrials from all the legends are climbing up and down. *Then*, in those moments, the peak of the mountain has a crown of leaden clouds which are like the apostle's halo, but a dark halo behind which – or inside which – one can guess that there are lights, tension, something that must not be seen or known. I manage to get a faint suspicion of the path to the top and to convince myself that I have to try. I am at the age when only the impossible is allowed me. The time I have left is only for things and attempts which are impossible.

The only note in the *Green notebook*: *Transparency in our days – a rape with the approval of the state.* I wonder what I was thinking of? In fact, the things I do, the notes in front of me, might also seem as obscure. Self-rape – you can't say that; masochism – doesn't cover reality completely. Confession, and confession has an exact correspondent in psychoanalysis. When will I catch up with myself? If I'm allowed to do it, will things be easier, I wonder? For the moment, besides the pain, I am also exercised by a terrible regret. I was, to a large extent, missing from my own life. Always for others, especially for others, and it's these others that I can't find, no matter how hard I concentrate on it. They don't have any consistency, they are no more than the vague memory of joy or reconciliation. Simple palliatives.

Mara left again in order to feed her animals, but not before assuring me that she would return as soon as possible, although her relationship with time is very different from mine: her clock is still the skies. I don't know exactly what her point of reference are, or what the skies could tell her in the days without any sun, but I see her raising her hand up towards an imaginary clock, a sign that the time has come, that here comes the time of her creatures: a cow, sheep, pigs, dogs. It seems strange that her frequent departures are not to my liking, they simply make me anxious. When I came here, to the mountains, she was not part of my calculations, she almost did not exist, except to the extent that I cared for the neatness of the house and, *look*, without my realising it, she became very necessary to me. The memories, the past, are no longer enough for me, as I used to think before, neither are the preparations for the road to the Margin of Life. Beyond these, I still have an immense space for something else, anything else. It is impossible for me to overlook this detail. There was a moment in which I had the impression that Mara was starting to interest me, I could not explain how, but it was more than that mountain which I looked at, today, with anxiety, because I do not yet feel prepared for the decisive confrontation, and time passes to my disadvantage. Should I walk towards death with eyes wide open?

Perhaps I'd like to live a little more, I often say to myself, and words don't exactly hide the conviction that I would be defeated like many others, but I have a need to study it some more and, maybe, to laze about some more. More recently, in Mara's absence, I seem to see my loneliness, it is given a guise, a material body which I feel is ceaselessly following me around, making ironies at my expense, getting transformed at times into a kind of encouragement to giving up. Anyway, I no longer have any doubts, the reasoning from back home, the projects that brought me here, seem not to match the reality on the ground. Before reaching here, the mountain was inside me; now, it is in front of my eyes, huge, mysterious. I have reached the age when nothing satisfies me anymore: neither life, not death. My friends, few as they have been, have disappeared. I can no longer find my place among the young, although, spiritually, I sometimes feel fresh, just like them. To be more precise: they don't accept me, they only tolerate me, and this horrifies me. Young, but with some special nuances. I know what is not possible, it is clear to me that everything is unstoppable and a loss, but, strangely, I persist in living as if I didn't know these truths. Fallen in between worlds, beyond ages, in a space belonging to no-one, forced to accept the unacceptable and yet with an absurd hope, where there is no lack of health and peacefulness, roaming inside me. This feeling had also visited me before, immediately after I recovered from my incomprehensible illness. It was as if I saw, literally, the distance between me and my relations, and their care bothered me instead of making me feel well. Now I feel a complex longing for them, the need to recover them, to bring them back into my soul, to remove them from the indifference and oblivion to which I condemned them. Without any intention, I found myself in front of the first concession made to memory, from which my son came to the forefront in a hurry. I can't say what age he was, I think that he was no more than two, but I see him running triumphantly towards his mother, plump and very bow legged, with a face that was always smiling, brandishing two photographs: "Daddy pig! Daddy wolf!"

Daria, who understood his language, laughed out loud because of the consternation that could be read on my face, but she didn't hurry to decode his few words. She preferred to laugh, waiting for my reactions. Of course, were I paying more attention, it would not have been hard to realise that the photographs had been chosen out of many others and, naturally, the child wanted to share, in his way, the joy of having recognised those respective animals. Since then, in rare moments of tenderness, when the hospital allowed me some time for myself, but especially in the numerous circumstances when Daria had condemned me, justified or unjustified, I admitted my guilt even when it was not appropriate, saying in one breath that sentence of the child: "Daddy pig!"

Nowadays, if I think hard about it, I would deserve even harsher words, because I didn't even know how time passed until I found myself having him as a student in his first year of Medicine. It was, I think, one of the happiest moments of my life: it was as if all my efforts up to then, the privations and humiliations – not few in number – had been rewarded. He had been successful in a mad competition, in an admission examination with 16 applicants for each university place, and his future had, therefore, become a little clearer. Equally, I was glad of his becoming more mature, of the fact that he treated me as a colleague from whom he needed, first of all, financial support.

"I bought myself a cranium, a femur and some vertebrae," he said to me once, and I was not surprised. I knew that each bone had a certain value, and especially the cranium, with that exasperating temporal bone – because of which the anatomy professor flunked students by the score – was the more expensive.

The sales from the start of the year, rounded out rather nicely the incomes of the lab technicians, but also those of the students in the higher years, who knew that the beginners, the *boboci* – the ducklings, the *balici* – the piglets, as they were called, didn't know the real price of the bones, the illustrations and the "serious" books that were passed down from hand to hand and from generation to generation. I was also consulted when it came to the various mnemonic formulae, inherited in their turn. The two names of the cranial nerve ten, called the *vagus* or *pneumogastric* nerve, were easier to remember with the help of an epigram: *Nerve ten, asks the professor feeling rather sarcastic, / and the student answers vaguely, but not pneumogastric!*

Our discussions in the first year of studies concentrated specifically on the psychology of the most capricious professors: the subjects that obsessed them, what you had to say to them in order to gain their goodwill, and what supplementary questions they asked when they wanted to fail you in the exams. The way you dressed was also a matter of great importance. With Professor Gaginski, for example, a carefully knotted tie and well burnished shoes were part of what caught his attention. This was the reason why the lab technicians, who were, more or less, bribed by the students with cigarettes and various other attentions during the course of the semester, in addition to everything else that was part of the passing grade, also looked after shoe cream, a shoe brush, and an electric iron which, always plugged in, was kept in a little room near the amphitheatre.

Another example, was Professor Ursu, who was particularly stimulated by the girls' cleavage. A more aggressive décolletage and breasts on par with it would create the good atmosphere that saved everyone's exams. As it happened, in the professor's room, where the girls who were the most decorative but who had less book knowledge were sent to meditate, there was, apparently by chance, a written motto 'forgotten' on a leather daybed: *"If you fall, you pass!"*

Outside of this matter, and beyond this sin which is so worldly and non-pedagogical, Professor Ursu was the first in what the students called the *Donkey scale*, their nickname for the list of the most rigid professors who flunked the greatest number of students for the semester, or for a repeat year. Dan didn't like any of the men I mentioned, but he managed to pass his exams without any problems. The marks, although very good, did not betray a special passion for any subject in particular, but they revealed him to be a perfect crammer, a man who wanted to be head of year. I was surprised, however, by the frequency with which I discovered on his table the books and studies of psychiatry from my library. With all this, or maybe because of all this, the discussions between the two of us took place as if between two professionals, not one word about his relations with colleagues, or with girls. Our relationship and any mutual understanding remained absent from the conversations, but I was content with the thought that, in this matter, the inquisitiveness and concern of his mother were more than sufficient. In this way, I discovered, with surprise, that he was making confessions to her, and as long as Daria was content, I could be at peace.

In his penultimate year in the university, on her insistence, he came home with his great love, Luiza, a student in Philology, who was rather disappointing, maybe because the difference between her intelligence and her incontestable beauty, good enough for a top model, was rather great. My wife, for a change, seemed extremely contented, a fact that surprised me and, even further, vexed me.

"How many people go to the Registry Office with their first love? Very few or none," she explained. "If he's a smart boy, he will find another, if not, he deserves his stupid girlfriend! Dan, for whom you don't really have much time, is, in my opinion, very intelligent!"

In the next few months, at Daria's suggestion, in order to leave the apartment free for them and, of course, in order to free them from the presence of the parents, we started to go increasingly often to the films, and the theatre, or to take little trips at the weekend. However, Luiza disappeared off his spiritual map at some point.

"Look, as I foresaw," Daria explained by and by, "she married the man who asked her, since ours didn't convince her that he wanted to get married. I told you once, long ago, that there would be nothing to come out of their story. This beauty, with the exception of her fanny, had nothing to offer him! I hope we see more idiotic films and make even more frequent excursions in the mountains by the time he gets married, that is, if he doesn't start preaching about the uselessness of the institution!"

Fortunately, we didn't have to wait long: at the end of the final year of university, he introduced Iulia to us, also a graduate, but from Pharmacy. He did as his other colleagues did: got married. He knew that marital status was important for the recycling of jobs, but, beyond that, he was also afraid of loneliness, as he was going to be in practice in a village or, in the best of cases, in some small town forgotten by the world. Iulia didn't look like the previous girlfriend, not by a long chalk, although she was also beautiful, but she was a different type of beauty, the type you can approach, in the beginning, with your mind, and only later on with the hormones. She was tall, blonde, with curly, rebellious hair which was not subdued by hairclips, hairbands or other means of constraint. She had big eyes which scrutinised you thoroughly, and which betrayed many questions she didn't want exposed at any cost. She was always looking for something, a greater understanding, points of support, a place in her world. On the other hand, as soon as she engaged in a dialogue or assumed some obligation, she totally changed. Her certainty, her concision and her clarity of ideas, together with the impression that she was talking in Dan's name, with his consent, had raised her so high in the eyes of her future mother-in-law, that Iulia seemed to be her daughter, rather than her daughter-in-law, and it was as if the marriage had taken place only to please Daria.

From what Dan confessed to me later on, he had met Luiza at a restaurant, where a group of future female pharmacists and another one from Philology, were celebrating the passing of some difficult exams. Dan sat at a table with the assistant from the Department of Gynaecology and, lacking subjects of conversation in common, they had both concentrated on the female philologists. In the absence of boys, who were very few in this faculty, these philologists had launched, together with the female pharmacists, a dance which was fashionable back then, the Penguin, a kind of Indian file which snaked around the tables. At odd moments, the assistant started to say, more for himself than anything else:

"I've slept with this one... not with this one, I don't remember this one... this one escaped me... the redheads we should bear in mind. I wonder who's giving her check-ups, because she doesn't seem like the type of woman who wastes time in church?"

The one that had "escaped" from the assistant's inventory was, obviously, Luiza, and, after Dan asked her to dance, they stayed together for some months. He had met Iulia before Luiza, at a debating society for literary psycho-pathology which was frequented by numerous lovers of good literature, and where people talked frequently of psychoanalysis – a topic which was forbidden in those times. Initially interested in the kinds of medication used in psychiatry, Iulia got closer to literature later on, and, through this subject, she also got closer to Dan's scientific investigations, which were interesting and courageous. One of them, maybe the least successful one,

The social reinsertion of chronic alcoholics, brought them together and distanced them at the same time, because Iulia's uncle was among the 50 drunks that Dan had to visit in their homes and their possible workplaces. He was a former Greek-Catholic[10] priest who, after his return from the Danube-Black Sea Canal,[11] in its first incarnation, had become a watchman at an alcohol spirit factory. The cold, the misery, the humiliations, the environment in which he lived, the lack of perspective – all managed to bring to his knees even a man who had resisted with dignity at the Canal. Alcohol, drunk daily, had become a necessity which was reinforced by the threats and by his fear of people who organised to steal great quantities of drink, even when they were convinced they had been seen:

"Father, if you chirp anything about this, the Lord on High will be seeing you soon – with your throat cut!"

Dan had met him some time before, in the alcohol rehabilitation department, but he did not suspect any connection between them at the time. Maybe this was because Iulia was merely an acquaintance with whom he liked discussing scientific matters exclusively, and only within the meetings of the debating society. He had learnt from Father Munteanu everything about his family, from which, bizarrely, Iulia was missing – that is, she had been given little importance. This was a fact which caused no small surprise when, at the address given on the medical

10   Greek Catholicism (a synthesis of Roman Catholic and Greek Orthodox dogmas) was severely repressed in Romania in the 1950s, with a great number of priests and prelates imprisoned and tortured.

11   Danube-Black Sea Canal is a project started by the communist government in the 1950s, where political prisoners and opponents were sent in labour camp, in very harsh conditions. The canal was abandoned in the 1960s, reopened some twenty years later and inaugurated by Romania's dictator, Nicolae Ceaușescu, in 1987.

observations sheet, he ran into her, too – the uncle being away in town, meaning at some boozer.

"He didn't have anyone," Iulia explained, "only his brother, that is, my father. My aunt passed away long ago with cervical cancer. Their only son had a tragic destiny, a great painting talent, ending up in the Psychiatry Clinic, with the diagnosis of schizophrenia. He is in a hospital for chronic patients, and for a long time you couldn't talk to him. From all they had – land, houses, cattle, etc., my uncle was left only with a studio flat that he sold when father proposed that he should move in with us, because the money put aside for a rainy day had started to transform into alcohol. Fate had saddled him with difficulties and troubles above his strength to carry, and his thoughts took him more and more often to the sins of the forefathers, to a past which was more suspected than known. A more complicated karma. As a Greek-Catholic priest, he was convinced that the Lord on High is patient and forgives you, even if you repent in the last moment, like the thief who shared Jesus' crucifixion. In any case, he wished for that final moment to be as distant as possible, although, without rehabilitation from alcohol addiction, his life would have ended in a ditch or under a car, long before he could think about forgiveness. He's started to drink again, but with some moderation. He is tortured by fear, a terrible fear of loneliness. He only feels good in the midst of a crowd of people, as many and as disconnected from reality as possible. We, the inhabitants of this house, are not of much use to him: he loves us, so he says, but he runs away from us. The boozer and the factory watchman's hut are the places where people talk about each other's sufferings and console each other."

I recall, without wanting to, the discussions I've had with

Dan about Father Munteanu's states of mind – oscillating between resignation, fear of sin, and rebellion –ending, most of the time, in tears. What is the background on which alcoholism was planted? Melancholy? The shrinkage of senile organs? Or - why not - is it only fear and humiliation that justifies his pleasure in drinking? In any case, I had never seen him, I had only built him up mentally from Dan's words, and Dan, who was at the start of his career, lacked experience and information. However, the fact that he was preoccupied by the cases of people who hide behind words made me glad. How much is real sorrow, and how much is for display?

"Lord, why did you give me only pain, nausea and misery, why this unending torture?" Father Munteanu found himself shouting, without caring in front of who he was. "I was punished before having committed any great sins. Was I perhaps judged for the sins of my neighbours, instead of being judged for my own? I do not doubt your right to punish me, but I am asking whether you've made me without that part of the mind or the soul which perceives joy. Maybe you are mistaking me for another? Or: is it possible you've made a mistake with the cross you gave me? Is it not too big for me? Is it possible you've forgotten, Lord, that you haven't endowed me with the strength necessary to carry it, too?"

In the end, horrified by his own words, by the sin he'd committed, he abandoned to his tears the attempt to be forgiven.

The special care for the "case" we discussed had brought Dan closer to Iulia. Father Munteanu was becoming, more and more each day, their "case". Unfortunately, that particular study was destined to be the end of a career, psychiatry, which he had not even truly started. Most of the patients visited by Dan had regained their interest in alcohol after several months, but he could not have foreseen the hardest thing. His professor had set a trap for him – he wanted to check his strength of character, his "resistance to sin". It was almost impossible for Dan to leave his house without having a drink, at least one glass, and his professor had anticipated this; which was why he invited Dan to visit him every evening and to describe the state of the people he'd observed. The road to the clinic had not always been clear and on a single, sober path, but the fact that the professor had numerous and unforeseen appointments and professional meetings had been helpful for him – and especially for his friendship with Iulia.

"I would like to accompany you," she had said. "You don't know how to say no, and this generosity may be your downfall. Women, unfortunately, have a lot of experience with this. They have to say *no* every day to various decent proposals, and especially to the indecent ones. You know the joke: a *decisive no* is the best contraceptive medicine!"

Dan had the inspiration to accept her offer, and, to his good fortune, he managed to pass the exam with a good paper, but with predictable results: alcohol proved to be, ultimately, stronger than the will of the great majority of the patients he treated. In the end, the most important gain from this adventure was Iulia, the point of support he needed so much. She was also the source of an inflexible will which, later on, was going to be the source of many disjunctions in communication, often painful. He introduced her to me as if I'd known her forever, proof that the wound called Luiza had healed, and I accounted for the fact that he had come a little too much under her thumb by putting it down to a love which was now completely established. I wasn't very certain, however. Something warned me that, at a later point, if she didn't find certain compulsory nuances, meaning that if she didn't make some concessions, even against her logical thinking, Dan would be tempted or even forced to escape.

In the end, after she moved in with us and I was convinced that my intuition had been correct, I strove to forewarn her, trying to draw the real portrait of my son, in the hope that she would come to the necessary conclusions.

"Dan," I said to her, "has the typical nature of the researcher. He has unrestrained curiosity, and patience and tenacity which are out of the common. Nothing can be imposed on him, but he caves in when confronted by argument, and he is even happy when he is given variants of which he has not thought. Any defeat, with the help of facts and reasons, of course, truly bring him joy. He files it under the category of knowledge. With the alcohol, you gained an easy victory because he was also aware of his error, but you have to pay attention to other things. Nobody ever managed to impose anything on him. Sometimes, convinced by an opponent's quality, by the uselessness of the discussion, by the lack of time, by boredom or pity, he goes so far as to say yes, but, in the end, he will do as he pleases; and another detail: it is good not to forget about your profession, and the most important thing here is what is not said, rather than what is. As such, you should not be surprised when you find yourself confronted by some facts, reactions or decisions you didn't expect. Taking all this into consideration, you will never cease to be part of the mutual relationship, but, in order to understand him, you will have to reassess relations with him during that period of time, and details matter very much. You can be very certain that he will never insult or attack you, but he will run away in his elegant, discreet manner, he will withdraw to an area, or even to a person, which you would never even suspect. Don't limit the freedom of a man obsessed by knowledge."

I had talked in vain however, the predictable cooling down took place. Lots of time was needed, and I was forced to hear endless rows before they managed to truly weld together. I think Iulia had a special charm, a warmth of the soul which was hard to grasp at first sight, along with a determination and power of sacrifice of which Dan was going to be convinced on numerous occasions. The fact that she managed to wrestle him away from the grip of Luiza, who had unexpectedly reappeared in his life, was, perhaps, her main victory – not only over him, but especially over herself.

Lord, I am closing my eyes, determined to lose myself, as deeply as possible, in my memory, in the years when I used to be alive, and time flowed differently, much slower, and hope had not become less scarce. That film gets brutally cut, however. The night behind my eyelids meets, and becomes identical to the night in which Iulia, Daria, and most of my friends were lost, without return. I miss Daria and Iulia terribly, and, even if I am visited by sorrow, by a terrible rending of myself, I am still afraid of having them pause on this capricious screen of my memory, because the feeling of loss turns against me. *Now*, *to lose* is connected only, and exclusively, with life. I utter the word involuntarily and, automatically, I think of the only loss that matters. It is strange; an entire life under the same dreadful omen: fear. We are fighting the fear of death following the moment when misery, with its multiple facets, has accustomed us to the fear of life. Yet, there are days when I manage to sneak through these terrors, days in which heaven is very close and, paradoxically, death is far away. Giant ice, huge ice floes, white mountains falling in silence, like a hallucination, a film lacking sound, but also without a beginning or an end. A strange world, in which the moon and the stars, huge and descended to earth, born out of cold and silence, are watching over new landslides and births, new shapes that have appeared only to be extinguished and then reintegrated into this absurd cycle. I am looking at this bizarre agitation and, as I strive to find out where exactly I am, I am enveloped by a terrible cold, the like of which I cannot remember to have ever felt. Confused, I open my eyes and, involuntarily, I say two words I don't think I've ever uttered: *the cold of death*. Could that paralysing sensation, that cold that sprang from the soul, glaciers and celestial bodies, be the coldness of death? The world to come or that which has been before? It was not, however, the things I could express which made me tremble so, but the images that stayed alongside the words, and beyond them, the things which have subtracted themselves from it all, the clichés and the useless struggle of that dead world, fixed in the most hidden nooks of memory, which I am living and which I bear in my senses like a grave infirmity. The fear of the sleep. The fear of dreams. The fear of the unknown to come. The fear of the very next moment. It seems I am obliged to look my failures and fear in the face, and everything that was and could still be. Punishment or liberation?

Even if she went to care for the animals three times a day, and the road from the Weather Station to me was not easy, you could read on Mara's face, each time we saw each other again, a great joy. She was probably happy to find me alive, and happy that her loneliness would have, for a while, the kindest nuances possible. Of course, I never planned to ask what exactly she was feeling, so that I might prevent, in the future, her controlling herself and dispelling the joy that enveloped me when she appeared in the frame of the door, or when I heard from afar the whistling by which she announced her arrival.

"Old man," she said at some point, "you must tell me what's in your mind. One: you move in at the Weather Station and then we make an excursion here every week. Two: I move in with you, but then I would have to bring my animals, too. Of course, that is, if you wouldn't want me to give them away to somebody or to sell them. Three: you go back and, in this case, you take me with you or, why not, you leave me here, where you found me, as, since you're not my father, you don't have any obligation with regards to me. If you want us to climb the mountain together, I also must do something with the poor creatures, instead of setting them free, at the will of the bears or wolves. I don't want to be a burden to you; that is, forcing you to shape your life according to mine."

"I will reply with the same sincerity," I hurried to offer, because our situation required a clarification, anyway. "I came here to climb the mountain, no matter what happened, even if I'm fated to stay forever somewhere on the road. It is my obsession, my curiosity. When I was strong, I was afraid, the stories about those who died did not encourage me, life had another price back then. Of course, and why should I lie, I've never thought of including you in my project. If we sit down and judge things honestly, the most rational solution would be the following. I'll take you to town, where my house is at your disposal, I can look for a workplace for you, maybe even in my son's clinic, and I will return to take my plan to its proper conclusion."

"Another version?" she asked, with a look and a tone of voice that cancelled this last solution automatically. "To stay just as we are, in one place or the other. This would be the worse solution possible. I have lived for some years, not a few of them, and you know well that at any time. I am very vulnerable, why not look the truth in its face? At what age did your father pass away? He was younger than me."

"You'd better tell me what are the maximum ages we talk about nowadays?"

"Around 120. Up to that age, you still have a lot of time," she laughed. "You need to step out from the ranks! Why not propose this performance to yourself? If other people managed it, that means you too have a chance! And, with this, our broadcast ends! We start training tomorrow, because the mountain is waiting for us!"

"It's waiting for me," I emphasised and she accepted it, her expression indicating that she was making me a great concession: "We'll see. We'll climb up and down until our eyes pop out, and we'll draw conclusions only after that. Otherwise, you can find simpler ways of killing yourself. At least, this is the impression of your intention that you are giving out, if we look at your wanderings back and forth up to now. I would like us to make another bargain. I'll stop telling you about life, because you know only too well that the things I have lived up to now don't look – not even by far – like what I imagined life to be, and you stop mentioning death to me. In any case, She will come, but let's not hurry Her, let's not remind Her that we exist."

"Unfortunately, the things which have happened to us, are happening and will continue to happen to us for a while, are called life. It's true, this is how it was given us. Good, bad, ugly, beautiful. I, too, would have liked it to be different, but it was not meant to be. I am neither a sage, nor a person resigned to his fate."

A short inventory of this moment. I don't want to leave here, and go away from the mountains, but I don't want to stay either. I don't want to abandon the Margin of Life project – the ascent that obsesses me, but I don't want to take it to its conclusion either. I don't want to invite Mara to move in with me, but I don't like her to stay where she is. I no longer like to be alone, but I don't want to move to the Weather Station for good. I don't know Mara's monk, but I find myself thinking of him more and more. I am missing my family terribly, but I don't want to go home. What I am living here is not life, but, with all its problems, I cannot deprive myself of it. In reality, I am just a sum of former desires, former sins, former joys, former ambitions and, of course, several different pains and fears. In other words, I am an answer no longer waiting for questions. As a consequence, it's neither good, nor bad; it isn't pleasant but it isn't unpleasant either. It is not, but it is.

"Old man," said Mara, "I thought this is the time to know you. With my mother, things were as they were, and they really were not, if I understood well. I took everything you told me to be true. Of course, I would be glad to learn she was happy, even if father might be missing from the story at times. As time goes by, I think more and more of her, and I try to explain to myself the reason why she stayed here, tormented by father's jealous crises, and why neither you or her ever managed to take one thought, one desire to its conclusion. Of course, you've explained it to me, but we've always returned again and again to your arguments, and something doesn't stand up, it's not part of the story. It is clear you didn't stay here day after day, since you had a profession, a family, maybe other creatures who desired you. Taking into account the fact that you saw each other only from time to time, and taking into account the fact that, in those moments, logic overruled the power of the senses, it means that your love could not have been so great. Can you love like this, like learning at a distance, or, how should I say, excluding, as it were, the body, the senses? Can such a love last? Was it real? Couldn't it be that, perhaps, you remembered mother only when you came closer to this area? Probably my questions seem idiotic to you, but I don't have the experience. I hope you grasp that. This is just what I've learned from your books and the films on the television, when it worked. I would watch some story in a stupor, I didn't understand the language, but I would invent subjects based on what I saw, and, in this way, I would subsume my needs, my loves, my desires. I would wander through various countries, I would listen to various languages, but, in reality, behind what I saw, I discovered my sorrow, again and again. You and my mother would have had the chance to be accomplished, to follow your feelings, because love and despair may force you to do exactly what they urge you to do, but it wasn't meant to be. Three unhappy people: you, father and mother. Sometimes I would run away from school and I'd see mother either standing in the window, or sitting on a big, round stone, gazing in a void, waiting for something. It's only today, when I find myself in the same places, waiting for something, I don't know what exactly, something that might change my fate or break the monotony of my days, that I understand her better. I stand in the window or on that stone and I gaze at the path that comes towards us. I sometimes see various animals that don't have the courage to climb up because of my dogs, but most of the time I feel my mother close-by. I have the impression that she'd like to tell me something, because now, when I look back, I am aware that, in reality, we never discussed anything seriously. She would feel the love, and I, in my turn, would feel it, and that was enough for us. On the other hand, how could a mother talk to her one and only daughter, who was actually inexperienced, about sorrows and issues which, generally, refuse to be expressed in words? I had to deduce everything, to notice how the two ice floes established their distance, slowly and certainly, and the words that marked this fact were foreign to me, and unknown. It was very rarely, at the times when she didn't manage to hide her tears, that she assured me that I was too green and I couldn't understand the suffering she was going through. He is your father, you need to respect him – that was more or less what she tried to tell me before she closed hermetically in herself."

Mara talked without breaks, as if, before she got the courage to tell them to me, she had rehearsed the questions puzzling her many times, and in a loud voice. I realised she had wanted for a long time to free herself from these questions, to which after all this time, I didn't have very clear answers. This is how things had been, that was all I could say to her. I had no other explanation, no matter how much she doubted my words. In the absence of Teodora, far away from her, logical thought and my senses assured me that next time I would take the decisive step because I wanted her with all my being. In my thoughts, which didn't care about the consequences, no matter how grave, I was swearing myself to her, but when we found ourselves face to face, the fear of consequences, our lack of courage, the entanglements in the thickets of morality again urged us to give up. I was thinking that my very well hidden antipathy for her father, and the joy of learning that Teodora had been happy with me, originated – more than certainly – from the truth that his entire affection had overflowed only towards her mother, and that she, Mara, had been excluded. It was precisely this fact that had created, in time, a strange solidarity: she was reliving her known and suspected sorrows. It was probable that, in this way, hidden behind Teodora, it was easier for her to talk about herself, or to bring me into an area that interested her. That was why I also felt encouraged to come forward, although I was not very certain that I had placed my finger on her bloodiest wound:

"And your monk?"

"You have forgotten the question I asked you," she hurried to answer with a strong reproach in her voice, "but I will remind you of it later on. As for the monk... he's disappeared for a while, but he'll reappear one day. This is how he's made. I think that not even he knows what he wants besides his temporary loves. I hated him, I detested him, but in the end I realised that I should be grateful to him. In reality, I had wanted this sin, with him or anyone else, out of curiosity, out of need, I don't even know why myself. I had to open or to close this chapter, too. All creatures and insects were doing it and it was normal that I shouldn't be the exception."

She talked with such detachment that she left the impression she was speaking of somebody else, or that she had been contaminated by the naturalness or by the lack of care from the creatures around her, from the living beings in whose midst she was living almost all the time. As for the matters which concerned me, I would have preferred her not to continue, that is, if the need to come to her rescue hadn't compelled me.

"In what way do you think I could be of any use?" I asked, trying unsuccessfully to skip over the episode which was not hard to imagine. "There are certain signs that make one anxious. Should I think of pregnancy?"

"Oh, no, I've gone through those emotions, too," she laughed, with no trace of restraint. "I told you about the first quiet night after father's death, when the monk came. He left without telling me whether he would return, but the next night he appeared just like that, out of the blue, to the despair of the dogs, who didn't like him. He brought me bread, cooking oil, tea, sugar, and – the best thing – a bottle of red wine. I cooked his meal, a *mămăligă* with sheep cheese, we talked little nothings about Dogaru, about the new forest rangers who'd discovered a shepherd with his head crushed. He drank half the bottle of wine by himself, as I was content just with tasting it, and after that he went into the building next door to sleep, but, after some hour, I heard a knocking on the door accompanied by the dog's agitated barking. As usual, I took father's gun. I haven't used it yet, but you make an impression holding it in your hands, you are intimidating. Surprised, I saw the monk but without his cassock on, dressed only in the few clothes underneath. I thought maybe he'd had a nightmare, that father's shadow had come to check things and it didn't like the person it found there, which was the reason the monk had run here, undressed; but I didn't exclude the possibility that some pain, some unexpected suffering had disturbed his peace. He didn't tell me what was wrong with him, he was content to sneak past me, and to sit quickly on the edge of the bed. I didn't have the power to stop him. In any case, the last thing that might have come to mind was that I might interest him as a woman. His uniform had contributed to this idea, the cassock, the fact that he'd buried my father and the fact I had welcomed him with all the respect due. Unfortunately, his intentions became very clearly visible in the following seconds. He raised up from the bed as soon as I closed the door, and his raging eyes, fixed on my breasts, forced me to think of some position from which I could defend myself. I couldn't come to believe what was happening. I was still afraid I might make myself seem ridiculous, or insult him, but he didn't give me the time for that. He immobilised me in a few seconds, turning and grasping my head at the back and pushing me down in the bed; he then started to kiss me noisily and to whisper to me through his teeth: '*Don't be an idiot, you've got nothing to lose!*'

Every time I think of him, I am invaded by a smell of sweat which is not at all repugnant, mixed with another smell, a sour one, of wine; and suddenly my shoulders and breasts were aching because of the terrible effort to free my arms. I didn't scream. I opposed what he was doing until I felt that my strength was draining little by little, then I was flooded by tears, and, later on, even became indifferent to all of it. It had to happen at some point, in the end; with him or someone else, it had no importance, I belonged only to the mountain and some animals. I had nobody who would hold me accountable, nobody would have cried for me or buried me, if it had come to that, if his madness had pushed him to become even more violent. So, I asked him to allow me to undress, so we could do the thing in peace, but he didn't want to. '*You are very strong and I don't trust you,*' he said, ripping the few clothes I had on me, in which I used to sleep. '*I am convinced the Almighty's made you for a thousand men, not just for one. We'll die together, but you're not getting away from me.'*

In reality, it wasn't his threats that calmed me, but precisely that need, awoken suddenly, from all my being, an unpleasant pain, not encountered up to that time. I called him and rejected him with equal strength, I needed what was happening, but I was also very scared. In any case, I let him do precisely what he wanted, and, from the dizziness of the senses, from the peace and peacefulness that had enveloped me, I was woken up by one of his hands slapping me on the face: *'But why haven't you warned me, you idiot? Couldn't you find anybody before me to make a woman out of you?'* Any answer would have been in vain, our sweat and my tears had been mixed, and I was now looking at him with a special interest, because nothing separated us, with the exception of some rags. He was a strong man, a handsome man, and I continued to follow him with my eyes, waiting for a sentence which, in the end, he pronounced. *'Will you ever be able to forgive me for the evil I caused? I am a bastard, a failure, nothing I did was ever successful. I've taken nothing to its conclusion, I turned my life into dust because of a creature whom I hope to be able to kill. You are a saint, I don't deserve you, only you could be able to heal me of my memories, of the shame that I live like a savage, like a man who hasn't known faith and morals.'* He then took the belt from my jeans and, with tears in his eyes, he offered it to me: *'Hit me, as hard as you can, help me forget the horrible wound I caused you. The devil, the wretched devil, pushed me from behind, and led my steps. You are so beautiful that I lost my mind. I'll be at your feet for all my life, if this is what you want. Don't spare me, hit me and spit at me, you have a ruin standing before you, a human piece of dirt, a nothing worthy of all pity.'*

He kneeled, embraced my legs with both arms and, crying, he started to kiss them. He recounted his loves to me, with unhoped for details, his road to failure, as if I should have forgiven him or given him courage myself. It was a terrible night, with love and tears, with hate and fury, a long night, and unique, like an illness from which I cannot free myself, like an illness. I started to cry in my turn, but from reasons which were completely different, as thousands of fears had started to torture me. A future child, condemned, just like me, to fear, to wretchedness and loneliness. Despite the tears and the details in which he had, in some of the moments, lost himself, I knew the monk too little, and the thought that he might carry some hidden disease or that he might not come back to me didn't give me any peace. All those stories were arguments in favour of his instability, and nothing, not even the tears, encouraged me to believe that, at least this time, he had been sincere. Everything was against me: the place he'd found me in, what I was, and who I was. In any case, I felt humiliated, vanquished, dirty, but free from any curiosity. I finally knew what I had not known before, I had somehow grown older, and time, despite pleasure, had uncovered new and unsuspected questions and anxieties; but it was not just the monk at their origins. This is why I didn't want to see him again, at any cost, and the thought that he might touch me again terrified me, so this hate, which grew like a storm born out of a little cloud, took larger proportions, increasing at the same pace as the time that passed until he reappeared at the Weather Station.

This time, the dogs sensed him from far away, so I had the time to grab my gun, which had never been used before that time. It was the only solution which would get rid of him forever. It was as if I'd lost my mind, I didn't have anything to hold me back, nobody took my hand off the gun. Sometimes, at night, I had missed him so much that it was precisely this sentiment, the explosive mix of love and hate, that accentuated my need to be ruthless – with him, and with myself. I warned him it would be good if he didn't come closer, I threatened a few times, I showed him the gun, I fired a shot in his direction, to convince him I was not joking, but he didn't stop, and continued to climb with calm, even steps, as if he was certain I wouldn't kill him. I unloaded another shot in the air and he, calm and almost indifferent, continued to advance, convinced I would not have the courage to kill him. And I didn't. What's more, despite my anxiety and the numerous questions without an answer, during the whole time he went missing, I could not find it in myself to blame him. In reality, if I hadn't wanted it, he would have never managed to force me to make love. All sort of people had come by this place – shepherds, foresters, day trippers, military men, geologists, students – and most of them had evil designs on me, they didn't give me peace with their insinuations, and even with direct proposals, but only he had found the solution. That time, he stayed with me for a whole week and he promised to me that he would forget his lovers, the monastery, his past, and 'until death do us part' we'd stay together because we suited each other, we had lots of similarities and common needs, and that, out of two great defeats, a victory might come. After marriage, we were going to sell the animals, also the few things we had, and, with the money we'd have obtained, with what I had left from my parents, we were going to go away from these places, to take life from the beginning, because things couldn't be worse somewhere else, anywhere else but here. Despite arguments and logical thinking, a shadow of doubt refused to leave me: maybe this time. How many defeats do you need in order to draw a conclusion? The monk believed in what he was saying, in his projects, but only when he was with me, and he stayed with me only for a week, a period during which I felt happy, although I was watching him anxiously, convinced he would disappear, like every other time. As it actually happened, anyway, I felt his impatience to go, the call from I don't know who, the call of a woman, of the roads, of risk, of other sins – and they could be read on his face with great ease. What's more, even when we made love, it wasn't me of whom he was thinking. One day he went to sell a cow and, as I expected, he forgot to come back. It was strange, though, that during all this time, I haven't missed him, but I thought intensely of those days which had been so different to everything I had lived up to that time."

"And did you welcome him back again?" I asked, wanting her to take to its conclusion a story which seemed to have obsessed her for a long time.

The moment had appeared to exclude this subject from our relationship entirely, but this moment also seemed to reveal her as she really was. I was also thinking that she was telling me her adventure with such unexpected detachment in order to force me to understand something beyond events and words, and also because she needed my forgiveness.

"I certainly did. He told me that his superiors in the monastery had punished him, ordering him to pull, together with other condemned monks, the thorn bushes off a wild crest of land bought by the abbot at a cost of almost nothing. He assured me he stayed there and suffered the whole punishment, which was extremely hard, out of the need to suffer for the evil he had caused me. I couldn't verify this, so, as a consequence, I took everything he told me as true. If I didn't have any hope before, there had appeared a very small one now, a hope maybe as small as one of my father's little clouds. With the money from the cow, as well as from foodstuffs, he bought me weekday clothes and Sunday clothes, in order to convince me that he was thinking of marriage, a gesture which didn't move my heart because I had numerous pairs of jeans left from my mother and, of course, many clothes with which I was prepared to resist the horrid frosts and long winters in these places. Wasted money, but the gesture fed my puny hope, and then he left with my consent, after he had helped me, for a few days, to gather grass for the animals I still had. He was going to find a place for us, away from Natalia and Madeleine, away from the monastery, away from the eternal temptations and, of course, away from the memories. Winter passed, spring came, and the venerable and pious monk no longer appeared. I thought of many things: that some beast had eaten him, that some husband, mad with jealousy, had killed him, after finding him with his wife in some more special moment, that he'd run away to Canada to follow his great love, but I thought, especially, that I wasn't up to the strength of his expectations. I could only offer him the thing he could find with any woman. At least, that's what I thought."

She stopped, but it didn't seem she wanted to hear my opinion because she wasn't trying to catch my gaze, as she used to do, waiting for a reaction from me. She seemed to be concentrating on other events which could be up to the task of drawing with even greater precision the portrait of the monk. I was looking at her closely, surprised by the fact that she was much more complex than I had imagined, when I discovered her in the cabin door, dressed in her washed-out jeans, with the jacket unable to cover completely her big, strong breasts. As I watched her and reconstructed her from the events she'd told me, it was increasingly difficult for me to understand what she was waiting on from me. At some point, I thought she missed the monk, that she longed for the pleasant moments that had taken her out of conventionality, showing her another facet of life; or that she missed the attempt of the instincts to keep him alive in her memory, to call him on a wavelength known only to him.

"As time goes by, I realise I judged you wrongly," I admitted. "Alone, far from the world, getting through insufferable winters, the mists that make you belong more to the skies than the earth, the frosty nights, the sieges laid by the wild beasts..."

"No matter how strange this might sound, I liked such nights," she said, as if waking up from a dream. "I would read, listen to the music, and I would be glad that I was protected by precisely this intemperate weather. Who could climb up here in such weather? And then, I am not afraid of animals, but of people. Seeing the enormous moon, having the sensation that you must watch your head so you won't touch it. Then, the howling wolves and the animals getting agitated in the stable, the dogs maddened by fury or fear, and the trees cracking because of the cold. Sometimes, I would sit glued to the window, father's gun in my hands, ready to shoot. I would wait for the dawn, with the hope that it would send the wolves away, but they sensed the smell of the sheep and they didn't quiet down, and I, out of despair, felt like crying, but no tear would manage to fall because of all the tension. In those moments I would tell myself that it wasn't worth staying here any longer for the sake of some animals, that the price was too great, and, when my decision to depart seemed definite, I would discover that I had nowhere to go, that I was feeling much more uncertain in town than I did here, and I would postpone again, convinced that a miracle would appear, that the One that gave us life would remember me, too."

"You are very strong, you don't need my advice – if by some absurdity you're waiting for it. Maybe you should tell me what you desire."

"I told you before," she said rebelliously, "and I haven't changed my mind: to die, to die, to die!"

"From your torment, from the state you are in, one can understand without too much effort that you loved the monk, that the wound with this name is still bleeding. Am I wrong?"

"I couldn't say one way or another. I loved somebody before, in the final two years of the lyceum, but you can't make a comparison. With this mad priest, everything was mindboggling, I didn't have time to think of him, to feel the love. When I got off the bed, the fear of pregnancy started, the fear of the thought that I might desire him and he wouldn't be there anymore. Curiosity or, if you will, the need was transformed into fear. So I don't know what love really is. Have you any idea? Can you tell me? If it is what I've lived, I don't think it's worthwhile thinking too much of it, waiting for it with despair. In a life like yours it is impossible not to have... in any case, even if a daughter wouldn't have the right to think like this, and, no matter what you might say or believe, I can't forgive you for what you did to my mother. There is no way that was love!"

Mara got closer to me, put her head on my shoulder as if expecting that we might shed tears together, but her touch woke up a completely different echo in me. I took her involuntarily in both my arms, but this time my gesture didn't mean protection, I wasn't offering my shoulder to her so that she could cry, although this was the impression I wanted to give her, but my embrace was the expression of a turbulent, equivocal feeling which denied itself to words, to sincerity. The feeling that was beginning to take shape was called shame, purely and simply, and, exactly at the same time, encouraged by the warmth of her body, I was frankly asking myself: why wouldn't I have the right? Why should I be ashamed of a feeling and a need which, in the end, meant life itself? I don't know why, I am often overwhelmed by the conviction that there are things which are forbidden to me. A deep, dominating feeling, a stupid and annoying "it is not proper" uttered despite the senses and needs. I've dragged it behind me during all these years, until it got to be a dominant element of my being. At the same time, I had noticed that Mara did not break away from me, that, instinctively, she had changed the position of her head, placing her forehead closer to my neck, which I then felt getting wet with tears. The woman's body, enveloped by a light tremor, no longer talked to me of sorrow or fear, instead it was a call, a terrible call which I didn't know whether I truly needed to follow, or whether I should be content to believe, like so many times, that my senses were lying to me. In the end, I stood still, unmoving, and, strangely, I wasn't conscious of the moment when we separated, but I remember that we looked at each other with joy, at peace, maybe because we had both passed a difficult threshold, in a very convenient complicity.

Loves that take one higher, loves that destroy. I am not the person most entitled to talk about my loves. A feeling of embarrassment, of indecency impedes me for the moment.

In this area, I do not feel in my territorial waters, I do not have sufficient words in order to seem convincing, and if – by some absurdity – I had them, I don't think I would manage to be very sincere. I am not yet able, or it is not yet proper– anyway, I don't want to destroy or unsettle the beauty that illuminates my memory, now when it appears that the night to come is testing my endurance. But, because I don't want to run away from the subject, Darius Pop came to my mind as a saviour. He is my father-in-law: white beard and long hair, a slight beginning of baldness, a kind of banal saint, tired, fallen off the icons of a country church, which he painted himself. The people who knew him in his youth swear that he could have been a painter of genius if he didn't have the bad luck to meet on a train, on the way to Berlin, Elisabeta Carol – Ella, as she was known. Ella and just that; a savage beauty after whom you turn your head without wanting to, irrespective of what age you were. Darius had graduated from Painting a year previously, and she had graduated, again in the great German metropolis, from the Faculty of Medicine. What's more, both of them were born in the same important Transylvanian city which, by the Diktat of Vienna, was going to be granted temporarily to Horthy's Hungary – but fate brought them closer only at the exit from Budapest, where they were both changing trains.

Ella had numerous and heavy bags, almost beyond her powers to lift into the carriage. Darius saw her toiling with them and, without asking her leave, came to her assistance. Her words of gratitude, spoken in a German with a light Bavarian accent, drew his attention to the person he had helped. Tall, supple, with rebellious curly hair, fleshy lips with strong contours, big, deep eyes, the face of a choice refinement that betrayed incontestable suffering, the traits of a tubercular – a doctor would have hurried to pronounce. With Darius, however, his thoughts led him immediately to the Bible. He was convinced this was how Judith, Esther or some other wonder conceived by the deserts of Judaea looked. The woman's face had become fixed indelibly in his mind, but he dithered for a long time about walking through the carriage, fearing he might not have the courage to look her in the eye. He was convinced he would lose his composure, that he would become embarrassing, and, because fate decided to take its workings to the end, Ella was the one who discovered him in his compartment. Surprised to meet his eyes, she strove to thank him for his help once again, by gestures, but her signs were translated by Darius as an invitation to a discussion. The woman didn't wait too long: after apologising for not thinking of inviting him outside, she told him that, purely and simply, "out of a reflex," she had shown him she was glad to meet him again.

"You can count on my muscles again when you get off, supposing that you're going to Berlin," Darius assured her – and she hurried to confirm, in Romanian, that they shared the same road.

"Is my German so bad that you've guessed, after the first sentence, that I'm not a German?" he asked, and Ella hurried to explain herself: "Not the accent betrayed you, but the gestures. A German would have been more reserved, he would not have hurried to come out from the first smile," she laughed.

"I do not come out for just any smile," Darius assured her, "but only for a smile I haven't encountered before. Don't be scared, I am a painter, I am interested by the psychology of the models, the portrait seen through this prism, but, with the unwanted risk of being interpreted wrongly, I would give anything to be able to make a few sketches of you. It would be the most difficult attempt and I think I would be left a resit student."

Discontented that he had hurried to confess a project about which he had not even thought one second previously, he didn't leave her the time to reply but explained to her, sincerely, the difficulties which he did not believe himself to be able to surpass. The traits of a face with a refinement that denies itself even to an experienced portraitist, the colour – faint sepia, a figure seen through an undulating veil, a shape, different, but always the same, the restlessness and frankness which call for a lot of study.

"All women like to hear that they are beautiful, interesting, unique, even mysterious," she said with a touch of irony in her voice. "This type of discourse precedes the road to bed, the most banal possible. But with you, I don't know why I believe you, I do not contest your sincerity. You probably wish to have the model at your disposition for a longer time. The truth is that I am sad. I am worried about what is happening in Germany at this moment. Fascism, war, anti-Semitism. I wanted to undertake my specialisation here, but it is impossible. My mother is Romanian, only father is half-Jewish and half-German, so according to the religious canons I am a Romanian, but you can never know in all this madness. I shall wait for a while to see what is happening, maybe some wisdom of the last hour, some miracle, the horror of the catastrophe that could start will determine them to stop. If not, I am returning home. I told father to change his name, but he asked me victoriously: was not the first king of Romania also called Carol? What about the third king? He understood that not all who bear this name also have the same rights, but his logic did not correspond to that of people who had conquered all and no longer got tangled up in details and nuances."

Her father was one of the owners of a large shoe factory. He held shares in another factory which repaired train carriages, and his experience had taught him that "greasing the axles," some money given to the party which won the elections, but also to the one that lost them, represent the best guarantee of peace and safety in business.

"Both the *legionari* and the communists, the liberals and the *ţărănişti*[12] live with the help of money! No politician has yet been born who will refuse some help. And if they do show independence, don't forget their wives do not have this habit. It is only when the sum is too small that caprices will appear."

Once Northern Ardeal[13] was ceded, Ella's parents took refuge in Romania, a part of the shares in the factories being left to her, and, of course, the apartment in the centre of the town.

"The people I supported – it's impossible for them not to remember me," said Ladislau Carol. "I did not desert them in their troubles, I hope they won't let me down either, no matter how hard it will be for them. Romanians make lots of noise, get agitated, threaten, but they have good souls and very rarely graduate to unacceptable deeds. And then, I feel it won't last long. You, Ella, have studied in Germany, you

---

12   The *Legionari* (legionnaires) were the Romanian fascists, so called after their official name of *Legiunea Arhanghelului Mihail* – Archangel Michael's Legion. They had a brief stint in government in 1940-41. *Ţărănişti* – name for the members and politicians of *Partidul Naţional Ţărănesc* – the National Peasant Party, a political force that ruled Romania on several occasions in the 1918-1945 period. The party was revived to mixed fortunes after the 1989 revolution.

13   *Ardeal* is another name for Transylvania.

speak the language perfectly, you know the customs of the place, you also have German roots, you accommodate with the new more easily. You are, whether you want it or not, one of them. On the other hand, you've mastered Hungarian language since you were in your cradle, anyone can help you cross over the border for some money. I know to whom I should entrust the fortune, if it should be necessary, the important thing is to survive."

Of course, everything was logical, coherent, but reality was taking a different direction, about which, in the beginning, they were too shy to talk openly, because they believed, deep inside, that things could not get out of control, that after the powerful people of Europe flexed their muscles, a compromise would be reached and everything would be normal again. Ella, especially, tried to convince herself of this, maybe also because the responsibility falling on her, once her parents left, overwhelmed her. Unfortunately, this presentiment of disaster, of uncertainty and of the imminence of the end – was not only his own, as a being who was about to exchange the easel for the weapon, but also the presentiment of the entire world – and it was daily reinforced by everything he saw. He didn't have anywhere to run to, he could not hide anywhere, because everything was vertiginously marching towards the catastrophe of a world from where reason, peace and calm had disappeared, and the dark night of the soul and the absurd had taken possession of everything. The most ordinary questions no longer had natural answers, and in this context the only thing left for him to do was to draw and paint desperately, as if he was going to disappear in the next moment. His obsession had become leaving behind him an oeuvre, a name, and the portrait of the woman he'd encountered in the train haunted him stubbornly.

In Berlin, on their separation – although they had not talked of important things to each other – they exchanged addresses, they promised to see each other again, but the chaos in his bags and pockets brought him to the apex of despair. The woman seemed to be definitively lost, or, in the optimistic variant, chance was going to bring them together again, some time, in the sad Transylvanian town. It's certain it was not just the unusual face of the woman that tormented him, but the feeling left in her wake, a correspondence and a call beyond his ability to ignore them, beyond the consolation of the thought that it was only a chance happening, the memory of which, he would, at some time in a near future, surmount. On the other hand, because he could not manage to forget her or to reconcile himself to the idea that everything was lost, he made appeal to his memory.

It was thus, that, at the time when she decided to come looking for him, Ella discovered herself in his flat, surprised, multiplied in tens and tens of sketches in charcoal, and even on canvas, in oils. Happy that fate had been so generous with him and that the sketches did not differ from the model who – look! – was in front of him, Darius embraced her with the feeling that he was making the most natural gesture possible. He had been terrorised, day and night, by the woman's face, he had looked for her continually, in all busy places in the city, in the show halls, everywhere, even in the sea of uniforms ready to fight chest to chest with the entire world, but he did not have the luck to encounter even one face that resembled her. Throughout all this, he had been stubborn enough not to give up the hope that he would, at some point, meet her again and, furthermore, he had tried to entrust to the paper this painful and inexplicable need for her. The fact that Ella had not given up on the idea of meeting again either, that she had really made this so unexpected gesture, gave him the courage to prolong the embrace which the woman did not oppose in any manner.

"Lord, how I missed you! I was certain that you were going to appear at some point, but because I lost my patience I had to take my heart in my teeth.[14] The madness around here scares me and I was afraid that, since you sent no sign, you had returned back to the home country. I would not have condemned you for it, but I admit immediately, with humility, that I would have been sorry. I don't know what gives me the certainty that I can confess exactly what I feel to you. If I am wrong, this would not be the first time I did that."

"I hope to convince you that I did not forget you, not even for a moment," Darius assured her, showing her the sketches with much enthusiasm. "Sure, I asked myself thousands of times why I tied myself to you, why you stayed in my memory, in my feelings, in all that I am, but I can only answer myself by this gesture."

Neither of them tried to break the embrace any longer. They lived intensely their rediscovery of each other, the sorrow of having sought each other with such vigour, their fear of the unknown, of the madness around them and, especially the feeling that the random event that had made them meet, could, with the same ease, part them. For Ella, the sketches were more convincing than any words, they told her that her instinct had not deceived her. As for Darius, the fact that he had been sought out, at a time when he did not have even a trace of hope left, convinced him that he must not hold back anything, although, in the shadow of the joy and surprise, this unexpected victory – too quickly and too

14 Equivalent to the English expression *"biting the bullet"*.

easily gained – troubled him. Why did she give herself to me? What will I have to lose?

Experience had taught him there is no gain without loss and, in that particular moment, besides life, in a world where threats and death had become normal, only Ella could have caused the greatest sorrow, especially because everything was too well balanced not to have the miracle of their meeting again paid for dearly. This fear dictated his next move, which Ella would not have ever foreseen. Darius broke the embrace precipitately and sat her in the armchair.

"Just for some minutes. I want to paint you. It will be the most difficult portrait, the exam of my life."

"Should I understand that I interest you only as a model?" Ella said, confused.

"You can't imagine the efforts I made in order to remember your features," Darius explained, over-excitedly arranging his papers, pencils and charcoal. "You probably did not notice it, but while we walked to the car carrying your luggage, I lingered with my hand on your back. We were talking about the dangers and dramas that were waiting for us, and it was as if I wanted to defend you, but I also felt irresistibly attracted to you. You stayed in the memory of my senses, you have therefore transmitted something of what you are, if I may say so; and, against any logic, I understood that you will have a role to play in my life, however absurd this may seem to you."

"But you have the original, the model," she said, surprised by his reactions. "I am, I hope, more than a drawing."

"Oh, mademoiselle Doctor, I would not want you to think I am mad. Or madder than I appear. This is something completely different. I will never encounter a moment like this again. It is hard for me to explain it to you. In this present moment, the drawing is done not just by my talent, mind, experience, or by my fear of losing you – but also by the soul, something in me which I did not suspect I possessed."

Ella didn't say anything more, she gave herself up to the will of his hands which arranged her in various positions, to the hurry with which he changed the sheets of paper and, of course, to the short, precipitate orders:

"Try to smile! Look at me with condescension, as you would at an individual who does not understand you! Even the bewilderment on your face is good. I am sure that you'll admit I was right, later on. Such moments do not visit me too often. It is only now that I have the feeling that I feel you and that I know you," he said, and Ella, as if woken up from a serene dream, laughed confusedly:

"Yes. You know my name, the name of my parents, you feel me and this all could only exist because I have the certainty that we belonged to each other even in our previous lives, but every human being has a story."

"Can you believe that, although I am naturally curious by inclination, I would not want to learn more about you? I have the feeling that both of us were born today, but if you wish to say something to me, I do not oppose it."

"Strange," she said, slightly beating a retreat, "I am talking to you and I am behaving as if both of us were getting ready for a long trip. In a few moments, all my barriers have fallen, although I used to like to be courted at length and insistently. But don't you think, for example, that each person is hiding something, and, I am convinced, it's not every day that you feel the need to confess. Maybe I do want to know something about you." She was trying to joke and Darius strove to come forward to match her.

"So, if it has any importance, I am the son of peasants from a village near Cluj, where I also attended the lyceum paid for by some acres of father's land. I disappointed him terribly, by the way, with my insistence on painting while he saw me as a doctor or a priest – it was for this that he had sacrificed his land. In the end, he accepted painting as well, with great difficulties, of course, after I held an exhibition of drawings in our barn, as in the house it was forbidden even to turn the conversation to it. *'What if somebody sees that, instead of the icons, you put our mugs up?'* my father said in amazement. *'Me, sitting in a place of honour, which is proper only for the Redeemer?'* The fact that not only my folks and those belonging to our house recognised themselves in my drawings, but also the neighbours; the fact that not even the animals in yard were left out of the sketches; plus the fact that, in reality, I was as good as a photographic camera – all this helped me win his trust, but not before I also copied, on his request, of course, some icons from the altar. *'In the end, you can paint churches and icons,'* father concluded, *'as there must be people who want such things, and you can win some beautiful money with church painting; but, since you have chosen this profession, go and learn it properly in Germany. The Germans don't deal with half-measures, you either are something or you are not, and a diploma from over there has value anytime and anywhere in the world.'* Father, like all the other peasants in the area, admired the Germans or, to be more precise, things which were well done, the German way. They saw the Germans as being above any errors, so that even the gravest actions, lacking in any reason, in the eyes of my father, had a motivation he would discover at a later date. There was one thing for which he did not forgive the Germans: the Diktat of Vienna, that is, ceding to Hungary a part of Transylvania, of which his village was also a part. This was unacceptable, especially because it happened without a fight. He, as well as several more peasants from the village, had been transported to act as spectators to the occupying forces' triumphal entrance in the city, and he was astounded when he saw that it was the same military unit going round and round the church, in order to produce the impression in those brought by force to the parade ground, that the occupiers were very numerous. The source of his sorrow, however, was different: how was it that the hands of the person who agreed to sign that act did not rot? That was the question that tormented him the most. It was even an obsession strengthened by the brutalities committed, on their way to Cluj, by Horthy's little army, in order to intimidate the people whose master he was going to be, but you know all this, maybe you are interested in my conquests, the women I've met," he concluded, and her wide, sincere smile reinforced the impression that he was not wrong.

"If I will tell you that I only had passing loves, without any importance and consequences, you would probably not believe me. I consumed a surplus of energy on Strada Cotită[15] and other brothels. There was a tacit agreement between father and I. He suspected what I spent my money on, and he had hesitation in his voice when he said he was concerned about my colours and canvases, but also about my health! Probably the specific street was not, or is not, such an unknown to him either.

Sometimes, I was waiting for him to tell me that I was old enough, ready for marriage, so that it might be about time to manage things for myself even without the money. Unfortunately, I was simply obsessed by my profession and tortured by history, by a brutal and unfair history. I did not

---

15 Literally meaning the Curved Street.

have time to look for my great love and not even for love itself. I had postponed it, just as, in the end, I had done with everything that had no connection to painting. Of course, I could talk in my turn about some ridiculous loves, the loves of a child or adolescent, but I am enveloped by pity when I think of the character I was back then. I was small, inhibited by my grandmother's orders – a harsh woman, merciless with those who did not respect her commands, no matter their age. She was a sort of force of nature. She woke up before everyone else, at the same time as the dawn. She fed the pigs, the chickens, milked the cattle, and when the bread was in the oven and the breakfast on the table, I heard her asking whether the sun was going to find us in our beds, that we were behaving like the village sloths. Prayers, meal times, fasting and feast days were her obsessions. Besides, she died on a Sunday, during lunch, when we were together with all the family. Just like that, out of the blue, her head dropped to her chest, and everyone belonging to the household believed she had fallen asleep and let her be, seeing about their food in the perfect silence to which she had accustomed them. It was only after dessert they realised that, in reality, she had passed over to the other world, as people used to say around our place. I did not have any special joys. I made my own toys out of pumpkins and apples; I added legs and everything else which was necessary. I imagined animals which, according to the case, I would call sheep, cows or horses. During summer days, when short and violent rains instigated tens of rivulets, I used to build small watermills, figurines made of the clayish soil with which I populated the citadels of soil and rubble; and during dry days – arrows and bows made of oak boughs, with which I laid siege to the numerous wasp nests. Regarding the first woman I've known, in the biblical sense of the word, I don't even know her name, or the face. In fact, I don't even think I ever saw it, but I am still haunted, even today, by her strange smell of abundant perspiration mixed with another, unexpected scent, the fragrance of baked bread.

"Later on I looked for it as if it was a necessity in the few women I met, like I just told you now. I remember too well. I was in the last year in the lyceum, on the winter holiday, and a colleague, who lived in the town and whose parents were away from home, invited me to his house. There, he had prepared a great surprise for me and another friend: a girl from Strada Cotită had been hired at a cost to stay with us for the entire night. I hesitated very long before I decided to go. In theory, we were all great heroes. In our stories we had tens of women on our lists of conquests. In reality the whole business was foreign to me, women had fallen conquered only in my imagination. The woman was a certainty now. I had consummated the act in question tens of times in my imagination, so I got there exhausted, without a trace of energy. My friend admonished me in a whisper for the delay and led me to his parents' bedroom, where the light was off, and you could feel a terrible agitation under the sheets. I was assured that my turn would come too, and a little while after I undressed, the woman sneaked in at my side. I was left, by that encounter, only with her smell, so particular to her, and the conviction that I had surpassed the hardest moment of my – let's call it mature – existence. The encounter, the first of its kind, was not as complicated as I'd imagined. On the contrary, and I had not brought more shame on myself than the others did. After this confused night, I went with more courage to the brothel in Strada Cotită and, of course, I no longer associated with other young men.

In time, it was still in that place that I found a girl with whom I met as often as I could. Her name was Elisabeta, but she was called Erji and many times I did not give her any money; she came to my house or she waited until I received father's contribution. I remember this one pretty well: tall, blonde, with curly hair, freckly, with enormous, green eyes in which you could lose yourself as if in calm water. She realised my lack of experience from the first moment, but she had patience with me, she did not hurry me up as it would have been normal to do – *you've paid, I did my job, each one to their own* – and we parted with the feeling that we'd had many things to tell each other, for which reason I sought her out in the shortest time possible. We met countless times in this way, but we never discussed what we felt we should. Each time she would wind herself around me as if she wanted even to forget she existed, and when everything was over I could not stop her crying. Unfortunately I never managed to learn why she cried like that: out of joy, out of pleasure, or because she recalled personal failures.

Of course, I went to see others, too. Two colleagues from my primary school come to my mind. Their husbands were away working in the woods, and they existed only in the memory of the senses. The passions, as many as they were, or, more correctly put – the couplings, were consummated in a hurry in the woods or maize fields neighbouring the village. The idea of these encounters belonged to one of them, with whom I had crossed roads by chance, on such a path. '*I think that no man would have dodged me like you did*,' Antonia said to me in an indecisive voice, between fury and irony. '*There are not too many solutions*,' I said to her, prompted by her courage. '*Come with me in the woods, I go back to the village, or we go nearby, in the hazel copse.*' '*Let yourself led*,' she breathed, feeling relieved, and on the way to the carefully chosen clearing I enquired whether she was not afraid of her husband, or whether she didn't have the feeling she was sinning, to which she burst out laughing. '*Something of the sin there might be here, as I've been following you for a while, but the road to hell is quite long. Do you think that Niculae steps aside when he meets a young woman in such a place? It's not that I'm not enough for him, but the things you steal are, or seem to be, better!*' The other peasant woman, Viorica, I also met by chance, on the hills where I withdrew for the sake of some watercolours. But I knew the lesson now, so that everything happened with no words. I took her in a field of maize and she submitted gladly. She had probably learned from the other woman that I was up to date with the customs of the place.

"Their tears after those specific deeds were consummated seemed strange to me, as well as the fact that they thanked me each time, as if I had taken a great suffering away from them. Things were rather like this. I remember these moments with a strange melancholy, as if they had been told to me in a moment of rustic peace. Of course, the fear of husbands, the fear of village gossip, but, before all else, the fear of history was not lacking. With my thoughts going to the war or any other absurdity of the times, everything seemed possible and impossible at the same time, I felt the need to know life on each of its numerous levels. I wanted to take, with thirst and fury, as soon as possible, everything I was sure that, sooner or later, could be useful to me, as if I was able to assemble some reserves of love, beauty and peace."

"I think I understand those poor women," she said to me, "it is so good to have the good luck to shed tears."

"How is it that it's precisely you who complains of such a lack?" I wondered, looking at her with unsated, animal lust. Cuddling up closely, she hurried to assure me that I was not dreaming, that I found myself in front of the most incredible and wonderful day of my life, because deep down inside, maybe more than any artistic success, I wanted a woman; not necessarily for fulfilment – or, more exactly, not for the always livelier bodily hunger, but especially in order to conquer the immense spiritual emptiness, the fear and anxiety that had taken over our part of the world. The sensation of being a lost wanderer in an hostile universe, of being a man without usefulness, of being a negligible quantity terrorised not only by the fear of death, but also by life – this had gained in proportion with each parade and march. These pushed me towards home, although home was no longer in my country. I contented myself with the thought that I would at least have somebody to whom I could talk and with whom to share the stable, to live fear, and with whom I might exchange a little hope. This was because the news that came from home did not amount to encouragement. The new masters of the village, who had come from other parts, had neither understanding, nor mercy. They tried to inspire fear, and they often even succeeded. This is what my father wrote to me:

"*From the few lines of my letter you will know about us that we live badly, may the Lord on High no longer endure it. We desire, with all our hearts, for you to come home, but I am sorely afraid that they will take you to the front, as they had taken all from the village, so it is better for you to stay there or go to another country, until this great trouble passes. This is what Father Gheorghe also advised, and he says you should run to America, where there is no war and hate. And neither is it a life to live in our village, as foreigners have come to the village hall and they do not know our customs and language and they force us to speak their language, which we do not know, and the gendarmes with cockerel's feathers threaten us and take everything they find in the house if we don't have the money to pay their taxes. In case you've found a girl, even if she is of good family, it would not be good for you to marry, as we do not know what tomorrow may bring. Your mother is well, but her back aches and she complains we are working too much, but I believe she pines for your presence, as she always looks at the paintings and cries."*

Darius was convinced that the girl of his dreams had appeared in the most unsuitable moment, in the same way that his father was thinking, and, as it happened, his father was a practical man, accustomed to foresee trouble and look for solutions in order to vanquish the difficulties of the times. He was grateful to Heaven, however, for sending him, in such confused and painful moments, the greatest joy possible, because, in a matter of hours, Ella had become north, south, east, west, night and day, life and death. She had become he himself, joy pushed to the upper limits of sorrow and tears, fear that the wonder would not be able to last, that he would be incapable of keeping for too long a gift which was so great and so undeserved. From that moment, they were no longer separated, but he lived with the feeling that everything was unreal. He looked at her continuously, and he found himself with eyes wet with tears, even in his sleep. She existed, she was real and no word had the power to express the nuances of the satisfaction that possessed him, but, for a while, it was only a spiritual accomplishment.

They slept together, they touched each other, they

caressed each other passionately, but for a long time they did not manage to go beyond kisses and tears.

"You must have patience with me. I cannot get used to the thought. No matter how curious this might appear. I am a doctor, I know human beings with all their details, but I behave like any nondescript wench. And I don't even manage to explain to myself why I am the way I am. I feel that it won't be long until desire will be stronger than the fear or whatever it is."

"When we met, you were disposed to tell me everything, and now..."

"I had invented a long and bizarre story. I had a mind to horrify you with the most insufferable nonsense that can be said about a woman, or which a woman can do. I wanted to punish you because you had not looked for me. My senses told me we were going to meet, but I condemned you because I expected to see you the next day and I had prepared myself in all possible ways. But you were impermissibly late, not hours, but days, so I had to step over my own pride and look for you. When I saw the drawings, I understood we had not been separated, not for one moment."

"Tell me at least the monstrosities with which you wanted to terrify me," Darius insisted, convinced he would know how to distinguish the truth from her inventions, but, just as he suspected, Ella did not hurry to reply.

"Most of the times, truth can appear implausible," she said, trying to confuse him.

"Of course, I am curious but I prefer to give credence to my senses," he replied, surrendering. "Given that you looked for me and you are here, nothing has any importance anymore. I am not interested in your former lovers and I am not interested in those you will love, if circumstances should decide something else, because you deserve everything. I am grateful to Heaven that I have you here, at my side, this very moment, and that you will stay for as long as you feel the need to stay."

What he said had been punctuated by gasps, as if after a great effort and, strangely, the words had arranged into phrases without his will. He had no doubt that he had said to her exactly what he wished to say, it was just that he had hurried. Confessions had no room in those moments, at the beginning of a love story, but much later, after the time when he would have known her with all his senses, and when time, as in any story, would have subjected them to its inevitable trials of endurance to vicissitudes. In any case, he had set aside even the most insignificant obstacle on the road to her and he was left only with the anxiety or surprise that everything had been too easy, almost unreal, as in his adolescent dreams, when he had not known properly any woman, and he only wanted his access to her – in fact, access to any woman – to be comfortable, taking into account his shyness and cowardice. Suddenly, the thing he wanted back then was about to be realised now, after many years, far away from his country, in a moment when anxiety and confusion had installed themselves over the world and terrorised not just the present, but also the future.

I reread the text horrified. What if I don't get to proofread what I wrote? What if I did proofread it? I am not writing for anyone. I started from the idea of looking at myself as if in a mirror, in order to occupy my time, and, from a need which is hard to explain, a kind of fight with death which I don't know how to turn into words. In fact, to write or not to write, from my perspective, is only a useless exercise, an attempt to keep the nerves permanently tensed. If you write, you grow angry it does not come out well, if you don't write, you grow angry because you are not at the worktable, as you planned, and you are left with an oppressive time which you cannot cover with something else because your own strengths betray you. Futility. In my case, it would be more rational that, instead of tomorrow, it should be eternity which arrives, as the Tibetan thinker says. With all this, I do not surrender yet, although I feel my will striving to create illusions for myself, and it flutters like an unfortunate rag in a breath of wind. Not in every moment, however. Sometimes I am determined to stop the struggle, to surrender. That's it, that's how long it was, it is useless, but, precisely at the same time I feel eternity. Not as a light, nor as a huge release, but simply like an asphyxiation, and the thought that I might not even be the way I am, tormented by impotencies, urges me not to give up on the nothing that keeps me hanging by the light, air and sky. Each step towards death, every second when we think about it, is an irrecoverable loss. We always lose everything that is dear to us, everything that is precious, everything we loved, even the memory of those loves.

Darius.

This is not a theft or a false memory; nor is it an exercise of imagination, but a phenomenon without a precise name. I simply attribute other people's adventures to myself. Adventures which haunt me. I don't know why, probably because they meant something to me. I have deciphered most of them, I know why they have stayed so alive in my mind. Others, although they have no explanation, I attribute to myself. In the village where I started my apprenticeship as a doctor, people did not say they stole firewood, although almost all of them had this as an occupation; they said they completed their necessities. This is rather what I am doing now, but not because I would be spiritually poor, but because – and I admit to this – I really need them. Those adventures, I feel as if they belonged more to me than to the people to whom they have in truth belonged. Furthermore, we also live – consciously or not – the lives of the people with whom we have come into contact, directly or indirectly, and who made an impression on us; in the same way as the books over which we lingered, in some way also belong to us, and compel us to return to them. Unfortunately I do not always also remember the authors, but I fuse so much with the various deeds and little histories, and even with the stories that could have never happened to me, that I cannot give them up. They are mine. What more can I say? I need them, although I don't know why. A very good friend hired, on the occasion of his marriage, a bulldozer which he parked in a corner of the garden. When he was asked why he brought it, he replied serenely: "No reason, just so there should be one there!" My explanation could be reduced to these words, too. There exists a hungry space in me, a need to know, a desire to fill up a painful, permanent void, which I cannot ignore in any way. Darius is the strangest part of my being: sorrow, fear, love, infinite candour, but especially sorrow beyond the tolerable.

In the end, marriage also came. They had both desired it with all their being, like a guarantee they would stay together forever. This is why they returned home, although the word no longer covered reality completely. This part of the country had been ceded to Hungary in a wretched manner, at the green table, without a fight, and the agreement was given during the ceremony, compulsorily, in Hungarian. The parents of the bride were missing, they were afraid to leave Romania, so that besides his folks there took part some friends and colleagues from the lyceum and some relatives from the countryside who had promised a proper wedding, in order to defy the provisory forces of occupation.

"How can you rejoice when your country is occupied and young people die for nothing in the war?" was the opinion of his father. "You should not have come home, but you should have searched for a way to America. This is not a time for weddings, but for tears! I know why you hurried: she is very beautiful and she is rich. And you were not picked up from the roadside either... After these folks will leave, we'll make a wedding to last three days and three nights, but until then only in the church, if the bride will accept to enter the House of the Lord."

"Why shouldn't she accept?" Darius was surprised. "God is the same for all."

Ella had nothing against it: "If this is what must be... I would have been glad if my parents also took part," she hesitated for a moment and Darius gave in immediately: "Maybe we manage to cross the border clandestinely and we get the religious wedding in their presence, in Bucharest or Brașov."

He had spoken without sitting to think and only after he saw her grateful smile he realised they were in front of a trial of extreme difficulty, with enormous risks, and death could not be excluded either. But his father did not seem scared, on the contrary.

"There are a few teams of peasants who know the forest of Făget like their own pockets. The illegal crossing to Romania costs a lot, but it seems safe. They make a contribution to the Hungarian border guards, so, if you happen to fall in the hands of someone who is the person you need him to be, you can consider you've made a simple walkabout."

And, because it did not seem to them to be an emergency, their plan was to take responsibility for dealing with the factory. They also planned, in particular, to be responsible for their relations with the surrounding world, which they, unfortunately, did not know too well. They walked around together, wanting to be seen this way, and the happiness of knowing themselves inseparable for life helped them ignore the fears that seemed to spring from everything around them.

"Let's live each day as if it would be the last," she proposed to him, possessed by a strange feeling of anxiety, of swinging between an immense joy and a sorrow which was just as intense, with a taste of loneliness and death. Ella's encouragement, however, could not bring anything new to the relations between them, it merely tried to transpose the things they lived into words. Unfortunately, they also felt, although none of the them had the courage to confess it, that this state of affairs could not last for too long, in conditions when the news from the front was not good and neither was the news around them, reports from which murders, brutalities and threats were not lacking.

Through the Romanian Consulate in Cluj, Ella had managed to get in touch with her parents, and they had fixed a meeting in Turda, where Darius and she were going to go, with the help of the clandestine connections of Făget, about which they had extremely good information.

The lawyer Alois Varga, true administrator of the huge fortune inherited by Ella, was the only one who had connections with the people who were going to take them to Romania. His assurances had made the two regard crossing the border in a matter of hours as an insignificant adventure, not even tiring. Darius's father, for a change, received the news with terror.

"It is not good what you're doing," he insisted. "Nowadays you should not trust anyone. Even your brothers may sell you. If however you manage to reach Romania, it would be best for you to stay there. Here it is the prison camp or the army that await you. You have to choose between life and the fortune. It would be a pity not to think of the only good solution!"

Although he could not ignore his father's advice, the decisive element in taking the decision to cross the provisional border clandestinely was the encouragement of the lawyer, whom the old man could not stand.

"This one, being such a big thief, did not even have the time to marry, although it would seem that he likes men more!"

Darius was grateful for the care he took of them, and, without a trace of fear or doubt, immediately after midnight, he took the road to Feleac Hill, together with Ella and Alois. The next night, after they received the blessing of the parents-in-law, they would return home in order not to have their absence noticed. Unfortunately, the things which were going to happen had not been taken into consideration in any way. So, Alois entrusted them to the guides he had talked to, three peasants from Feleac, wished them great success and established for the following night the place and price of the return – which, unfortunately, was not going to take place. Close to the border point, they heard violent whistling, and the barking of dogs. The peasants started to whisper very agitatedly.

"Run back, they've discovered us. Each one save himself as he can!"

Subsequently, there was one detail that Darius could never explain to himself. What happened to him, how come he was left alone, where did the others scatter to, and why did Ella leave with them as well?

He only remembered that the noises stopped suddenly and he found himself paralysed, as if under an immense bell jar, without air, without light, incapable of taking a decision or even of taking a step back in order to run, as the peasants had urged him to do. He whispered "Ella!", his thoughts, probably, wrapped up in the emotion of meeting his parents-in-law – with a view to which he had constructed numerous scenarios, all to his disadvantage – so that the peasants' shouts had disorientated him to such an extent that he simply no longer knew where he was. The primary sensation was that of confusion, followed by the fall.

He had somehow exited the time and the reality he knew. He had entered a space without sounds and without pain. He was terribly alone, a stranger, and incapable of understanding what had happened to him. When he came to himself, the dogs were barking violently at him. The weapons and flashlights of the border guards which were pointed at him drew his attention to the fact that any attempt to run or to oppose them was useless, dangerous, although the blows he received, given with the feet or the weapons' butts, might have encouraged him to try. He did not know what to say, and he did not know the language of the people who had placed handcuffs on him either. They bombarded him with questions he did not understand, and he tried to ignore the pain and the yells of these people who seemed to rejoice in catching him as if it were a great success. He looked for Ella and he didn't know if he should be glad she was not there, if she had got away, or whether he should be afraid that something worse than he could imagine had happened to her. Anyway, her absence had created a feeling of finality in him, of dissolution. From love, he had slid brutally into death. This is what he felt as his eyes became clearer and the blows forced him to understand the real situation in which he found himself. It became increasingly clear to him that his life had taken a different course, that he was facing a new beginning, a painful, confused one in which physical and spiritual suffering reached maximum intensity. Somewhere in the depths of his soul a tiny hope had germinated: that Ella had managed to escape, in the end, and that her interventions with the authorities would not be late coming, and that, without any doubt, she would make that man, Alois Varga, find the most appropriate solution to set him free.

At the headquarters of the gendarme unit where he had been taken, between kicks and words he did not understand, he had tried to concentrate increasingly on this man. What did he know about him? Why had he entrusted himself to him with such ease, without doubting one single gesture or word, and why did Alois fail to win the confidence of his father – on the contrary – although at that festive meal that had marked their marriage, his father had conversed the most with this man?

In a narrow room where numerous people slept huddled on the floor, sitting on the only iron bed, on which he had been thrown without having his handcuffs unlocked, Darius started to reconstruct from gestures and words this individual who, in reality, was responsible for the entire fortune of the Carol family. In any case, there was a good sign: neither he nor Ella were in the neighbouring room where the gendarmes continued to bring people. Of course, Darius was not in the best moment to recollect the man, but, beyond this, he could not understand why he had always ignored the lawyer, why he had left all the business of the house and the family to Ella. As a result, apart from a perfect politeness and the wide gestures that always accompanied Varga's words, he had not managed to recall a great deal, because even the details connected to their escape had been discussed only with Ella, and his trust in her was beyond any doubt. Alois was increasingly revealed to him under more guises. When in groups of Romanians, he condemned the brutalities of the occupiers and said to people that such an injustice could not last. When he was among Hungarians, he imitated their exuberance and arrogance, rejoicing that the injustice of Trianon[16] was finally repaired.

The following morning, Darius was investigated by an officer who spoke German. He did not admit to wanting to cross over to Romania, but he said he was walking around, and got lost looking for a border post or somebody who could show him the road to the main highway. He had been away from the country for a long time and he did not know the area.

"I could have not returned at all," he said to the officer, "or it would have been more convenient to go directly to Romania."

These were explanations with no effect, as he had been found there, a few steps away from the border, and this was important. He was then challenged with two peasants also

---

16   The Treaty of Trianon, in 1920, established the Hungarian state in its current borders. Parts of the former Kingdom of Hungary with ethnic majorities other than Hungarian were ceded to neighbouring nations, including Transylvania which became part of Romania.

caught the same night. They were probably the people who were going to help him, but Darius did not know them. In the end, convincing himself that his insistence was useless, the officer filled them with abuse about the defects of Darius' and the peasants' nation, and ordered them to be taken to the prisoner camp at Someșeni. Here, it seemed to him he had landed in an authentic Tower of Babel, in which he found everything: political prisoners, thieves, innocent people, perverts, and everything else imaginable, but especially individuals who had not agreed to the new order which had been installed, as it was said, for a thousand years. Surrounded by all this, he did not become friends with the peasants and he did not discuss with them the event that had doomed them all, either. This was not out of prudence, but from a terrible feeling of revolt. He almost felt forced to give himself one more chance: to escape at any cost and try crossing of the border once more: and, while the sequence of his departure and capture ran through his mind, it was impossible to understand how Ella and Alois had disappeared with so much ease. He especially couldn't understand why had he entrusted himself to them, without any of his senses warning him of the danger. Did Ella wish perhaps to get rid of him in this manner? Had there been an older connection between her and Alois, and, from the moment of their return home, had it been brought up to date? Did Alois wish to remove him in order to stay with her and, of course, her fortune? He believed the answer was no, but the questions had to be asked. In any case, it was clear to him, a chapter of his life had ended, the shortest and most beautiful, and the fact that a lawyer, hired by Alois, naturally, failed to appear, or the fact that he had received no sign, no matter how pallid, from Ella, convinced him that he had entered an entanglement from which the only exit was to break out. In the giant barracks, tens or maybe hundreds of people slept on straw, among them Hungarian soldiers who hit the prisoners with the weapon butts at the smallest attempt to talk, and from these there seemed to be no chance of escape. He looked closely and obstinately, however, at the hills he knew so well, at the spires of the churches, which he saw with the strange feeling that he would never get to be next to them, but especially at the barbed wire and the guard posts over which, or near which, he did not see how he could pass unnoticed.

The number of the days he had been ignored had grown, and he had entered a dangerous automatism. He washed, he cleaned the so-called toilets. He swept the yard. He took his small portion of food and mockery from the warders. He slept a little and, he researched, in particular, the possibility of running away. One morning, however, he was called for a medical checkup and the joy that something was finally going to happen, that he would have to have an explanation from somebody, gave him confidence that his relatives, and Ella especially, had found an avenue of rescue. He presented himself in front of two military men and a civilian, the doctor, who asked him to undress. After the doctor took his measurements and listened to his heart and lungs, the two officers, who knew German, got in the queue. They were interested in his connections with the Romanian Consulate in Cluj, what he had transmitted, why he had wanted to run, and what connection he had with the Romanian information services. Of course, they did not want the truth, but to confirm their speculations; but they commenced the brutalities because Darius did not give in. Stretched on a table, after several blows from which he had lost consciousness, tied by the hands and feet, he was subjected to the most unbearable torture about the existence of which he'd had no idea. For example, being beaten with a stick over the testicles. It was night before he reached the dormitory, crawling along the walls. He was covered in wounds, confused, but dominated by a single thought: not to forget the faces of the two military men, on whom he had sworn to return the torture, at any risk; and as the time passed, his need for revenge took larger proportions, made him stronger. It was strange, with his senses tensed, close to paroxysm, he relived his days spent with Ella and tried to understand what had happened. Something didn't come out in the calculations: the disappearance of Ella and Alois and the fact that only he had been caught and arrested. It was a bafflement which did not leave, and there was just one step from there to asking himself whether there could be a hidden connection between the two persons. Something intrigued him however. Nobody had forced her to marry, even more, the marriage had been her desire. Anyway, a relationship such as theirs, in an old provincial town, could not be passed over out of sight. The concept of honour was above everything else, so, as a consequence, they either married or separated. Was it possible that Alois had arranged his capture, which meant taking him away from Ella, perhaps at the suggestion of his parents? Following the tormenting investigations, another lack of understanding started to insinuate itself in his mind, until it managed to replace everything else: why, with all their money and relations, did they not look for him, to discover him even here?

Taken over by his unnatural, devastating passion for Ella, by the feeling that his life was finally in order and made sense, he had lived each moment with all his being – so much that he had not thought even to ask himself at least one of the questions that tormented him at this time, when it was so late and he only had one wish: to break out. Day and night, despite the brutalities and the endless investigations, he looked, with infinite patience, at the exits, at the change of the guards. He listened tensely to the voices outside the camp, he strove to get acquainted with the prisoners whose release was rumoured, convinced that he would find, in the end, a solution by which to communicate to Ella or, in particular, a way of leaving that place dominated by humiliation and pain. He now knew the route to Romania and he was determined not to entrust himself to anyone's will. At the same time as this project, he was surprised to discover the new feelings that came to him: hatred and the thirst for revenge. His energy, instead of being ground down by the beatings, focussed on escape. He had connected himself to no-one, in fact he had no means of doing that, he could only exchange a few words with somebody in the kitchen or when he washed the toilets; but he was afraid of everybody, not because he would have had anything to hide, but because he had the impression that he had not studied the things happening around him well enough. Beyond everything else, the ease with which he had left for the border scared him with each additional recollection. He knew there were snitches among the prisoners, but this did not scare him. His own desire, almost savage, for revenge, frightened him, and he could only do it by himself. He believed strongly that Ella could not have cheated on him or forgotten him, that was his only certainty, and her absence, or at least the absence of any sign from her, no matter how insignificant, exasperated him.

The officer who had beaten him cruelly was convinced

he was a communist, and after he found no evidence with which to accuse him, things were left at that – that he was a communist, but also a Romanian spy. That was a given. As a consequence the officer gave him one last chance. Apply the penalty himself, instead of his interrogator, and he would be free. Darius, of course, could not imagine himself in that particular situation and he didn't even want to think about the proposal, as he had been advised to do. He refused the substitution immediately, violently, and for a while, contrary to his expectations, he was left alone. After a while, the same officer informed him that he was free to go. He didn't give any explanation and Darius did not think of asking for one either. He behaved as if his release was the most normal thing possible. He had concentrated on the officer's features; he did not want to forget him because he had a debt to pay. He owed to the officer a feeling which, until he'd met the man, had been unknown and a stranger to him – hatred. Big moustache, black, upturned, deep black eyes, strong jaws, pronounced brows and a slight beginning of baldness. He remembered him, also, because the officer informed him he was free and, then, accompanied his departure with a hard-to-forget peal of laughter, which made Darius believe that, in fact, they had prepared another surprise which would stop him from getting out of the yard of the camp. He did not respond in any manner, contenting himself with stepping slowly, prudently, convinced the surprise could not be long overdue, since even the soldier escorting him tended to lag a little behind him. Because nothing happened until he reached two or three steps from the gate and the barbed wire that separated him from the world, he was convinced that the evil he suspected would overtake him with no delay. The temptation was to hit the soldier and run, but, as he had not slept for long – for a very long time, he had no trace of energy left in him, not even to hurry his steps. Nothing happened by the time he reached the gate, he was simply given the identity documents, the soldier made his way back and Darius, abandoned in front of the huge hangar, stayed put for a while, confused, not understanding what had happened to him, because of the fact that he no longer expected anything good lately, not even normality. Suddenly, a thought crossed his mind: that particular evil, the miserable surprise, was waiting for him at home! He could not understand otherwise why they had let him go, how was it that from the daily violence, from the arrogance and brutality with which he had been treated, he would find himself suddenly freed. He was tempted, for a moment, to go to his house in the countryside, to see his parents, to learn from them the news which could not be good in any way, but the conviction that something bad had happened to Ella urged him to postpone the meeting with his relatives, to risk, to look the truth in the face, as it were, no matter how painful it might be. So, expecting whatever could be worse, he dragged himself along the side of the road until a peasant agreed to take him in his cart.

Once he was left in the town, he sneaked behind walls, attentive to any gaze or word uttered around him, aware that he was in a foreign place, without anything familiar besides some walls and the stones on which he stepped, and he made it home with difficulty, extinguished by tiredness. The servants received him with a reserved joy, telling him that "miss" was reading in the bedroom, after which they retired and he hesitated a long time before opening the door. Suddenly he was afraid of the meeting with Ella, and it was not because he needed more time in order to familiarise himself with the thought that he was, finally, one step away from his wife, a meeting he'd dreamed of in every lucid moment, especially during the time he'd spent in the camp – but from other reasons. What if, after this painful experience, Ella should seem to him – or would even be – different? He was punched unexpectedly, violently, by his own smell and, in the same time, he discovered with all his senses the wretchedness in which he found himself: the grimy clothes, the dense, overgrown beard, the broken shoes, so much so that the only clean thing about him was his feeling for her, but even this had crouched under the pressure of filth. He thought for a moment to announce his presence, but even the words had deserted him. They had become incapable of expressing anything, reminding him of the tree trunks from which, during his lyceum studies, he could not manage to create much, and never anything he had intended; amorphous materials which refused to submit to his inadequate, poor tools.

All of a sudden, he felt a stranger in that room, which had been beautiful and welcoming until recently, a room in which everything was as he had left it, except that the air given out by the objects was now rejecting him, and, because the postponement, the hesitations scared him, he tried to utter the name of his wife, but the shout or whimper remained unanswered. Then, with a last effort, he pushed open the door and, from the armchair in which she was seated, Ella jumped, frightened: "My God, you? But where have you been until now?"

She had started decided to embrace him, but she stopped after her first steps, as if she was not sure that it was Darius in front of her. She then gave herself up to the will of her feelings, of her tears and uncontrolled gestures, as if wishing, in those moments, to recover the kisses and embraces that she had missed for such a long time.

"What happened to you? Where have you been? Why didn't you answer?" she repeated desperately, but when Darius tried to talk, Ella covered his mouth with a hand and asked him to postpone a little, after which she did not want him to speak again.

She felt good in his arms, crying with a despair he could not have ever imagined. His joy had been immense as well, but between them there sneaked, little by little, the terror and sorrow accumulated in the days of the prison camp, and, especially, in the overwhelming moment of loneliness he had felt there, in the forest of Făget. Even now, after the circumstances helped them to find themselves together again, he could not free himself of anxiety and doubt. As if chained to each other, they started towards the sumptuous bathroom guarded by two giant mirrors, as big as half a wall. He allowed himself to be shaved, then washed, and in that place, and later on in bed, at every attempt of his to give or receive explanations, she covered his mouth hurriedly, imploring him to have patience, not to ruin the joy of the reunion.

It was a night without words, a night when they made love, they cried and they caressed more than any other time, as if each one wished to discover with the aid of the senses that which the words would never, ever manage to express: the things that had happened during the time when they had been separated, and the intensity of the love which they had not lived up to that time. In the morning, before the tears and sweat could dry, two soldiers and an officer brought his army conscription order which compelled him to leave immediately, under escort. This was a war and they admitted no excuses, delays, discussions. Yet again, Ella stayed behind defeated, confused, without tears and, probably, without the hope that they would see each other soon. They promised nothing to each other, given that everything had happened against their logic, and also against any power of theirs to withstand the absurdity which dominated everything. He did not see Ella again. He was sent a short time afterwards to the frontline in a regiment with many Romanians in it, sent to clean up with their bare hands the numerous minefields left by the Russian soldiers during their retreat.

I wander through my own memory. Nothing impedes me, nobody urges me to do anything else, I simply give myself up to the will of a strange desire of not being in the today, of reliving the times in which I truly existed, or, to be more precise, the times which I missed. Now they all belong to me, happenings, dreams, desires – mine and those of others – which I still remember. An irrepressible flux helps me to be as far as possible from what I feel at this moment, when I am writing, and the words which would describe the state that chases me to the past are sorrow and fear. Both of them are connected to death, because She can come at any moment and it is only now that I realise how much I've lost. I even lost life, and I realise this now, when my senses seem to me to be more alive than any other time, my senses and my lucidity. They give me a state of being which neighbours on suffocation.

Mara also means sorrow, a terrible sorrow. As she tells me the number of years, she shows me the distance between life and death. She fidgets near me, she is annoyed that I am writing. I can swear that, if I don't stop a reasonable amount of time, she will leave home and tomorrow she will be late, she will make me wait for her. I do not understand what she wants to say to me, but I feel her quiver. She hesitates, she gathers courage and then beats the retreat again, only for me to feel her nerves immediately, her tension, the reproaches she addresses to herself or to me. I look at her with pleasure, in some moments when I forget about myself. I am overwhelmed by the joy of not being alone, but then I ask myself what can I be to her, how do I seem to her, and, in order to free myself of illusions, I am intending to place myself on the spot she reserves for me, wherever this might be. I would wish – enormously so – for her to tell me the truth, the way she feels. I realise there is enough insincerity in my relationship with this person, but there is also insincerity in her way of behaving with regard to me. In fact, each one must have – or seem to have – a project for the future in which the other is also included, but the steps taken by one towards the other are very small and uncertain. If I would proceed with this sincerity to the end, I do not understand what I am expecting from her or, more precisely, I am not capable of formulating what I feel, what I would tell her if nothing stayed hidden in me, if the sentiment that possesses me had a clear name. This accentuates the sorrow and the fear, because, for me, time means something else, but I have no means to make her understand. Of course, both of us are heading towards death, but I am compelled by time to meet Her very soon. Death is so close that I even hear Her breath, I feel Her shivering cold. This is why I cannot wait until the feeling that possesses me in my relationship with Mara should acquire a name, but what would it mean for me to hurry? What would be the risk if I suggested to her that she interests me, but she is not a beautiful woman?

I still have: the sky, the trees, the ridges of the mountains, the always changing mist, the storms, the wild animals, the numerous nameless bugs, the sun, moon, stars, the books scattered around, the memories, the mountain of the saints, and Mara. I depend on each of them, but especially on her, because, in her absence, all the others are parts of the loneliness.

> *"You should expect death daily so that, when the time comes, you can die in peace. Calamity, when it occurs, is not as dreadful as you feared. (...) Die in your thoughts every morning and you will no longer fear death"*
> Hagakure (after Marguerite Yourcenar)

> *"To the gods alone old age and death never come; but everything else sinks into chaos from time which overpowers all. Earth's strength decays, and so too the strength of the body; trust dies; distrust is born; and the same spirit is never steadfast among friends, or between city and city"*
> Sophocles [17]

> *"The body ages because it is time, as does everything that exists on earth."*[18]
> Octavio Paz

I close my eyes and, without any effort, I get closer to Darius, my father-in-law, the painter of churches, who might have become one of the great names of the country, if... and this last word covers a sorrow which, in the end, he could not defeat. Suffering gave him added vigour and

17 Sophocles, *Oedipus at Colonus.* Translated by Sir Richard Jebb, Cambridge: Cambridge University Press, 1889

18 From Octavio Paz, *The Double Flame.* Translated by Helen Lane, London: Harvill, 1996

depth to his talent, refined him and enriched him in an
initial stage, but the imbalance, which is so necessary to
art, was too strong, the shocks very hard to endure. I try
to express him, to substitute myself for him. This comes
after I had deduced him, for a long time, from gestures,
tears, syllables and barely started sentences. After summary
instruction in a language he did not know, he was sent to
the frontline in a unit with many Romanians who had to
clean up, with their bare hands, the minefields left behind
by the retreating Russians. Ella was left somehow outside
of him, because his permanent company were: fear, hunger,
and rain. He knew that he could err at any moment, and
here mistakes could not be put to rights, they were paid for
with your life. Sometimes, when fear reached a paroxysm,
he wanted to free himself from it by death. In reality,
the Russians or some undiscovered mine would end his
anxieties definitively. As a consequence, why should he
not die at that moment, why prolong suffering, when the
finale was already known for a long time, expected? He
had reconciled himself to the thought he would not return
anymore, even from the moment when, after endless days
of advance through the fields of Ukraine, the train stopped
in a station without a name, where they were disembarked,
and the Russian artillery received them with unimaginable
violence. In fact, from that time, confusion and chaos had
become the tutelary gods under which all his days on the
front rolled on, but it continued also after that time. There
was no day without deaths, no day without amputations and
horrible wounds caused by mines, and, more than death, he
was scared by the possibility of being maimed, of infirmities
of any kind – hence his desire to die. In his short life, he'd
had almost everything that he wanted. He had known love

of the kind he could not have imagined, not even in his most optimistic moments. He had seen some of the vastness of the world. He had studied in a foreign school of great renown. He'd had highs and lows. He had been locked-up, beaten, humiliated; fate had maybe given him more than he wanted, so, as a consequence, he waited for death to come – naturally, somehow – before its time. Many times, he had decided to go out to welcome her, especially since the war seemed far from ending, and being in the advance line, cleaning up minefields, any mistake could be fatal. Hunger, sometimes desperate, also made him wish for death, especially when the kitchen was destroyed by projectiles or when, because of the explosions, it was impossible for him to reach it, although the distance was covered easily by the smell of hot soup. There was also the rain, which exasperated him. Forced to sleep on a ground sheet, his clothes soaked by water, he only dreamt about that prolonged, often unbearable torture being over by any means. Silent, alone, almost grown wild because of the many months since he had been far from her, he had moments when his memories forced him to think of salvation as well, because all his senses evoked Ella. It was just that he no longer knew where to position her.

He had kept in his mind all the details of their life together, but, as he remembered them and looked for a point of support in them, the peace and beauty which he did not want to give up, he also felt, in parallel, how the fear of death had invaded him. From books or from the things said in his region, in the countryside, he had learned about the calmness and peace preceding passage into the next world, and, when the sequences with Ella became increasingly luminous, he said to himself terrified: "Lord, this is death!", and he looked around him for a spot where he could hide or he listened tensely to the noises coming over from the Russian area. At other times, with the woman's face in his mind, winning out over his fear and pain, he called to her from all his being, as if she was the only possible salvation, and, with his senses tensed, frozen in paroxysm, he had the certainty that he heard her steps, that death was very close. At this moment, bizarrely, he experienced a great happiness: he was going to go away, to disappear together with Ella's image, forever. But, when he was looking for landmines, when his desire could become reality in a matter of seconds, he gave himself another chance; the entire organism, even the pain, became bearable, they obstinately refused death, and there was another sorrow that accompanied him. He had not given much attention to his parents, ignoring them in some way. During all the previous events he had lived with the impression that there was still time for them to await reconciliation, and that, very soon, he would devote himself exclusively to them, but he had also avoided the discussion also due to his father's very different way of seeing the world. For him, everything was clear: things that were, things that are, and things that will be. He had not been too happy that Darius had come home from Berlin, instead of leaving for America. Neither had his marriage, in the present moment, in the middle of a war, produced too much enthusiasm. Of course, his father had not confessed this directly, but he had made him understand it, even though nothing could be changed anymore. Not even Ella's unusual beauty softened his feelings:

"Only ill-advised men take beautiful wives, so that they may have something to guard," was his opinion.

There also was embarrassment between them, and the awkwardness of conversation, but Darius was especially uncomfortable because of the resignation with which his father met every event, including the war. Evil was a punishment from God for the sins of mankind, good proceeded from the Lord on High as well, a sign of undeserved magnanimity in a moment when the world, he said, was closer to Sodom and Gomorrah than to the Kingdom of Heaven.

From the trenches, the face of the old man was lit up by a strange light. Sometimes Darius was happy to have him at his side in the madness and misery of each moment. At other times, with no connection to what was going on in the mud in which he found himself, or in the snow desecrated by oils, ash and blood, the most surprising events from his childhood or adolescence came to his mind, and his eyes became wet. He did not know what might be better: to live for them or, through death, to free them from the new illusions which, inevitably, he would have caused – especially since, after such a long time, his folks must have accustomed themselves to the thought that their son no longer existed. In his few hours of sleep, it was strange that he dreamed of his mother, more than of Ella, in the way their last meeting had fixed her in his memory. Inevitably, she told him various stories which he forgot on waking up, but he was left with a bitter feeling of sad resignation, of resigned waiting, in his soul. These moments reassured him, to some extent, that he had not become a complete wild man, that the terrible loneliness experienced under the threat of death could be temporary, interrupted or at least attenuated.

In the end, he received three letters from Ella at a time that he no longer wanted them, since he had convinced himself that their life, definitively ended, had been left somewhere behind, like the streets of Berlin or the lanes of his village, and like their astonishing story with everything that it had meant. From this point onwards, he was under the dominion of another star, the star of death, and the lines she had written – which were otherwise conventional, as permitted during times of war – only managed to make his fear and wait for the end even more painful, because, every time he had tried to renounce Ella, her face, which had become even more luminous, refused to take its place among the other memories. Strangely, this horrible fear of dying, this crawl among landmines and cadavers through Ukraine's fields seemed to be the payment, the punishment for an excess of happiness, the other side of the coin with Ella. After several readings, he was left obsessed by some banal information sneaked in between assurances of her love. She had started to practice her profession, she was, therefore, a doctor, and the medicine she had conscientiously learnt in Berlin helped her – she was telling him – confront the difficulties which are unavoidable in times of war.

He replied on the usual postcard and, besides the repeated words of love and good wishes for her health, he asked for a series of explanations connected to her new situation, given the unexpected absence from the period of the military training, but he never received another answer. Furthermore, the blood spilled from a wound in his shoulder had stained both the letters and the only photograph of her he had saved from the mud and rain. The bullet that strayed to his shoulder had been a warning, because he had talked too much about death, and he had provoked it too much; or maybe it was the sign that this was all he had to pay in this war he waged in the name of another country? As for Ella, he had not tried, as in other times, to appeal to his memory in order to sketch her face, although her features were even

more alive than they had been, once upon a time, in faraway
Berlin. He looked, however, at his dirty, heavy hands, full of
calluses and wounds of all kinds, ugly and infected, which,
started to shake even at the thought they might hold a
pencil, a paintbrush or a piece of charcoal. Although he had
no evidence for it, he felt things were not the way he had left
them: something was amiss, but he refused to think about
what it could be, because, with each succeeding day, the
questions without an answer increased worryingly. He often
tried to confront these questions, in the name of what had
happened between them, and in the name of love without
limits, of which he had never been in doubt. Most times,
however, the huge pedestal on which he had placed her came
crashing down noisily, a *what if...?* insinuated itself among
his memories and then everything transformed into painful
indifference. He was more frightened by death than by life,
a life without her and without everything which had lifted
them above the misery of everyday. In any case, from there,
the trenches, he perceived Ella with his senses in particular.
He lacked the conversations, the phrases – not because
they had not had them, but because, in Berlin, it was their
bodies and the terrible fear of Nazism which united them.
Back then, in those days, when they explored each other
with unsuspected curiosity, they had discovered feelings and
states of spirit which were absolutely new, which denied
themselves to words because they came from a dialogue of
the bodies. They embraced with energy and thirst, as if their
life depended on those moments and gestures. They thought
the rest of their lives would be enough for words and that it
was essential to give themselves up to the will of the always
unsatisfied senses, a state from which they then woke up
completely unprepared later on, forced into awareness by

the circumstances. Suddenly, violently, the unforeseen set them on an entirely unwanted orbit, from which Ella was absent for a while or maybe forever, as he was increasingly tempted to believe. What then? An empty space, deserted, as big as a whole life. It was impossible for him to believe that fate might offer him, later on, at some point, another love, just as intense, after he had escaped from the war, if, by an absurd possibility, he did escape, and the thought that without Ella all that awaited him would be a banal slog through life terrified him. Then look, unexpectedly, the fate he always invoked placed him in front of a new beginning.

He was in a tent, a kind of improvised infirmary where he had come to change the bandage, when a huge explosion covered him in a wave of sand from whose pressure he extricated himself with great difficulty, after a long time. He had lain there under the bodies of the medics, and when he woke up it was night. He managed to reconstruct later, the chance that had brought him there, at the edge of a deep hole made by a projectile, after he saw himself alone, away from the noise of cannons, under the unsettling sky of the most oppressive end of summer. In that precise moment, he had a great revelation: he had been saved in order to return home. *In order to run away home.* He was convinced that his perseverance and the intensity with which he loved were rewarded in this way, but, at the same time, the Saviour had forced him to discover how much suffering, sorrow, injustice surround us and how insignificant we are when facing history. Of course, he had known this truth, but he had not lived it with his own being. From all the cardinal points he had been welcomed by Ella's love, and this had disarmed him. In a way, it had blinded him, it had shielded him from the brutal atmosphere of the events. Now, a confusing question: which direction was home, his home? Which was the right direction? Death in front of him, death behind, death everywhere. At least if his movement took him one step closer to Ella, at least one step, it would be the correct direction. Placing his hand instinctively on the breast pocket in which he kept, such as they were, stained by blood and mud, the photograph and her so-conventional letters, as if received from an unknown woman, he felt their moisture and he could not tell for a long time whether it was his blood, from the still unhealed wound, or the blood of the medic under whom he had lain. It had no importance anyway. With eyes closed, he tried to imagine the road back, the huge distance which he was about to walk, especially at night and, suddenly, instead of feeling free, he was tried by a terrible, overwhelming fear. Later on, after a time which was as long as a century and hard to bear, in which he gathered whatever he could from the pharmacy reduced to dust by the explosion, and from the food and objects found on the cadavers that surrounded him, he had a strange feeling. It was as if he saw, and not just with the eyes of the soul, how the man in him began to suffer, and how instead of the man there grew a terrible animal, a predator, obstinate to survive and to reach home at any price.

"I am everyone or no one. I am the other / Who I don't know I am, who has looked / Into that other dream, into my vigil. / He judges it / In resignation and smiling. / Resigned and smiling."
Borges – *The Dream* [19]

---

19 From *Atlas*, New York: Dutton, 1985. Translated by Anthony Kerrigan.

"Death is not to be shunned, for the Son of God did not think it unworthy of Him."
St Ambrose – *On the Death of Satyrus* [20]

On they went dimly, beneath the lonely night amid the gloom, / through the empty halls of Dis and his phantom realm, / even as under the niggard light of a fitful moon / lies a path in the forest, when Jupiter has buried the sky / in shade, and black Night has stolen from the world her hues"
Virgil – *The Aeneid* [21]

Over the story of his tormenting return – of the running away from the front, to be more precise – my father-in-law always passed very hurriedly. Only when he was drunk did he happen to "remember" details about which he had not talked before, but he never managed to complete the story of the desertion and of the return itself. Often he left the impression that it had been the gentlest part of the nightmare in which he'd found himself.

Over and over again, time changes the colour of events, attenuates hardships and, in the majority of cases, gives back to things their real dimensions. As far as Darius is concerned, I had the feeling that, from his biography, something was left out, unsaid, irrespective of the time of day or night he related it to me, sober or drunk – as it happened, in recent times, he got drunk increasingly often. This was either because he did not have the right words, or, probably, he did not believe I could have the sensitivity

---

20   From *Nicene and Post-Nicene Fathers*, Second Series, Vol. 10. Edited by Philip Schaff and Henry Wace. Buffalo, NY: Christian Literature Publishing Co., 1896. Translated by H. de Romestin, E. de Romestin and H.T.F. Duckworth.

21   From *The Aeneid*, Book VI, in Virgil. *Eclogues, Georgics, Aeneid*. Harvard University Press, 1916. Translated by H. R Fairclough.

and experience which were necessary in order to understand him.

Darius recalled: There was only one direction, sunset; and the road had to be travelled at night, without the uniform and unarmed. Armed or not, you could have been killed by the partisans, by the locals – who had also grown wild, or by other deserters like me, and a pistol was yet another piece of evidence against you, faced by possible accusers. I had kept a very well sharpened bayonet, though, serving as a knife, at the bottom of the rucksack, along with a razor, some scissors and a shaving soap. I had also discovered by chance some good boots and, in order to start on my adventure, I needed nerves of steel plus flawless indifference, neighbouring on cynicism, not to care that you could die or, even worse than dying, that you could be left an invalid. I told this to myself as if to a stranger, whom I was striving to convince that, against logic and feelings, he had chosen the best solution. You just need to see the end of the road and to remember that others had successfully gone through more difficult situations, therefore, as a result, the return on foot, at night, was possible. The truth was that I did not have the courage to start immediately. The more I thought about it, the more the arguments against this attempt increased. If I stayed put, I would be found in the end, either by my people or by the Russians, somebody would have to take an interest in these cadavers who had belonged to a military unit. None of the variants was brilliant, irrespective of who found me. Prisoner in a camp in Siberia or mine finder, this was all that could be waiting for me, but, actually, the chances of staying alive for another little while increased in both situations. In the end, I was chased away by the maimed faces of my comrades, images of a nightmare superimposed on the faces of my dearest whom I was trying desperately to bring back to my mind.

I started with hesitant steps, convinced that I wouldn't be able to get too far from that bizarre area, dominated by immense projectile holes, by trenches, by corpses of men and horses, by abandoned cannon and houses still on fire. Free, surrounded by death, as I assimilated the unknown around me to death, this being its visible face, I felt the contact with the earth in all the fibres in my body. It seemed strange that nothing hurt me and that nothing stopped me from waiting with stoicism for the stray bullet, my bullet which would punish the madness of having chosen this solution, that of desertion; or the bullet of captain Kalnoki, "*the mother, father and godfather of all stinking Wallachians*"[22] sent to clear out the mines with their bare hands. Wallachians who did not welcome with friendly eyes the victory of Admiral Horthy, and the occupation of northern Transylvania, an occupation which was going to last for a thousand years at least. I did not know whether my unit had fallen back or advanced. I was welcomed everywhere by the marks of death and destruction, and in the places where I thought it was behind me, I could have been waited for by the captain himself, who always bragged about his pleasure in shooting Wallachian deserters. In any case, gradually emptied of feelings, attentive to noises and footsteps, I turned back, although it also could have been forward, possessed by the absurd conviction that I could be saved, that God would guide my steps home, just as He had helped me live, despite the landmines and the death present at every step.

---

22 Wallachian is an old name for ethnic Romanians. In this context, it is a demeaning term.

My arguments, besides the blind faith that, in the end, I would manage to cross that immense space that separated me from home, were puerile. Since the Creator had given me talent, he would also give me the chance to exploit it, to realise something. I could not ignore love. How could I destroy a love that surpassed words and conformed exactly to the love preached by Jesus? And then, although I had been on the front for such a long time, I had not killed anyone, what's more – taking away the landmines, assuming the major risk each second, I had given other people the chance to live. Above all, I did not desert, terrorised by the thought that I was going to die. Instead I was imbued with the conviction that I would reach the end of the road. I think that all these arguments were crystallised during the way back, travelling only at night, on the darkest paths, with my thoughts on the hungry wild things and the partisans who could appear from anywhere. What would happen when I would no longer have tins of preserves? What about when I would have spent my strength? Can it be possible that, in order to survive, I would have to kill, that is – to defend myself?

"Every person is chained to his loneliness and condemned to death. He lives – it is not known why – alone, with desires unsatisfied, grows old and dies. It's terrible! The only salvation is to free oneself from one's 'I', the love for the other. Then, instead of a quota, there will be two more chances, and man, without wanting to, tending to it, loves mankind. But people are mortal and, if in one's life there will be more bitterness than joy, then the same will be true in the life of the others. And it is for this reason that the situation is so desperate. There is only the consolation that death in front of the world

229

is beautiful. The only total salvation could be the love for the Immortal, for God. But is it possible?"
Tolstoy – *Diaries*, vol. II

Darius said: The first days were horrendous. I would walk only at night and I was thinking, terrified, about the landmines forgotten in the ground and the unexploded projectiles or about other deserters, whom fear, hunger or madness could push into murdering me, so that, above and beyond the desire to go on, I was haunted by the obsession of returning to the trench near which the medics' tent had been. I was thinking with increasing persistence about this, but I never had the strength to take the first step back, although I was overwhelmed by loneliness or maybe a much stronger and more savage feeling than that, which I did not know what to call. During the day, hidden in the bushes, but especially in the holes left by projectiles, I would slumber, concentrating on the noises, so that no danger of any nature should find me unprepared. At night, I would walk on ground which had been minutely researched with my eyes during the preceding day. Everywhere around – the signs of destruction and of the end. I remember well that, at some given moment, I heard some light noises around me and, after hours of tense waiting, I saw an animal, a wolf or a dog, a wolf rather, it was impossible for me to see it from any closer, who was looking at me without having the courage to approach. Scared by the thought that an accident could put me in the situation of not being able to defend myself, I grasped the bayonet with all my strength, ready to confront the animal, but after some hours of fear and exhausting waiting it disappeared. I no longer heard it, although the hallucination or maybe the animal – whatever it was – stayed imprinted on my senses for a long time, so that I was afraid even to fall asleep. More than a few times, in my immediate neighbourhood, I heard shots and sinister noises, but I was lucky, and later on I started to get used to night and to the road. Absolutely alone, under the open skies, in an unknown space, in which everything had the taste of death, I was often taken over by strange fits of terror and suffocation and in those moments, defeated, I would sit down and call my memories to my assistance. I would make a kind of inventory of all the people I had known, but I wanted Ella especially, with all the strength of my being. It was a call and a prayer, a run and a fear of death. During the day, because I did not have the courage to walk, I would take my notebook, the only thing that reminded me of what I had been, and, like the times when we met, I tried in vain to reconstitute her from memory, but I also tried, especially, to write to her what I felt. At times I managed to describe the squalor in which I found myself, but, in particular, I wrote of my longing for her, terrible, desperate longing. At other times words deserted me and I would then make appeal to my parents or acquaintances, because – bizarrely – I could not really find friends when I was looking back. Maybe that was why I had invested in Ella, not just all my thirst for love, but also for friendship, which I had neglected. I don't know why. I discovered now, unexpectedly, that I had not connected in a special manner to anyone, during the lyceum or at the university. I was friends with everyone and no-one.

My parents inspired in me, like the saints in a church, a sort of mystic love, meaning respect and affection mingled with fear. They had told me what was not good to do and, despite the kindness in their voices, I had perceived all their words like orders which, even if I did not agree with them, I did not have the courage to contradict. Later on, I don't know why, they considered me more mature than I was and, very seldom, father in particular, commented on my mistakes and naiveté in a manner different to what I expected, like some unsuccessful explanation, *a sort of.* This was also a variation, but not the best suitable, immediately followed by the reassurance that such errors could happen to anyone.

I once asked him directly why was Ella not to his liking, but of course he defended himself, saying that he would not have liked it either, if somebody had chosen his wife for him, even if everything would have been against it. When they arrested me, I saw his face for a matter of seconds, rising from the depths of my memory, and it was possessed by a sadness without bounds:

"Can a woman deserve so many sacrifices?" he seemed to want to ask me, and my answer would have been unquestionable: "Yes!".

I had lived something which denied itself to words, and the light of that meeting changed the course of my life, adding a dimension which had been unsuspected up to that time. I walked, accompanied by father's face and, very close, two steps behind, my mother, who – despite her firm contours – came silently, and sometimes she even lightened my darkness, helping me see beyond the squalor and the ugliness in which I had thrown myself for Ella's sake. My mother, strangely, had not left in my memory any words, events, dramatic struggles, but only gestures, warmth and a strong sensation of certainty, of a call: "There is a little more, try, you must not give up!". She would have quoted father another time, she would have assured me he wanted this, that he had ordered it, but she had now come out of her habitual shadows and tried to help me. Thus, guided in turns by one, then by the other, I passed, with infinite precautions, through frightening, unknown spaces, getting to the point when I identified with the road, being myself a road, night, fears and, again – I have no way of avoiding the word – death.

...Lord, I feel it and I tremble. Although the body such as it is tells me the saddest story about the person I am, and about how I am in this moment, although I know my age and all which is connected to it, I cannot believe that I, too, will die. There are no exceptions here. Planets, constellations disappear in order to be reborn some other time, some other way; all the roads lead, inevitably, to death. In the long moments of insomnia, I cannot manage to think of anything else, I close my eyes and I try to imagine the giant struggles of stellar matter, the terrible clash of suns and galaxies, the explosions and writhing that precede a new birth and, with all this, I cannot manage to accept that I, too, will be no more. What if now, in this second, the heart should stop? A flutter, a powerless struggle and that's it, light is getting thinner, disappears, in the few minutes the crust decomposes, there is no way to return, nothing...

The spiral-bound notebook...
<u>Immortals facing Death</u> by <u>Isabelle Bricard</u>.
Edison: *"It is very beautiful over there."*
Christopher Columbus: *"Lord, my soul is in your hands."*
Lope de Vega: *"Dante always bored me."*
Cicero: *"I never forgot I am mortal."*
Dostoevsky: *"The end, the end, I am sinking."*
Léon Bloy: *"I only feel one thing: an immense curiosity..."*
Goethe: *"Can you see this beautiful head of a woman, with*

233

black, shining locks, there, in the dark background? Light...
More light!"
Renan: *"Take this sun off the Acropolis."*

I take my pulse at the carotid artery, I feel the rhythm of my heart, it's normal, I don't have any reason to grow anxious this moment, but the messengers of death, seem to be cold perspiration and animal irrepressible fear. I wish it would end once and for all, now, this very second, as death cannot be more brutal than the suffocating fear. It chases me away to the window, because I can't have enough air. I often try to save myself from the death that looks imminent to me and, suddenly, I discover the fir trees in front, the strange contours of the mountains, illuminated by a huge moon which, in its turn, has entered the age of decrepitude. The cold air of the night wakes me up from this nightmare. I discover, step by step, that I am alive, that I am still alive, but the joy that invades me is crushed by a few parasite questions: "How much alive? Until when? Could it be, perhaps, that the forest, the moon, the air and firs are only the good part, meaning the good part of the endless nightmare which is my reality?"

Darius recounted: As time passed, I was getting used to reality, with that bizarre sensation that I had been there forever, abandoned, hunted for, not fully dead but neither alive, a desperate entity always searching for food, often followed by creatures which were even hungrier, more imagined, more felt than seen, which did not have the courage to attack me. Vagabond dogs, wolves, I could not understand what, maybe even people. Nothing seemed to exist besides fear, death was lying in wait for you from all sides, from the holes made by projectiles or from the ammunitions abandoned everywhere. Only the sky was familiar, to some extent, with its large stars, shivering, or with the clouds which were lowered to the ground, often covering the holes, the squalor, the corpses of animals in putrefaction, accentuating my sensation of loneliness in that foreign, hostile space. I was no longer even accompanied by the memory of those for whom I had deserted. I could do anything, laugh or cry, I had all the time to create for myself various roles for the numerous circumstances in which I could find myself. I was in the most humiliating situation possible and any madman or idiot had ascendancy over me, even the wild animals which followed me, or, which I only feared followed me. I had even lost the count of the days since I started hunting around like that, and in the end animal hunger made me go closer to the abandoned houses, and even to force open some doors. I wasn't expecting mercy or understanding from the possible inhabitants. I could not be a welcome guest and, in need, not even capable of defending myself, but there were moments when I did not care for anything, for life, for Ella, whom I had no way of informing that I was still alive, for my parents who, probably convinced I had died, had made or would make a grave and a funerary service in keeping with the grief that visited them, according to custom. In one of the houses I discovered a child who had become savage with fright, whose age was impossible for me to establish. I didn't know his language, but one of the two tins of beans which I kept for the time when I wouldn't have any other solution left helped me tame him, and even to improvise two wooden splints for him. He left some beans for me as well, after which I decided to leave, feeling that the masters of the house or the neighbours could not be far. The child accompanied me for a good part of the road through the village, but at the first lit house he split from me, just as I had wished, in fact. Although I was convinced he was following me, I was enveloped by a strange nostalgia, a feeling which only tears managed to express. Could it have been my lost humanity, another facet of life, which was calm, domestic, or the complicated state of feeling which had a constant name, *Ella?* For a few moments I'd become a human, and not the hunted animal, terrorised by fear and the need not to forget what I had been and for what I'd deserted. After more desperate days, in which hunger was equal to the measure of fatigue, I saw a train station or what seemed to be a real train station. The closer I got, the more distinctly I heard the whistle of locomotives and I could make out the pallid light of light bulbs on the lamp-posts in front of what had once been a solid building, now with the roof and top floor destroyed by bombardments. Without stopping to think about it, I decided to go round it, as the trains might have been loaded with Hungarian troops meant to hurry the advance in Soviet territory.

I went round the train station and I sat somewhere close to the rails, trying to see what was in the carriages, what languages the rail workers or the travellers spoke and, in particular, where I found myself after all these days of walking. By good fortune, two shadows jumped from a bush and, pressured by the feeling that I was not wrong to imitate them, I hung on to a freight carriage, in which I later discovered two more people, the same age as me, who looked at me terrified. Neither they nor I had the courage to say a word, we looked closely at each other with infinite prudence, trying to guess our intentions. Later on, one of them smiled and gestured to me he was going to sleep, a gesture to which I hurried to reply, but I could not fall asleep in any way. The sudden stops in the middle of fields, and the distant roar of aeroplanes created a state of panic in me, tempered in the end by my neighbours' indifference towards to any noise. I did not know in what direction I was going and I did not care either. It was important that I was going somewhere and that I was seeing two people. For the rest: stops, bridges, never-ending bridges and whistles of sirens foretelling attacks. At some point I fell asleep, too, and I woke up with the sun towards noon, shaken hard by one of my neighbours who gestured to me to get off quickly because a station was getting closer. I thanked them by gesturing as well and, as the train was rolling very slowly, I jumped, but I could not manage to join them from behind. The men simply got lost. I think they too were deserters, if not locals, because they seemed to know the route and the area was not foreign to them. I thought that the train also could be a solution for salvation in the future. Far away from the rail line, but with my eyes fixed on it, I waited for the night to fall, in order to look for other empty carriages. I had caught some courage, starting to believe that, if I had a little more audacity, I could reach home.

After another few months of wanderings and fears, of risks and squalor, out of which the single pleasant memory was of a field of potatoes abandoned to the autumn cold which ensured my sustenance for a few days, I reached a sheepfold in Bucovina. The shepherd, a Romanian, updated me on the course of the war and, for more than a week, he fed me with generously. At our parting, he confessed that he had lived with fear in his bosom that I might rob him. I was not the only deserter, there had been others to come that way, Romanians, Hungarians and even Germans. He had treated them all with the same humanity, he told me, but one of them, one night before leaving, had threatened him with a pistol, asking for all his money – which, in any case, he did not have. In the absence of money, the man had been content with a change of clothes. The shepherd's adventure did not surprise me. In a situation where life and death compete, if you have chosen life nothing should surprise you or stop you, and no sin can be excluded. Only when you are very close to your goal you are enveloped by the dread that you cannot touch it, and at that point you become a beast.

The true story of my father-in-law's return had many unknowns, which I never managed to clarify. With each remembering, something got added and something else, from the story he had told me a little while previously, was missing, and the hurry with which he passed over when it came to the last part of the journey made me suspicious. Had he killed somebody? Had he stolen? Had he got mixed up with some other kind of lawlessness? You cannot even imagine what you are able to feel when you hope you might live, when you think that the dangers have decreased, he answered me once when he'd had a bit more to drink. This was a kind of reply too, but not the one I expected. I thought he would tell me about that part of his return, doubtful or obscure, like an event he'd heard from somebody else; that sooner or later it would be impossible for him not to free himself from the psychological pressure of a deed of such gravity, but it did not happen. He was content just to tell me that there had been days when he hated Ella, and, he'd cursed the moment he'd met her, but there were also days when he was tormented by a ferocious jealousy. She had not received news from him for entire months, and, as a consequence, he could not exclude the possibility that her patience might have reached an end, nor the fact that he could be caught after he'd seen her or even before. Other times, when he discovered his face reflected in the water of a bucket where he happened to wash himself, he was overwhelmed by despair. Lord, who am I? How did I get here? Why did you punish me so harshly? But what if my parents no longer live, what if grief brought them down? The questions and the revolt against destiny, against heavens and earth had not helped him cool off. On the contrary....

Darius recounted: Fear increased in proportion as I got closer to the town. I would avoid main roads, villages and towns, and the thought that I would have to pass the Romanian-Hungarian border that had brought me the most terrifying bad luck, changing the entire course of my life, truly obsessed me. This seemed to be the harshest injustice, and that was why I did all that was possible to be informed about the safest crossing areas, having always known that smuggling was blooming in certain points on the border, and the people I had taken counsel with – having entered an area in which Romanian was spoken – had explained to me that it would be best to make my way towards Maramureş. Here, with the help of firewood thieves, who were otherwise very generous, and whose involvement in a case of this kind was not their first, I found myself, without understanding how, on the other side, "in the country". From here on, the road was easier, as the inhabitants on the edges of villages had become used to people hiding in the woods and, equally, to deserters. Because of all this, the fear that tested me was infinitely greater, as the Hungarian administration and the gendarmes with cockerel feathers in their hats were extremely vigilant. They did not speak Romanian and they tried to rule by fear and terror. Above all else, deserting in times of war finds no forgiveness or understanding anywhere.

There came a moment when I intended to stay over in Romania. I could look for my parents-in-law and get news of Ella from them. This would have been the clearest plan. Once inside the country, I would have been free of any risk, but from where I found myself, Ella was much closer and I had, in any case, lost my patience. After so many months when I had only been an animal terrorised by death, the face of the woman, of my wife, was more present than ever in my memory. Despite the time and distance, I was trying to imagine our future meeting. It was possible that she had been informed that I had died or disappeared, and then it would have been her right to remarry. In this situation, I had no choice. Marriage was logical, legal, I had nothing to blame her for and, in the end, she might well love my replacement even better. The new spouse, Ella herself or, more certainly, the mysterious and insufferable Alois could denounce me for desertion, and then my journey would have resulted in the most ruthless punishment for some unknown crimes. This would have been a huge sorrow, which wouldn't kill me, but it would have been hard if not impossible to remain unaffected. Sometimes I thought it was possible that she'd run away to Romania, called by her parents, and not returned, but, no matter how hard I tried, I could not imagine her as a Penelope crushed by sorrow and waiting.

As I got increasingly closer to home, all Ella's gestures, details of her face, of her body, which I was sure that only

I knew, were becoming clearer in my memory, so that at a sheepfold, close to the town, I managed to draw her. Her image on the paper torn from a school notebook, on which the shepherd kept a record of his milking, encouraged me to continue my journey. Look, I could not make it anymore. I was blind and mad, I had a hole in my soul, a need for her, a need for peace and beauty which I was still able to control.

I chose a market day, as the shepherd advised me, and, losing myself among the peasants leading their cattle, pigs and horses to market, dressed like them and with a basket of food "for sale" in my hand, I reached the town, vanquished by emotion, not even a kilometre away from Ella's house – that is, our house. I had thought of father too, who often went to the cattle markets. I had looked for him everywhere in vain, and, as normal, I should have gone home to my parents first, in order to reduce the risk of being found out, but I could not master or organise myself. It was as if somebody was spurring me on from behind.

I waited for the evening to fall and then I took my heart in my teeth and left the market. I met no-one on the road, what's more – by good fortune – there was no light in the house, as a consequence of which, finding the key in its hiding place, I opened the door stealthily, putting the key back afterwards. Once in the house, I had no time to see what had changed in the meantime or to look through her things, so dear to me, since I was possessed by an inexplicable tremor, as if surprised by an intense cold in the most vicious of winters. A great miracle had been accomplished – I was living, I had made it alive, and look, I was now facing another miracle. I had reached home after a long and tormenting journey, and fate had offered me the chance of some time to get used to my own house, and to the thought that I wouldn't transform

241

the meeting with Ella into a confused or even embarrassing moment, which would then haunt us for all our lives.

I hid in a closet near the bedroom, where we used to keep our old clothes and the winter clothes. This was a useful place from which to spy her movements, to observe her surrounded by all her things with the eyes and the thirst of the man I had once been, when I met her. I had hidden myself in there before, tortured by the stale air mixed with that of lavender. These were the moments that I wanted to see her in her intimacy, as she undressed and stayed naked for a while, before sprinkling herself with perfume under the arms and on the neck, moments in which, because of the slow movements, I had the impression she would fall asleep before getting dressed in the silk pyjamas which she never buttoned up. Of course, she had threatened several times that she would replace the door with another one, massive and padded, but she did not keep her word. She liked to know herself admired, desired.

What's more, she had borrowed my habit as well: "I want to see if you're waiting for me, how much you miss me and what you do when you miss me very much!", she threatened me often, when she did the impossible in order to reach home before me.

This time the tears, which I could not control, and the darkness, hampered me from seeing the potential changes in the bedroom, but the paintings of the colourist painters of Baia Mare were in their place, just as I had left them, a sign that very big and important changes had not taken place. While I tormented myself in order to moderate my emotions and to accommodate myself to the space in which I found myself, I heard her voice. It was her voice, but also that of a man, and they were speaking in Hungarian about the door. She was anxious because she had found it unlocked, and he assured her that everything was alright, that before she put the key in its place she had forgotten to turn it in the keyhole, but, since everything was in order, as she had noticed after a short investigation, Ella admitted that it was possible for her to be mistaken, to have only imagined she had locked it. When she turned the lights on, I was convinced that she had not changed at all apart from her hair do and clothes. She was just as I knew her and the way I had kept her in my memory for such a long time. Indeed, she now had shorter hair and she wore a very elegant, black hat, which gave her a severe and distant air. First of all, she hurried to the windows, drew the large black, camouflage curtains, and then she looked around in order to convince herself everything was in its place. The man who accompanied her, a captain in the Hungarian army – tall, well built, with a black, well groomed moustache, seemed to be familiar with the room and he seemed very used to Ella, too, to her way of being, to her most intimate gestures, because they did not talk too much, they knew only too well why they had come and what they had to do. Back to back, they both undressed, in something of a hurry. He went to the bathroom, from which he emerged naked, then sat on the bed with movements which were as natural as possible and, waiting for the woman, he lit a cigarette. Ella, just as I knew her, used to linger a lot in the bathroom, because it was only there that she remembered her innumerable creams and perfumes about which, during the day, she would forget completely.

One might have said that the officer knew everything about Ella, about her pleasure in letting herself be waited for, because he opened the nightstand near the bedhead, took out a bottle of drink, took a swig – quickly and thirstily – then carefully filled two small glasses which he placed on the same nightstand and, feeling relaxed, he splayed himself as he was, naked, on top of the cover, his manhood covered by her hat, and, of course, his eyes pointed at the bathroom door, from where Ella was going to appear. When we were together, the bottle in the nightstand was not part of our habits. The cover was also new, with its unsuccessful drawings: strange plants, with big, very green leaves, something in between vine leaf and maple, scattered in disorder as in an abandoned garden. Ella did not seem amazed by the surprise prepared by the officer. She took the hat nonchalantly, threw it far off and, with mad lust, she threw herself on the area it had previously covered.

I retained every gesture with infinite precision. From the moment I saw them getting undressed with such ease, my emotions had practically disappeared. I was spectator to a grotesque spectacle I could not have imagined, not even in my darkest moments. Nevertheless, I don't know why, I felt obliged not to lose any detail. In fact, as soon as I saw them naked and I had the certainty that what was happening under my eyes was not a hallucination or a sequence from a nightmare, I was brutally overwhelmed by the absurd sensation that my head was growing. The light had disappeared and I felt the need to shout, to run, to do absolutely anything in order to remove myself from that nightmare. Unfortunately, I no longer had the energy, or the light, and air. I was incapable of jumping on them, of killing them, the way a parasite thought urged me, because – isn't it so? – death was familiar to me, it had accompanied me everywhere.

As time went on, it was increasingly clear to me that

my life had to take another route, and not a good one. I no longer cared for anything, because nothing had any importance anymore. At a certain point, the slide into the void, towards nothingness, ended just as unexpectedly. I had disappeared from this experience, it was no longer my experience so I could look at them with relative detachment. Even more, incredibly so, I looked with the desire to find evidence with which to forgive her. Lord – I prayed – , why did you save me? Have I travelled such a long way, have I endured so much hunger and fear in order to see what is going on under my eyes? Am I perhaps paying for the mistake of loving her madly, of risking everything for her sake? Should I have refused to believe in love, in people? But what should I believe in, my Father? The feeling of a huge, irrecoverable loss invaded me step by step. Then came the counterarguments. Ella had no means of knowing I was alive. I also felt guilty for having taken only ourselves into account, and for our unsated need to sacrifice everything for love, to entrust ourselves to others with condemnable ease or, in other words, for considering history to be more understanding than it had proven to be. I told myself that, being threatened, forced by circumstances or human needs – which are understandable up to a certain limit – she had to do what she was doing. Unfortunately, the fact that the man in her bed – our bed – was part of the army of the people her parents had run away from contradicted my excuses. In addition, the way in which Ella had come out of the bathroom, the way in which she had hurried to him with an appetite which had no pretence about it, had scattered any trace of generosity to ridicule. I recognised her in every gesture. She was now repeating even the hesitations, the shivering anxiety with which her hands seemed to search for something unknown, a certainty, or the way in which they expressed the joys of the fulfilment that had already started to possess her.

The unbridling that happened under my eyes amplified to a spasm the conviction that I had been betrayed in everything, in feelings more than in deeds, and, of course, my defeat was definitively sealed. Another person inside me had become lucid, calm, as if I had seen everything from the height of the heavens or in a dream from my distant childhood. There, in that closet – I died. At least that was my sensation. A more difficult death, harsher than all I had felt and known about Death. I was another person, and I had no possibility of leaving the room. I had just heard them close the door and, as a consequence, all that was left for me to do was wait and see what else was going to happen.

Since the love scene had been immediately consummated, I told myself that the officer might go and, in the tens of minutes while Ella used to stay in the bathroom, I could sneak outside, where the danger of being asked for identification documents by the gendarmes was extremely great. I could have stayed even close to daytime in one of the four rooms on the ground floor, but I didn't know when the servants were coming or whether she still had them. She could not maintain the eight rooms by herself. Another possibility would have been to kill the officer and then tell Ella that she could just go ahead and denounce me. I would have probably put this into action, but, as I watched their moves and heard Ella's increasingly insistent moaning, my good angel assured me that it was not worth staying tied to her through this secret for the rest of my life. If I had the strength to assume so many risks, including that of dying, I would be capable of confronting the loneliness that would follow. In the end, I chose the wait, and look – luck was on my side. The officer dressed in a hurry, without washing, and the promise made to Ella that they would see each other the next day made me believe that their relationship was not exactly public knowledge. Ella, naked, just as she had got off the bed, walked him to the gate. After that, with slow and tired movements, she returned, smoothed the sheets and, finally, walked into the bathroom. I didn't leave my hiding place until I heard the water running, a sign she had entered the bathtub, but I left the door of the closet open, a petty punishment, which could not pass unnoticed in the end. It was the only one, anyway, which my defeat dictated to me at that time.

The street was deserted, but, by good fortune, a horse-drawn cab crossed my way. In one jump, I found myself behind the man who drove it. It was a moment's inspiration, a reaction due to despair, but also to the need to live. I found myself, it was evident, facing a new beginning. Life had thrown me once again, brutally, into the unknown. So, the lesson was not yet ended. I could see that I still had something to learn, but I had neither the strength nor the patience at that time to look for answers. I was very afraid and, apart from that cab, I saw no other solution for salvation.

"I have just come from the front, I have no money, I have no valuables," I confessed to the cab driver, "but you have to take me to the edge of the town!"

Determined, I took my wedding band off my finger and put it in his hand: "This is all I have!"

The cab driver was not surprised, he didn't refuse it, and he was content to whip the horse, but feeling him overtaken by anxiety, I took the knife I had received in exchange for the bayonet from the last shepherd with whom I lived for a while, and I assured the driver that if he called for a gendarme he was a dead man. He only replied after we reached at the foot of the hill of Feleac, far away from the town.

"Yet again, it's the woman," he said, looking at the wedding band as if my despair was transmitted to him through it or through the tip of the knife which he felt, without any doubts, in his back. "No woman deserves tears and headaches," he said encouragingly before offering the ring back to me. I did not take it, as he probably expected me to do.

Ella existed no more and, if it were in my power, I would have taken her out of my memory too, for good. Possessed by a mixed feeling of release, hate and defeat, I started towards my parents' house. The fact in itself produced an unexpected pleasure, although I was simply a beast, capable of killing. Beforehand, love had a name, a face and an address. Now, nothing held me back.

I reached home, just as I desired, at night. My family had not gone to sleep, the uncertain rays of a petrol lamp came through the edges of the camouflage paper that covered the windows. I had reached home and I felt like kissing the ground, the door, the posts of the veranda and the trees, but fear told me that there was no time to lose. I had to enter, although the tears, which father detested even when they were tears of joy, slowed down my movements.

"All must be faced with dignity, both the good and the bad. Even death, because it mediates the meeting with the Creator."

Father was usually happy if, before going inside the house, I went to see the animals, whom he would show me again anyway, describing their qualities in turns. Now I felt

I had no time, and, before everything else, I had no idea if he kept the old customs or if, overnight, he had hosted who knows what strangers. I knocked on the door gently enough and I immediately heard a "Who is it?", very short.

I said: "Father!", and the door was unlocked immediately, but before giving him a fiery embrace, after such a long absence, I sneaked past him. I was afraid to have been seen by anyone. Strange – the time I looked at him, for some seconds, before having the strength to say one word to him – I felt like the child of other times, who had come to tell his sorrows, to hand them over to the stronger one.

"Have you run away?", he asked, and I hurried to confirm it. "It is not time yet for people to know you have come. Your mother sleeps in the other room, with the child, I'll go in first so that she doesn't get scared."

"What child?", I wondered, and he added insistently:

"The little girl. Haven't you been around home?"

"No," I lied, "I was afraid I would be asked for identity papers or seen by anyone."

"Your little girl," he remarked, surprised. "Haven't you known? She is one and a half."

"How come she is with you? Was Ella capable of giving her up?"

"Eh, she did not give her up. I went with the old lady and asked her to leave her with us for a while, as we are alone and we want to rejoice in her too. She did not oppose it very much, and she comes to see her periodically. Sunday she'll be here. The child grows up beautifully, she is sprightly, she eats well, she's never been ill."

"And what is she called?"

"As is proper: Daria!", he replied with the most natural air. Because of her joy, my mother was speechless, she cried and she held me in her arms until father intervened.

"He is home now, we mourn no more. We'll be better off giving him food! And I'll heat up water for you to wash. I think you've gathered all the lice and fleas in the world on you!"

It was hard for me to leave the girl's side. She slept holding with both hands a ragdoll made by my mother, with eyes, mouth and nose drawn in chemical pencil – even though she had other, more beautiful ones on a shelf under the window.

"This is the one she likes," father assured me. "It doesn't close its eyes and that's why she holds it in her arms trying to put it to sleep. Its name is Mau, that's how she baptised her. It's the night doll, but eat something. Your mother dreamed of you all the time, she was sure you were alive and that you would come. She kept all your drawings and she looked at them all the time and she cried."

The atmosphere, very charged, hindered us from talking. There was so much to recount that nobody knew where to start, and it seemed nobody wanted to learn any truths at that time either. I was looking at the girl gently and, as I traced the features of her face, the peaceful, rhythmical breathing, my memory of the "encounter" with her mother became unbearable. I had risked my life in order to be able to see her, but she had no means of knowing this banal truth, just as I had no means of suspecting, either, that at the end of my adventure I would be awaited by the little girl, to whom I was not yet allowed to say who I was. It seemed suspicious they did not feel the need to talk to me about Ella, which made me suspect that, in reality, they did not want to ruin my joy at our meeting again. In the end, I felt it was not good to leave anything suspended. I felt a kind of 'come what may, everything can go to the devil now'!

"What about Ella?" I asked.

"She is working... maybe not in the most appropriate place, in a prisoner camp for communists, at Someşeni, she is a camp doctor..."

"Did something happen, did she remarry, what do you know?"

"She didn't tell and we didn't ask, but she is Jewish, it wasn't easy for her."

"Well, how can she be Jewish? Maybe one quarter, she's a catholic."

"That is the quarter which matters," father repeated, after which he changed the subject. "You will sleep in your room until near to morning time. Until then, I will think to see what we do. It is not good for people to see you. The occupiers haven't left yet, but people say they won't stay for long. They are very nervous. Requisitioning for the front, prisoner camps, digging trenches. I would not want anyone to see you, as this is what happens in life, half the world loves you and the other half hates you. And you can't know to which half the one that sees you belongs."

I ate a lot, followed by their inquisitive and, at the same time, peaceful gaze. "You've had the courage to desert and to reach here. This means you have become a man and that you will be able to carry on your back the hardships that will come. This is not bad at all," father concluded, preparing for me the tub of hot water.

My parents left me alone, to splash all I wanted, but I came out quickly, fearing I might fall asleep there in the water. Despite the bath, I did not crash, as would have been expected, into a deep sleep. I dreamt of great explosions, barbed wire, mud and people fallen under the fire of weapons; distorted figures, as if coming down from the paintings of Goya, stopped for a while in front of me, as if they wished me to remember them, and only fell after that. Ella was also there; but not as I had seen her that time, with the Hungarian officer, but as she had been once and as she would never be again. The joy that reality could not offer had been given me by my dream in the first night after the catastrophic disillusion. A late dream, obsolete, which expressed the things I had wanted to happen. Instead of the officer who made love to her furiously, as if he wanted, at any cost, to prove his ascendancy over her, to humiliate her, there I was, as I'd dreamt so many times, and I felt in the ninth heaven. A state that followed me even after my father woke me up.

"I am going to a friend to get an agreement with him about what to do in order to help you. You take care that nobody sees you, not even the little girl. Not to mention the wife. She comes on Sunday to the girl, but you shouldn't trust anyone but me and your mother. Who knows whether she'll make a slip and tell someone. Out of joy or by mistake."

I did not contradict him. I was convinced that he knew the truth, but he wanted to spare me for the time being. Satisfied, dressed in clean clothes, I followed him into the attic of the barn, where, until evening time, when he returned, I continued my sleep, leaving untouched the bottle of water and the food my mother had placed in a wicker basket.

"I am leaving you in the hands of a cousin of mine, a forester in the Cucului area. He will explain to you everything you need to know until our people return. He has a radio on accumulators, you will hear what London says too. What was too much has passed, you have proven you are a man and I trust you. The gendarmes do not have the courage to leave the village lanes, they fear the partisans and the people who ran away from the army conscription. From time to time I will come there myself, because we have much to tell. You have a little more to bear and that's it!"

It was not a "little," instead it was more like a lifetime. The fact that I was home – defeated, but home – in places that I knew, had moderated my suffering to some extent. I could extract from these places the energy necessary to resist the "little" which father believed I still needed before I was truly free.

Epictetus: *"You are just soul carrying around a corpse".*

"In a sense, every life that is recounted is offered as an example; we write in order to attack or to defend a view of the universe, and to set forth a system of conduct which is our own. It is none the less true, however, that nearly every biographer disqualifies himself by over-idealizing his subject or by deliberate disparagement, by exaggerated stress on certain details or by cautious omission of others. Thus a character is arbitrarily constructed, taking the place of the man to be understood and explained. A human life cannot be graphed, whatever people may say, by two virtual perpendiculars, representing what a man believed himself to be and what he wished to be, plus a flat horizontal for what he actually was; rather, the diagram has to be composed of three curving lines, extended to infinity, ever meeting and ever diverging.
Marguerite Yourcenar – *Memoirs of Hadrian*[23]

I am writing with great effort, with tension and dread. Each word is a burden capable of crushing me if I don't find its sense and place. I can't understand what will come out of it, why I drag myself among these events, why am I so

23 From *Memoirs of Hadrian*. New York: Farrar, Straus and Giroux, 1963. Translated by Grace Frick in collaboration with the author.

frightened of Death. I am writing in order to postpone it, to lie to her that she has to have more patience with me. I write, although with the feeling that I don't have anything to say. For tens of years I have only discovered questions without an answer. Fear, hunger, waiting, love and the other states of feeling were useless since I could not find any sense in them, a deep motivation, not even now. I am because I am. I lived because I lived. My life, composed of tens and hundreds of saved, read, assimilated lives, or even lives stolen from others, squeezes along with difficulty in the shadow of questions. I am writing stubbornly, allowing the events and the people to develop as they wish. I cannot understand why so many strange connections are made between events, what precise importance they have, and where they want to take me. I feel like a mundane, powerless spectator who watches, defeated, a film in which it is impossible to intervene. However things are, it is clear to me that nothing can be repaired, changed, understood. Emotions can't measure an old, ruined organism, which has no future. I mean an organism which feels more like a punishment. To end by my own will this torment, would be the gravest act of disobedience to the Creator. I should write what I feel, to describe the fire that tortures me, but I have no words. I don't have the necessary force, I only have states of feeling without a name, suffering without a name, fears without a name and a scream inside me drowned in the soul. The organism no longer replies to commands; between it and the will an impassable chasm opens. The soul is whole, alive, lucid, it has needs, and desires. The flame is unchanged, but the wax of the candle is almost finished. I am not glad to be alive, but I lament pathetically the fact that I will die. I know only too well that everything progresses towards death, towards being extinguished, but, no matter how strange it might seem, I am not used to the thought that I, too, will die. I often look at the starry sky and its galaxies, aware that many of them are dead, and that their light continues to come to us just like the reminiscences which can no longer be held in memory. What do they want to tell me? Why these ones and not others? I must find sufficient strength to vanquish my fear, and to accept the unacceptable.

> *"What a small portion of vast and infinite eternity it is, that is allowed unto every one of us, and how soon it vanisheth into the general age of the world: of the common substance, and of the common soul also what a small portion is allotted unto us: and in what a little clod of the whole earth (as it were) it is that thou dost crawl. After thou shalt rightly have considered these things with thyself; fancy not anything else in the world to be of more weight and moment than this, to do that only which thine own nature doth require; and to conform thyself to that which the common nature doth afford."*[24]
> Marcus Aurelius

Darius's account: Father's cousin, Alexandru, nicknamed Boboc – duckling – because he was the youngest of three brothers, had a beautiful house in the village, not far from the church, but during the war he had enlarged the cabin in the woods and, step by step, had also built a barn and a stable into which he had moved his fowls, animals and everything he possessed that he held most dear. The permanent

---

24 From *Meditations*. Project Gutenberg, Available online at http://www.gutenberg.org/files/2680/2680-h/2680-h.htm

requisitions, the mad order to concentrate youngsters for the front, and to assemble everyone who was able-bodied for labour, and, particularly, the fear of what might happen once the Germans and Hungarians withdrew, had compelled him to be prudent. The road to the cabin was difficult and, apart from himself, it was only rarely travelled by those who had run away from conscription, or by their wives when they brought them changes of clothes. I slept there from spring to autumn. In the gorges nearby a good part of the village was hidden, because the front was near and people were afraid of retaliation from the forces of occupation. I had laid down a long antenna and our poor "Marconi" radio set, a strange contraption with the speakers on the outside, was working non-stop, to the joy of those who needed courage and hope. Boboc took care of me, as I had run away from the front and I was spending the time gathering strength; but I had to tell him, in exchange, if other radio foreign language stations, broadcast the same information as that from Bucharest. After the ceding of Northern Ardeal, he had lost faith in the sincerity of the national station; but step by step the cannon and heavy bombers announced the same things to us, the liberation seemed close. Until that time I had to hide from people, so that neither Ella nor the local authorities should learn I had come back. It is true, I had not dared to go home either, although I could not take my mind off the little girl. After I had slept sufficiently and rebuilt my strength, I tried to have a discussion with father who, terrorised by the thought of forced labour, spent a great deal of time here, at Boboc's. I could not hide from him that I had seen Ella and, considering the preparations he made for me, he didn't have it in mind to be endlessly silent either. He wanted me to get used to the truth that my wife was no longer the same as I had left her and that I should take whatever decision I found appropriate while fully in possession of the facts. I was the first to break the silence which encouraged him to tell me openly all he knew and what he believed.

"I was not opposed to your marriage," father told me, "although I felt that you would not stay together for long. But it was not my opinion that was important. I could be wrong, like any other man. Yes, Ella is a very beautiful woman and you cannot keep her kind only around yourself. They escape, they are curious, they think nobody can resist them. But you were too intoxicated and it was not my business either. I was thinking that, in the end, you would run to Romania and from over there, with the money of your father-in-law, you would find the best solution, the country where you would stop. Especially because the front was coming this way, with the communists and all."

Although father talked a lot about the world in which he remained, in the end I had to recompose his story and that of Ella from fragments. He once told me that after her parents fled, Ella was left with three servant women, and, of course, with Alois, about whose business around there I knew nothing for a long time, until I managed to make the acquaintance of one of the girls, a smart peasant from the neighbouring village, who helped me understand Ella's suffering and complications.

"Immediately after you were sent to the front, Ella fell into a state of depression. She didn't do anything, she cried, she walked around desperately in the house, not knowing what was happening to her and to the world around.

Alois informed her parents, and they advised her to leave everything to him and to run away to Romania, but she refused. She had not forgotten, not even at that time, the things that had happened when she tried to cross the border clandestinely together with Darius. She then followed another piece of advice: she was a doctor and she had to practice her profession. The colleagues and the sick people with whom she was going to come into contact could not harm her, and, by working, time would pass quickly and thus she would bear more easily the suffering of the separation. Her father had asked her to leave Cluj immediately, to find a position as far away as possible from the big towns, where anything could happen, and Alois was, as usual, the person instructed to accomplish his orders. How well Ella's parents had known Alois before they left for Romania is hard to say. In any case, nobody would have suspected a facet so different to that he had shown until then. The boundless euphoria that possessed him immediately after the Hungarian administration was installed happened to be, among other things, an unexpected manifestation of his. The kind man of other times, the conscientious, precise employee who had not had any opinion besides that of his boss, now tried to know the newcomers, to befriend them, and, as far as possible, to enter their good graces. Being a well-known character in town, his gesture – made on the day the occupation forces filed past the stand where the new officialdom stood – did not pass unnoticed. He was among the first to spit on the two bishops, Orthodox and Greek-Catholic, who had been forced to be spectators as representatives of the Romanian population, at the parade of the unopposed winners. One day, he came home accompanied by a Hungarian counter-information officer who, without beating around the bushes, proposed to Ella that she should work as a camp doctor in Someșeni, a locality near Cluj. In some blocks which used to belong to the Anti-aircraft Defence, they had organised a camp where they interned the communists, in particular, but also various members of religious sects. It was there that Darius had also stayed for a while, a sufficient reason for her not to listen – even out of politeness – to the officer's arguments. Although he had left the house very irritated, he returned after a few days. The proposals he made to Ella were unacceptable: doctor in the camp, doctor at the front, or sent to labour in Germany.

To all these, Alois added another one – crossing into Romania clandestinely. The memory of her husband's tragedy, in which Alois was present, had evidently made her refuse the proposal. Especially since, due to the numerous successes of the Jews, the number of border patrols had been increased. On the other hand, it had seemed strange to her that she was given the opportunity to choose, in circumstances where the army of occupation, as well as the administration that had come into being overnight, didn't step aside from anything. They sent people to the front or forced labour, they claimed fortunes that had never belonged to them, they intimidated in any manner and by any means. In the end, scared by the categorical tone of the officer and also convinced by Alois, Ella accepted the variation that gave her the right to stay in her native town and, of course, in her own house – doctor in the prison camp."

"From closer to closer," Alois encouraged her. "No camp lasts forever. And then, after you know the new masters, you might hope for a transfer to some clinic, and, you know too well, parents who ran away to Romania plus your Jewish blood are not exactly the best calling cards!"

She was greeted by the officer almost with the same words, on his third visit, when Ella decided to accept the job in the camp, about which she knew nothing, not even its appearance.

"Have you heard about the Party of Peace? Does it really say nothing to you?", the officer also enquired. "According to the information we possess, Mr Carol, your father, supported this party with some serious sums, and, as the communists hide under this name, you have the opportunity, in the camp, to find yourself in the line of the family, and continue to help them!"

A little while after Ella was compelled to accept, Alois left her for an important position in the town's administration, the factory and the fortune of the Carol family being left in the hands of a German, who, because of extreme sight defects, was not apt for the front or for digging trenches. Ella had thought of Alois as an ordinary family man, an obscure employee of her father's, instead of as a single man, even if he were older than most, and this had been a costly mistake – that was the opinion of the woman who knew only too well the relationships in the house. Ella's encounter with the camp and with the investigators, led by Juhász András, terrified her, but she could not turn back, as she was constantly reminded of her parents' situation and especially about her Jewish blood. How she got to tolerate and then to love Elemer Marton, the counter-information officer, the woman could not understand. Fear, was the woman's opinion, but also beauty – since he was a tall, well-made man, with a black moustache, carefully trimmed, and with eyes that would have melted the strength of any woman. In the end, she stopped receiving him with loathing, obliged to submit to his caprices, but with much affection, giving him to understand that she belonged to him without reservation, although she knew that the officer had a wife in Budapest.

When she came to the countryside in order to see her daughter, Ella told Darius' father what went on in the camp, as if she was exonerating herself in front of her husband, but she had never talked about Marton.

"I think that I will soon have a nervous breakdown," she said to her father-in-law. "A huge military barracks, big rooms, with tens of windows. Empty walls, and no trace of furniture. Men and women altogether, many acquaintances and friends of our family, sitting one near the other on piles of hay arranged on two rows, among which soldiers walk incessantly. Their eyes followed me night after night, hoping in vain that I could help them or at least bring them news about their families. After a while, sympathy and hope transformed into hate. Nobody is allowed to talk, any look, to the left or to the right, is punished by violent kicks with the foot or with the rifle's butt. At the most insignificant attempt to talk I could expect any punishment, even that of taking a seat near them, on the straw. Investigations are terrifying. The handkerchief or the socks stuffed in the mouth, and the prisoners, lying on their bellies with their legs bent in order to be beaten on the soles with the rubber truncheon. Then beatings over the palms of the hands, with the same truncheon, until they faint. After some buckets of cold water thrown on top of them, the investigated man or woman will come back to their senses, only for the beating to continue with a chain, people being forced to run around a circle drawn with chalk on the floor until they fall again. Others are hung by their feet, their heads down, and savagely beaten with the ox-vein whip, and it is not just a few, in one stage of torture or another, who are beaten over the testes with a conductor's baton until they lose consciousness. My role is to tell the bruisers when to stop and to minister to the wounds left by chains and truncheons. Who is not afraid of such treatment? Especially now, when people are picked up from the street and taken to the front or to labour in Hungary and Germany. You would do anything, just not to be sent here!", Ella confessed, excusing herself.

Her fear was understandable. Resistance to torture is different from one person to another and, seeing daily what she saw, Ella's nerves naturally gave up. Hoping that, in the end, I would understand her and I would forgive her, which seemed normal to him, father incessantly found excuses for her. War destroys everything, lives, families, loves. Those who have the strength will look forward, those who don't will continue to lose. The most serious argument was implied: the little girl. We had to reconcile for her sake, we were not to blame for the world in which we lived and, anyway, after a while, oblivion falls on everything.

At the same time as the arrival of autumn, military planes and the pounding of cannon, increasingly stronger, announced the approach of the front. Radios were fixed only to the frequency Romania, which had turned its weapons[25] round, and the fury of the occupation forces was fiercer than at any other time. They started to arrest priests and local

---

25   Romania switched sides against Germany on 23 August 1944, when the pro-Germany government led by Marshal Ion Antonescu was deposed by the young King Mihai I.

notables who were going to be taken away as far as possible, to Hungary and Germany, to gather the crops, to harvest turnips and sugar beets. One night, the gendarmes with cockerel feathers disappeared from the village, and then the administration also vanished. Because of all this, I did not go home, fearing they might return or that, in the retreat, they would make many victims and great destruction. My mother and daughter had stayed in the village, but thieves and deserters were not rare visitors and, aware of this, father slept in the barn, his pitchfork at the ready; at dawn he went to Boboc's again. It was strange, the image of Ella and her lover did not fade and, as much as father urged me towards wisdom, the more her guilt increased in intensity. I had thousands of arguments aimed at forgiving her, and all of them were valid, but after I told myself that I forgave her, that it was the only real and reasonable solution, my feelings were running amok, contradicting me. I was back again to where I had started, to that scene of love-making, to the passion with which she gave herself to the officer, and my gaze and mind darkened:

"I must kill him. For as long as he is alive, I won't be able to take a step towards forgiveness."

I imagined some scenarios, and, at the same time, I felt I had entered a different world, with other rules than those of the front. The enemy was no longer somewhere in my proximity – the unknown you had to kill in order to live , he didn't have a face, a biography, you didn't hear his breathing and you didn't smell him; you fired madly, without looking into somebody's eyes, without seeing their suffering. Even if he was presented to us as a monster whom, in the name of humankind and future, we needed to get rid of, the enemy was also a human being and, in the same way as ourselves, his courage was stimulated by his superiors. In the short period of military instruction, the same voices ordered us to imitate the leap of a frog, with the suitcase in our arms, or they yelled at us: "Enemy planes in the dorm room!", to which we needed to fall flat on our bellies, compelled by the same weapons found in the hands of those who did not seem to know mercy and understanding. On the front, each hour and each day were gifts of which we had become aware, and we suffered the miseries for the sake of the life which had been spared.

I had condemned that specific officer, Ella's lover, to death; but I had also placed in the balance the possibility, equally rational, of being defeated by him. Curiously, I did not regret too much; my sorrow was a little tempered because I had the certainty that one of us was unnecessary. It was my duty to solve the problem. I don't think he cared about me: too insignificant compared to his position, from where he could dispose at any time of anybody, without being responsible to anyone. For him, it was probable that my wife was a passing adventure, a way of calming his nerves, which were already too tense because of the military defeats that did not stop. For me, however, Ella was everything, no matter how much I denied it. When I took the decision to kill him, I had been lucid and calm as if I was going to make a commonplace gesture which was going to normalise my life, my thoughts. The weeks since I had come home could not fill the immense void in my soul and, despite my efforts to forget her, nobody and nothing could seem to take her place. Not even drawing. Ella always existed and, at any moment, everything reminded me of her; each line of my countless sketches, my dreams, my gestures, my different expressions, the waves of warmth kept in my memory. Our past now also had another name: Daria. The idea of leaving the officer alive in the end, waiting for the imminent retreat of the Hungarian armies, did not satisfy me. He could always return, after the world settled down. As I had seen them in those moments of love, it was not hard to suppose that he too was contaminated by her and desired her with the same intensity. As a consequence, I did not foresee another way. Under normal circumstances, I would have provoked a discussion between the three of us; but now there was only one solution: death. His death. This is what I thought about, first of all, and, when the decision seemed irrevocable, I felt a strange transformation. I suddenly calmed down. I existed only in order to kill, with my thoughts subordinated only to that urge, and to it alone. No collateral project, nothing except the decision to kill him and the desire to stay alive. In the wake of this craziness I did not have the courage to confess to father. I could anticipate his reaction:

"For a woman? You are young, handsome, full of strength, you can choose another one, whoever you like. Or others. It wasn't you who gave him life, you have no right to end it!"

I felt as I had on the front, in Ukraine, when I was sent on my first mission of mine clearing: "Let us pray while we still have the time and while we're alive! Let's not forget that here a second mistake is not possible. Lack of attention and hurry mean death!", the sergeant that led us said. "Increasingly few return after each mission."

Attentive to the news broadcast on the radio, and especially to the increasingly loud noises of the cannon, I did not realise when summer passed and autumn started to takeover. On the feast of Saint Mary, the leaves of the poplars on the edge of the valley had started to rust and fall; then came the turn of beeches, and the sun was increasingly weak. Waiting for the Romanian army, announced by the few radios in the area, the village had taken refuge in a hidden valley watched over by two abrupt, precipitous banks, far away from the main road. Only the old women, old men and the young children had been left at home. Father was hiding during the day, and at night, as I was saying, because of worry for my mother and daughter, he returned home, carrying his customary hunting gun, which he had kept hidden up to that point. During one of those days charged with wait and anxiety, when the appearance of the Romanian army seemed imminent, father summoned me to see my little girl.

The Hungarian army and administration had left Cluj and, together with them, some of their fanatical supporters also left. About Ella he had not told me a great deal, merely that I had to think ten times before taking a decision. We had all our lives in front of us in order to wash away our sins and, first of all, a little girl who needed parents. It was good that I had escaped whole from the war. In other words, he suggested to me we should reconcile and I could not deny that I had deserted for her sake, for her sake I had travelled thousands of kilometres on foot, with her in my mind I had cleared mines, and, I had borne the unending rains and snows. She had saved me from depression and every kind of fear, which other people did not have the strength to confront. Any one of these things, by itself, weighed in the end heavier than the sin she had committed; but my units of measure were different and, no matter how hard I tried, they did not match the situation in which I found myself. My state of spirit was fluctuating: it depended on the moment of the meeting, of the first impression, of her reactions, which I could not foresee. We were separated not just by what I had been destined to see, but also by a confusing, long and turbid period of time. Going home, father warned me that Ella had arrived a little earlier in order to see her daughter, so, as a consequence I could not have suspected, in a matter of minutes, I would be – just as I had dreamed for such a long time – together with her. She had not been prepared either, so the surprise of the meeting was total.

"My God, you are alive?", Ella exclaimed through tears, but she did not make any move to show that she would like to embrace me. She just slid down near the chair on which she sat, continuing to cry heartbreakingly, with hiccups, in a way I had never seen her do before. The little girl followed her immediately, then my mother; only I and my father stood still as rocks near the door. I did not run to calm her down or kiss her, as may have been natural. It was impossible for me to move. I waited without knowing why, and time passed with terrifying slowness, everything had transformed into an unbearable tension, until father took the girl in his arms and, after he had made a sign to mother to leave the room, he took a long look at me, as if he wanted me to understand that he trusted my lucidity, my power to take the wisest decision.

Unfortunately, I wasn't capable, even after their departure, of making the first gesture, as would have been proper. In my mind, I was looking in vain for the woman from before, the young woman in the train who barely dragged her suitcases, or the woman from whom I had never been separated in any circumstance. Now, bizarrely, she seemed even more beautiful than in my memory: the features of her face, the reflections of her hair and the deep, dark eyes were livelier, they allowed themselves to be discovered immediately, and her body was even more accomplished, provocative even.

She was and she was not Ella, the one I had known with all that was hers, but I did not have the strength to go closer to her. I waited, pinned to the ground, until she stopped crying so noisily, but even afterwards, when, her head lowered to the ground, supporting herself on the chair, she managed to get up. Of course, I should have helped her, but it was impossible for me. I continued to stay stiff, out of time, deserted, incapable of concentrating, even on the light that flooded the windows. In the few weeks since I had come home, I had imagined all the situations in which we could have met, even this one. I had thought of all of them, it was merely the powerlessness that tried me now that I had not foreseen. After another period of confused waiting, she came back to herself and, after she had wiped her eyes for a long time, she looked at me somehow accusingly:

"When did you come?"

"For some four months," I replied in a whisper.

"And you haven't felt the need to come looking for me or at least to send me a sign that you were alive?", she enquired in a tone which was slightly firmer.

"It was impossible for me."

"I came a few times to see my daughter."

"Yes, I knew."

"And a sign you were alive, at least this?," she insisted, increasingly confused. "Help me understand you!"

"You really want to know?", I replied, to which father intervened in an appeasing manner:

"You have not seen each other for long and I think that after this long, bitter time it is not the right thing for you to start arguing. We go to set the table. I would like us to rejoice that we've escaped whole from the madness that has passed over us!"

My parents retired, looking worriedly behind them. I felt their pain, and it helped me, in some way, to realise that I could not stay there to the bitter end, in the middle of the room, avoiding her eyes, trying hard to get used to the strangeness of the situation in which we found ourselves. In the end I sat on a chair. A short while after that, Ella also sat down. We were finally, after such a long wait, face to face, without having touched each other, without having smiled – even falsely and automatically – incapable of miming the joy of seeing each other again. Each one of us was searching for the shortest road to the other, in order to free ourselves from everything that had separated us.

"And so many months without sending me a single sign? Does the little girl at least know you are her father?"

"She doesn't know," I replied as naturally as I could.

"Not even her? But what kind of man are you?", Ella revolted.

"I know too well how I am and who I am. Just like you, moreover. But I have the feeling that the individuals who are meeting now are not the same as the ones that were before."

"But what could these people tell you that makes you afraid of me? Could you think that I, your wife, would betray you?"

"Yes, I could. My parents didn't tell me a great deal about you, just that you are well and that you practiced your profession. But what I saw myself, with my own eyes, was enough. I deserted from the front and I risked everything. I trod thousands of kilometres night after night, hungry and with death in my soul, but with my thoughts only on you. Don't let me tell you how many landmines I had to dig with my bare hands, or how many roads I wandered like

269

a haunted animal, among holes and corpses, through how many camouflaged rail stations, through how many trains of horrors, with carriages pulled on blocked sidetracks. Nor about the people I could have killed if I had sensed the smallest hostility coming from them. I abandoned the idea that I was human on the day I entered the barracks, and during the moment we started to do that parade step, *diszlepes* or 'Enemy planes in the dorm!'. We weren't sent on the front to fight, but to die, to be killed by other people. I entered the house thinking that I would do you a great joy, and I assisted, without wanting to, the most painful sequence of love in my life. You and a man with a moustache. At the end, when you walked him to the door, you were surprised only that you'd forgotten to lock it. If you'd done it out of fear, under threat... but you gave yourself to him with passion, just as you gave yourself to me at the beginning of our story."

I think that I never uttered some words with more difficulty, but I was not sure she was listening to me, as Ella was crying with her face buried in her hands. I was convinced that as soon as I ended my recital, she would leave without looking back. With all this, I no longer felt the need to explain myself, to make appeal to nuances. I was pretty much at peace that I had managed it and that was that, but to my surprise, Ella recovered quicker than I expected and mowed me down with her gaze.

"You have convinced me, I remember how it was with the door," she said. "You are right, that time I did it with pleasure, but you have no reason to be surprised. Or, to be more precise, with despair. I wanted to forget, to lose myself, to die. I was living out of inertia. I no longer had friends, close relatives, the people who courted us and whom father had helped were now avoiding us. From the position we had, in the centre of attention, defended by money and by the authorities, I woke up alone, helpless, even attacked. Nobody believed that I had no way of helping many of our friends who were in the camp, apart from little nothings that would hurry the healing of some wounds. As for Marton, the first time I was purely and simply roughed up... a blow in the middle of my head... then I did it out of fear, under the threat of the camp; but afterwards I deluded myself, even if it seems absurd, that I was doing it with you. After all I got no news, although other people who were on the front communicated now and then. The families were notified about those who disappeared too."

"I had deserted, I had no means."

"Yes. I thought of everything, but not of this," she admitted, continuing her explanations. "I told father about the story with the Jewish blood. Alois convinced him how grave, how great a sin this fact had become. Apart from this, the help given to the Peace Party – in other words, to the communists – also weighed heavily. It was a truth which was impossible to deny because the person who had transmitted the money to them, in order to buy the printing works, had been Alois himself. After that, he left us in order to become a great clerk at the town hall, and from there his tracks got lost in Hungary. Father asked me not to have regard for money, to run away to Romania, but I no longer had the courage. Alois had denounced us once before. Of course, people talked about all sort of clandestine connections, but I no longer trusted anyone, since the man to whom father had entrusted all his business had betrayed us. I am convinced that I owed Alois, both for the story about the Jewish blood, which Marton also took on board, and your departure for the front. The officer had come to accommodate other officers in the house, with just one room being left to me, only for him to change his mind and to do the things which you saw happen. He'd chased away my servant girls as well, so that it would be just the two of us left, without witnesses, and, most important, without Romanians around, as he didn't trust them because they could inform their Consulate. There was a principle of reciprocity. Any aggression against a leader of the Romanians from ceded Transylvania – journalists, important personalities – automatically triggered the same treatment against their Hungarian equivalent in Romania. What's more, the man was also married, as I was to find much later, after the unpleasantness between us had become more blurred. I do not know what one could call the things I was fated to live. At night, my Marton would come, and during the day I was a spectator at the horrible beatings which a different Marton, Marton Dede, administered to the people detained in the camp. I had to tell them when to stop, or to revive the people who had been mistreated when they fainted. Of course, no-one listened to me but, despite the threats, I tried. I had many acquaintances among the people in the camp, and I was forced, powerless, to assist in their torture. In the end, I ended up being hated by all, because I could not manage to help them. Their suffering made me think about what could also happen to me."

With dread, she told me about all the methods of torture, about the infernal camps in which they kept, on a provisional basis, the Jews who were going to be sent to Auschwitz. Periodically, they summoned her there in order to certify some death, and, in the same way, as if by chance, her officer reminded her about her Jewish blood, although, after the brutalities of the first days, he started to behave more and more nicely to her.

"He inspired fear in me, as well. In fact, all of them inspired fear in me, and yet, his was the only voice which was more humane, and, when he no longer reminded me of my blood, he was delicate, tender and handsome. He was the only one to whom I could make an appeal, in case others discovered what blood ran through my veins. I wanted to commit suicide many times, but I thought of the little girl. As for you, I still did not feel you were dead, but a prisoner in some mine in Siberia. I brought Daria here, to the countryside, so that at least she could escape if they put me in those terrifying trains of death, or if fear and despair forced me to take my own life. I don't know why I haven't done it as yet. There are moments when fear, physical and psychological torture, force you to stop being responsible for your deeds. I have reached the point where I live in a town which will chase me away, dwelling among people I detest. They all accuse me, but nobody offered a finger to help me. Nobody felt obliged to say a kind word to me. Although I was born here, I feel more alone than in the most insufferable desert."

"And Marton?", I asked, stirred by the old thought of killing him.

"I don't know. He disappeared three days ago. Maybe he felt the need to see his wife, maybe he was driven by fear as well. He is a military man and he has bosses and duties. Anyway, he did not say anything to me. I don't know what could have happened to him. As you see, I have no luck with men," she was trying to joke, and at the same time mother opened the door carefully to call us to the table.

We both stood up instinctively and went to the dining room, followed by the puzzled gaze of my father, who did not know what had happened when he left us alone and could not deduce whether we'd taken any decision. Mother put Daria in my arms, but she got frightened and started to cry.

"It's father," my mother repeated, pointing with her finger at me; but the little girl, on hearing this word, stretched her arms to her grandfather, from whom she expected help. I did not have the courage to get closer to her, although my mother took care to underline our physical similarities, and not just those between the two of us, wanting to assure me I was her father, because that was what mattered.

Unfortunately, sorrow and despair had settled solidly between us, so there were moments when I regretted my return. Ella was right, in her own way. I had not discovered a lie in her words, or, to be more precise, I had not felt anything false, but in my mind and my imagination there was just one thought that remained. I was telling myself that I should be grateful to her because it was due to her that I was whole and home. Also it was due to her I truly discovered love. Or even more than love. Unfortunately, she could not propose anything, everything was confused, painful, nothing was connected. My mother recounted Daria's adventures, my father talked about the future, but nobody seemed to take into consideration the atmosphere of joy, sorrow, hate and confusion that floated above the words. Ella proved to be the strongest in the end:

"No matter what you chose, if you have chosen anything, you will at least have to come home, to your home, at least in order to pick up your clothes, because you cannot stay like this!"

It was at that point that I discovered myself in father's peasant clothes: trousers of a black, impermeable fabric, grey *suman* coat, made of wool, a cotton shirt with embroidered shoulder pads, which came out from under a wide, leather belt with small pockets in which there were not only the keys from the two houses, but also flint, flint steel and tinder which are necessary to build a fire when you don't have matches.

"Yes," I said to her, to my parents' joy, "you are right, we are going."

On departure, Daria looked at me with a little more curiosity, but didn't allow me to embrace her. Ella kissed her little girl and parents-in-law, after which she said to me: "if we hurry, we can still catch the train…"

Her words, spoken naturally, in a warm voice that seemed to come from somewhere in the past, made me feel emotional beyond measure. We did not talk about important things on the train. We talked about the landscape, the temperature, the late autumn and about the people who, a little more lively for being rid of the war, had recommenced the habit of going to the market. Baskets with food, hens agitated by the movement of the train and an oppressive smell of bad pipe tobacco. The time that had separated us, which had been so long, was interposed between us like an impassable wall. I remember – watching her from the corner of my eye, trying a reply to an absurd question: "When was I wrong: then or now?" All my adventures, and hers as well, had been concentrated on two feelings which alternated rapidly: rejection and mercy. I could have shown my superiority by forgiving her, and by trying to reconquer her. She had not lost her beauty – on the contrary, and the suffering she endured had added a shadow of sadness and profundity to her face.

Unfortunately, however, I realised I was not able to do

it, and instead of worrying about how to reconnect the threads, even if they were so distant from each other, I was more obsessed by Marton, and the sequence of events which increased my urge to kill him. I had not been capable of such a thing on the front, but now there was no law that could compel me to forgive him or to postpone my decision. At least, that's what I believed, although I was not too certain that, with his disappearance, the memory of the moment in which I took his life would not stay alive. Once we arrived in front of the house, we stopped instinctively, and, after we had looked at each other in confusion, Ella asked me to unlock the door:

"The key is in its place," she said, seeing me hesitate.

"Are you alone?", I asked, remembering Marton.

"Yes," she replied. "I am alone for the moment, my parents stayed in Romania, they were scared of a possible return of the front, but they should arrive soon. Marton, since it's he who preoccupies you, has run away without a single word of goodbye. Try and get used to the thought that it is our house. We must start from another beginning or separate like two lucid people who loved each other truly, without taking the madness around into account. We need to be tolerant, to look at each other with understanding and patience."

Despite her calm voice, and the certainty she tried to transmit to me, I stepped with dreadful fear, as I once did on the minefields, careful about any noise or suspicious move. I recognised every object. I relived the impressions of my first visit, when she had introduced me to her parents: the same obsolete décor, charged, stiff, uncomfortable. In order to gain time and not to meet her gaze, I took my jacket off and, feeling very inhibited, I entered the living room.

"I tried many times, thousands of times, if you will, to imagine the moment when we would meet again," she said with more assurance, "because not even in the most horrible moments of misanthropy have I felt that you were dead. I can now confess to you that I was afraid you might return an invalid. In fact, I imagined you in every manifestation, even without arms. Tell me, I whispered to you in my thoughts, and I will draw the line myself, I'll apply the colour. Describe the landscape or what you wish to paint and I will repeat it until you're satisfied. Dictate to me, I also whispered in my thoughts to Darius the invalid, and I will write the letters myself, or I will read to you in a loud voice the book that interests you, you only have to listen and to tell me what you are waiting for. We are a single being, it won't be hard for us. Only this meeting I failed to imagine. Because, in all the versions, the meeting began with a kiss, with tears and tender words. Of course, you have the right to consider me a liar, a wretched woman, a sinner, whatever you want, and I am. After all that happened to me, I could not stay clean, with an unblemished soul, the way I had started on the route the moment we met each other in the train. You don't understand that this is because that I was also afraid. I always lived under threats, without knowing, on the other hand, what was happening to you. I am not cut out of the fabric of a hero and I was very lonely. There, in the camp, I took care not to be seen crying, out of fear that I could be detained too. But at home I would cry like a madwoman. I was afraid to walk on the street because they could perhaps pick me up and send me somewhere, to some camp or even worse, because I might be attacked or even killed by the relatives of the people in the camp, at Someşeni. Maybe our love was not as strong, as intense as we believed, but it is hard for me to believe that, as much as it has been, it has trembled at the first difficulty. The experiences through which we have gone do not give us the right to lie to each other, nor to postpone that which must not be postponed."

"Yes," I admitted, "it is true, I do not doubt anything, but it is above my powers to reconcile my senses with logic. I need a little time."

"There's a few months since you appeared in the village, sufficient, I believe, to be able to take a decision, any decision."

"During all these months, I only saw you making love with gusto. Our gestures, kisses, caresses, and all I believed that belonged only to us – I saw you repeating them with your officer. I could not think of anything else but those moments in which I was watching you from the closet."

"I don't have much imagination, that is how I learned them with you. I was afraid he might be discontented with me. Can't you understand this? As it happened, I was glad he never opened a discussion about the little girl, he did not ask a thing about her."

Then, suddenly, she changed the subject, she asked about everything that happened to me at the front and on the road back, and I told her everything, in detail, even if it did not produce any pleasure. Suppertime also arrived, and while she set the gold-plated crockery, used only for festive occasions, as in the olden days, I walked though the other rooms, thinking that Marton could be hidden in one of them. I no longer wanted to kill him, but I asked myself if perhaps he might not catch me unawares in my sleep, thus resolving the dispute. When I returned to the living room, Ella smiled, understanding, and assured me that the Marton chapter was now closed for good.

"It would be madness for him to take the risk. He is an intelligence officer and he probably knows well how to defend himself. If he was caught, Siberia would be the closest destination, if not death. He simply ran away, without telling me a word. And then, he has a wife. I was only an adventure. Of course, I cannot convince you to forget, but you should think of what more we can do now. We have a child, in the end. And we are still young. Maybe, after my parents return, we can try to move to another town, without memories. Maybe even another country, if... here, I can no longer stay, everybody hates me because of the things that happened in the camp."

We ate in silence, quietly, concentrated on the plates, and after that I was invited in the bedroom of her parents. We were going to spend the night there, but before that she called me in order to check if the all doors were locked and if the camouflage curtains were closed. She probably wanted me to make sure that we were alone in the house. This gesture told me that she did not exclude the possibility that Marton had not left the town, either. I didn't tell her what I thought. I was content to follow automatically the old ceremony of preparing for sleep. In the olden days, after we had dinner in a solemn atmosphere, the servant girls checked our side of the house. They asked whether we had clean towels, whether the soap was new and sufficient, whether Ella's countless powders were in their place, with the last question – whether Mrs had need of anything – closing the evening. This time, all the objects of the house exuded a strange air of desolation and confusion. Incapable of taking any decision, it seemed best to give myself up to the will of chance, meaning not to make any gesture which I might regret afterwards. I followed her into the bedroom, where I found the pyjamas, as usual, folded on the pillow. Sat on the side of the bed, I was content just to wait, dressed as I was, while Ella lingered – again as usual – in the bathroom: but that evening not even the face powders had managed to hide the traces of the tears and the redness of her eyes.

"This is not how I expected our meeting to be," she said in a faint voice. "Sleep in another room if you want. You do not feel at home, I can see that. I have a single request: to let me lie at your side, like a thousand years ago, when I agreed that we should sleep together. I've been wishing for this since you left. After that, you are free to do what you think fit. And I the same."

I got undressed and Ella huddled into me sobbing out loud. I kissed her for the first time since I'd come back and, unexpectedly, although she had wanted it, she shook as if I'd forced her. I did not explain the rejection to myself, although even back at the time I first met her she had asked me to be patient with her as she had to pass a spiritual threshold which she never mentioned again. This time, I was the one who could not go further. She was the same as always: the same eyes, the same big, round breasts, the same lips. Nevertheless, each part of her body, all I had possessed and which had intoxicated me once, did not say anything to me anymore, and even repulsed me. The man in me no longer wandered the roads of the return, but seemed truly dead. I no longer squeezed in my arms the woman I had dreamed of such a long time, but the woman who, under my eyes, had slept with the officer, and my physical senses proved to be more cruel, more unforgiving than reason. She did not try to spur me on like she used to either. She probably felt that it was in vain. Between us there also was Marton. For the moment, he was the winner. We stayed glued to each other, without speaking, and, after we had enough of crying, we fell asleep. We woke up early in the morning with our sweat and tears frozen on our faces and, surprise, with my father-in-law sipping his coffee in the living room. He was so happy to see me whole that he appraised me with his eyes and seemed not to believe that it was me. For Ella he had great admiration: she had managed to survive in the maddest of worlds and, on top of that, she had also stayed beautiful. I went home, to the countryside, assuring them I would return in two days, but when I did return, determined for us to search for a road back towards ourselves, and determined to take life from the beginning, I was greeted, instead of Ella, by a letter.

My dear Darius,

I left, I don't know where I'm going, but I am certain you will appreciate my decision. The rejection I felt in each one of your gestures and in each word convinced me to do what I must. I want you to know that I loved you madly, that you were with me, no matter how strange it might seem to you, even when I was kissing Marton. I wanted you to find me alive, here, ready for us to see about our life. It was, I think, the only way to escape prison camps or forced labour camps of who knows where, in Hungary or Germany. That's how things looked like to me then and I do not think differently, not even now, when you have returned. If they had caught me running to Romania, the camp would have seemed more terrifying than anything. I lived in it and I can bear witness. Furthermore, they would have condemned me as well because of father's unhappy idea of helping the communists. Anyway, as a sign of my love, I leave Daria to you, until the time a corner of the world should wish to receive me and to allow me to find a life for myself. In our town I can no longer stay, even if (at least you have to believe me) I was blameless. Unfortunately, I was not prepared for the terror, aggressiveness and hate. I am not alone. Marton assumed the risk of crossing the front line in order to take me with him: he has documents for a country in Latin America, where we hope that we can at least get far from an unjust history and from the nightmare which, in these last years, was called life. Up to now, there has only been love, a blind and unconditional love for you; from today onwards there will only be life. God keep you and Daria in His care. I hope that, not after a long time, we can meet as two good friends, I even have the mad hope that we will love each other again, that all the blows we have taken will help us understand that love is also forgiveness. If the Lord on High united us, it will be also He who separate us.

I would be glad to know that you would have at your side a creature who will measure up to your power to love and understand.

Ella

Her letter, unexpected, was like a death. It was only afterwards, when I felt the pain of loneliness, the waiting in vain and the hole in my soul she left, that I realised how much I loved her. I would have forgiven her anything at that time. Love is validated especially in difficult conditions, but her pride and vainglory, and my jealousy and confusion, weighed much heavier. I think Ella did not forgive me, especially for the fact that I had sent her no sign after I returned home.

After some two years and a bit, I received another letter: this time, from Paraguay. She told me that Marton had left her after he was employed on a big estate together with some SS officers. She had become a nun, she was in a

Roman Catholic monastery which she wanted to leave if I would send her the smallest sign of life.

"I can cry and pray from anywhere," she wrote to me. "God is everywhere, and monastery life convinced me that even here there are rather more humans than saints, with the same qualities and defects. It is not what I had imagined and, in the end, it is impossible for me to give up on life. I am not made for loneliness and meditation. Nor for unconditional obedience. There is such a loneliness here that it makes my ears ring. But it was here, once I was left only with myself, that I discovered the wretched pride that tested me when I was so stubborn as to give up on you and the little girl. Your behaviour, your somewhat natural reserve determined me to run away. I ran away, but I did not believe I was going to get so far. Nor did I believe that, wanting to punish you, I would punish myself. Despite what you saw, I always thought of you, and I never stopped loving you, even if I did not know whether you were alive or dead. I was afraid. And I wanted to live. To wait for you by any means and no matter for how long. I'm staying here for nothing if I can't do anything except always think of you two. What kind of mother have I been? How does the earth still bear me? Even if Daria would forgive me, I know only too well that I don't deserve it. I cannot imagine how you are, what you are doing, how you bore my disappearance."

The remembrance of the little girl tormented her, but also the doubt that after such experiences we would still be able to forgive one another. Unfortunately, she did not write the address of the monastery or anything else. I only knew the country, which seemed little enough to test the enormity of the ocean with my finger. At that time, that unfortunate night, it had been difficult for me to forget the affair with that particular officer, and then I did not forgive the fact that she had left me with such ease. After a while, just like a flower that appeared in the most repulsive heaps of dung, her face at the beginning stayed there, the face from Berlin frozen in my drawings and, later on, when lack of money forced me to paint churches, in all the icons that needed a female saint.

Daria allowed herself to be convinced, in the end, that her mother had died and this type of death connected us intensely. We became very good friends because our wounds had the same origins. We felt alone in a sick world. My parents-in-law became distant from us, step by step, and when communism started to take root they left the country for good. Some maintained that it was for Israel, others that it was the United States, but I think they chose Germany – first, because they spoke the language, and second because the products of my father-in-law's factories were orientated towards that country. If I had maintained the connection with them, I'd have probably been the inheritor of a great fortune and could have re-established the connection to Ella; but, like ice floes, we progressively distanced ourselves, until we ignored each other completely. The truth is that I could never forgive the fact that, in some way, they thought Ella was right, agreeing for her to leave with Marton and, later on, because they neglected Daria. I had to see for myself and check through my own experience that everything starts beautifully in our country and ends horribly. So it was with the peace after the war. And the same with my life. Once I saw myself alone, meaning without Ella, I started into the forest and I yelled until I lost my voice. Defeated, I dropped to my knees and I cried in despair: "What did I not understand,

Lord, to make me keep on being vanquished? Who else do I need to lose? And why? Have I lost the way so much that I am no longer capable of understanding what is happening to me? Why did you punish me, Lord, with so much loneliness?"

"Those who are born will die,
and the dead will live.
The living will be judge.

Reality does not mistake,
does not forget and does not take sides,
and does not allow itself to be bought.
Everything is as it should be, there is no escape.

Against your will you are formed,
Against your will you are born,
Against your will you live,
Against your will you die,
and against your will you are destined
to give a judgement and accounting for your own deeds.
So continue."
Rabi Eleazar ha-Kapar – *Pirkei Avot* [26]

"The pain of life is much stronger than the interest in life. This
is why religion will always hold the balance over philosophy."
Vasili Rozanov – *The Apocalypse of our Times*

"Fight as though fight served for something; work as though
work served for something".
Bhagavad-Gita

---

26   From the online version of *Pirkei Avot*, published by Chabad.org.
http://www.chabad.org/library/article_cdo/aid/5708/jewish/Translated-Text.htm

"We're done with laziness, with papers and books," Mara said to me with the air of having only just discovered how much my poor papers inconvenienced me – in this desperate, final confrontation with myself. "You have come here to climb the mountain, not to laze about. When winter comes, I shall declare that it's alright to read! Because we'll have nothing else to do. The wind and the frost are hard to endure, so we'll stay in the house with a lit fire and hands on our weapons because of the wolves. But, until then, we have to gather grass for the animals, to feed the pigs and the chickens. And, before everything else, you have to get used to making an effort." Without giving me the time to hesitate, she placed a jersey on my shoulders and offered me her father's old gun.

"For the unforeseen, but also for my priest," she whispered to me in the most serious manner possible, pointing towards the east, where, by the by, there was also the mountain... that mountain. "Old man," she said with the air of sharing a great secret with me, "I am not joking, you know I have no-one, but really no-one, and I won't ever forgive myself if I don't take care of you. I have looked at you with attention and I could swear there is absolutely nothing to stop you being healthy! You have muscles showing, your skin is taut..."

"Nothing besides the age," I replied in all sincerity. "At my age, I have nothing else to wait for, apart, possibly, from dying suddenly, in my sleep, without any torments. It's almost as if all my desires are reduced to this. Of course, I should have kept silent, you are at the age where it's hard to understand true pains and fears, when everything ends: days, energy, projects. Only the desires remain to torment you and to make you understand your own powerlessness."

"Stop the whining," she said, probably unhappy that she

could not find another answer, something to contradict me. "There are other joys, too," she continued. "Seeing the grass, the mist, the fawns, the birds of the skies, the sun when it raises... the ants. Long ago I would sit for hours on end to watch as they built their anthills. We have to rejoice in what we've been given. Mother showed me the leaves and took me to the places where the edelweiss, the queen's flower, grows. These are idiocies, you will say, but things are not quite like that."

"Of course everything can appear to be idiocy in front of death," I said, speaking more for myself than for her. "It's not good to count the days you believe you still have to live – as my father used to preach at me. It might be that the Lord will give you fewer if you try to set deadlines to His will. Death is a mystery which we don't have either the mind or the power to figure out."

While talking to her, one of the nightmares I'd had before leaving home came to my mind. I was in the dining room, at the table, together with some of the ever-present friends of Dan, my son. We laughed a lot, as we were joking about politics, and in a milieu of psychiatrists it's hard to find any politician normal, or any idea which can't be interpreted. Claudia had assumed the duty of serving and, attentive to her gaucheness, I decided to help myself to water, which was not being shown much favour in its competition with beer. Suddenly, while I made my way to the kitchen, after my first steps, I had an absence, a hesitation of a few seconds, and at that moment I said to myself, defeated: this is the end! I didn't have the strength to oppose it. I thought with infinite curiosity about the following sequence, when, according to the things I'd read long ago, I was going to see my entire life again. Instead, an immense emptiness took hold of me, accompanied by dread. Indeed, words couldn't help me, because far from being able to suggest at least the things I was feeling in those enormously dilated seconds, the heat, the dread, the need to ask for help – they proliferated exasperatingly, but they stopped in my throat, as if I'd forgotten them, and only the cold, abundant sweat had a name; it's simply that I could not pronounce it then. After another second, during which I had the impression I was falling slowly and certainly into a void lined with total silence, I felt a wave of warmth followed by the terrible revolt of each cell, of everything I was, but which I had not taken into account until then. It was a heave of my organism, a storm, a kind of being pulled from the void, an effort to stop the fall. I could not realise whether I was closer to life or closer to death, in any case I had reached the boundary between the two in the moment when they confronted each other with obstinacy. I looked around, in the hope that somebody would eventually see me and give me a helping hand, but they were far away, unmoving, as if frozen in an ancient photograph with sepia tones. I then felt something solid which stopped my fall. I would find out later on that it was the wall to which I'd glued myself and where, absurdly, I was waiting for help. In fact, time had disappeared, it was neither later nor earlier, or, if time still existed, everything was happening in a second that was dilated to the maximum, over which dread had stretched in a suffocating manner, and this event had another name as well, maybe the only true one: death. Each nuance of dread surpassed my powers of endurance. The devastated and vanquished spirit waited for help from a terribly fragile organism, but help was delayed dangerously, and I knew where I found myself, I perceived the line between life and death, but also their insistence on taking me, and nothing depended anymore on my own will. I then felt a strong hand on my chest and another one on my back and, in that space terrorised by panic, Dan's firm, baritone voice came through to me: "Father, what's wrong with you? Come and lie down!" and after I felt myself to be helpless in his hands, there came another order to Claudia: "Quick, a glass of water and the blood pressure monitor!" Lying on the bed with a cold compress on my forehead, placed there in a hurry by Claudia, I rediscovered the faces of those at the table looking at me worriedly, and the physician in me felt the need to calm them. "A panic attack," I told them. "A warning, maybe. Another world, another reality, which you have no way of grasping."

My blood pressure had calmed down, my heart as well, so that I only felt exhaustion now and the need to sleep, but sleep terrified me, thinking that I could fall into that void again, that the panic could return. Also, in parallel with the looks from the people who continued to observe my reactions, I rediscovered the true colours of the objects around, and the feelings without a name I'd had earlier. The panic and the obsession with death retired slowly to a space in my soul in order to wait for another, more propitious moment. Because the people who looked at me with patience were physicians, I could only get them back to the dining room by proving that I had come back to myself, especially since they did not even suspect the moments through which I had passed. In any case, their presence made me feel uncomfortable, and created an increasingly insistent complex of inferiority. "You don't have to get anxious," I assured them, "it was a banal panic attack, which can't be mastered. With age, you find yourself facing impossible states of feeling, obsessions and terrors which all have the same banal cause: the closeness of death. You are alone in front of death, nobody can help you anymore, you have to look her in the face and, of course, you are afraid. I wrote some studies, I have read even more but they helped me with nothing, although I knew this is how things happen, this is the way you have to feel, that panic does not yet mean death."

Finally, in order to convince them that I was whole, lucid, and master of myself, I talked to them about the numerous authors who have researched, or at least circled, this subject. From Freud, Pierre Janet, Kierkegaard or Jankelevitch to lesser-known old names, from my distant student days, who helped me understand these states of feeling, such as Landsberg, Jacques Choron or Maurice de Fleury. I was trying to demonstrate to them and, in the same time, to demonstrate to myself, that I could master myself, that I had surpassed the moment, although my body, exhausted because of the confrontation, no longer answered to commands. I only felt thirsty, a terrible thirst, along with a fear of sleeping and of a new invasion of the panic.

Dan had understood the recent moment better than his guests: he asked me whether I wanted him to stay near me and, of course, I would have wanted it, as I felt his presence would diminish the fear of a new crisis; but, I don't know why, I preferred to lie to him, and, somehow, he knew it. "Claudia will stay for a while, only until the guests leave. She has to change the compresses, to keep you chatting. Maybe you will want something and your strength doesn't seem to have returned. But do you believe that it was only panic? Are you sure? I can take you to the clinic in order to make a general investigation."

"There's no point," I assured him. "It was just panic."

"And you don't believe that this has been enough for you?"

"We shall see," I said, putting him off.

Contrary to expectations, I fell asleep immediately, with the woman's hand on my forehead. She seemed to have freed me from the wait for another crisis, giving me something of her energy.

Nightmares steered clear of me that night, but I was tried by other ill-boding dreams which had haunted me on previous nights. I was running through foreign cities, without an identity and without a point of reference, searching for a room, for a space that would belong to me and where I could settle down. I was alone, as per usual, not a trace of people or other beings, everything was tiredness, waiting, disillusion. I would wake up exhausted, vanquished by the thought that the dream foretold the eternal night and rest that inevitably follow the search, the agitation. There would be the time, it seems, for me to get used to this thought but I can't. In fact, in the most unexpected moments, even when by chance I am visited by some happiness, there come to me absolutely insufferable sequences connected to that irreversible moment of death. How will it be? I would take all possible variants one by one, for example, the vital organs that could abandon me, and I would try to imagine that specific sequence. How will it be, what will I say, how will I act, will I try to look for salvation, for a postponement of death? More than a few times I would also bring into the discussion the variant of the suicide: poison, a bullet, the rope, the train. In fact, the solutions were numerous and, like any physician, a good connoisseur of this specific casuistry, I would comment on them with relative detachment because death did not seem imminent to me. Now, I avoid the subject as much as I can because it seems to me the time has now arrived.

I got dressed with care, with Mara watching over me, and we started haphazardly towards the Meteorological station from whose vicinity I could cover the entire area with my eyes. I walked with small steps behind Mara, who was more or less hurrying, as if she'd proposed to herself to reach some place as quickly as possible.

"What do I actually want from this woman? Alone, on a mountaintop, far away from the world. What would be immoral, after all?" I asked myself, looking at her profile, after which, with humility, I addressed to myself – in my thoughts – all sorts of reproaches. On the other hand, in their shadows the need to live gained shape with speed, a kind of painful thirst, an energy that seemed to come from the innermost depths of the mountain and, bizarrely, tended to contradict everything I knew about life and death. "What would be immoral, after all?" I repeated the question and, for a moment, I had the certitude that Teodora herself was there in front of me, with her provocative gait – inexplicable haste and slowness – with aggressive looks thrown at me followed by total detachment, as if she were alone, without a single care. Her hesitant walk betrayed her character abundantly: incapable of deciding whether, at the first stop, we should pass beyond the exasperating kisses with which our walks through the mountain's thickets would end. She always postponed that moment which, in reality, both of us wanted. Unlike Teodora, Mara was much more physically rounded out and her shape obliged me to forget the years, which separated us, and to ask myself questions which I barely dared to formulate. Was it a mistake that my story with Teodora remained unaccomplished? This is how I feel now. I am no longer satisfied by the thought that I was moral back then. Had she been satisfied with her family relationships, it would have been more than certain that she'd have denied me her meaningful smiles, the madness with which we kissed, and all those things which pressed us into being together. Fate seemed to be offering me another chance: what should I do?

I needed Mara's warmth, and everything that might take away from me the thoughts of death which followed me everywhere. But, at the same time, all known and unknown interdictions came tumbling down on me, and the confrontation between them made me hurry my steps, to be as close to her as possible. Bizarrely, it was not very hard, although the woman seemed to be in a hurry and walked without looking back or encouraging me in any way. I had understood that she wished to test my endurance and, in a way, I was glad and I did my best to match it because after this exercise, probably the first of the numerous which would follow, I would have the right to talk to her about my mountain, about what I had set in my mind to do. This trial was a success, at least in Mara's eyes.

"That's not bad, old man," she said to me after we'd reached higher than the Station, on a ridge whose climb had raised enough problems for me. "You would need more training till the top of the mountain. In any case, you show some promise, but, since we're talking of this, it would be the time for us to be sincere with one another, because there is quite a lot to talk about."

"I don't think you should suspect me of insincerity," I replied immediately. "But, if you have a criticism or if I transgressed without realising, do tell me! It's just the two of us, I don't know for how long, and we should shorten the distances between us."

"Do you have the impression I am hiding something from you?" she hurried to ask. "I am only hiding the things which you haven't asked. I'd also like to confess the fear that visits me when I'm thinking of you. I admit immediately that I am afraid to allow you on the mountain, although this is your dream. If you haven't managed it when you were young..."

"It's true, but I do have the right to try?"

"Even if you are aware that you don't have the necessary physical preparation?"

"Death comes either way. Here, in the bed, at home, in your cabin, somewhere on the road to the mountaintop."

"And why would you commit suicide? Because this is more or less the place you're circling. We are being sincere now, aren't we?" she threatened me.

"Yes. Maybe I won't die, meaning that I won't have the strength to decide on my own the moment when the end of the tragedy will come. I don't know yet. This is, too, an equally valid hypothesis in which I believe at times. Of course, I am afraid of diseases, of decrepitude, of paralyses, I think I've told you before. And I don't find enough serious reasons to drag myself through life either. My wife, my best friends have disappeared. I don't find any meaning. My relatives treat me with too much understanding. They make too many concessions to me. Above all else, the world I am living in is not my world, and it scares me. An assassin world dominated by packs of primitives who come tumbling on top of you, penetrate your mind, your way of being, under the blanket, in your bathroom and in the hiddenmost depths of the soul; and it compels you to be like it and if you can't, if you are not able, it destroys you. A standardised world. In this country or in the faraway lands where the devil's mother dwells, there are the same rules, same magazines, same manners, same schedule for all TV stations. Hate, sex, violence. As far as I'm concerned, it is impossible for me to stand its noisiness, its insensitivity and the spiritual muck in which it wallows. But it is a cheerful wallowing. It kills you spiritually, sometimes without your feeling it, without your singing or laughing. It seemingly protects your life while it kills you. My world passed away, or it has not come yet, and nothing makes me hope that it will come soon. I am sad, very sad and alone. A lonely old man terrified of death, this seems to be the summary of the story of the man who keeps you company. There is no going back, nor salvation, not even the chance to lie to myself. I am advancing in death with my eyes open. I am quoting from somebody, but I don't remember who. I am advancing but not with the appropriate dignity. I cannot be dignified, as I should be, and I can't manage to lie to myself either. Wherever I look, I discover her shadow and I feel her sinister breeze. I am closing my eyes and I am trying to pierce with my mind the night that will follow. I convince myself once more that the end is not a true end. I am acquainted with all the theories, I know all the paths of the spirit from Christian, Egyptian, Tibetan perspectives, I am up to date with scientific research connected to people who have been brought back to life – and yet my mind doesn't cross through this night, it cannot accept that there is a salvation, although my soul, and my senses tell me this. Were I not to have a mad confidence in the future, I should have died in the Revolution, at the same time as my wife and my daughter in law. It would have been enough to go out in the street. What did the future in which I believed passionately offer me? Squalor, material and spiritual wretchedness and a country led by pygmies, in which I can't find any purpose anymore. Freedom has become the most precious ally of the liars, the thieves and the impostors. People of value, those who mean something, live alone; the impostors live in droves, in packs. You cannot understand what life truly is when everything is forbidden to you: food, love, sport. Forbidden not by ideology or lack of freedom, but forbidden by biology, by the debility of a body that can no longer keep its soul intact. The feelings stay the same, the needs are unchanged, maybe they are even greater, more intense. What I lack is the power to satisfy them. In fact, there is not a great deal left from all that I once was. I am purely and simply a sentiment, and what once used to be called my body was transformed, in its turn, into sorrow. A fear and a scream. It is terribly sad. What is left to you, so it's said, is wisdom. But what can you do with it when nobody takes yourself into consideration? And especially in our country, where nobody is interested either in the past or in the future? Wherever you are, you drag behind you the world from which you've run away, the wretchedness that tormented you. The cogitations of the person in front of the guillotine. The guillotine of time, if you prefer a rather ridiculous expression. The definitive answer to all the perplexities and searches of a lifetime is the guillotine. To live out of a sense of humour, to see up to the point where the degradation, and decrepitude go. To probe the depths of pain? Not to surrender as long as you still have a living cell in you? Words. I don't know why I'm telling you all this, when, on the contrary, I should encourage you to enjoy life, a blade of grass, the gusts of wind, the clouds which – look! – threaten us with a storm. Your father taught me to fear those little clouds on the horizon."

As I continued to talk, Mara followed me with increased

concentration and, in the same time, astonishment. At some point I lost the connection with her, I simply did not care who I was addressing, but in any case it was not her. Anyway, I was convinced that after this episode the relations between us were going to change. I could not understand in what way, but it was absolutely certain they couldn't stay as they had been. I had proved myself weak and, strangely, it seemed I had entrusted myself to her, although I did not have the certainty that she'd understood what I told her in that moment, when I don't know through what mechanism, all fears and pains were transformed into words, and I would have spoken in front of anything: the trees, the ants or the savage beasts, the heavens and stones, the deaf and the blind. I was sorrow, only sorrow, just like old age is sorrow, after all. I felt as if I had broken free from the corset of all intellectual and moral restraints, from the saddest and most aberrant prison. I had become a sort of lava which had defeated the rigid constraints of the earth. From the moment I came here, to the cabin, I had the certainty that Mara expected some salvation from me, a resolution for the absurd situation in which she found herself and, lo, her possible saviour proved to be scared of life and death, powerless, vanquished. We were now only two fears, two despairs in an aggressive space periodically terrorised by devastating tempests, by fogs and wild beasts.

Her eyes had turned red, and she suppressed her tears with difficulty, although she tried to start joking: "What am I going to do without you, old man? I see you are fixated on death. Train a little bit more and I am coming with you on the mountain, whatever happens. I can no longer stay here. From the moment you turned up, panic enveloped me: I can no longer stay alone. And you don't know what it means, how each moments passes, how the winters and blizzards are, and how terrible it is to fight with the wolves or with all the kinds of bloody wretches who pop up around here at night time or when you don't expect it. I feed them, I let them sleep in warmth and, after they get better, what do you think they want to do to me? Since you don't want to live anymore, we'll die on that blasted mountain. I am not staying here anymore! Maybe some lost saint will find us up there!"

I had nothing to reply to her since I myself had triggered uncomfortable confessions, so, pointing at the little cloud that I feared, I started back to the cabin. "I don't think I'll have the time to return today," I said to her, and Mara smiled. It was the saddest smile I was ever fated to see.

"All life is punctuated by deaths and departures and each one of these causes great suffering which it is better to experience, rather than not knowing the presence of those people while they still existed. But each time our universe heals itself, and we also know that it will not last to the infinite either. In this case, we may say that life and death take us by the hand with firmness and kindness."
Marguerite Yourcenar – *With Open Eyes*

"Only to you, Death, our soul and our faith and hope turn, and our greetings!
Lady of Last Things, Carnal Name of Mystery and Abyss – caress and encourage the one who started on the search for you, but who does not dare to find you!"
Fernando Pessoa – *The Book of Disquiet*

I wrote: *panic attack* and, unexpectedly, the fear or the

disease with a name which I don't yet dare to write brought in my memory the face of Claudia, my son's lover. More correct: his concubine. In fact, not a concubine either, but an obsession, a chronic disease, impossible to heal. Brown hair, with blonde strands, big, black eyes, plump lips, big, provocative breasts, mini dresses in lively colours, red in the days when she is upset with Dan and he needs to know that she has bad days, turbid days, cold days, dry days, days with demons, days without demons, days of celebration, days of getting out in the world, days when she slept in our house and days for hiding in the house, days dedicated to aunts, uncles, distant cousins and close cousins, days in which she does not have any honourable dress worthy of going out in the world and, of course, days in which the stores bring new models. Of course Dan knew all the shortcomings that tormented Claudia, but he absolutely did not cotton on during some days when she simply disappeared. To Dan's reproaches, which were otherwise natural, she showed herself to be very revolted: "I can't bear being suspected! I have very bad days, too, when I am upset by my mother, my brother and, in general, the whole world. This can happen to anyone. Purely and simply, I am unbearable and, as a consequence, I do not wish to see anyone, so not even you. The feelings stay the same, it's just the fact that I can't stand myself anymore that keeps me away from you and the world in general. I sometimes try to punish myself because I only manage to disappoint everybody, because I am unable to master this impossible character of mine. It often happens for me to feel the need to punish you all for diverse insults and humiliations to which, without being aware, you have subjected me". It was strange that he never found her home during these black days, irrespective of what time he called her. "Her days with demons," her mother excused her, resigned, trying to leave him with the impression that she too was a victim of Claudia's nerves. After those obscure days passed, my daughter-in-law returned and did everything that she could in order to erase the impression that she had left. She did not separate from Dan, she overwhelmed him with attentions and, of course, she convinced him to go to sleep earlier after having given him, beforehand, the customary red wine that made him forget everything and not insist on the reasons which had provoked her demons.

"It's your madness to look in a person for something you know precisely that you won't find. I do not have secrets, but only needs and desires. Don't ask of me things for which I don't have a vocation. With me, you can make love for as long as your hinges hold up, you can go to shows, because I am decorative, I raise your male prestige, but don't ask sophisticated things of me. If you are jealous, I am sincerely glad, but you are not. Because of your suspicions, a furious love, like the one there was between us, may collapse into a bearable friendship."

Of course, I did not leave them with the impression that their story would interest me in any way, but Dan's exaltations and subsequent depressions could not leave me indifferent. In one way or another I had known all his loves following the death of his wife, but it seemed to me that he cared the most for Claudia, although she suited him the least. So it was not just one time that I asked myself whether the pain of not having her was somehow less than that of having her. What was more important, in the end: the life she gave him or the life she took away from him? A useless question, just like the answer, after all, although the jungle in which my son was lost had to be explored.

Dan had stayed friends with his former lovers, and some of them, although they had married, continued to visit him. Even though she had found out the truth about these friends, Claudia had a liking for them or, in any case, she did not feel disturbed by them, and with Natalia Georgescu, an extremely well-known paediatrician, she even got to be friends. She seemed to be attracted both by her humour and by the advice Natalia gave straight out, in a loud voice, without feeling embarrassed that I heard her, too:

"You need to set out your intentions, even if you don't tell them to him. And I would not advise you to do it yet. There will always be an even better man, although this is not a rule. My first love was an Audi, followed, at a close distance, by a Mercedes convertible, and only after that came Jean's turn. It was sufficient to see him for a few moments for me to start praying, all of a sudden: Lord, give me the strength not to fall in his arms! And what do you think happened? I didn't even have the time to say the prayer and I simply fell down! A true doctor, Jean gave me first aid. I told you before, I think, that I fall pregnant even if I place my overcoat in the wardrobe under that of a man, what more can I say if he takes me in his arms?! Unfortunately, my Jean did not invite me in his bed, as I would have wanted, but to the library. The reason was simple: he lived in halls of residence, there wasn't any place where he could take me. And you know how socialist morals used to be in those days. There could be a woman breaking into a monastery now and then, but it was impossible to do that in the halls of residence, and we did not have the money to live in town. Our luck was that summer also came, when the fatherland's forests received us with open arms. We couldn't take things to their logical conclusion not even in this way. Speaking for ourselves, we

301

didn't have anything to live on, what would we say if we found ourselves with a child? So all roads led to the library. That was where we talked, caressed each other, sometimes we would find a thé dansant, so that, without having intended this, willy nilly, we both discovered ourselves to be book people.

Later on, when we had the freedom to have sex, meaning after marriage, between me and the *British Encyclopaedia*, Jean rather chose the *Encyclopaedia*. It doesn't get pregnant, it doesn't ask for dresses or shoes, and since he cheated on me with the post-Freudians and the *Encyclopaedia*, why couldn't I find something according to the measure of my needs? And this is how Dan appeared. He immediately understood what I lacked. Books – I had as many as I wished at home! It was a simple, beautiful story, without complications and promises. And it ended the same way, without tears and sorrow. I found a younger man, because life is short and it is good to taste of all the fruits of the earth. Sometimes I propose to myself behaving as if nothing would be forbidden. Jean didn't cause me any problems: it was sufficient to ask him some smart question, or for him to have a scientific paper to finish or something new to read, and I simply disappeared off his radar. I could go to the theatre, or to some other man. I had the time to read or to see a film. I like to cry at bad and patriotic films. Sing a march to me or the national anthem, and I immediately exhaust my entire supply of tears. Unfortunately, the woman in me can't take being ignored for too long. After all, I told Dan the entire story about my young lover too: 'In case of need, don't avoid me and don't look around elsewhere too much either,' I encouraged him. 'With me, if that's what you want, you will always find a warm and well trodden path.'

With the younger one I mentioned things lasted even less time. He was too emotional, we had diverging opinions on the actual act and he was not that well-endowed either. Before me, however, I realised that he'd had a rich sexual experience. He had been kissed by a woman about whom people said that she was a whore! But I did not come back to Dan. Neither he nor I like warmed over meals, although we both know skills and, in bed, we were well-matched."

In the region of secrets, Claudia was situated at the opposite pole. She had nothing to recount. She had apparently lived an uninteresting life, under the sign of misery. When the conversation turned to her past, she immediately changed the subject: she had nothing to recount about childhood or adolescence, nor of the men she'd met before Dan.

"Everyone comes with their past," she explained. "No matter how much I look behind, I don't think there's anything worth being known. I made mistakes, like any girl my age. As for the rest, I passed exams, I had a scholarship. I had likes and dislikes, like any other female student. I learned very good English and French. I didn't like it in the educational system, so, for the sake of an income, I opened a translation office. I wanted to make money and to leave for the other end of the earth, from where I wouldn't return. I worried for my parents, so I had to keep postponing the project, but one day, when I won't be able to stand it any longer."

Her mother was a secretary at a school, the father – an officer in the firefighters, and her younger brother, Valeriu – Vali, as he was called, a mature student who accomplished with difficulty the requirements of a civil engineering college. There existed between the two of them a sickly solidarity that intrigued everybody. Claudia defended him in every circumstance, even against her parents, and, it goes without saying, she struggled to drag him out of every mishap. Between him and Dan there was a terrible antipathy, which is a natural occurrence, easy to explain even if you don't have any knowledge of psychiatry, but, lucky for both of them, they met pretty rarely. The constant feeling between Dan's son, Radu, and Claudia was again called antipathy. He was a top IT specialist and a hacker with the risk of getting imprisoned, and he did not lose any opportunity to pick on Claudia.

"*Măi,*[27] father," I heard him say, "do you think this mother of ours has anything to do with the kitchen? Does she love us like that, in general, because we are part of humankind, or does she have other, more domestic interests?"

"Go and wash your ickle hands 'cause baby's food has been ready for a long time now. Use the liquid soap 'cause it's also a disinfectant! And blow your little nosey while you're at it!"

"You are good," Radu admitted immediately. "You've had me. I'll come around again. I hope to find you in this house, because women nowadays like their domiciles to be as diverse as possible."

"Can you reveal a secret to me just now? From where do you know women so well?" Claudia enquired in a loud voice, so that everyone else would hear her. "The way I see you, you don't seem to have known too many of them. Have you by chance gone beyond number one? But let's pass over this. What is certain is that you will always find bread and butter in this house. For anything else, let me know one day in advance. I shall cook especially for you, irrespective of the domicile I find myself in! I can give you free consultations

27 *Măi* (also *mă, băi* or *bă*) - informal and discourteous mode of address, equivalent to some extent to "Oi!"

about the matters you don't understand!"

Radu did not like Claudia's challenges and he was content to look at her at length, without any other reply, and with a smile of contempt on his lips, after which he got lost in his exploration of the fridge. But Claudia, happy in her victory, decided to be more appeasing. He was, after all, Dan's son and she did not want to make him feel bad in any way. As a result, she went closer to Radu, willing to assist him, but she didn't have much success as he took a bottle of beer and came to me.

"How is the eagle of the alpine ridges?" he said, but, because of the hurry with which Claudia insisted on sending him away I did not manage to reply, and that was for the best. Back then, I was very fragile. I felt defeated because after such lows I experienced a terrible lucidity. I felt the passing of every second, and thoughts always arranged themselves so that I would go and meet the answer which, in that precise moment, I would not have liked to hear. Another I, ignored or chased away up to that time, chose the shortest road in order to tell me in one breath that nothing could be changed, reformed or saved anymore, that instead of dignity I had chosen the ridiculous, the fear. In fact, I didn't chose, but this is simply how things turned out, I only managed to be ridiculous. As in other times when I was visited by sickness or fear, I lost control of my body. I was deserted, it seemed, by everything that was matter. Or that was living and growing. I was left a mere sentiment, an immense pain or tormenting fear; very seldom a healing hope.

Claudia's hand had been unexpectedly accompanied by hope, as well, and, without wanting to do it, I thought that even Dan had his moments of weakness when a hand – hers or that of any other woman – was a bringer of reconciliation.

In fact, after the death of his wife, Dan's life had become very agitated. Sorrow had betrayed his fragility, and the refuge he found in his work, especially his research work, had not managed to heal him. I could have said that chance placed Claudia in his way, were it not for the certainty that nothing happens by chance.

One nondescript spring day, Dan had decided to go by the Surgery Clinic, where his friend, Dr Cazimir Tudor, was on call. It was a way of wasting his time because the deserted house and our shared housekeeper, Simina Bob, did not encourage him to hurry, especially since there were the same lye-like soups, which even I was exasperated by, waiting for him there. Back then, I had not yet moved in at Dan's, I believed in my health and I valued the peace which, not very long afterwards, I was going not to want anymore. Massive, silent, with an exasperating power to work despite her age, Simina had been my medical assistant, and my dialogues with her were very short and rare: "The Lord on High took him!" or "The Lord on High didn't take him yet!"

After she was pensioned off, her completely insufficient income had forced her to do other jobs as well, among them that of housekeeper. I had also reached a point where I no longer had the appetite to haunt the restaurants, nor did I feel like putting my things in order by myself, so Simina seemed a good and necessary choice. As a consequence, I recommended her to Dan as well.

Unfortunately, Simina Bob assumed the role of master, step by step, imposing on us her culinary preferences, and also the customs and rules of her own family. While Dan was less patient, I, for a change, had to endure her until the time when, forced by illness, I moved in with him. I would see Claudia there often, he had met her in the practice of

Dr Cazimir Tudor. She had come by herself, crying. She had a small injury at the temple, her blouse was torn, full of blood. She was very scared, always looking at the door, as if she were followed. She said, through her tears, that she had been assaulted on the street by an unknown person, a thief who tried to steal her bag and to tear the earrings off her ears. She had managed to save her belongings since, upon hearing footsteps, the thief broke into a run. She had not retained any details, the person had his face covered, a thing which seemed rather unlikely to Cazimir, and the spasmodic crying which followed after he washed her injuries made him whisper to Dan: "I think this one is part of your parish! Since we're lacking the patients now, see whether I'm wrong, because we have the time."

Dan knew his profession very well, and, with a little patience, he managed to establish a dialogue with her, although she had rather surprised him in the beginning. She didn't want to call a taxi, she didn't feel like going to the police and she didn't burn with the desire to leave the emergency room either. In the end, she agreed to be accompanied home, especially since they were both going in the same direction. My son was convinced that he was dealing with a serious person who'd had the mischance to encounter a thief in a badly-lit city, with few or lazy policemen. Unexpectedly, as she was nearing her dwelling, the woman's hesitations increased:

"How can my parents see me as I am now, covered in bandages and blood? My father is a military man and, as he is very stubborn, he'll wake the entire town up, he'll make such noise that he'll agitate the newspapers which are already desperate for scandals."

"So what then? Should we look for a hotel or do we stop

at some man's place? Because, with your age and beauty, it's impossible not to have a lover."

"I had one once," she admitted, "it's a story I'm right to forget. It was only when I became involved with him I realised I had no aptitude to be a wife."

"You can't stay in the street, anyway. Won't your parents get alarmed if you don't go home?"

"It's happened before. I have a bed in my office and, when I have a lot of work, I sleep there."

"In that case I'll accompany you."

The office was installed in an apartment situated on the ground floor of a new block of flats, a sort of filler among the handsome houses built after the first war, in a pretty good area, not far from the town centre. It was well arranged, new furnishings, paintings of good taste, nothing improvised, a sign she'd had enough money and that, ultimately, she was functional. She regained her confidence there, so that she got dressed quickly in a black, very sombre suit which she used for ceremonies and for shows. Only the bandage round her head struck a different note, as did, of course, the blue-black eye.

"There are many variants by which you can justify yourself in front of your parents: you slipped down the stairs, a cretin on a bicycle slammed into you, some painting fell on your head. You can invent anything, but the most plausible thing seems to be what you've told us at the clinic. I am a psychiatrist and, since we are here, alone, I would be interested in the truth. Knowing it helps you invent the most convincing lies."

"Do you somehow believe I've lied to you two?" she enquired in a voice which was not sufficiently revolted. "What reasons could I have for it?"

"My colleague bandaged you, that is to say that he did his duty. He's not really interested in explanations. He bandaged you, he recorded you in the register and that's it! These things are part of my profession. I simply want to verify my own knowledge, to see if my intuition still helps me. We are going to separate in some minutes and it is possible that we won't ever see each other again. Our discussion ought to take place under this aegis. It will be, I swear, without any consequence. Just a banal story of psychology. So I do not think that what you've told me is true."

"And why would it not be?" Claudia asked him in her turn. "What reason would I have to lie to you two?"

"This, I really can't know!"

"So, then?"

"Simple. The signs have shown something else to me. To my colleague, they were neutral and indifferent. But not to me. Is it true?"

"I do not have a too wonderful imagination, so I wouldn't know what to invent in order to confirm your supposition, but you tell me what you believe and I will immediately say if you're right."

"And, if I show you the evidence, will you admit it?" Dan persisted, and the woman immediately approved. "You don't have to say yes, only if I convince you," Dan encouraged her, undoing, under her worried gaze, the buttons of her jacket. "The traces of these fingers above your breast are telling me the truth. I don't think it was theft, but an attempted rape or a love story in which more passion was poured than it was necessary."

"Wouldn't you want to leave the answer suspended?" she invited him. "I am not in the most appropriate moment to tell you too much."

"In that case, we'll bury the mystery for fifty years, when I'll be no more," Dan tried to joke, preparing to go.

"No, I am not going to stay here alone," she ran to Dan. "I am scared. Do what you want, but don't leave me, especially now!" Claudia implored him, reaching the door before him.

"And what do you propose?" Dan said, confused.

"It would be improper to propose to you to stay here with me because I am very afraid, but I can ask you to leave me at the train station. There are all kinds of people there, ill and healthy, nobody is surprised at anything, not even at my bandage, so I could fall asleep unnoticed on some bench."

"What is left for me to do is to take you my house," Dan tried to joke.

"And the wife?"

"She died together with my mother in the Revolution. They were going to the hospital, they were doctors, and some bullets fired by an unknown person cut their lives short. I have a very intelligent and crazy son, but prison awaits him. He is a hacker and they will catch him out one day. For each smart person you will find another one who is smarter. He doesn't live with me, we see each other very rarely. As a consequence, I am alone, I am not accountable to anyone."

"In that case I will come," Claudia hurried to assure him. "I will only stay until dawn. Please believe me I do not have any contagious disease and I am not a street professional either. I do not suffer from TB, AIDS or anything else. And, what's more, I am rather hungry. How can I go to the restaurant with this horrible bandage?"

Dan called a taxi and thus acquired a woman who was going to make, every now and then, his life impossible. The immediately following day, when he returned from the clinic, he found her home, to his surprise.

"I arranged things with mother, father, with Adriana, my office colleague, so I can stay another day. If you didn't have any mirrors, I would have gone away. But as it is, I look like a monster. What can I say to them? I put a bit of order into things here, in order to pay to some extent for my food," she tried to joke. "If you don't wish to see me, I found a little room with a small telly, where I can stay until tomorrow evening without bothering you. In fact, ignore me, do what you think you must do. As a military wife, mother always prepared us for what could be hardest. She even managed to teach me to cook! I would be glad for you to see that I am able to do something else besides getting beaten up."

Of course the exam to which she had submitted herself was passed with flying colours, especially since Dan was not a gourmand, he didn't eat for pleasure, but out of necessity. In the end, bored with crawling through the restaurants and cantinas, where waiting was an iron rule, he had started to specialise in what he could buy from fast-food outlets. But it wasn't just the kitchen which was the only point gained by Claudia in her relationship with Dan.

"You seem a good man," she said to him, "and easy to please. You deserve more than you have."

"I am waiting for you to tell me your reasoning," Dan insisted and she hurried to underline his goodness, the fact that he'd received her in his house in a very difficult moment for her.

"And what will you do now?" Dan enquired. "I don't think you are afraid of the person who tried to steal your money, but of something which is much more complicated. In this kind of situation, you have to have more options for defending yourself. But, since I do not know what this is about, I'll abstain."

"One must be in a certain state of mind in order to be able to relate various wretched circumstances into which life throws one. Maybe later, after my wounds heal, if you want to see me."

"You know the address, the telephone number, the occupier... The door stays open," Dan emphasised.

"In that case I would be bold," she insisted. "I'll stay for another day or two, until I get well. I don't want to give explanations to anyone and especially not to my father. He is a rough man. I always talk to mother on the phone and she understands."

Unfortunately, or fortunately, Claudia left only after a week, because of a nightmare that complicated things even more. It was late at night when he heard a series of confused words, moans and screams from the room in which Claudia slept, which made him believe that a certain someone, the unknown who hurt her, had located her. Scared, he took an old sabre inherited from his great-grandfather on his mother side and, deciding to confront the unknown, he entered the woman's room. Confused, incapable to extricate herself from the nightmare, she cried out in despair, huddling against the wall, trying to defend herself from an apparition of the night only she could see, so that it was very difficult for Dan to wake her up. The moment she recognised him, she cradled herself against his chest, asking him to defend her, and not even later, when she came back to herself, did Claudia have the courage to separate from him.

"Don't go," she implored him, "please stay here."

Dan stayed, and that night was the beginning of a story whose end is hard to foresee. In the morning they looked at each other ashamed of what had happened, without explaining themselves and without being able to confess the untold happiness that came over them. Dan told me that she was *something else*, different from everything he had known. It was just that he did not know how to describe that state of feeling, or exactly how she was so different. The next day they both behaved as if they'd known each other since forever, and he felt that this woman deserved any sacrifice, although something whispered to him that he was taking things rather quickly. In Dan's absence, Claudia had washed her clothes, taken off her bandages and, since he had gotten home too early, he found her dressed in his bath robe, pottering around the kitchen.

"I am trying to compensate in some way," she explained. "It is time for me to leave. I'm trying my best not to show my wounds, and to convince you of my gratitude."

"We both had luck," Dan assured her. "You for meeting me, and me for you having that nightmare. In any case, I've had some happy days for which I thank you." The next day, Claudia left him a letter and disappeared.

My dear, I did not have the strength to wait for you, to confess openly how grateful I am for giving me a hand when things were very hard for me. You are a wonderful man and you deserve a fate and a woman better than me. If I had stayed a little more, there was the danger I would fall in love with you, a thing which hasn't happened to me for some years now. Other words don't come to mind now, and they do not make sense in any case. C.

The echo of this encounter surpassed any expectation, as Dan confessed to me later on. For a few days, hoping she would return, he stayed home, kicking himself for not asking for her phone number and address. He then went to the Emergency ward, where he found her address and, although he doubted it was the real address, he took it and circled for a long time among the blocks of flats, with the hope that luck or chance would put her in his way. But it was not to be. Claudia had not left the numbers for the entrance or the apartment, but only a number which Cazimir's assistant had written down in a totally negligent manner. In the end, he found her office, but it was closed both in the mornings and in the evenings, and, when he had lost any hope of finding her, one boring evening, when he wasn't even thinking of her anymore, he heard the doorbell and, to his surprise, Claudia was standing in front of the door. Instead of expressing his joy at finding her again, Dan raised his voice at her: "From now on, you don't disappear without my approval! Understood?"

"Yes, *să trăiți,*[28]" she answered, very satisfied that her instincts had not lied to her. "You convinced me... I saw you twice in front of my block and I knew we'd see each other again."

"And why did I have to wait so long?" asked Dan, to which she started to laugh:

"I, too, have various bits of business to look after, plus some questions which I had to answer for myself!"

"And?"

"This is the answer."

Claudia entered the house and, for a while, she stayed with Dan. She went to her job, then home, to bring changes of clothes, and, with the most natural air in this world, she returned, assuming all household obligations. They seemed united, body and soul but, with all this, he could not learn

---

28   The words are part of a military salute to a superior. Literally, 'long life to you'. In common parlance, it has passed into every day speech as an equivalent to a phrase such as 'yes, boss'.

too much about her. On the contrary, with each conversation she seemed to deepen the fog in which they were sinking.

I have to say this relationship made me glad from several points of view, but, as the time passed, it vexed me. Claudia was young, very beautiful and, anyway, more silent than the other women who'd tarried for more than one week in Dan's apartment, who were some kind of geese for whom the word *discretion* was categorically foreign. I do not understand what she tied him with, how she made him fall in love with her in a pathetic, adolescent manner. I don't understand either in what her strength lay. I don't think that, sexually speaking, she was more of an expert than Natalia Georgescu or, even more positively, the blonde woman from Biology, whose name escapes me.

Clearly I only speak from hearsay, as these women bragged without embarrassment, sometimes even in front of Dan. They did this without talking about the other hussies, just as young and maybe more beautiful, who had frequented his bed. Of course, at first sight, Dan could seem a cynical adventurer, a person who could never have enough of sin, but, in reality, the death of his wife had changed him a lot, accentuating his fear of loneliness or, to put it better, his horror of loneliness. Before his entanglement with Natalia Georgescu, he only left the clinic and the library with difficulty, so much so that she rather pulled his leg about it: "Here is where the savant laid! And me, chasing you from back in the ancient days because you seemed more of a man than many of those with whom I crossed paths."

Natalia took him out of the library, for a while, but it seems she was not quite what Dan had dreamed of in the chapter called women. Claudia, I think, defeated him by the fact that she told him next to nothing about herself. She had avoided any direct answer, everything that had happened to her was lacking in importance and did not deserve to be retained: a grey life in a grey world.

"Beauty? In an era dominated by boorish people it takes you away from the world rather than bringing you closer to it. Men only want one thing: to sleep with me! And into this fight they throw their cars, their houses and all the nothings that surround them, but not even a drop of intelligence. Of course I, too, have sinned. Curiosity, the need to experiment on myself, to pass over this threshold towards maturity, because in my group at the university I was the only virgin. So I didn't do it out of love, but out of curiosity. About my erotic experiences I don't really have much to say, I lack the most pleasant memories, so this is what it comes down to. You go to bed once and you are scared for a month. Maybe I haven't found yet the man from whom I can expect more than I have received up to now. And then, in a corner of the subconscious, there was also my father, with his aberrant ideas of morality. A single life, a single man and intercourse only after you are blessed by the priest! In the village he came from, you were forced to wave around the sheets stained with blood on the wedding night! If not, divorce, shame and the disdain of the more experienced women who, if it came to it, made use of chicken blood."

Claudia talked with great conviction, as if the most rapid conclusion of this uncomfortable subject depended on each one of her words. This fact seemed to have spurred Dan even more, as he was annoyed by the silence into which the woman sank if he didn't finish the conversation whenever she deemed it appropriate. I had many discussions with him, but I could not understand whether he lost or won in the months that followed. Step by step, he had given up prolonged investigations and prolonged documentary research. He was content to be the third or fourth signature on some banal scholarly papers meant to declare, to all those who were interested in his fate, that he was still the same passionate researcher. The time he'd consecrated to science previously was generously given to Claudia and I was glad, convinced that he too had the right to a little folly. Unfortunately, in the end, after she moved into his place, his folly was more than a little. Claudia had taken not only his time, but she had also exercised his skill and spirit of observation to the maximum. He had the feeling he was defeated, without quite knowing why. The woman did not abandon him but disappeared periodically for two-three days and returned feeling tired, saddened, but as mysterious as before:

"Later on, we'll be able to discuss all this. You must be certain that I love you, that I am not cheating on you, that, in my soul, I am always with you and that I do not wish us to part. The rest is words which do not have any point right now."

"You – I don't know why – are calling for bad luck, and I want to protect you. When you disappear, I can't work and I can't sleep, I am afraid something bad happened to you. I pass by the Emergency department. Is it hard to let me know you are going? And then, telephones have been invented for a long time now. At least tell me when you'll come back."

"When I explain it to you, you will understand why I didn't give any signs. Just don't worry, that's essential!"

Dan forgave her, convinced she wasn't lying, but, when everything seemed forgotten and peace had descended on their home, Claudia disappeared again without warning. Annoyed, and taking care they wouldn't recognise his voice, he called her parents at various hours and they gave him the address of Dr Dan Robert, assuring him at the same time that they had spoken to him not long ago. One night she returned bloodied again, with torn clothes and, this time, Dan didn't reprimand her, didn't ask what had happened to her, simply content to care for her. He refused to sleep with her, as he had done in the beginning, although her nightmares reoccurred, and the sedatives got to the stage where they replaced him.

"It seems I no longer interest you," she said to him after her latest disappearance. "I think it's time for me to go home."

"I didn't say this, but I've got used to seeing you come beaten up every two-three weeks. I think you cannot live without this. I feel like a mug. I don't have sadomasochistic leanings, but I can give you a good beating periodically, if you need it so much."

"Next time, if you continue to keep the same distance from me, I will come with my health tests done, so you can convince yourself I don't have AIDS, gonorrhoea, syphilis."

"Tell me, if I came home like you, beaten up, and with my money taken away, how would you react? What would you believe?"

"I would have faith and patience and I would wait for the day when you have the disposition to tell me!"

"I would feel better if I was freed from any shadow of the past. It doesn't seem to me that it is sufficient for us to be naked only in the bed!"

"I will no longer come here," said Claudia, "since it is so important for you whom I slept with before knowing you. I didn't ask you to get married, so it is my right to sleep with whoever I like. As it happens, I got to love you, but this does not concern you."

"I don't think you have been too careful. I only asked you to tell me who beat you up. You don't have any obligations to me, but it would be, in the end, a sign of trust."

"As long as what is happening between the two of us is not enough for you, whatever I'd tell you could not change the relationship, it wouldn't make it perfect. If I am not here, if you don't see me daily, you won't think of my entanglements. As a consequence, I'll simplify things starting from the very next moment."

"Since you're leaving with such ease," Dan riposted, "I have absolutely no comment."

"Everything was beautiful. Once again I built illusions for myself in this life. May it do me good, but now it's good for me to go."

Dan didn't stop her, as Claudia would have expected. He remained still, as if turned to stone, convinced that, in the end, she would come back. She probably waited for a single word, but she did not hear it.

After some days, Dan found her at home: she had cooked, cleaned and, very emotional, she was waiting for him to appear.

"You didn't make a single phone call," she reproached him. "And look, stepping over my pride, humiliating myself, I have come – although, I think, you had made peace with the thought that I had left for ever. You gave up on me with remarkable naturalness. And here I am. I am ready to be despised, but I had such a need for you as I don't think you can even suspect. With your twisted psychiatrist mind, you've shoved me into one of your boxes and that was that! Seen, classified, indexed. And forgotten!"

"Would it calm you if I told you that I missed you? I missed your presence terribly, if it comes to making a full confession. But, if you should want to leave, I will never call you back!"

In the presence of Claudia, Dan's mood suddenly changed: he was cheerful, communicative, attentive, generous all the way to stupidity, as if all the world had to be glad of what was happening to him. Even more, his research on schizophrenia tended to transform into a synthesis that deserved full attention. But, as one can see, happiness doesn't last too long. Claudia was ever changing – something hidden, unconfessed, an obligation, a mystery forced her to leave, so Dan's exaltations and depressions were precipitous. He could not do without her, but the question marks she raised in him, her stubborn refusal to give an explanation, no matter how insignificant, worried him. He felt something was not right, so that their relationship could only be in a state of suspension, under the sign of fear of the future. Unfortunately, Dan did not have the strength to cut through the knot, but he was not capable either of contemplating it to infinity, so he asked for my advice – but only after I confessed to him that, involuntarily, I had started to keep a check on him because his state was worrying me somewhat.

"It is clear that you love her much," I said to him, "you can see from a distance that you are not sending her packing, as you did with the others. Even more, you have started to depend on her. In her absence, you ignore yourself, you don't have an appetite for anything. I believe that you kind of started to suspect what she is hiding, but it is hard for you to reconcile yourself to that thought. To me, it seems useless to postpone. It is mandatory to be trenchant! You are at an age when this kind of wound hurts much more, and experience, as rich as it might be, doesn't show you the right path. Her secret, or at least her unconfessed biography, can be found even without her help. The country is full of private detective offices. Why not hire one? Just like that. To know the truth or verify your suspicions. You've been living together and you have had sufficient time to study her. If you haven't learned yet what interests you, if she is hiding certain chapters of her life so hard, it means they will permanently sit between you two, like an obstacle. The truth or, well, what you are going to discover cannot force you not to stay together. I do not exclude the fact that things might be much simpler: she is probably terrorised even by her parents! But this could just as well be about an older connection with a man or, why not, she could have a double personality! Because she has told you next to nothing about her past. And she doesn't look like a woman without experience to me."

Dan was a very generous man: he had done everything to make her feel good, he had offered her all his trust, he had accepted her in his house without any natural suspicions, only according to what his senses had dictated to him, and he had not received in exchange, as he would have deserved, the equivalent trust he needed. During the time she had gone missing, he would have accepted even a plausible lie. That's how much he missed her.

Although the idea about the detectives seemed necessary to him, Dan did not have the courage to hire them. He was trying to convince me that by doing this thing he would pass beyond the limits of fair play, that maybe she would solve by herself the history, that, without any doubt, incommoded her to the same extent. The idea was not convenient to me either, because I would have entered into their intimacy more than was proper, and I would have probably learned things I didn't have the courage to tell Dan about, especially since up to that time I had left everything up to him. I hadn't asked questions, I had censored my curiosity. Instead I had deduced the gravity of the situation or, to be more precise, the profoundness of his pain, more from silences and from his need to ask me for all kinds of opinions on Claudia.

In the end, unable to bear seeing him upset, and out of professional curiosity, I risked – without telling him – giving two detectives from the best known agency in town the necessary information, not only the photographs, but also a very reasonable sum without which they wouldn't agree to discuss it. In that agency, former Securitate secret policemen and militiamen from Vice who were out on pension had linked arms and, of course, knowing the entire town from various positions – both the people at the top and the underworld –, they had not failed in many investigations. That was especially because, before being classed as retired, they had prepared systematically for whatever the future might have thrown in their paths. A sin which is known beforehand is a useful point to start from in any investigation. The former Securitate major Ion Moraru even started his investigation with Dan. Since when, where and in what circumstances did he meet her and, especially, how did he behave with other women; and as Dan was a known person in the town it was not too hard for him to gather the data of his temporary relationships. Nor, on the other hand, did they fail to consider the following hypothesis: was it not possible that Claudia had run away precisely from him? How did he behave with her in intimacy?

"The doctor is not unknown to us," the major mentioned. "He is, and I hope I am not wrong, the man with the lysergic acid."

That was a story I had forgotten. Dan had made friends

with an American lecturer from the University who procured for him the latest novelties from the field of psychiatry and, especially from psycho-pharmacology, in the United States. This is how he was in possession of some studies on lysergic acid, for which he conceived an overwhelming passion.

"The relationship with the American gave us big headaches," Moraru said. "We had recorded a conversation in which he was promising the doctor to send him the said substance under the stamp on a letter. We worked until we became sick. Not knowing what this could be about, we decided not to give him any of his letters. We simply burned them. Well, that's how times were, orders were severe, a mistake could be enormously costly. And the nonsense of some doctors was the last thing we had an appetite for!"

The other one, the former militia captain Mitică Oprea, only asked for Claudia's addresses: home and office, and he asked if I wanted to be kept up to date with the progress of the investigation or whether I only wanted the conclusions. I proposed to them to let me know when they had the first certainty, and to decide only then whether we should continue with the investigations.

After the first week, the two detectives invited themselves to my home, so that I would be prepared for anything, and, I confess, the things I was fated to learn would not have even passed through my mind. One of these black days, when neither Claudia or her mother answered the phone, she left the house with infinite prudence, as if she knew she was being followed, and got into the first taxi that came her way. She was very elegant, as if she were going to a concert or sophisticated dinner, as in fact also happened. She stopped at one of the new restaurants in the forest on the edges of the town, installed in a new, superb villa without any signage, so that it looked more like a private club than a public house accessible to everyone. The owner, Guță Boierul, used to have a doughnut stall before the Revolution, but in the post-revolutionary days he had won an important sum from commerce in second-hand cars from Germany and Austria, after which he diversified his businesses, investing a lot in real estate and restaurants. Many people suspected him of commerce in drugs and the procurement of prostitutes, but nobody had proved it, being afraid to try because of his relations with the police.

Claudia walked inside in a hurry, holding the arm of the owner, and passed on into a private area from where she exited, after two hours, arm in arm with her brother, a mediocre student at the Polytechnic. They sneaked into the owner's car, and it took them home, but Claudia didn't stay there, as the detectives expected. She returned in the same car to the restaurant they had just left. The detectives withdrew around two o'clock in the night, when the last party goer left, but not before noticing that the windows of the motel were still lit. Claudia was staying, probably, in one of the rooms. The relationships in her family hadn't said much to the detectives. They were quiet, hard-working people, rather silent and not terribly sociable, but very correct in their dealings with the building administrators and neighbours, whom the two detectives had approached in the various shops and oftentimes in the park where her mother walked their poodle. In their vision, Claudia's story was even simpler. She was going to get married immediately after finishing her studies to a student of the visual arts, but he got drowned in the Danube during an excursion about which nobody knew too much. She had stayed sorrowful for many years and, maybe, because of that accident, she had lived with the obsession that she lacked any luck, especially since a relationship with one of her professors lasted only for a few months, after which he migrated to Canada, where his tracks were lost. As a consequence, as the two detectives found out, Claudia was an unhappy, silent, hardworking person and, despite her beauty, she had not emerged from the run of the mill, and she was not present in any way in the evidence of the official "organs". They had to unravel a mystery: precisely what was she looking for in Guță Boieru's motel? It was more than certain that it was an adventure with another man, so they were left only with the opportunity of pronouncing who the surplus person was when they were in full knowledge of the facts. Who was she cheating on: Dr Dan Robert or the man baptised as N, meaning Not-Known?

"All this effort for a poor little slut for whom one man isn't enough!" had been the first conclusion of the former militiaman from Vice. "The doctor is a high class man and might not have quite what this one needs. But let's not be in a hurry: maybe he does, but she doesn't like it! Or it may be that conman has her in his hand with something. Guță never did anything clean in his life. Anyway, Claudia's path to such a motel must have been strange!"

The following day, dressed in an impeccable hunting suit, kitted out with a solid moustache and a female colleague who had served the same institution as himself, Mitică Oprea presented himself at the actual restaurant and, being to all extents hungry, curious and, seemingly, in love he also asked for a bottle of wine which he managed to get the best of by evening time. When he was close to losing his patience, the woman for whom he had waited so long put in an appearance, accompanied by a muscly man with a shaven head, and the figure of a high performance rugby player. She had come down from a room, accompanied him to the door, tarried there for a few minutes and then, encouraged by the owner, she got lost for a while in the motel's kitchen, from where she didn't return – a sign that there was another exit, but also a sign, especially, that between her and Boieru there was some complicity.

The second day, it was the major's turn to take his meal there and Oprea's to do surveillance work on the building from the forest. Moraru had a Turkish passport, spoke Romanian badly and was very tired, he only wanted food to be brought up to his room. He said he had come to Romania to do some business, and he was worried by the fact that Boieru might bring up another Turk in order to check on him. Before concentrating on the neighbouring rooms, he asked to be served breakfast, after which he started on forays to the reception desk and the kitchens, unhappy that the waiter had not brought various foods which, by the way, he hadn't asked for. When all his desires had been accomplished, he asked the waiter whether the room he had might benefit from a warm soul as well, to which the waiter smiled enigmatically: "With patience and wisdom, all wishes can come true, but I am just a simple waiter!" In the end, the owner was impossible to be found, the same as Claudia.

At lunch time he said that he had to go on a purchasing expedition, and he left the motel with a feeling of failure, but the much pursued woman had returned to Dan without special marks on her body. Instead she was rather shot through with fatigue. She had been in the countryside, where her office colleague had a little summer house. Her mobile phone had been stolen or lost on the road, anyway

– there was no signal in that specific area, but the way in which he had welcomed her, his unconcealed joy and warmth, confirmed to her that the telepathy between the two of them was working. Claudia's explanation and the witness statements of the two detectives encouraged me not to put a stop to their investigation. My son's future and peace seemed important to me. Furthermore, the number of hypotheses about her unknown life increased worryingly. Why was she doing it? Older debts and entanglements from which she hadn't managed to extricate herself? More than any moral failings, I was concerned about the state of her health and especially about the spectre of a malady whose name was not of a nature to calm me: AIDS. When Dan considered the question or discovered the malady, it would be too late for the both of them. Of course, once you enter the area of uncertainties and speculations, reason directs you to the worst and, many times, after you have seen the outlines of the evil at the end of the road, the most evil evil, you behave as if it had already happened. And there was something more: Dan, who was also more fragile than me, did not deserve to suffer for a creature who was incapable of repaying his affection or at least of understanding it.

During the week when Claudia stayed with Dan, the investigation by the two detectives had only Boieru as an object. "The warm soul" mentioned by Moraru in the discussion with the waiter from the motel made him suppose that there could be a small illegal brothel for moneyed people or for foreign tourists, and this had to be looked at more closely. He was no longer an employee of the state, and it was not his business to discover facts that disturbed society's state of health, but such information could always be exchanged for something else, as he had never neglected the relationship with his former colleagues. And, in the end, a warm soul, even that of the woman they were trailing, could not count as surplus. But there was another question left up in the air: what was Claudia's brother looking for there? What business did he have? And why had they been there together? The detective had reprised the role of a Turk, but his biography needed to be adjusted. In order to be able to face the unforeseen, Moraru was no longer a real Turk, but a Romanian who had fled to Turkey during the years of communism, and he had become a Muslim there. Even from the first evening Boieru had sat down at his table, but he had been very evasive about the satisfactions his establishment offered for its customers' desire.

"There are all sorts of creatures coming by here. My care is for them to pay for their meal or room and, of course, for them to feel good, because I care for my business. For the rest. Only the communists watched for missteps, for people's trespasses, so that they can blackmail them. If you come with a charitable soul, that's up to you. I do not deny it, there are plenty of lonely girls, and they are up to making a profit they work for! Morals is one thing, but need is a different one and, most of the times, they do not meet. Of course, there's no harm putting yourself in the situation of the person who comes with one of these creatures. With some lost female soul. Nobody takes a step to the left or the right if they don't have a great need for it. Maybe a man is tormented by what is called sexual boredom. He might have, probably, spiritual pains which are impossible to calm otherwise. I have met many serious people, whose wives were infirm or denied them. Do you have the right to condemn them for the things you are not destined to know? It is better not to know and to be glad that you're not in the situation of those people who are cheating on themselves. The eyes see, the heart desires, but you are forced to think first of all of the spirochetes or the virus. With me, honesty and discretion are above all else. This is why I told this to you, you have probably not thought of the numerous difficult situations through which a man can go, irrespective of his age!"

Judging by the intensity with which the cafe owner watched his eyes and the hesitations in his voice, Moraru felt he was suspected of something, so he changed the discussion, showing himself interested in Romanian cuisine and especially the red wines. Boieru brought him some, without asking, on the house, so that he could assure himself of being in control of the situation, after which he sent the waiter to the table, contenting himself with smiling from a distance.

For Moraru, this would not have been too lucky an evening if it hadn't come to mind that, in the end, the real key to the problem could be Claudia's brother. In a town where, from morning to evening, people were digging ditches only to cover them up and have them re-dug by a different company, it was very simple for him to wear a high visibility vest and to post himself in front of the block of flats where the brother lived. During the former regime, tailing various foreigners among other targets, Moraru had played the role of a fisherman or hunter in various hotels, and also masqueraded as an employee of the Telephones – so well that not even his wife recognised him. Now, in the confusion of town and country, nobody had an eye to spare for a poor workman who was looking at manholes.

Chance helped him only on the third evening, when, having decided to interrupt the surveillance, he saw

Claudia's brother getting in the car and driving away at great speed, only to pull up precisely at Boieru's place. He didn't stay for too long, but when he made his exit he was accompanied to the car by Boieru. Their discussion couldn't be heard but it did not seem too friendly since it finished with the slamming of doors and a nervous takeoff. Moraru followed the brother up to the alley at the edge of the park, where one could find rent girls and boys and especially drugs. He lost the track there because of some girls who circled him offering their services and, of course, quoting the prices. The fact that he'd had the idea to hang around among the lost souls there was of great usefulness because he had discovered, much too quickly, the interests in which Boieru and, probably, Claudia, were involved.

Moraru again asked whether he should continue with the business or not. This time, I needed time to think. Of course, it was not good to tell Dan the things I learned, although he had asked for my advice, because we found ourselves on unstable ground. His disappointment at being lied to colliding with her fury for being followed around could cause a real catastrophe, especially since, and I had no doubts, their love didn't seem to be superficial – on the contrary. As a consequence, I proposed to myself looking closely at Claudia in order to be convinced whether she used any drugs, because Dan, being in love as he was, would have noticed only if she made a childish error. I invited myself to their place, and, although I paid attention to their eyes, speech, and psychological state of mind, I was not destined to discover anything besides the multitude of barely perceptible gestures which connects lovers. I thought that, for reasons which escaped me for the time being, the woman was prostituting herself, but not with just anyone, and for a lot of money, hence the connection to Boieru. In any case, the investigation had to continue for her own good, because I did not exclude the possibility of her being blackmailed. When I left, Dan insisted on driving me home, a sign that he had some matters to clear up. In fact, immediately after we got home, he asked whether I had noticed something special about Claudia, because I'd given her a quite unusual attention, in the confrontation where he had been convinced for a long time that I didn't strive to be polite and exaggeratedly amiable.

"I didn't do anything special," I told him. "It's just that I asked myself what is happening in the disappearances you told me about. I wanted to sense her and to exclude two variants of the many possible ones. Whether the man that preceded you doesn't want to separate from her or blackmails her with something, and if she is using some drugs."

"Yes, this is what I thought too," Dan admitted. "For the moment, none of these seems to be supported. She goes to her job, she comes home, she waits for me with dinner. For the moment everything seems alright. Which does not mean that I won't continue to pay attention, because, I admit it, I have a great need for her. Maybe it's also because she reminds me of Iulia."

The fact that he had not lost his lucidity completely made me glad, but I also thought that any matter, once it is begun, must be taken to its proper conclusion. I didn't have any doubts that, sooner or later, she was going to disappear again, and Dan's suffering, which was inevitable, could be moderated only by convincing testimonies; but, beyond everything, we were both doctors and we had to offer her a hand when she needed it. This is what I thought when I asked the two to continue with their investigations and, looking at all facets of the situation in which the three suspects were found – the girl, her brother and Boieru – I had started to believe that Claudia's brother was the most vulnerable. Men or drugs – that was what he might have been looking for there, in the park, at that very late hour. When it came to drugs, we still had to find an answer to the question: was he selling or buying? And given the hypothesis that he was selling, Boieru could not be missed out from the equation.

Claudia had not left the house yet, so as a consequence they had the time to study the young man with close attention, especially since he seemed pretty imprudent. Mingling among the gays and whores, after following him when he came from Boieru's, Moraru and Oprea tried to make friends, haggling for the prices and type of services which the numerous girls offered – girls who, lacking clients, risked being molested by "fishes," the pimps who watched their movements closely. Among those who were idling away their time there, Oprea discovered, more or less to her surprise, two colleagues from Vice and another one who took special interest in drugs.

"If you need something warm, I'll give you a list with some other, better quality girls, who are not forced to be on the pavement beat. And for a little crate of whisky I can suggest what you must whisper to them so that they won't complain to us about you!" said one of them.

"Are following somebody?" the other inquired. "If you hold a place for me in your unit for when I get pensioned off or fired, I'll reveal all that I know, just tell me what's the name of the one you're looking for."

"I want to find out exactly what a certain boy is spinning. Come and see him and, if you know him, tomorrow I'll pay my debt to you," Oprea said.

She showed him the man, told him the name, and made an appointment to meet her colleague the next day at a restaurant in the centre.

"That specific boy is not profiled on girls, neither on boys, but on... weeds!"

"Is he selling or buying?"

"The one and the other, both, but he belongs to somebody important who has in the palm of his hand all the people you want, and those you don't. There are proofs that he owns more prosecutors and officers than two counties taken together. The clincher is that the specific individual likes law suits so much that, many times, he wishes to lose – only so he can rejoice in a bigger victory later on. I advise you not to continue digging, if you don't want to regret it later on! He is very vengeful and he has some boys who can leave indelible marks on you! He takes perverse pleasure in manipulating people, in elevating and destroying politicians..."

The mysterious personage was, as suspected, Boieru himself. Had Claudia become a simple distributor? This was the question that waited for a reply, and the fact that the siblings had been seen together in Boieru's restaurant seemed to relieve him from any other questions. They still had to wait for a new disappearance from Claudia in order to definitively close that chapter. The thing I didn't know at the time was that Dan had also proposed to himself to solve the enigma, at any risk, despite her numerous gestures and declarations of love. As a consequence, watching her reactions patiently after various telephone conversations, he had understood that her agitation, which she tried to hide, announced the next disappearance.

In a moment of great inspiration, he'd said to himself that the unravelling of the mystery depended on somebody to be found in the contacts' list mobile phone, so, while

Claudia was bathing, he had copied out all her numbers, including those accessed in recent days, and, even further, he had decided to meet the people she talked to on the phone. Engaged in the most complicated adventure, Dan had thought of the situations in which he could meet those people, studied the various chances of possible failures and, furthermore, had managed to keep the secret – meaning that he lied even to me, saying that there was another woman on stand by, in order to explain his own absences times when Claudia was missing from home. "One nail can push out the other,[29]" he said, and I believed him for a while. I had even made excuses for him at the clinic, from where he had absented himself without justification. But he had come home accompanied by Claudia.

The woman's clothes were torn, she was unrecognisable because of the blood on her face, but Dan had solved at least one part of the enigma. What had happened? He had waited for an entire day in front of Claudia's block of flats, convinced that she was going to return home at some point, at least to change her clothes, and this happened after he had conversed, with more than half of the people from the long list in the phone's memory. Some were university colleagues passing through the town, some were people for whom she hadn't finished translations in time, but there had been two of them who enquired his reason for trying to locate her and, even further, called him back for other details, since his number had stayed in their phones' memory. Dan had the courage to tell one of them, among other things, that the memory of that woman was strongly fixed in his senses, and after he mentioned this, he gained an invitation to *Popasul ingerilor*, The Angels' Stopover, a bar he had never heard of before and which, to his surprise, was not listed in *Yellow*

---

29   The Romanian version of the saying Fight fire with fire.

Pages. A policeman deciphered the enigma for him. Very expensive girls and cheaper weed, if you managed to gain the trust of the owner, a singer of *manele*[30] music behind whom one found a rather important ranking officer, but was, otherwise, an influential businessman.

"I have no idea how you need to proceed, or what paths lead to his trust. In such cases, I do not entangle myself with this type of *piloşi*[31] except on the orders of my boss. For the moment, all these people feel fine and it is said that, bored with their wives, many make use of the services of working girls in whose company they are filmed during their happiest moments. This is all I know, this is all I'm saying. It's simply that I take pity on them for the time when they will have to pay for keeping quiet!"

In the end he found the bar with the help of Claudia herself, by following her. He didn't know what to say about who and why invited him there, he uttered her name a few times and, even more, he tried to force the door open, for which deed two bodyguards immediately threw him in the street. After a while, seeing that he refused to leave, in order to teach him a lesson, they provided him with some solid bruises after which they threw him in a taxi which took him to Claudia's address, as he had asked the driver. He waited there until dawn. The decision to wait for her no matter how long it took was taken in the only moment of inspiration for that day, as she appeared close to dawn, accompanied by her

30 *Manele* is a style of urban-Gypsy music with Balkan influences. In Romania, this style of music is generally associated with a lack of good taste, based on the so-called "aspirational lyrics" making reference to spending and giving away loads of money to one's friends, enemies dying of envy, being "Number 1," and enjoying "living it large".

31 *Piloşi* (sg. *pilos*) is a pejorative expression meaning well-connected people, normally with connotations of nepotism and illegality. Also, *o pilă*, a connection. Normal meaning of the word is *file* (the tool used for filing); the origins of the expressions are unclear.

brother. Seeing him on a bench, all bloodied, as he had been abandoned by the taxi driver, Claudia ran to him, desperate, trying to learn what had happened to him and where, while, on the other hand, her brother seemed very scared.

"At the angels'," Dan replied to her, trying to push her away with contempt. "If you needed money, I could have given it to you without your doing this. At least tell me how much you're asking for the night. How much do I owe you for the time we've been together?"

Instead of giving him a reply, the woman snapped at her brother: "You idiot, this was the last time. Either in the hospital, or in jail!" she yelled, pulling a fistful of money from her pocket and throwing it in his face. "I hope that next time you'll pay your debts!" Taken over by nerve racking, unrestrained crying, she helped Dan stand up: "Lord, what they did to you! Come home, don't sit here, just see the way you look! I don't want you to forgive me, I don't deserve it, I am trash and I only wish to take you home and that is all! I am disgusted by myself and the world in which we live. I hope to find a proper length of rope or a plane ticket, so I can disappear as far away from here as possible."

In the end, Claudia took him home. I had not moved in to Dan's yet, but it was not only a few times that I had slept there, because the woman's absence produced great anxiety in him. Loneliness and the most absurd questions overwhelmed him. From the moment she appeared, he had lost his sense of humour. He could not find in her, after profound analysis, any quality; and yet, he could not be without her. His vanity was killing him. He didn't want to admit his defeat, the fact that a woman, a nobody, had left him. Alternatively, behind the nasty words, he tried to convince himself that her departure was a chance, a deliverance.

He made no reply in an open manner, but his inner state betrayed him. Now, my surprise was not insignificant when I saw them together, with her being very attentive, tending to his wounds, trying to wipe the congealed blood off his face, and him being downcast, incapable of looking at her but also unable to master his feeling of rejection. Because Dan's silence seemed impenetrable, I encouraged him to go to the bathroom, to wash off the blood and to take off the torn, dusty clothes, which smelled strongly. In the meantime, Claudia came to my room.

"I don't think we'll ever meet again, this is why I would like to explain to you why we are the way we are. I believed I could solve on my own the misery in which I found myself involved, but it was impossible. My brother started by selling drugs, but ended up by consuming and getting into terrifying debt. When he didn't have any other choice, when he almost got killed or mutilated, he asked for my help. I went to the supplier, who, in exchange for his life and in order to cancel the debt, asked me to sleep with him, and then with others from the high class milieu. And I did it out of fear. When I refused, they sent to me some animals who brutalised me or picked me up by force and took me brutally, or else they beat up my unfortunate brother. The policemen asked me to recount everything, in writing, but when they heard who we were talking about, who I was complaining of, they encouraged me to leave the paper with them. Some tore it in my face and advised me to leave for another town, and some simply tried, to sleep with me. And, when even the police didn't get involved, to whom can I appeal? How can I save the idiot? Of course, I cannot be called otherwise. I am a whore. It was natural for them to ask such a thing. This is why I want to get my

337

brother committed to a hospital before my parents find out what we're doing. Here is where I would ask you to help. He must be saved! Then, I will disappear from the country and, probably, from the world. I love Dan enormously, in this wide world he is the only one who gave me a hand, but I am not worthy of him. I have become a rag, a wretch, I know this, but it was impossible for me not to lie to him. I was sure I was going to lose him, but I wished that this would happen as late as possible!"

Committing her brother as an in-patient could be managed, but we were still left with their story. However, over Claudia's great sorrow there floated a shade of peace:

"What a relief it is over! From now on, whatever might happen to me can't be worse than this! Not even death."

"I don't want to butt in on your story," I lied to her. "You must solve it between you two, no matter how painful it is. I would be interested, though, to know the name of the man who coerced you. The drug supplier's name. If, in the final analysis, something unpleasant happens to you again, I will then know where to look for you. Does your brother still have debts?"

"I don't know. He never tells me the whole truth. The man with the drugs: Boieru. As far as I could understand, this individual is stronger than the police and prosecution services taken together. He gives them money, girls, and even drugs. He has them all filmed, the people who called for his girls' services. Not even one of them suspected they were filmed."

"And have you been doing this for a long time?"

"For about a year now."

"And are you indeed connected to Dan? Do you truly love him? If you feel something for him, you have to tell him the truth no matter the risk."

It was not the most intelligent discussion I strove to maintain. Dan's sorrow, his bad luck, the fact that in his choice he had excluded any trace of reason – these pained me, so much so that I asked myself many times: how much love, how much pity and how much pride were hidden, in reality, within this story? Where did the fixation on her come from? What distinguished her from others? And, because I could not forget I was a doctor, not for one moment, I found myself facing the same question I would often ask certain patients: "If the lucky goldfish[32] could grant a single wish, what would that wish be?"

"Lord, help me not to lose Dan !" she hurried to reply, proof that her prayer was very sincere, especially since the result of the investigation by the detectives was no different from what she had told me without my insisting in any way on it.

I allowed the two former officers to continue their investigations: I was interested to see what would they do when they discovered the drug connection:. Would they allow themselves to be bought or would they try to put their foot in the door? Or, following a good tradition, would they say like so many others: it is not our business! As for Claudia, I could not say anything much anymore. She had buried her face in her hands and cried desperately. This is how Dan found her after he decided to come out of the bathroom. After a period of uncomfortable silence, when it seemed that nothing could be said any more and everything was happening beyond the reach of words, Claudia was the first to snap out it:

"I ask your forgiveness because I could not master myself.

32 The Romanian equivalent, in popular anecdotes and jokes, to the genie in the bottle.

We'll have, I believe, to part as people who loved each other truly. And the love meant a lot, at least for me. It saved me, to some extent, from the wretchedness in which I found myself involuntarily. Now, there is nothing more to say, because not everybody who fights and wins gets to enjoy the results of the victory, because it's especially them who lose. I only wanted to live and to do exactly what I'd always wanted."

> *"I often tell myself that my life is a book from which I do not understand much."*
> Julien Green

The priest's proposal arrived, as a consequence, in a moment when I was tormented by such thoughts, and it was the beginning of a road against fear, a road I had not believed myself capable of until that moment. We went to the priest's house and, on the road there, he didn't stop telling the people who saw us together that his lady wife wasn't feeling well and that she needed emergency care. I did not really understand why he needed to explain, as if he was walking alongside the person with the worst reputation in the village, but I did not know him well enough so to be able to judge his gestures. But I explained them to myself later on.

In the priest's house, I was greeted by a man I'd never seen before – a red, rough face, unkempt, with deep creases, the hands of a lumberjack, as big as shovels, with which he always gestured as if words didn't seem handy to him. When I was ready to ask the priest's help in order to put some order into the loose exposition by the man who talked as if I knew what this was all about, Dana appeared from the bedroom. The surprise surpassed any expectations, not only because I saw her now after such a long time, but especially because she had lost a lot of weight, her big, black eyes were sunk in their sockets and the white, taut skin lent her a strange beauty.

"I stayed in the other room because I first wanted to get used to you after such a long absence," she said without coming closer. "Andrei is very gravely hurt and needs help. In this situation, I had to come here myself because I did not trust anyone. They all fear prison or bullets, and I understand them. I would not blame you either if you refused me. I cannot ask anyone to risk their lives for my husband. But because I care for you, I want to ask you not to ignore the fact that your gesture could cost you your life. The Securitate secret policemen only think in terms of the class struggle."

Seeing my confusion, the priest hurried to mention that Dr Oniga was gravely wounded and was somewhere far away, in the mountains, in the area of the Meteorological station, in a shelter dug in the ground. If I accepted this trip, we were going to be led there to him by the man who had also notified Dana, the forester in front of us. Evidently, the priest was going as well, but not Dana. The risk would have been too great and, in the physical condition she was in, she would have hindered our getting there in time. Equally, at the same time, she would have attracted the attention of the numerous Securitate men disguised as geologists and hunters, who were haunting the area. People were accustomed, to some extent, to me and the priest, we didn't impact too much on the retinas of the people, although anyone who entered the forest automatically became a suspect. From what the priest confessed to me, you can't trust anyone in the village. The Securitate and militiamen beat up some of them until they lost their endurance, for some others they found the most absurd blame in order to send them to prison, and they simply bought some of the rest. The partisans aren't kinder with the traitors either, so that terror floats in the air and nobody is excused from its threat. The priest told me stories which, up to that time, I had avoided discussing with my numerous patients. As such, I had manufactured for myself the role of a tired, overworked physician who only wanted to approach subjects that had to do with health. I had dreamt about tip-top performance and, as a consequence, I was forced to leave the village as soon as the opportunity presented itself to me, but I had found instead that I must survive, at any cost, and return to war-time medicine: that is, to save lives without having the least significant equipment and, if I could not make them well, at least I would not make things worse, just as Hippocrates had asked from us. Certainly, I would have liked to stay with Dana longer, but she, as seemed normal to me, behaved as if she didn't remember the two days when we had been ourselves, and her worries for her husband knew no limits.

I was looking at her with nostalgia and lust, although between us there seemed to stretch the Arctic Ocean. The eyes, the nose, the lips were the same, just like the hands, too, but the entire warmth from back then had stayed only in my memory. Yet, there was a moment in which we found ourselves alone, and the desperate, defeated figure she made killed off my hesitations.

"Please, help him," she whispered to me, swallowing her tears. "Andrei is different from the times when you knew him during the university years. Despite appearances, you know yourself that he did not love you. I mean, you felt it, and then he also had reasons. I made an inventory of the colleagues appointed to work in this area, but it's only you who are closer to the mountain and... to me. I don't condemn him for what he did, I am just trying to explain him. His father did not send him to veterinary school just by chance. Having a lot of land and numerous animals, he encouraged him to attend a faculty which would not distance him from agriculture and from home. But the lunacy of the collectivisation arrived and, being an influential man in the village, the greatest pressures were exerted on my father in law – endless fines, beatings, suits at law, humiliations of all kinds. With all these, nobody managed to convince him to join the collective farm or to scare him, after which the party activists asked him to donate the land, and he refused again, with even more obstinacy. There was a joke doing the rounds in the village, which he had told to the party secretary after this latter had explained that the land would still belong to him, even after joining the collective farm. 'It's just like you'd cut off my c***... after which you'd give it back to me: take it, since it is yours!'

In the end, losing their patience, the party activists and Securitate men took him to the regional centre where, for two weeks, they beat him up until he lost his memory. They then threw him in the yard like an inert bale. The old man's become a vegetable – he doesn't remember a thing and it is still hard for him to retain the names of the people around him, or even his relationship with us. But the suffering was far from over with my father in law's situation. Andrei's turn had come, and he had already lost all trace of patience and hope, his father's health bringing him into a permanent state of irritation. He was doing his job with great difficulty, but he had some strange reactions when various people who looked suspicious to him made an appearance at the practice and he rejected them. I don't think it was chance that brought home the first secretary for the region together with an activist who was responsible for our village. This man showed him where we lived and then left. I am convinced that Andrei had promised him that he would join the collective farm, otherwise I can't see other reason for the party secretary to agree to come precisely into the house where he had brought misfortune on a man. He probably didn't remember anymore, or had done this out of despair. People said that the party activists had pledged themselves to inaugurate the collective farm to honour the day of 7 November,[33] but experience showed them that not even terror could increase the number of people who joined in. They needed an influential man and they were convinced that fear is a good counsellor, so they came without taking any precautions. What followed simply horrified me, especially since Andrei didn't forewarn me, and he didn't even suggest what he had a mind to do. Later on, by myself, recapitulating every moment of that visit, I realised that I could have suspected what was going to come.

The fact that he had prepared even the food by himself, without telling me who would be our guests, then the strange sneaky glances filled with anxiety, the uncertainty of his gestures, along with everything else taking place in an overwhelming silence, should have made me question things. But it was one of those confused days when nothing is connected, a time when you feel a stranger even in your own body. I didn't ask myself any worrying questions, not

---

33 The anniversary of the 1917 socialist revolution in Russia. In the Russian Julian calendar then in use the date was 25 October, hence the official title of the Great October Socialist Revolution. The modern calendar equivalent is 7 November – leading to some confusion and slightly absurd situations when people had to say "We celebrate the Great October Socialist Revolution in November" with a straight face.

even when I saw the Party secretary opening the gate to the street. My husband welcomed him with great warmth and invited him inside the house, assuring him he had taken the right decision. Once there, he led him to the room where my father in law was. 'He's my father,' he said to the man. 'I think you haven't forgotten him. He, unfortunately, doesn't recognise you anymore. He doesn't even recognise me. He was a real man, now he is nothing. Apologies are not enough.'

In a sudden move, he twisted one of his guest's arms behind him, and with the other hand he placed a knife to his jugular. 'At the smallest move, you are dead,' Andrei shouted. 'Why did you do this to him?' he enquired, pointing at his father who, frightened now, had huddled on the bed and, through the tears, emitted a sort of moan like a wounded animal. Terrified, I asked him to stop, not to start on a road where there was no turning back. He didn't hear me, his face had changed, he looked terrifying. In that moment, he didn't care for anyone or anything, he was not interested in the man's attempts to explain himself, nor in his threats. He banged his opponent's head powerfully against the wall until the man, his body limp, slid lifelessly to the floor.

Once the secretary's moaning stopped, Andrei seemed to wake up from the nightmare and said to me with total lucidity: 'Lord, what have I done? How could you let me lose my mind?' Then, with calm, sure gestures, he abandoned the secretary, kissed me with despair as if he were convinced we were seeing each other for the last time and, with tears in his eyes, asked me to give him quickly all the money we had. 'I am going,' he said to me. 'Maybe I'll manage to go into the mountains. I am sorry I brought you misfortune. I don't know what happened to me. I could no longer bear seeing father in the state they'd brought him to. Take care of him, if they'll let you do it.'

He kissed his father, he then lifted the secretary on his shoulders, slammed him inside the abandoned jeep and, at great speed, he disappeared before I had the time to come back to my senses and understand what was going on, or how Andrei's fit was possible. The militia post in the village, the few Securitate officers and the village hall clerks found me where I had fallen in the hallway of the house. I had wanted to run after Andrei, to stop him before he committed a new error, but I had barely managed to pass the threshold before my energy suddenly deserted me. I fell without feeling pain or terror. I had suddenly understood that the next step could only be death and, in the few moments of lucidity, before I fainted, I had wished it as the easiest and most comfortable liberation.

I was woken up by having water thrown generously over me, as well as by the encouragement of a militiaman who handled the bucket energetically and, from time to time, kicked me with his foot, but not with all the strength he could muster: 'Wake up, you whore, and tell us where the comrade is! Is he still alive?'

I got up with very great difficulty. Disorientated by the water and the kicks, I tried to master myself and to coordinate my movements, but after I came back to myself I heard the militiaman repeating obstinately, mechanically, the same encouragement and the same name calling. Without thinking too much, stimulated by the cold and the pain, a horrible pain, both in my body and in my soul, I threw myself at him: 'When I saved your wife from dying, I was a whore then, too, you wretch?' I asked him, but I was no longer capable of listening to his reply. A powerful kick helped me lose consciousness, just as, in fact, I had desired.

The militiaman's wife had appealed to a crone in the village to help her have an abortion, but a catastrophe had come of it. He asked me not to tell anyone, and to assume the risk of caring for her. Which was what I did. Pity and human kindness do not always consider the laws, and neither are people as you'd want them to be. I woke up in the car, with my hands tied tightly, between two men. Despite the pain and physical exhaustion, I didn't want to draw their attention to the fact that I was conscious. I tried to concentrate on the painful areas, to isolate and then eliminate them from my own body. I was performing a sort of psychological surgery, if I may put it that way. I had somehow abandoned myself, since the pain surpassed the limits I perceived to be in one place or another. I had become pain and scalpel at the same time. I had read many years previously of the terrible experience of some inmates from Sing Sing who, as a punishment, were inserted into a rubber tube which denied them any movement. In order to surmount this, they concentrated on various muscle groups, then on the whole limbs, until they managed to cancel their pain, and they felt nothing.

My experiment was not successful, but for the entirety of the road I did not emit a single moan, although – alongside their fear of being sanctioned for the disappearance of the comrade secretary – they were interested in my shape, in the fact that my husband could abandon such a 'morsel' and other comments of this kind. I am no saint. I have sinned, and not only in my thoughts, you know this, but there is a level of discussion or a level of inter-human relations below which I cannot lower myself. As a physician, I understand many things because they appertain to diseases, and not to the state of a patient's constitution. On the other hand, as a woman, when I am dealing with verbal aggression of the kind suggested, I feel defeated, incapable of reacting, other than with a tool for defence. We have nothing in common, we belong to different worlds! I know their vocabulary. I could have confronted them on their territory, but the sentences refused to come together, even my vocal chords were paralysed. I couldn't stop asking myself, then as now: where did these human specimens come from? Are we perhaps descending back into the caves, and I didn't realise it until this misfortune happened?

Once we got to the headquarters of the Securitate, I allowed myself to be dragged inside because I imagined I would escape for at least a few hours from the unusually brutal interrogations everyone talked about. I moaned and involuntarily opened my eyes only in the moment when they were struggling to untie the rope with which they had tied my arms behind my back. For two weeks, the same thing happened to me almost constantly. I was interrogated day and night with small breaks during which, they sometimes gave me something to eat: bread, water and, often, some translucent soup. The same questions, about Andrei's connections to the partisans and foreign agencies, the same lightbulbs directed in my eyes, the same buckets of water in order to wake me up because I was becoming dizzy more and more often, especially when they hit me on the soles of my feet. Water, straw and beatings, said a platoon leader who woke me up by throwing bucketfuls of water on me, in order to bring me to my senses after what they called an interrogation. It is true, there were calmer hours when I was given real food and I was advised to work with them, on the promise of a position in a hospital of the Ministry of Internal Affairs. They proposed to free me, on the condition that I would go searching for Andrei in the forest. I would be accompanied, naturally. I always refused, even when I was threatened with not even being allowed to take part in the burial of my husband who, so they said, had lost his life during a fight in the mountains. 'He is not that courageous,' I tried to taunt them, 'but I will go immediately after I escape from here!'

In the meantime, eavesdropping on their discussions, I learned that the secretary had been abandoned together with the car some tens of kilometres from the village, at the foot of the mountains, where Andrei had probably felt safer. For two weeks, they hadn't managed to convince me to sign an agreement with them, despite the beatings, the promises and the threat of a trial, so they let me go. I think they planned to follow me so that they could get to Andrei, or to what they called accomplices, through me.

I arrived home with great difficulty, especially since I went on foot, or through the mercy of some cart drivers. I didn't have any money on me and I felt a terrible hunger, but I was afraid to beg in case anything happened to the people I approached. To my surprise my father in law recognised me, since he started to cry as he was coming to welcome me. I gathered that he had been fed by the neighbours. They'd also fed the animals.

Because nobody stopped me, I presented myself to the dispensary, where I restarted my work. For a change, the moments of loneliness, and especially the nights, had become nightmares. I would review Andrei's madness, sequence by sequence, and I would try to guess whether he'd invited the man to our house by chance. Not even later, when I had become accustomed to the thought that I'd lost him for a long time, maybe forever, did I know how to interpret the news from him brought to the dispensary or home by various people in the village or elsewhere . Which one had truly met him, and which one had been sent by the Securitate? I asked everybody the same questions and I communicated the same encouragement to him: turn yourself in before it is too late, as he had to choose between prison and death. For the rest, nothing special. I would work until exhaustion and I would try not to cry and pity myself. I knew that I was finished with life, even more so since I was permanently haunted by a strange feeling of powerlessness and of the end of the road. It was hard to understand how it was possible that I had jumped from a youth wasted reading so many medical books straight to death. The fact was that life under the terror which I could not ignore – not even for one moment – was harder than death.

I had moments when the woman I still was to some extent remembered her physiological rights, and in those moments I condemned Andrei for not thinking of me at all when he decided to hit the secretary. This was an aspect of himself he had not even allowed me to suspect. In those moments I would dream of *Făt-Frumos*, a Prince Charming who came from nowhere, threw himself at me and left me without energy, and even without life. At other times I proposed to myself assuming the risk of searching for him, anticipating the difficulties of the road, the fear of travelling alone at night, through the woods, without knowing where I could find him – and I gave up.

This is how, waiting for a miracle, the days – many, and very long – huddled one on top of the other without hope, without news and without a trace of light in the soul. I have nothing to fight for, and nothing to expect – I said to myself, overwhelmed by the increasingly bad news that came from the mountains. Increasingly greater numbers of partisans were caught or killed. The villages at the foot of the mountains were permanently in mourning. The wives of the fallen needed my support, so I had managed to build an exact image of the disaster in the most natural fashion. It was clear to me that after they caught or killed Andrei, then it would be my turn to go to prison, or to undergo one of the numerous humiliations the families of those who'd fought were subjected to. All this might still be ahead of me. I wanted to come to you many times, because I was incapable of carrying my sorrows by myself and, despite our agreement, I dreamt not of two nights with you, like that time, but even two hours. I no longer cared what we had promised to each other. Sometimes, in order to break the night, you only need a single lit match. Its light can stay in your mind for a long time. And it tells you that there exists something else besides darkness. I felt the need for a strong shoulder, but I gave up looking for you, convinced that I would harm you, so I contented myself with crying alone. I didn't believe the forester here, who notified me that Andrei was gravely hurt, until he brought me his wedding ring, because, naturally, a letter from him risked falling in the hands of the Securitate men. In a serious confrontation with those people, Andrei was shot in the shoulder and the hip. He can no longer move. He lost a lot of blood and needs urgent help. He lingers hidden in a shelter, but he is not safe. We must do something, but I am simply paralysed. I am afraid that I am perhaps sending you to your death."

"For the moment I am a doctor and somebody needs help," I replied to her. "That's all. A doctor never cares for the political orientation of the sufferer, for their nationality and creed. Could I ever be at peace if, because of fear, I stayed home?"

Dana didn't make other comment. She looked at me with gratitude and, with her eyes in tears, followed the priest's urging to sit down at the table. After she did so, he said the

351

prayer, as was the custom.

That moment – it was impossible for me to ever forget it. I had saved numerous people from dying because it was my profession. I was ready, even from the first student year, for this confrontation, but it was at just that time that I felt the presence of death with my whole being. We were not speaking about others now, but about me, and I perceived her cold, terrifying breath for the first time. I was suddenly discovering that in those circumstances it was not enough to be a doctor; because if you were truly a human being, you could not hide behind your profession during those confused days. Fate had sprung a new provocation in front of me, the hardest. She had probably wanted to convince herself, once and forever, about who I was, and I could not dodge the challenge. I had died and was reborn in the same moment. I had felt a break, an illumination. I had made a somersault which denied itself to words and, finally, I had understood that, from then on, it would be impossible for me to be as I had been before. I no longer said to myself, resignedly: "Whatever the Lord gives us!" although I committed myself to His will, but I was without any doubt that I could not have forgiven myself any trace of hesitation, not ever.

"I hope to bring you good news," I whispered to Dana. "I think it would be better to manage to convince him to come to a hospital. Certainly, they will lock him up, but in prison he will at least be alive, he might have some hope, whereas in the mountains he has none! Time, theoretically speaking, is ahead of us and, as Nastratin Hogea[34] used to say, either

---

34 *Nastratin Hogea* is a humorous folk character based on a real person, also known as Nasreddin or Nasr Uddin, believed to have lived in the 13th century Ottoman world. Humorous moral tales and anecdotes featuring him are known across the Islamic and Ottoman sphere of influence, from Afghanistan to the Balkans. In the story quoted above, Nastratin received a large sum of money from the sultan, saying he could teach a donkey to speak.

the sultan croaks it, or the donkey will start to talk! Evil cannot endure forever, but I would like you to know," I said, as if foreseeing a gust of death, "that nobody forced me, and should I not return, you won't have any blame for it."

Dana came closer to me and kissed me with gratitude, but not as a woman, like the woman she was once, but as a friend who replaces the words they have in hand with a kiss: "I don't know what to say to you," she whispered, "I should stop you and go there myself, but the Father doesn't even want to hear about it. Neither does the forester, the man who will accompany you to the hideout in the mountains. And, on top of that, I can no longer control myself."

"I feel this will be fine," I said to her in a whisper, regretting that a more intelligent phrase didn't come to mind, but when faced with any separation, gestures – no matter how gauche – are not ridiculous.

In the following minutes, the priest took command: "You have taken the most appropriate decision. Don't look back," he ordered me, "because if you do you won't go anymore. Leave everything in the care of the Almighty and they will be safe. The reasons for you to stay, not to take the risk, are always stronger."

He then explained to us what difficulties awaited us on the road, how to confront them and, especially what I should say to the Securitate and militiamen if we got caught. Then he talked about conditions in the custody of the Securitate and what tortures they employed. The forester had to leave earlier and wait for us in a place known only to the priest – who had undergone a transformation impossible to suspect a matter of minutes previously. He had become harsh, authoritative, while his appearance and manner of being in those moments seemed to have no connection with his real profession. Each of us prayed before setting out and, following the priest's advice, I didn't look back, although the noise of crying from Dana and the priest's wife stopped me from leaving immediately. I had the certainty that I had forgotten something, but I could not point to what exactly it was. In any case, besides the fear, the doubts and the hesitation in my soul, regret at not finding any soothing words for Dana had also increased. I owed her more than anyone could imagine. Now I was presented with the chance to repay her trust, her friendship, and even our mad unfettering of those two days. Furthermore, I didn't believe anything different than she did about the life to which we had been destined for us here, in this part of the world subject to every failed social experiment.

"Life is a series of parallel deaths."
Flaubert

"Punctual or not, we live according to life's timetables. Death, however, is time without hours. Can one imagine a greater privilege than believing one's own death is unique, just for oneself, a private box reserved in the great theatre of eternity? There are people who are waiting for death to liberate them from their own memory. Many suicides. There are people who will regret for all their lives – that which is still left to them – that they haven't paid heed to the creature who is gone forever, for not giving them their hand, for not listening to them. There is the silence of virile love that must wait until death in order to be manifested – the whisper addressed to the dead person, whom, out of shame, we haven't talked to while living. [...] There is no word which is not charged with forgetting and memories, a nuance of illusions

and failures. And, without any doubt, there is no word that cannot defeat death, because there is no word that doesn't bring its imminent renewal inside it. Words fight against death, because they are inseparable from death, they trick it, they foretell it, they inherit it."
Carlos Fuentes – *This I Believe*

The road to the shelter where Andrei was, the first trip of this kind, was free of any incident, but to me it seemed to be never-ending. All the lights in the village were out, the petrol for the lamps was procured with great difficulties, only exchanged for foodstuffs and especially for eggs, according to an epigram that circulated from mouth to mouth:

> *"Come to mother for a kiss, dear hen,*
> *Cause your arse gives off our light.*
> *Glory to the Russian people*
> *For sinking oil wells down inside it!"*

Electricity was mentioned only in a slogan of Lenin's: "Communism is electrification plus the power of the Soviets." The Power of the Soviets, as is known, had been installed in our country with the help of the "Glorious Red Army" and with the decisive contribution of the four great powers in Yalta, but there was still a long way to go before electrification. The country lanes were deserted, only the dogs did their duty by announcing the proximity of wild animals. I had gotten accustomed to their barking while traipsing night after night to the houses of my patients, but I felt their agitation differently on this occasion. It was as if everybody was lying in wait for us. I was waiting from one moment to the next to be stopped by the flashlights and the yelling of Securitate men.

Fortunately, we reached the edge of the woods without any incident, but we felt a little safer only when we were in the shelter of the beeches that watched over a very narrow forest road. This led to a clearing where there were a few hunting cabins which nobody had used for a long time. The forester whispered to us that we had found ourselves in an unsafe area and he advised us that, in case of "something," we should throw ourselves to the ground and not get scared if there were any exchanges of fire.

"The Securitate men do not have the courage yet to walk at night through these places, nor to attack," the forester assured us.

Despite the animal fear, the exhaustion and the flashlights that blinded us from time to time, we finally reached unharmed, after a few hours of walking, the shelter where Andrei was. Surprised, he tried to smile at me:

"Thank you," he whispered to me in a faint voice. "Now it's too late, you should not have risked."

In the pallid light of a small lantern held with trembling hands by the priest, I opened in a great hurry the thing which could be called bandages. Rags of hemp cloth, strips of peasant shirts soaked in blood, covered two wounds – in the shoulder and the hip, deep and dangerous. I started to talk to him in order to distract his attention from the painful manoeuvres I was going to perform, and the priest, understanding it immediately, started to talk both about Dana, and, naturally, about his father. When he moved to the political situation in the country and the approaching military help of the English and Americans, Andrei gave a nervous start: "There is no discussion about it, father! We are dying here like fools. I wish at least they didn't promise it."

His facial expression and the way he had reacted reminded me of the old Andrei, who was always irritated, discontent, reproaching the whole world for his own non-achievements. In fact, even with me, despite the friendship he showed me, I felt his air of rejection, the desire not to get too close to me.

Suspecting the question which, logically, we had to ask, he came forward to meet us: "My mind had simply gone dark. I could no longer see father like that, a kind of shadow without memory, incapable of understanding what had happened to him, a defenceless creature. I was thinking of how many things he'd given up for me so that I could finish my studies, and at the injustice done to all people from around here. When I reached the end of the village with that party activist, I intended to kill him. I knew that I would pay with my life for my revolt of one moment. In the end I thought that, in reality, the person in front of me was a wretched tool of other tools and I took pity on him. Especially since he had soiled himself and stank so badly that, at the edge of the village, I was forced to throw him out of the car. The luck of cowards. They either strike you with pity, or they stink! It was only here, with the partisans, that I discovered we have no hope. A handful of men may furnish an example, but doesn't have the power to replace all the mindless ones or the cowards. And we are doing bloody well, both with one category and the other! Now, since I know them better, I am convinced that, deep inside, these people didn't set out to win, but to survive. In any way."

His voice got extinguished little by little, the energy that was still left in him was kept only for moans and in order to keep his eyes open. After I explained to him that I was going to perform the cleaning of the wounds and extract the bullets, I administered an analgesic and asked him to bite on a thick piece of rubber I took from the clinic back in the day when the professor of psychiatry taught me how to perform electric shocks on patients. The wounds were deep and, after I looked at them carefully, I realised that I didn't have the minimum required means to make a surgical intervention, nor the required skill.

"We'll have to take him to a hospital," I whispered to the priest, who had convinced himself on his own that, in the given conditions, I could not help him more.

"This means that our turn to go to prison has come as well, even if we don't die. But as we cannot close our eyes in front of suffering and injustice, things will be as the Lord on High will decide. We shall do everything we believe it is good to do!"

To my surprise, Andrei shrugged his shoulders resignedly, as if we were talking about somebody else. He had left all responsibility to us, or maybe we had come to meet his unconfessed desire to leave the mountain and to give up the increasingly numerous and brutal skirmishes with the Securitate.

"If we make it whole to the village, I will say that he was abandoned by somebody in front of the church. As a priest, I naturally called on the doctor, and the doctor, just as naturally, took him to the hospital after he realised he had no way to help the man. The important thing is to find a plausible explanation for him as well, especially since people know his story with that party secretary."

"Yes, but after he abandoned him on the edge of the village it wasn't necessarily the case that he had run off to join the partisans. As a proof, he left him there and didn't take him as a trophy or an object to exchange. As for the wounds, he happened to be in the wrong place at the wrong time," I answered, and the priest immediately accepted the explanation; he then asked the people around to improvise a stretcher which was going to be pulled to the edge of the forest. Andrei opened his eyes less and less, he seemed confused, lacking interest in what was going to happen to him in the following hours. In the end, thinking of the jolts to come, I administered a dose of morphine and, while the men fixed the two blankets on the pieces of wood that formed our so-called stretcher, I explained to the commander what we would say to the Securitate men if we were about to be caught. He then gave us four companions and, hurried by the priest, we started downhill:

"We should reach back while still dark," he explained to me. "Otherwise we'll have to wait for next night or for some miracle so that he passes unseen. Even so, in the state he is, I fear he will not pull through."

As for me, from all the states of mind that God gave us, with the exception of pain, the hardest one to bear seemed to be that of waiting: dead time, a torture. Experience had taught me not to see the good aspect of things, but only the bad one. In situations of such great tension, waiting exhausts you. "Now that the suffering of these men made us brothers, I have to confess sincerely that I've beaten this track many times, but the greatest fear normally gripped me on the way back."

The broken boughs, the gritting of leaves under the brutal weight of our steps, the terrors of the night birds, as well as Andrei's moans seemed to cause great avalanches, which our companions appeared not to take into account. I stopped at short intervals in order to read his heartbeat and blood pressure, then, urged by our companions, I would run after the men, fall, get back up and, terrorised by the noises I caused, I would try to concentrate on the road, convinced that my senses, sharpened to paroxysm, would warn me of dangers. At the edge of the woods our companions left us, and the forester started on ahead in order to prepare the cart on which we were going to take Andrei to the hospital. So it was only me and the priest left with the stretcher and, to my surprise, I pulled through. In fact, we didn't care if we were seen, and maybe we were. What seemed to us to be important was to get home as soon as possible so that we could save him.

To our surprise and joy, Dana had not left, her instinct had urged her to wait for news of Andrei. It was a painful meeting, but one which I interrupted without mercy. "We don't have the time, Andrei can't wait anymore! I don't think that an Ambulance car could reach there quicker. And I am not sure there is one!" The forester brought the cart, inside which we had improvised a straw mattress, the priest took over the reins of the horses in a hurry, and Dana and I checked once again the state of his wounds, the blood pressure and the heartbeat.

All preparations took place in a funereal silence. The priest's wife said no word: resigned, with lowered head, she gave some sandwiches to him along with two big bottles of tea, and then led us to the gate. The forester returned home, he had to be protected because, as the priest had explained, he was our only connection between the partisans and the few people in the village who helped them.

Dana's presence was good for Andrei. Probably feeling guilty, he enquired, as far as his energies and pain allowed him, about the state of his father and that of Dana. Feeling happy to hear him and for the inspiration not to go, as

Father Goga had advised her, she told him everything that came into her head about her father in law, then a great deal of happy events, but it was impossible to decipher from his face whether he believed them or not. She avoided telling him of the two weeks of torment.

"I don't know what came over me back then," Andrei said, trying to justify himself. "It was as if I had lost my head. In the mountains it was even harder. The partisans didn't trust me. They put me under the care of one man who seemed to be decided on killing me at the least significant sign of disloyalty. I felt like killing myself many times. Instead of being inspired by the thought that I must live, I found myself crying. I didn't wish to live in a world the way I used to anymore, it had made me sick, and another world refused me. I am well now, for the few kilometres we still have to travel together. I think that never in my life have I felt calmer, more at peace."

In any case, for a matter of moments, a deep, wordless state of communication had been established between us, and a silence such as I had never encountered before had installed itself all around. It was as if we had entered a space of great serenity, so much so that, in other circumstances, I would have thought of the peacefulness that precedes death. But back then I was convinced that, no matter what happened after the unavoidable surgical intervention, we had still obtained the greatest victory: we had vanquished our fear of dying, of prison, of all that could happen to us. I was grateful to the priest for the things I felt and I confessed to him how much I was morally in his debt.

"These people give you five years of prison even if you haven't done anything. What about us, who have saved from death 'an enemy of the people'– as they say?! If you didn't know on what side justice resides, my advice would have probably not been of any use to you. But as things are."

"I realised that all people know it, but they lack the courage. Instead of fighting, they adapt and thus increase their suffering. I am convinced that, for the simple man, no regime can be good," I told him, but the priest concentrated on the horses. It seemed to him that we were driving too slowly and that, with sunrise, traffic was going to increase and, as such, so would people's curiosity.

"Don't deceive yourself. In the end, they will sell us too, either the squealers in the village or some partisan who won't withhold torture, or some friend – as usual. But if you think of the possible punishments, then you should know you are lost. Let us thank the Almighty that we can help the people who haven't forgotten on what side justice and courage reside."

Having reached the Emergency Hospital, Dana introduced herself as what she was: a doctor, but also the wife of the wounded man, with the hope that professional solidarity might work. I was just a nondescript companion, especially since, after such a night, I looked worse than a horse-coach driver. Still, I stayed nearby until I knew Andrei was on the surgery table, and then, urged by Dana, I left the hospital in a hurry:

"Go, you can still help others. And please rest at peace that, irrespective of the difficulties, I will never admit that you've helped me. I suffered their brutalities once, I know what to expect. Of course, they will notify the Prosecutor's office, the Securitate, the Militia, the Party. A great scandal will come out of this. But the important thing is that Andrei will live."

I no longer had the time to kiss her or to give her advice. I was just a chance acquaintance. For my part, I cannot bear separations and especially those where you realise there might be so much more to say and that no other possibility might appear again. Then, I was also thinking that some doctor or who knows who else might recognise me, and experience has taught me that friends or colleagues can often be more dangerous than enemies. Fear spurred me to leave quickly and to lose myself in the turmoil of the city.

I immediately went to the barbershop, to the public baths, the restaurant and the cinema, where I saw a Soviet film about the competition between two teams of sailors: meaning which one could wash the ships' decks quicker and better. I will never forget this film, because it was one of exasperating monotony, and very long, equal to the measure of my need to sleep. After this, I went again to the restaurant: I had the certainty they would arrest me, since it seemed impossible to me that we hadn't been seen and, I don't know why, I wanted to gather energy. I was lucky. Later on, when I reviewed the events, I regretted that I did not stay longer to talk to Dana, although it was useless to assure her that I would always stand by her side, in all circumstances. It was a burdensome separation, heavy like a death, and it was also the beginning of great losses, the kind that make your life more confused, more incomprehensible. Dana was arrested immediately after the surgical intervention was over, and Andrei stayed there with three soldiers at the door of the ward until he got well. There was a trial as well, as expected, after Andrei went out of the hospital. In fact, it was not a trial, but a party meeting in which everybody brought accusations, including the defence team, with the punishment being known in advance. She, as wife and accomplice, was condemned to five years of forced labour. He, for sedition against the social order, received by some miracle only twelve years, although they could have, just as easily, condemned him to death. He was freed in 1964, together with the other political prisoners, as many as were still alive. A short time after his release, Andrei crossed the Danube into Yugoslavia, establishing himself later on in Austria. He had risked his life and got lucky. Dana followed him after some two years and the family was made whole, if I can use a word which was fashionable back then. They returned to the country sometime later, after the Revolution, a little while before Dana's passing away after breast cancer. In fact, she wanted to die at home.

He then suffered a change which was hard to imagine at the time, but which was almost natural in those years. He had become malicious beyond measure, and he believed, as many others do, that the whole world was guilty for his suffering – which had been real. I, especially, was the guilty one, the person who seemingly took him to the hospital by force after I had an agreement with the Securitate men. He never wanted to meet me, to talk openly, for us to explain to each other, although there was nothing to clarify in my opinion. I didn't know about Dana's death, to whose funeral I would have gone, irrespective of the risk. In the balance of his judgment the only matters that weighed were the things that I didn't do for him, or I hadn't suspected that he had expected me to do. Since they hadn't also jailed me, that meant I was guilty. That was his most important argument. The priest and I have escaped prison, whereas he... I went many times to the mountains – together with Father Goga or on my own, as necessary. Usually, the priest buried them, and by the time he finished his job I encouraged or treated whatever could be treated. Why didn't the people in village betray us? I often asked myself. They had a need both for the priest and the doctor. At least that's what I believed, but, in spite of all this, I lived every day with the certainty that it would be the last one I lived outside prison. In any case, both of us breathed a little easier during winter, because the mountains were emptied of the partisans before the fall of the first snow. They descended into the valleys or took refuge at the other end of the country, because Securitate men guarded the sources of water and hunted for them by the tracks left in the snow. Some of them, disappointed that the foreign aid – the atomic bomb about which President Truman had spoken previously – was delayed, no longer returned, and worked under false identities on the "great building sites of Socialism" or cutting down the woods. Others preferred to die by bullets rather than shame, as a monarchist officer I had cared for told me.

After this first experience with Andrei, I no longer had the sense of risk. I was a doctor and I was doing my duty. The rest was up to fate, up to the Lord's will, up to luck. In any case, I enjoyed each day I lived outside prison, each Sunday and feast day I spent in church. I built the cabin much later, near the grotto where Andrei had been hidden. Because it was *from this place* and *from those moments* that my life took an unsuspected turn. I wanted not to forget that, in a very difficult circumstance of my life, I had been not necessarily courageous but I had been dignified. Courage also contains a dose of irresponsibility and haphazardness. I had been truly dignified. I tried later on to become like this, and many times I had the conviction that I had managed it..

"World, even if I knew I was dying,
I would still not ask for your help!"
Folk song

"Meditating upon the treacherous moment
I conquered the citadel of deathless Eternity.
Now, the fear of death can find no bridges towards me."
Milarepa

I write with fierceness, although, looking back, I don't feel more relieved and I don't discover anything able to take me out from the confusion in which I find myself, either. I don't even know why I persist in writing since words do not help me at all, and it's not because Mara would not allow herself to be described, but because my feelings for her are contradictory, impossible to draw. It is not the first time that I don't look at her through the lens of my age, but as a woman. Through the lustful, sinful eyes with which I looked at her mother once. Suddenly, it feels as if a fault in time has just opened and we are again face to face, exactly the persons who, despite our desires, we haven't managed to be, and fate, knowing me weak and undecided, gave me another chance. The last one. Absolutely certainly.

Looking at her, the feelings that try me bear various names: confusion, sorrow, mad, animal lust, terror, powerlessness and, on top of that – unbearable – morality with its ancient or not so ancient principles, ready at any moment to circumvent their substance, to draw my attention to the fact that I am, and it is hard for me to admit it, the person who is looking shamelessly at the shape of the woman who's moving here and there in front of me. This is a person who thinks that, after all, this is her meaning, to provoke you by everything she has, to draw your attention by each one of her cells to tell you she exists in every state, to inundate you with her pheromones in order to demonstrate to you that you are closer to the animals, than to the angels. I am very tense in front of this very beautiful creature belonging to nobody, who seems not to have any trace of restraint: she says what she thinks, she does what she thinks, with the most natural air possible. Free like the wild things among which she lives. She has known sin and she didn't hide it from me. Or maybe she behaves like this in order to express her gratitude to me because I promised I would take care of her? Does she want me to be indebted to her for the same reason? I don't know, and I should not even care. She has giant strength, a power of attraction that forces me to feel my frailty, but, at the same time, also forces on me the hope that I could still live, that life has numerous well springs from which it feeds. Leave the initiative to her – this would be the most correct solution, the cowardly option, but this thing has started to gain outlines inside of me: fear of her hesitations, fear of the fact that she might give up on defeating my restraint, my terrors. In those moments, Mara meant life, and, simplifying everything, I had to choose between morals and life.

There was just one answer I was missing: what would happen to me, or in me, if I chose morals? What if I gave free rein to the senses which had now awakened after such a long time? I must not forget that I always stumbled on morals, and what had I gained from it? I never stepped on the lawn, I never pulled the flowers, I didn't spit where and when not allowed, I forbade myself everything that was required of me to forbid. So what? Suffering, regrets and discontent are the only consequence of all these interdictions, and my life has been just a never-ending postponement and a waiting. A sort of failed suicide. I think that my profession defeated me definitively, since I understood everyone. I accepted that there existed not only the sick, but also various evolving states. Most of the time it has been up to me to impose my point of view, to be a human also, not just a psychiatrist, but speaking for myself, I never had the courage to take the step, that particular step, no matter how small it might have been. Most of the time I didn't know how to start and I didn't even try, so that the event was consumed in my mind before it started. And yet, with my eyes closed, among the tears, I often look behind and I am welcomed there, with the embraces of old, by almost all my dear ones, those who are no more. Suddenly I feel a sickly yearning for Daria, for my family, and yet I seem not to be able to conceive that, on this earth and with these weakened eyes, I will never see them again. Absurd longings, sometimes tormenting. I rediscover Mara, for a change, who – with sure, lazy movements – makes the bed for me, and I, despite everything I could be told or everything people could believe, I try to explain or to justify myself, in front of those from whom I cannot manage to separate myself fully, that I am very lonely and that I'm trying to live, with all my might. Trying to live, even like this, tormented, as it were, by the overwhelming feeling of ridiculousness. In the end, I decided to leave everything up to the woman. Or to the cowardice of always.

> *"All those who are unhappy are so because they looked for their own happiness;*
> *All those who are happy are so because they have looked for the happiness of others.*
> *What use comes of so many words?*
> *Just look at the fool obsessed only with his own interest*
> *And the saint who works for the interest of others."*
> Shantideva

"The landscape of my days appears composed, just like mountainous regions, of different materials thrown with a pitchfork. Among them, my nature – already a composite, formed in equal parts of instinct and culture. Here and there the granite of the unavoidable comes through; and everywhere the landslides of chance. I strive, jogging through my life, to find a plan, to follow a vein of lead or gold, or the bed of a subterraneous river, but the devised plan is just an illusion of memory. From time to time I think it recognises the hand of Fate in an encounter, a foreboding, a certain series of events; too many roads will lead nowhere, too many sums can't make an addition."

Marguerite Yourcenar – *Memoirs of Hadrian*

Before being Dr Cassian Robert, consultant in psychiatry, member of various scientific societies, respected psychoanalyst and author of numerous specialised articles etc. etc., my name used to be Vasile Robescu. My father, Gheorghe Robescu, formerly Robu, hailing from an obscure village on the shores of the Danube, had read commercial studies, but he had not advanced in the ranks, he had been happy with the position of head of office and with the madness gained from his wife, Eufimia Câmpeanu, an energetic schoolmistress from a village near Cluj. This madness was to do with buying land, as much as possible, because land meant power and independence.

The Câmpeanu family had produced numerous countryside intellectuals, local erudite men kept in the memory of the area. One of them had written a history of folk dress and customs in the village, and of oral traditions; another one, over-passionate for the Transylvanian School,[35]

---

35 *Şcoala Ardeleană* in Romanian. An 18th and 19th centuries Enlightenment-inspired school of thought and intellectual action of the Romanians in Transylvania, then part of the Austro-Hungarian Empire. It played an important role in the creation of modern Romania, its literature and culture.

discovered different writing implements which had seemingly belonged to the intellectual Samuil Micu Klein, the bag in which historian Gheorghe Şincai had carried around his celebrated history and other, smaller things, for which he wanted to make room within a museum that was going to bear his name: *Eusebiu Septimiu Câmpeanu Museum of National History*. Unfortunately, because of a journalist "who a pure Romanian was not, and a pure Romanian heart beateth not in his heart," as Eusebiu Septimiu Câmpeanu had written himself in a reply note, the idea had fallen into derision. The last article of the journalist in question convinced him to give the idea up for good. A national museum or a flea-market? Vasile Mureşan asked.

"The underpants which Decebalus was wearing in the moment of his suicide, the fork with which the Persian King Darius ate quails, the belt on the trousers of Scorilo together with the jug in which Dochia, the hypothetical daughter of the great Dacian King Decebalus, had gathered her tears – all these will be seen in the museum of the schoolmaster Eusebiu Septimiu Câmpeanu. In the near future, the exhibits will be augmented by the skull of Attila the Hun, aged 16, a rib of Hungarian King Árpad, the engagement ring of Romanian Prince Menumorut and, maybe the most interesting item on display, the wooden spoon with which Empress Maria Theresa ate wild bees' honey in a village near Năsăud. In a separate room, Mr Câmpeanu will display the paper on which he is going to comment on the history of each exhibit, as well as, in a first translation of its kind, the travel journal of Emperor Trajan in Dacia, annotated by Emperor Aurelian, the man who left us prey to the heathen hordes coming from Asia. These are just a part of the numerous surprises, which I learned with great difficulty from his neighbours. But we shall be there for the inauguration, and we shall recount to you all that seems interesting to us."

That journalist, "found in the pay of the millenary oppressor," also expressed a few times afterwards his anxiety that the inauguration continued to be delayed, but Septimiu Câmpeanu was content to shut up and say in a lowered voice some harsher words addressed to his nation:

"Woe to you, Romanian nation, who allow yourselves to be guided by fools and scoundrels. Because the millenary enemy sleeps not."

As a consequence, the museum was left to oblivion, but the heirs got possession of numerous old manuscripts, diplomas and deeds of real value, newspaper collections, objects belonging to important Transylvanian personalities, with the notes made by some priests on the capriciousness of the weather for the past tens of years, as well as with various folkloric collections.

In the end, two members of the Câmpeanu family, Octavian Augustus and Lucrețiu, crossed the mountains to the Old Kingdom[36] and, following the example of the Gheorghe Lazăr, the Transylvanian educator, they opened a school in Bucharest itself, "in order to help our brethren to step away from the customs of the Phanariotes[37] which bring anything but honour onto themselves." Then, the two brothers died in the First World War at the head of some military units, in the effort of liberating Transylvania from the Austro-Hungarians, and the trace of their families was

---

36 The expression Old Kingdom is used in Transylvania to refer to pre-1918 Romania, which did not include Transylvania as yet. The shape of present-day Romania is more or less the same since 1918.

37 Literally meaning people of the Phanar. Phanar (present-day Fener) was a neighbourhood of Istanbul inhabited mainly by Greeks. Various members of prominent Phanar families have been appointed by the sultans as rulers of the Romanian principalities of Wallachia and Moldavia, from 1711 to 1821. With few exceptions, they are held as prime examples of venality. This is a period of great Ottoman and Hellenic influence over Romanian customs and culture.

then lost. The transformation of Robescu into Robert and of Vasile to Cassian took place during my university studies, at the insistence of my grandfather, Ioan, who had grown angry because of the jokes made by some course assistants from History of Medicine. Robu – meaning "slave," and, as a consequence, Robescu as well – could not be anything but the expression of a social status, so as a consequence my folks had been slaves, meaning Gypsies from the south of the country, freed by Kogălniceanu.[38] What's more, my grandfather, Ioan Robescu, was not too tall, had thick, dark hair, a slightly swarthier face, and eyes of the same colour as the hair. On top of that, his very beautiful baritone voice had helped him to decent earnings as an extra in the choir of the Opera of Cluj. My qualities as a science researcher, my height and my chestnut-coloured hair would have come from my mother's side, as often stressed by my grandmother, who was proud of the past of her forebears, "patriots who sacrificed themselves on the battlefront for the liberation of Transylvania, so that thieves and scoundrels can nowadays sully the blood of these heroes with deeds of shameful memory." As for my grandfather's resolution, besides these malicious deductions, nothing made him regret his decision, even if the ironies were now leading towards the Chosen People – a fact which made him immeasurably glad: "It's much easier to bring an argument here: in case of need, if a representative of the weaker sex might have any doubts, we can whip out the argument. Men will be forced to ask for references from their wives or lovers." In any case, under the communists, nobody called me a pederast anymore when

38 Until mid-19 century, the Roma Gypsies were kept as slaves on the great estates. Mihail Kogălniceanu – revolutionary, liberal statesman, historian and publicist – is an important figure in the creation of modern Romania. He supported and pushed forward legislation for the abolition of slavery in the Romanian principalities.

we sang the *Internationale*:

"Come join the great struggle,
Slave with slave we shall unite..."[39]

People got used to my new surname quickly, but not to the madness of history. The prisons were overcrowded, books were burnt in plain sight, nobody felt safe, and people whispered that there was no family without a member in prison. As was natural, the fear reached the university as well. A number of professors had been arrested or removed to some forgotten villages in Moldavia, and numerous colleagues had been expelled or imprisoned for having unhealthy social origins[40] or for not declaring biographical details. Step by step, we were faced with the fact that there was a type of medicine which was uttered in a loud voice during lectures, and another one which was whispered, in the sense that, during practical work hours, our professors suggested, or whispered to us, that various theories they had just taught us were not true, and did not have a scientific back-up, but that they had been forced to teach them to us. For example, Pavlovian thinking, in which everything was cortical-subcortical-endocrine-visceral reflexes, Soviet scientists Michurin, Lysenko and Lepeshinskaya with the transformation of non-cellular live matter into live cellular matter, and other similar theories which were straightforwardly childish and bizarre. When the Securitate picked up a roommate in the middle of the night – for the reason that, during his holiday, he had

39 The Romanian version of the *Internationale* chorus "So come brothers and sisters / For the struggle carries on".

40 Expression denoting the bourgeoisie and former higher classes, but rather more precisely anyone who was not of proletarian or peasant origins.

helped a fighter in the mountains with some medication – I thought of my family, well-off people who had lots of land, and the thought that they could arrest me or expel me from school as well, as happened to many others, terrified me. Because of this, I started to learn like mad in order to be the best and, as a consequence, indispensable. An idea of incredible naivety, but it was, more or less, all I could do. At least they'll be sorry for me, I told myself. When they proposed joining the Union of Young Communists, I did it immediately, convinced that I would be better defended this way. Although the most frequent warning was: *"Shut up so they won't hear you!"* the contact with suffering and death protected me from it to some extent, and so did the student tradition, from which nobody deviated. The football matches between the fat and the thin, the fights with the students from Agronomy, the lists of sterile women – married or not – to whose generosity we sometimes appealed after their hospital discharge – and, of course, the tour of the central square in three hansom cabs. I was driven around in the first, I would place my shoes in the second, and in the third there was the booklet with the marks obtained in the hardest exams, with the most demanding professors. Hunger, misery, colloquia, exams, practical works, loves lasting one moment in borrowed rooms or in hotels paid by the hour, or medical work performed in some better off provincial hospitals helped me not to feel the speed with which my student years went by. Because I had very good marks and numerous papers delivered within the scientific circle of psychiatrists, they kept a place for me in a laboratory of judicial psychiatry in a little town nearby, following which, after half a year, I was going to be transferred within the department at the university. Unfortunately, or because this is how destiny decided, a colleague with paperwork filled in for a job of prison doctor changed his mind and, because he was married, with a child, he chose the position before me and this is how I ended up being a country doctor in the Commune of Pădureni, formerly known as Valea Boului – the Ox's Valley.

It was only here that I realised it would have been good to marry during my student years, because I didn't really have anything to choose from in the village, except picking up what had been left in the wake of others. There was only Florica, a drawing teacher who also taught, in absence of specialists, history and music. Among all the women I was fated to meet up to that time, she seemed the most easygoing creature of all I've known. Incapable even of brewing a cup of tea for herself, she had got to the point where she got tired even at the thought she had to go to school; even more, she always complained she was sleepy, even when she was making love. The curious thing was that nobody ever found her sleeping, and she was visited by sleep only when she was not alone. When it came to love, people said even more. She didn't choose her men, she accepted almost all of them without asking them to love her, without forcing a promise from them, no matter how insignificant. She left the impression that choosing a man depended only on her own senses, and the most important exam was held in the bed, without communicating any sign that the partner interested her. The woman had a beautiful face and a pleasant physique, that of a high performance sportswoman, and it was very rarely, when she wanted to talk and she didn't offer her body for you to do almost everything you wanted with it, that you discovered a very pleasant interlocutor in her. It is probable that, as a consequence of the gossip on her account, I would have ignored her completely if she hadn't looked for me in the dispensary. From what she told me, reading the symptoms, she seemed to suffer from a crisis of the sciatic nerve, for which complaint I proceeded just the way I learned in my student years: asking the patient to undress. I asked it mechanically and she executed the request without being surprised.

It was only when I saw her stretched on the examination table, ready to check the mandatory signs of sciatic fits, that I discovered under my eyes, without wanting to, an interesting woman whose body didn't leave me indifferent, a fact she noticed as well.

"You are very expressive," she said to me while dressing slowly, her face turned to me, "one doesn't visit the doctor empty-handed, but as my salary is not so big as to push me out of the house, I would be glad to make your portrait. Although I am not a very good painter, I don't think I'd disappoint you."

I thanked her for the invitation and I assured her that I did visit my patients. She liked my answer. "As a woman, I don't expect special treatment, especially since I've heard you are not really interested in the weaker sex," she said in a provocative tone of voice as she departed. I didn't try to contradict her.

I didn't feel the need to describe the previous night during which the noise of car engines, apart from the sound of the other traffic, agitated me. Waiting for the moment when the Securitate men could burst into the house literally exhausted me. Who could I have told this thing to?

In any case, more out of inertia than anything else, we set up the meeting for the following evening, but I wasn't very convincing and my assurance didn't seem more than simple politeness to her. *"I'll go, if they won't arrest me,"* I was saying in my mind. *"It might be possible to discover another aspect of the locality from which it would be possible to escape as soon as possible."* Of course, I was not too convinced that I would go looking for her, but because the day passed without any special events, I planned not to disappoint her.

I found Florica dressed in a bathrobe, a sign that she had not thought I was going to keep my word. After she locked the door, she returned quickly to the bed from which she had just gotten up, assuring me that, after the cold she felt would pass, she was going to deal with the promised drawing. I didn't wait too long and, defeating my restraint, my fear even, I undressed quickly and, without saying a word, I sat alongside her. The woman clung to me, almost with despair, as if we were in water and I was trying to save her from drowning, and our bodies didn't refuse each other – on the contrary, they seemed to have met many times, and got along wonderfully.

After a short nap, we started again with even more energy and with regret that I had ignored her up to that time. It seemed strange that, for me, she existed only at the moment I was touching her and, many times, when my fears overcame me, or I returned from the mountains, not totally convinced that no one had spotted me, I would go looking for her because Florica had become the most appropriate remedy for this state of mind. The only one which was truly efficient, able to mollify to some extent the despair that came over me at the thought of never leaving the locality. If she hadn't existed, or to be more correct, if chance hadn't brought her in front of me, in order to be like everyone else, I would have been left only with alcohol – the mandatory refuge of all born here. The portraits sketched by

Florica were not too successful, so much so that even she reproached herself for the lack of talent with which she had been endowed.

"Maybe if I practiced more," she said in excuse. "But it doesn't come to me to do it. I feel fine, alive, only when you are near me, in the bed, glued to me. I would be happy for us to stay like this, until the time when we were no more, and only this would satisfy me completely. I don't feel the same thing with all men, but, in any case, it's better than hunger and fear. I often think that a bullet straying in the mountains, or somebody grassing on you could take you to prison or death. And you can't tell anyone what you are thinking of, you have nobody to protest to because you don't feel safe anywhere. I am convinced that I was mistaken in my century, my country, my sex and my profession. I only had one certitude: the moment I saw you, I knew what would come!"

I think this was the longest discussion between the two of us. Convinced we had the same anxieties and needs, we didn't construct any project in common, not even for the next day. We didn't look back, we didn't poke into our common fears, we left ourselves at the mercy of our senses and of futility. On leaving, I saw her cry most times, but I didn't ask for explanations, I was probably visited by the same state of mind during the empty nights terrorised by loneliness or when, out of the blue, I found myself tormented by the foreboding that I would be arrested in the next few minutes. Once, she almost tried an explanation, which she nevertheless did not take to its conclusion:

"In the midst of the chaos in which we live, we have met for one moment and I lied to myself that we could have a future together. But after the first night I convinced myself that you were not making love with me, the woman with a mind and soul, but with a certain part of me on which you concentrated. You haven't looked in my eyes once, you haven't been attentive to my reactions, but it is very well like this, too."

She said no more and it would not have made sense anyway, we all lived, even if we didn't admit it, with the feeling that every gesture, joy, moments of love, eating, sleeping or anything else could be done or lived for the last time. Who could think of the future, a future detached from threats and death, at the times when bullets were wreaking havoc and the cars of the Securitate disturbed everybody's nights?

The three years in the countryside passed with extreme difficulty, with great snows, with hunger, anxieties and waiting. I always promised myself I would study, but as time passed by I was increasingly farther away from studying. The woman who cleaned for me had locked my books in a wardrobe in order to protect them from the dust and, knowing that, I had abandoned them there, until one day when I was surprised to find, at the door of the dispensary, my psychiatry professor, Silviu Albu. I'd had to assist in two births and, faint with tiredness, after a sleepless night, I only thought of finally making it to sleep. But sleep went away as soon as I laid eyes on my professor.

He, as I was to find later on, had visited in my absence, with the help of the cleaning woman, my house near the dispensary – the premises in which I slept and worked.

"It was enough to see your room, the equipment of the dispensary, the books on the table and on your shelves in order to convince myself that you have abandoned it all," he said in the most natural tone possible, as if we'd parted only some minutes previously. "But I don't blame you, I only reproach myself for attributing to you more passion for psychiatry than you have in reality. I am rarely mistaken, but this time I am convinced I overrated you."

I wasn't expecting such a hard blow, but, after a while, which was actually quite long, I decided to play my last card.

"I suppose that not even you believe what you say. If I were just a nobody, one of the thousands of students who passed through your classes, you would not have remembered me. If you judge me by what you've seen here, you are perfectly right. I'm just a banal country doctor, a future alcoholic, just like the men on your list. A list in which people drink a terrifying lot, especially methyl alcohol. I got to the point where I am keeping medical spirit under lock and key, because the cleaning woman and the coach driver steal it with impunity. Sufferers from cirrhosis, blind people, handicapped and violent children. As far as I'm concerned, for the moment I don't drink, I am allergic to alcohol, but I fear that one day I will let myself go. Not in order to be like everybody else, but out of fear. If you only knew what happens here in the mountains. Sometimes I jump at the smallest noise, at other times it is enough to think of what could happen to me, about the broken door, about the fury of the Securitate men."

I told him in detail about the Securitate and the partisans, about the arrests and the informing that had turned my nights into an inferno, but I did not have sufficient trust to confess to him openly that I had helped the partisans, that I had been in the mountains with them at least once a week, with Father Goga. Speaking of help, I asked what would he do if he were me, and he said, resignedly:

"That which I believe you have already done!"

"It is increasingly hard for me to accept what is happening. The world seems to have entered a stage of decomposition. You never know who you are talking to, whether they are coming for you to examine them or whether they are here to coax words from your tongue, to examine you. And I am not afraid of what I say, but of what others understand. I am convinced they will ask about you as well. It is sufficient to give the coach driver or the cleaning woman a mouthful of *ţuică* plum brandy or medical spirit, and both of them are capable of inventing or declaring, without hesitating for one moment, everything that someone might ask of them."

"I imagined that," said the professor. "I was careful to explain to people at large that I am your boss and that I am here on a supervisory mission and, of course, for an exam. In fact, you've done your exam now, in a way. What you did not say is, and I am convinced of it, much more important than what you've tried to suggest to me. As for me, I can't understand what would be better: to risk your life in a desperate action without a chance of victory? To die, that is, together with these wretches who delude themselves that they will be helped, or to be useful for the larger number, becoming a real performing professional? The country has a terrible need for true heroes, too, but also for really high performing professionals in all fields. In any case, were I to choose, I wouldn't go for heroes. Unfortunately, the few high performing individuals we have are lingering in prisons."

I was in a confused state because, on the one hand, I felt the need to tell him all my anxieties, and on the other I realised that he had no means to help me, and that by telling him I could appear even weaker than I was in reality. This visit, however, disturbed me for a reason I didn't understand too well. The professor had reminded me, by his simple presence, of another world which definitively denied itself to me: that of research, of tense struggle with the unknown – the one inside man, in the world of those times, and in world which was to come.

It wasn't just about research, but also about a world of something undefined, unclear, which had once given me the feeling of an achievement. It was like a reminder of a life I had lived at some point. The fact that the professor had visited me gave me the feeling that I could still exist, that not everything was definitively lost, even if life over here had forced me to think often of my biological survival. In spring, the waters of Râul Negru, the Black River, came in torrents, sometimes for weeks on end, making the exit from the village impossible, and that compelled me to try interventions of the most difficult kind in order to save the lives of the patients I could not send to the hospital. In addition, because food provisions were getting scarcer, I ended up living from poaching or, in the worst case, counting the few potatoes that I still had.

It was impossible for me to ignore the look on my professor's face, the pity with which he looked at my clothes. It is true, my clothes had not met with an iron for a long while, as this was not part of the items found in the inventory of my dwelling place, but I often called on an old tailor who looked after my attire when I was visiting some patient in town. In fact, it was only then that I could eat until I was full. I would lay about for whole hours in the public baths and I planned to return to my books and to the plan of conducting, as much as I could, some research. Of course, after this I was going to leave the village, a desire which had seemed unrealisable until the moment when the professor left.

"A new open position in judicial psychiatry has cropped up," he said to me then, advising me before parting. "A chance which you must not lose. The competition will not be formidable because you don't make money here and, furthermore, you need a special sense; some even call it talent. After half a year, I will try to second you for the university Chair".

The professor's attention, unhoped for, made me feel over-emotional, but unfortunately I wasn't able to thank him or to assure him that I wouldn't miss this opportunity because I simply didn't believe I would be capable of winning the contest. His arrival obligated me, but it was only after he left and I had the courage to recapitulate each detail of the professor's visit that I realised how pathetically I had presented myself. I didn't tell him anything about me. I didn't take any discussion to its logical end, but, with the exception of the squalor in which I lived, I hadn't proved in any way that I was still interested in psychiatry and that, despite the poverty in which he'd found me, I had not surrendered intellectually, or that I had not been definitively defeated by the terror either. I didn't want to seem different than I was in reality, but this is simply how things happened.

His visit gave me inhibitions, it was like a cold shower, a punishment for my inability to look forward, to at least dream, since I wasn't capable of committing myself to a project. But I was tormented by the clarity and certainty of failure only when I found myself near Florica, after we made love, and my aggressiveness was lessened for a while: "Lord, what have I ended up being! What a failure of nature, what a stupid mix of powerlessness!"

It was strange that Florica was also crying near me, probably terrorised by the same anxieties. I felt her tremors, her bitterness, but I wouldn't ask her anything and she didn't seem curious either, because neither of us was capable of admitting their defeat.

In the end, I managed to leave the district, but I did absolutely nothing to deserve this success. I had lots of luck, instead. Professor Albu persisted in believing in me. So I was leaving, but I hadn't managed to leave there, in the village, the memory of the numbers who had died in the mountains. I never wrote down their names, so that no possible house search by the Securitate could find them and, without wanting it, cause bad results both to the survivors and to myself. But I know their graves, even those of the people who were left without a cross. Sometimes, at night, there appears in my mind, with no connection to the psychological moment or any other natural state of mine, various sequences in which I was a participant. I never talked to anyone about them, which is why they sometimes torment me more than I can take. I didn't have friends, apart from the priest who had fallen in a strange state of resignation: everything was a punishment for our sins. Suffering and good deeds from here would be rewarded Beyond. He saw everything from the heights of eternity. To me, such a goal seemed much too distant. I had needs, unsatisfied desires, the man in me claimed his rights, for the moment only on a theoretical level, because my shyness went before me, with every move I made. As in Pădureni I was afraid of the living. I got into a situation where I maintained that my true friends, the only ones, were the dead, the people among whom I lived in reality. During the nights, especially, I stayed among them and somehow together with them. We tried to understand what had happened and, in the end, why I was fated to bear in my memory only events from the realm of cruelty and sorrow? Besides the trees, grasses, flowers, skies and stars – can there be nothing beautiful, nothing soothing? Look, I am haunted by the face of the fighter who they called Moise. Irrespective of the circumstances or the seasons, he did not part with an old, tattered Bible, from which he always read, trying to convert the others to his faith. Nobody had learned to what sect he belonged, and too few knew what his name was, but his zeal in bringing them "to the right path" had irked all of them.

"How can you not kill, since you walk with a weapon in your hands and you are hunted by day and night? If you want not to let yourself be killed, you must defend yourself with the weapon, killing in your turn. If you don't kill, the communists kill you! And then, you haven't come here, together with everyone else, in order to convert to nonviolence some desperate people from whom their lands, their freedom were taken away. Is it not normal for them to defend themselves with the weapons with which they had been attacked?"

One day the priest called me with urgency to the mountains for a special case about which he didn't know much himself, although he had been informed that there was an absolute need for us. These imperative calls disturbed me profoundly. I had become very superstitious since I started to live in this village, especially because I could not take counsel with anyone. There was a special significance not only in what I dreamt the previous night, but also in many other signs which were important only to me.

I went silently beside Father Goga and, more than other previous times, I reached the place physically and intellectually exhausted. The commander who was waiting for us in front of a cavern showed Moise to me: thrown to the ground, with a gag in his mouth. His hands and feet were tied with pretty thick ropes.

"He is sick, the poor man," he said to me. "Maybe you can calm him somehow. He's been complaining for a while now, he gets agitated and he also wants to convince others to surrender. He's consumed by dread, he doesn't have any control of himself anymore, he yells, and threatens with the weapon, so we had to take it from him and tie him up. If he surrenders, he will say everything about us, what weaponry we have, how many and where we are, what our connections are in the villages around here. If he cannot be calmed down, we only have one solution. That solution. No matter how painful and unusual it might be."

The priest went closer to him, said a prayer and Moise's face suddenly became serene: as if he had come out of a nightmare. He had a kind gaze, a grateful gaze, so much so that, convinced that he needed our help, we asked them to remove the gag. He didn't reply to the priest's questions, nor to mine, but he complained that the ropes, tied too tightly, had chafed him, and that it was hurting badly. I asked the Commander for permission to untie him because I wanted us to discuss his state of health between ourselves, and Moise thanked me with his eyes; after which he stood up with great difficulty.

He stood in one place for a while in order to massage the joints chafed by the ropes, then, emitting a bellow like a wounded animal, he started running downhill with incredible energy. The others, confused for a moment, took their weapons and hurried on his tracks. After a time which seemed unending to me, I heard the same terrible bellow followed by a weapon firing and, after a long wait during which nobody said a word, I saw four men dragging Moise, placing him down at the priest's feet.

"God rest him and forgive us, if He can," said the Commander making the sign of the cross, after which, without attempting an explanation, he stood with tearful eyes waiting for the priest's decision. The priest, although he had seen many things in his life, as he was going to confess to me later on, was haunted for a long time by Moise's madness and execution.

"What happened to this country? We kill our leaders, we hurl the best we have deep inside the prisons, we chase away abroad the people who should be guiding us. How many devils are haunting us, I wonder, that we ended up killing one another, living in shame, in panic and hatred?"

Father Goga often asked this of himself; and, with each passing day, he seemed increasingly old and overwhelmed by the events he had to face. Sometimes, at night, after this kind of journey, he got horribly drunk and his face, usually bathed in a calm light, became darker, became more fierce. I heard him gnashing his teeth, yelling, as if the failure to bring order to his inner world would end later on in tears: "As the Lord wills it. We shall carry our crosses until He deems we have paid for our sins!" His meekness and resignation were followed by great tempests and doubts: "Lord, what will become of us? We have a bad shepherd and the sheep have scattered. Lord, do not leave us to oblivion!"

I returned home with the feeling that was our last trip, because it seemed impossible for the authorities not to have heard the noise of the weapon that had taken Moise's life. Imagining all sorts of scenarios about what could await us after we were caught, I was suddenly visited by a strange joy. I was discovering the pleasure of walking, of seeing and feeling the trees, the leaves, the wind. I had become, that is, very aware of these details while thinking of the prison cell, which seemed unavoidable in my opinion; and it was this obsession still which urged me to stop by Florica's. In fact, when I had left, it was only her and the priest that I felt the need to say goodbye to, before swearing that I wouldn't return to those places no matter what happened. Back then I hadn't yet heard of Ian Fleming, who said that you should never say never.

> *"Yes, but the dead are everywhere. They cannot be so simply evaded. One feels them pressing their sad blind fingers in deprivation upon the panels of our secret lives, asking… [for a place] they bequeathed us by their failure to use up life – alignment of an eye, responsive curve of a nose; or in still more fugitive forms like someone's dead laugh, or a dimple which excites a long-buried smile. The simplest of these kisses we exchanged had a pedigree of death. In them we once more befriended forgotten loves which struggled to be reborn. The roots of every sigh are buried in the ground. And when the dead invade?"*

Lawrence Durrell – *Clea* [41]

The departure from Pădureni didn't set me free me from my fear. On the contrary. I had entered another world. I was living according to new timetables. I had cares which were different from those of the village. I was learning again with the conscientiousness of a researcher. I could eat and especially wash how and when I wished. With all this, however, things had not changed inside me. I continued to live according to the rules and customs from over there, especially since, from a distance, the events in Pădureni had other meanings, they had changed colour and, in the end, they only maintained my fear, which received better contours with each remembering.

41   E. P. Dutton & Co., Inc., New York: 1960, pp. 229-230

The pressure of the Securitate was increasingly brutal as the skirmishes in the mountains intensified and, instead of forgetting or detaching myself from the village, I would always enquire after what was going on there, because, as I was now realising, my connections with that place were much stronger than I imagined when I was back there. The captured partisans, their relatives, the connections – they no longer needed me. While in the end, the tortures didn't have limits, and, with their aid, they obtained the most fantastical statements, so I expected that, one midnight in the near future, I would wake up to the feared black jeep at my door.

There was something else that maintained my feeling of discomfort: the atmosphere in the clinic, and the discontentment of my colleagues. By coming over there, I had created it involuntarily. I had become the foreign body that disturbed the hierarchies and balance of the university department. Who was I, in fact? Had I been brought over by the professor to be his successor in the Chair? Why did he do special exercises with me? In fact, they wanted to know what extra qualities I had, compared with the others and, of course, whose *pilă* I was. How did I appear just like that, out of the blue? It was well understood that the questions didn't stop there, all my movements and mistakes of all kinds were followed closely, including mistakes in diagnosis, which are unavoidable in any case, but they were all much exaggerated. They did everything so that they could maintain in me the feeling of being tolerated, or the feeling that I was a man who had to be placed in the queue for the queue – as the majority of them suggested.

As was natural, before declaring me a homosexual, gossip had been circulated that I had been sent by the Securitate, since nobody was able to be hired in judicial psychiatry unless they were undercover Securitate agents. My observation sheets were read covertly, as well as my prescriptions and treatment plans, my diagnoses were verified, and also the way I behaved with the patients, in order to convince the professor that my place was not at the head of the queue, and that, in my turn, I had to understand this willingly if I wanted to stay in the clinic.

I knew only too well that, in a greater or lesser measure, they had all passed through a similar process. As for what concerned me, I only had two solutions: to confront them or to ignore them. Of course, each variant had its own disadvantages, but I felt more prepared for the latter, the most difficult one, because it required more attention and patience. I had to be attentive to all the moves, so that any attack might find me prepared. As for confronting them, I had no means to do that as I was not exactly a master – either of my profession, or of my tenure – and the professor didn't like to get involved in the disturbances fomented by his underlings. On the other hand he would not have been too happy to see me defeated after he, with a lot of personal sacrifice, had brought me to the clinic.

Maybe it was because of this atmosphere, but also from a natural physiological need, that what hurt the most was the absence of Florica. While I stayed in Pădureni, we had never discussed the emotions that visited me, but there, in bed, she answered all my anxieties and questions, her caresses came at the appropriate time. The reactions I needed were the vibrations of her body, so well built, or her tears. I was not in love with her, but I wasn't indifferent to her either. In any case, I had no doubt that, near her, I could have lived for a long time without us communicating through words. She seemed an easy-going woman, she gave me everything without asking anything of me, but it was precisely this silence that, in a strange manner, left me obligated. I felt the need to tell her something, to promise or at least to explain in some way how much she'd meant to me. When I left the village, she didn't ask anything of me. We were both content to wipe our tears and to make each other understand that we should never see each other again. I think that there were only a few times in my life that I have felt more miserable than at that point. As if to increase this feeling, Florica made a gesture that made me over-emotional. She ran after me and, somehow hesitating, gave me a portrait in charcoal for which I couldn't remember to have ever posed. Later on, after several years, my wife looked at it with great attention and said briefly: "She must have loved you very much this creature!"

I explained to her that we weren't talking about anything like that, not even in a roundabout way, at which point she gave me a look of chastisement, "In that case, this is very grave. That means you've never looked at it with attention. The finesse of the lines, the manner in which she concentrated on all the details, the care not to allow anything to be lost of what she felt you might be... and she's felt it deeply."

I didn't contradict her, but I never mentioned how much I thought about it either, or what a need of Florica I'd had after I left Pădureni. I had planned a great many times to return to Pădureni, even for one day, but the thought that I might reopen a wound which had probably not yet healed cut off any enthusiasm. There was also the fear of reminding those people who had taken up hunting for special friends of the partisans about my existence. This was because the partisans had been chased away deep into the mountains, and others had scattered around the country or had been caught in their attempts to cross the Danube to Serbia, while the villages at the foot of the mountains had become a paradise for snitches, for those who had various old scores to settle. The fear caused by the Securitate, along with some material advantages, had contributed especially to this state of affairs. Thus, I did not have the courage to go to Pădureni, but I thought of the possibility of finding a woman, and the opportunity popped up finding me unprepared, with the dining table not already laid, as the saying goes.

We are talking about Natalia Plopeanu, a medical assistant from Neurology who always accompanied the patients sent to me for diagnosis. I had seen her a number of times. I had noticed her beautiful body, the body of an athlete – and she had done everything to show it off , but I had never addressed any other words to her besides those that had a connection to the patient sent for the investigation. During one such circumstance, I held her back in order to ask more information about the female patient who in my opinion was trying to simulate a neurosis, because I suspected that, in reality, under the cover of this diagnosis, she wanted to get rid of a pregnancy. The administered medication was forbidden during pregnancy, and the patient had insisted in drawing my attention to the fact that she had taken it of her own initiative, before she came to see me. I asked the nurse to take her to a gynaecologist then bring me the results, and I was going to tell her the conclusions only after that.

"I wouldn't have thought that you were going to exchange one word with me," she said. It was only then that I noticed the shortness of her dress, the beauty of her legs, but also the warm, clear voice, just perfect to read stories to send children to sleep.

"I was thinking about pretending I was ill as well, and

asking some colleague to accompany me to see you."

"Well, you can come on your own whenever you need it," I said, surprised at her words. "Even now, if you are not in a hurry. What can I help you with?"

"It's a rather complicated story. Terrible insomnia, and when I finally fall asleep I am tortured by nightmares which are so terrifying that I immediately wake up. And I am very afraid."

"For how long have you been suffering? Do you have a family? Husband? Lover? Do you live alone? I must know more about you.."

"In that case I'll come back," she said, kissing me with unexpected familiarity. "I am sure you can help me. Now I need to go!" I assured her she would be welcome any time, and I followed her with my eyes. The woman's body – which was straight, provocative, with a well-studied sway – didn't leave my mind, but after I put together what I'd seen and what it seemed, the conclusion was pretty brutal.

"This one might also need an abortion, or she's just been abandoned! Such an interesting woman can in no way be alone, unless she is hunting for another man, in order to take revenge."

I didn't think she would come back and I hadn't retained her name in my memory in order to enquire with other colleagues if they knew anything about her. In any case, beautiful – or at least interesting – women are always at the centre of attention: everybody wants to possess them, but nobody wants them for a wife. After exactly three days, to my surprise, I woke up with her in the consulting room and only at that moment I apologised for forgetting her name, a fact which Natalia let go of with great difficulty.

"This means my person did not interest you," she said,

hiding her feeling of anger in the shadow of a pretty and provocative smile.

"I confess sincerely that, after you left, I didn't think you'd ever come here on your own. There are many very good doctors in our clinic. I don't understand why exactly you've chosen me."

"If you remember, I have accompanied a number of patients to see you and I was convinced that you are a good professional, and, beyond this, I trust you. I don't know why, but I do."

"In that case, all that is left for me to do is to not disappoint you," I replied, with the feeling that I was facing a defeat.

Of course, I did not realise what it would consist of, but I would have preferred it if she had found another doctor, or if I'd met her somewhere else completely, but under no circumstances as a patient. I'll admit it. I also thought of the fact that she could have been sent by some of my more benevolent colleagues in order to check the strength of my relationship with medical ethics. I am not unaware, either, about the siege laid by spinsters against young doctors. In any case, I imposed prudence on myself, although the manner in which she, by mistake, often uncovered her legs and breasts urged me to anything but restraint.

"What do you think I should know about you?" I enquired, concentrating on her green eyes, from which it was hard to deduct her true state of mind.

"I am the daughter of a doctor, my father died some time ago. The eternal infarction. I did the entrance exams to Medical school but I failed, then my father died, there was nobody else to maintain me. I resigned myself to a sanitary school for nurses."

With precise movements, she handed her ID booklet to me so that I could fill in her medical record, then on seeing me concentrating on the piece of paper, she decided irritably to start on the monologue, but not before asking me with light irony: "Should I start with medical antecedents? Hereditary-collateral antecedents? Ailments?"

"So many observations sheets have passed through your hands, you know the drill."

"I had all the childhood diseases, except whooping cough and mumps," she started ironically, "menstrual cycle aged 13, neither too early nor too late, sexual life started aged 18 and a day. I had just celebrated my birthday, I was tipsy and, as I didn't feel well, I went to a friend of my father's, also a doctor, who, after he performed a general check-up, invited me to look him up later on in the evening so that he could get me rid of a problem.

"Isn't it possible now?" I enquired, somehow suspecting what he was going to do to me and in fact desiring it, especially since nobody, up to that time, had seriously proposed such a thing to me. It was neither good, nor bad; the emotions were greater than the pleasure. In the end, I was convinced that beautiful women have no luck: interesting men are, without exception, married, impotent or homosexuals! Sever is in the course of a divorce, he lives with me because his wife's found somebody else as well. He told me that they see each other once a week and they do an exchange of experiences. They tell each other the adventures or displeasures, as the case may be."

"And is there something that displeases you? Because we all have good parts but also bad ones... Will monotony somehow come and eat you up?"

"No, that's out of the question," she hurried to reply. "I

don't lack anything, Sever is good, attentive; he feels guilty at times towards me, at times towards his wife, that's why he behaves in an extraordinary way."

"And yet, as a man, doesn't he sometimes neglect you?"

"He is a manager for an information technology business and, he comes home tired sometimes, but this doesn't have any connection with our intimate life. I can assure you that no woman, no matter how demanding about this subject, would be dissatisfied with Sever."

Of course, I enquired about how long she slept, how well or how badly she was sleeping, what she was eating, what discontentments she had in her work, and in the end I asked her to describe to me the nightmare to which she kept returning.

"I normally sleep in Sever's arms. After the hour of love, I slumber immediately only to wake up all sweaty and horrified in a little while, half an hour – an hour at most –, but Sever sleeps deeply, he doesn't sense that I am scared. I then try to calm myself down, I read for around two hours, I watch the TV or I walk through the room like a madwoman until I get tired. The nightmare wakes me up," she said. "Night after night more or less the same thing. I am swimming through mud, a black, thick mud, from which I struggle to get out. And I do get out with great difficulty, exhausted, only for me to be then unable to go any further. The river of mud is edged by a forest of spikes. These are sharp spikes, maximum half a metre in length, forcing me to run on their tips which stick in my feet. And, despite the pain and the blood I leave behind me, I still move, I try. Every time, I wake up drained of strength, terrified, as if I'd just escaped death."

"How does Sever react when you tell him the nightmare?"

I enquired, to which she burst into a nervous laughter:

"He has the same answer for absolutely all my fears. He immediately undresses me, and crushes me in the bed. The same one and only treatment for all my pains and fears!"

"And do you dislike it?"

"How can I dislike it?" she wondered. "I am a normal woman, after all. Not even the frigid refuse a man, especially if he has Sever's qualities!"

"So what should Sever do, then, in order to make you happy? What do you think he doesn't understand?" I enquired, and, I admit it, her reaction was the one I expected. She suddenly stood up, then she glued herself to me, kissing me again with the calm and contentment of the woman who has just got out of her bed.

"I think I retained you for rather too long," she whispered. "You allowed me to look for you whenever I desired. And it wasn't hard for me to learn when you'd be a little freer."

Strange, she didn't look back, she seemed to come out of a dream and she left the room quickly. It was impossible to understand why she'd really come. Her nightmare, easy to psychoanalyse, somehow contradicted her eternal references to that man, Sever, whose virility I had started to doubt, but I was just at the beginning of the discussions with her and I had to leave the conclusions for later. Inside me, if I should proceed with sincerity to the end, it seemed that the interest I showed her was rather outside of my ethical framework, and I was going forward without thinking of the risks, or even of the next move. I had tens of patients I had to deal with in the clinic, and hundreds others from the various inter-clinical check-ups, so I could not explain to myself exactly why I was preoccupied with this creature. Of course, she was not the only woman who had learned I was unmarried, nor the only one who made me to understand that she was ready to have a relationship of any kind – a decision which depended only on me alone.

I don't know why but I always had a feeling of restraint or, to be more exact: as a doctor I ran away from any closer connection to a female patient, but in this case all prohibitions had stopped for a while; that is, until after the visit which she made to my house, without letting me know. She had memorised the hours when the cleaning woman worked in the house and she barged in on her.

"I am the doctor's girlfriend and I'll continue the cleaning myself. You are free, leave the key to me and go."

"Everything is possible," the woman replied. "After all, I don't know you, but the concierge tells me all sort of whores are looking for him." For her, any woman's voice on the telephone was, it is well understood, that of a whore. The women who brought my correspondence or my clothes from the laundry were, evidently, from the same category.

"Look, I'll leave my ID booklet with you," Natalia had insisted. "I'll recover it from Cassian."

"And how should I know if you are something else and not a thief?"

I dropped in during that discussion and, seeing me enter the room, the woman gathered her utensils, apologised and, before I become aware of what had just happened, she left the room in a hurry.

"I wanted to make a surprise and that stupid woman didn't allow me to wait for you. Today is the day when I cook *sarmale*, and cakes. This way, I thought that I would help you tell me that at least I am a good cook."

"You asked for my support as a patient and, as you know, I do not give medical consultations at home," I hurried to tell her.

Inside me, I had dreamt of such encounter, but now, when it had become real without me making the least effort, I felt disturbed, unprepared, incapable of finding the words and gestures by which I could restore myself to normality.

"If I suspected I wouldn't be well received, I would not have passed by this side of the town, not even in my thoughts," she said to me, deeply offended, while trying to gather her packs of food. "I regret it sincerely, but I will release you of the burden in a matter of seconds. I notice we have very different ideas about surprises."

"I didn't want to upset you. Now that you're here," I sounded the retreat, "let's continue what we've started at the clinic. And then, I don't hide this from you, I am truly hungry."

"What a twisted man you are!" she said, a little more relaxed. "I shortened the road to what I felt you wanted, but I see you are getting upset. It's not just you looking at me. I too am paying attention to your eyes, to your reactions. You haven't unglued your eyes from my breasts for one moment. Look, I am now in your house, place your hand on them, take your thought to its conclusion," she encouraged me, putting my hand on one of her breasts.

"And Sever?" I enquired pathetically, to which she burst into laughter:

"He has a wife, after all. Furthermore, I am accountable to no-one. I am vaccinated. I do my medical analyses periodically. The best times are those that you live. We don't know what will be tomorrow. Or whether there will be a tomorrow."

"And yet, I am obsessed by Sever. Does he not satisfy you as a man?"

"Can't we make love without mentioning him?" she

enquired, and, seeing her slightly annoyed, I didn't hurry to offer her the only explanation that interested me, since I wanted to know her indirectly, through him.

"You are still a psychiatrist, at a time when I need the understanding of a man?".

She didn't wait for a reply, she caught my head in her strong arms and started to kiss me with mad lust. I was not capable of reacting in any way, of denying or agreeing with her when she reminded me of my gaze as I lay asleep on her breasts. I should have said that what I did was only to test her reactions and that the only thing I could do was to appreciate her sense of observation; but back then I left myself to the will of her arms and lips, like the youngest teenager. And it was as she had wished it.

I have to admit that the hesitation and remorse appeared only the next day, around evening time, when questions and insomnia took the place of joy at having known a sort of woman that I didn't know existed. After two days, Natalia looked for me at the clinic. She was the embodiment of meekness and politeness: she kissed me, but differently – like an old friend, without anything going on between us. I hadn't learned either if she had told Sever about my existence, or if she justified the previous night's absence by lying to him that she had been on duty. In my consulting room, in my white coat, I persisted in being a doctor only in order to clarify the story of the nightmares, in which I continued not to fully believe. Also, that prudence which is typical to psychiatrists had regained the terrain lust had temporarily forced it to abandon.

"The night we slept together – did you have any nightmares?" I enquired, sliding immediately into a joke: "You didn't have any! The conclusion, I believe, you'll have to draw by yourself."

"Starting today?" she asked, her face turning suddenly red.

I hurried to assure her that was what I desired, although all my senses urged me to postpone, to continue studying her. The feeling that I made a mistake by saying 'yes' didn't leave me for one moment, but with all this I was going ahead without thinking of those alarm signals, or of the consequences.

After three days of mad loving, I felt the need to see more clearly at whose side I had spent my nights and energy, but I didn't have any great surprises in connection to her biography. She almost repeated the things I already knew and, if we set aside the madness with which she knew how to make love, I persisted in finding out whether her spirit played any role in her life. I asked her to tell me a verse she loved especially and, after a long pause, she said as a joke: *"Little dog with curly hair..."* the children's rhyme. In many circumstances, when I wanted to get an idea about somebody, I asked them to tell me a verse or at least a proverb they cared about the most, and because I was in no mind to let myself fooled by her laughter and her preferred verse, I insisted she should tell me whatever she thought could be said about her lovers. Again, I wasn't able to learn too much. With the lovers of her school years she'd only had bodily relations, she told me. An endless search for a room where they could make love, because they were asked for an ID in the hotels or, more rarely, blackmailed by the concierge or cleaning women. She had also had some passing associations with some doctors and medical assistants who had risked performing abortions on her. She could no longer have children since that time, so she was, as she insisted in telling me, a safe woman.

Her true love was called Sever: rich, smart, virile, generous and, before me, the best at everything. I had nothing with which to reproach her. Each person came with their past, nobody could suspect what fate had in store for them and, as a consequence, each one could say as much as they wanted to and their morals allowed them; because every one of us has happenings we would like to forget, to erase from our minds. She then promised that, at the right time, she would acquaint me with her great love, Sever, who had preceded me.

Then came my turn to tell her about my lovers and, from the first moment, I had the certitude this was what she wanted to hear. I told her, fleetingly, about my small school-time adventures about which I didn't remember a great deal and I insisted on my only story from the time of the lyceum, in which Luiza had played the main role for a long time. Fleeting kisses, walks on darker streets, holding hands, some failed attempts to go beyond these and, immediately after graduation, the separation. Luiza got married urgently to a military doctor and, after seven months, she gave birth to her first child, a sign that, at the peak of our love, when I was tormented by questions about our future – mine and Luiza's – she had not had the courage to even suggest to me that she had already chosen a different path. In our last meeting she explained that everything had happened because of her parents and that, whenever we met again, we would rejoice together and I could do exactly what I wanted to her. A little time afterwards, I strove not to lose the opportunity. I didn't do it with affection, but from a natural physical need of her. It was clear to me: she'd been forced by her parents, she didn't have the strength to oppose them and, in the end, she was neither the first, nor the last creature lacking a will; but her proposal had seemed strange, almost impossible to understand. Did she want to take revenge on the husband? On the parents? Or to repay me for what I had meant to her up until the time she met the doctor?

In any case, she had died inside me, despite all my efforts to recall how much I had wanted this moment. The woman I made love to was just a nondescript woman, more gauche than the two or three wives ignored or neglected by their husbands: lonely women who, in their spare time, understood they could do whatever they wanted. Due to them, I managed to discover in the same time as my other colleagues those guilty pleasures, taught with much skill by creatures who were extremely diligent and sad: "Don't get emotional, *tanti* – that is, aunty – will help you! It will be better in an hour!"

One of them was called, I remember, Tanti Țica. From the name of Lenuța, Lenuțica, Țica. Her husband was a civil engineer, who had managed to get a contract in an Arab country and had forgotten the way home, for which fact she managed to assuage her impulses by taking in pupils and students as lodgers. I had been recommended by a teacher and Tanti Țica didn't hesitate for one moment. A short time afterwards she started to walk in on me in the bathroom. I am not saying that I didn't like it when she helped me soap and towel myself, but later on, with me dressed in one of her house gowns, she guided me to the bed, where she jumped on me, crying and sighing like a desperate woman saying she could no longer wait for her husband, that she was a healthy woman, with lusts, like any forgotten wife. Everything would have been terribly well were I not terrorised by the thought that her husband might find us in the conjugal bed. I left tears behind me, and I then regretted the stupid idea of leaving that house in which I had known some facets of sin. Our female colleagues, as I managed to learn later on, had overtaken us in this task a long time before.

Of course, I could have also told her about other little and ephemeral conquests from the time of my student years, but Natalia's curiosity was connected with more recent times, to which I, at least, was afraid to steer the subject. One moment when, left without any energy, she especially wanted to enquire whether my landlady had been better in bed than her, she insisted I should continue with the story, but I couldn't imagine where she wanted to go with it. "What about Florica?" she enquired in the end in a hollow voice. In the first moment, this name told me nothing, I couldn't remember a lover of that name. Later on, as I was confused by her suspicious gaze, she started to laugh and repeated the woman's name to me: "How come it doesn't say anything to you? You will do the same with me after a while. Florica? You don't have to go too far in your thoughts."

Suddenly, I woke up as if from a dream. I had never told her about Pădureni and, absolutely certainly, never about Florica. And so? I recalled, as far as my memory allowed me, each sequence I spent together with her, absolutely everything we had talked about, but I did not remember telling her about Florica or Pădureni. So where had she learned about it, and why had she insisted on me talking about Florica? In any case, all the memories from that village were, as I always repeat, accompanied by fear. Without any doubt, I was not ashamed by my deeds, but the thought that the trials continued, that people were being pursued, threatened, and that, in my turn, I could be locked up, tortured and humiliated for the simple reason that I had done my duty as a doctor was not the kind of reflection to calm me down. Despite the cold shivers down my spine, I wanted to learn what she knew, where she knew it from and why she had insisted so hard that I should talk about Florica to her. Could she have been to Pădureni? Could she have a connection around there? Of course, I could have talked to her with pleasure about the teacher, but I persisted in not saying anything to her, with the idea that she would up the ante in the end, as actually happened after a long and pathetic tiff.

Irrespective of my reactions, Natalia didn't hesitate to maintain that I had told her about this former lover and, even more, in the fire of this confrontation, she also, unwillingly, mentioned Dana! It was not important that I would not remember ever uttering their names, she didn't want me to make any step back. They probably forced her to learn faster about what I knew, or what I admitted, about the things that had happened in Pădureni.

"Not all women I had a love affair with at some given point have also been my lovers. If I mentioned their names, perhaps I told you other details about them as well," I insisted, and she exclaimed, feeling liberated:

"It's good you remembered. In any case, you were a great gentleman for helping her with the trial!"

After the terrifying shiver that ran down my spine, I was very certain that Natalia had not come looking for me because of her nightmares, but because she had been sent by somebody, probably by *that institution*, the sinister one. What else could she want? Things being as they were, all that was left for me to do was to shut up and smile enigmatically until I could gather more facts, if, of course, I was going to be given the time. In any case, in the days immediately following, I did everything in my power not to touch her anymore, although, I admit, it was very hard for me. There was still my curiosity to learn what she really knew, how and from where, about Dana and Florica, and especially what it was about Sever which simply obsessed me. All subjects of discussion had suddenly become pointless, as long as fear and distrust were interposed between the two of us, and she had to be kept ignorant of what I was feeling, as well as the fact that I was dragging behind me, wherever I went, the same fears. But what decision did I have to make? Nothing was certain, concrete or at least foreseeable. We went together to the restaurants and, because nobody came looking for me, no Securitate men and no party activists were interested in me, I restarted the nights of love. Physiological needs were a good sign: stronger than fear. With all this, however, the anxiety and uncertainty floated above us each day, and their weight always increased.

Then came one day when Natalia no longer looked for me, and, for a while, I did not phone her either. Instead, for a change, I was waiting to be taken over to the Securitate or, in one of those embarrassing trials, to be accused of helping the partisans. After her departure neither one thing, nor the other took place, however, so I took my heart in my teeth and went to her workplace, and then, with even more courage, to her home. She had not been seen in the clinic for a long time and, as a consequence, they had rescinded her work contract. Given that situation, I went to her home, but the door was locked and the curtains drawn. I immediately thought, horrified, that she'd died. She had committed suicide or been killed, but the family that had let the studio flat to her told me that, exactly at the time they had decided to notify the militia, they had received a phone call from her, from somewhere abroad. She was happy for making whole again the family she had never talked to anyone about and, as a consequence, she had behaved as if she had nobody who could hold her accountable.

At that moment, a thought passed through my mind: that Sever really existed, but in another country! And because in our country no secret can be kept, the news spread in the end that she had asked for forgiveness from the neurology professor for the wrongs she had caused. She had then added, briefly, that she had managed to arrange a trip to Hungary, a socialist country, from where she had run away to Austria. "For a beautiful woman, there are no barriers of any kind, if she puts her mind to it," the head of the clinic is supposed to have said. "When you think people believed she was one of the Securitate people! When even Securitate agents are running away, that means that the whole ramshackle construction is going to the devil!"

This, too, was a kind of encouragement, because, during those years, we extracted hope from the most insignificant gestures or words. In the overwhelming darkness that had been installed everywhere, any spark was a hope, a source of faith. I then tried to assess our relationship from this perspective, only to ask myself, in the end, in confusion:

"Was Sever truly the husband? The lover who had run away from the country? The Securitate man who had procured her passport and, between two love matches, had her pull my tongue? Could she have been sent by the Securitate, and I was just a banal study subject, a nondescript person on whom she had practiced her skills?"

Who could answer me, since Natalia had not sent any signs of life to anyone? But with all this, the terrors healed by time, and connected to the skirmishes in the mountains, just like my doubts, she stayed forever alive in my memory, just like Florica. I was going to discover later on that fate had placed us in an absurd world in which anything could happen, especially for the worst. But unfortunately the fear and mistrust stayed deeply imprinted in my soul, as well as the caution. This is the reason why I really didn't have my share of friends, although, strangely, I felt I had the vocation for friendship.

> *"The kingdom of plants is very easy to imagine as the closest neighbour of the kingdom of death. Here, in the greenery of the earth, among the cemetery trees, through the stems of the flowers grown from the beds, there are, perhaps, concentrated the mysteries of transformation and the enigmas of life which we try to untangle with so much labour. Mary did not recognise Jesus risen from his grave, and, in the first moment, she took him for the gardener who walked in the cemetery ("She, supposing him to be the gardener...").*
> Boris Pasternak – *Doctor Zhivago*

It is impossible for me to avoid or ignore the things around me, the great or insignificant world in whose midst I live. This satisfies me, although the most appropriate word for such a state of spirit doesn't come to my mind right now. I mean, I feel it but I can't say it, because none of the words I know cover this state fully. Here, absolutely everything has importance: small, red ants about whom I don't know how they manage to sneak in under the window or through various cracks which are impossible to cover, and the fine, brown dust that settles step by step on everything I don't touch, and the abundant, untameable grass that throbs from between the wooden beams of the cabin or among the stones of the foundations, and the small or violent clouds, and the mist that appears and disappears especially early in the morning. Then, the pine trees and the birds, diurnal or nocturnal, the sun, the stars and everything that I feel but only see with the eyes of the mind. I have the strange feeling I depend on them and that, in their turn, each one belongs to me, becoming an essential component of my being. The light and shadows are changing unceasingly, the same for the taste and temperature of the air. It is a continual, liberating movement, which integrates me and helps me, at the same time as them, to become equally heaven and earth, to pulsate together with the universe, to feel accomplished and, for a moment, immortal, invincible, stronger than the death I ignore although, in any moment, it can annul my senses and the illusion that I have managed to surpass my limits. As so many times before, the soul which has escaped control is looking for something outside words, it knocks with fury and despair on a massive gate that refuses to open. I am here and I am there, especially there, still undefeated. I have the certitude that beyond the gate lay the salvation, the miracle, the un-fated mystery of the words, that something which attracts me and repels me with equal strength, the source of despair and nostalgias. I wish with all my might to stay there forever, in the same place: a beggar at the gates of eternity... Me – who?

I looked in vain for the most fitting words in order to suggest what we both knew should happen, but neither of us had the strength to utter them for a long time. The gestures, once routine, now seemed impossible to me because, as in my very distant adolescence, I was trying to anticipate my own moves, to look for the phrases with which I could resist the most absurd situations. But Mara did everything she could in order to save me the wait. Without hesitating or asking for my consent, she urged me with a gesture to climb into the bed, then turned off the light after she first took the ancient hunting weapon and laid it on the table, barrels pointing at the window. I naturally thought of the monk, then the wild animals that circled her own animals, but she didn't leave me the time for other suppositions as she undressed hurriedly, as if she were afraid I was going to stop her, as I was otherwise inclined to do in the first instant. I didn't see her eyes, but only the contours of the body dressed in a greenish light by the rays of an enormous moon, frozen in front of the window. She then nestled at my side, but I didn't try to distance her from me, except in the moment when I felt her abundant tears falling on my face.

"Was it alright for you?" I asked her, trying to free myself from the terrible feeling of guilt which had overwhelmed me, and she hurried to reply as was her wont, with a light aggression:

"What are you afraid of?"

"Of myself, of you, of my own instinct," I replied immediately. "Of everything. Of morals, of faith. Of the memory of Teodora. I always ask myself what would she say if she knew."

"She would be at peace. She would be happy that I am no longer alone."

"For how long?"

"It bears no importance. We do not owe anything to anyone. If you leave me here alone, do you think we'll accomplish the will of God in testing my strength to endure, and my faith? It is possible He doesn't even know we exist. Did He tell you not to sleep with that girl? Do you think our purpose is only that of respecting some laws? What did

I do wrong, since I have been forgotten here, among the clouds and animals? What if it was precisely Him that sent you in order to save me? Why do you feel compelled to find explanations for that which cannot be explained?"

"Haven't you noticed I am almost dead?" I whispered, taken by a fury almost impossible to hold back, to which she burst into nervous laughter:

"And how can I prove it that you aren't, or that at least I am alive? But we can discuss this tomorrow as well."

"In that case close your eyes," I requested, full of embarrassment, taken over by a mixed feeling, partly composed of the need to pray, to ask her forgiveness, to rejoice, and to desire to leap, somehow, over what was going to come in the following days. She whispered something to me, but I no longer heard her, I had allowed myself to be taken down by boundless joy and peace, so that for a fraction of a second I said to myself, in confusion: *"Lord, this is death!"* but it was only in the sense I'd wanted. Once I closed my eyes and allowed myself to go with the will of my senses, words simply disappeared. I would have liked to talk to her, because the happiness that overwhelmed me was amplified, one by one, with other states. I felt like a bastard, flooded by boundless happiness, odious, a liar, pathetic, immoral and again a bastard.

At dawn, I got dressed in silence, I ate the breakfast she had prepared and, in the same silence, I left home. Mara didn't hold me back, she was content just to smile at me in her strange way like an accomplice. She behaved as if she was with a man who she had finally got to know:

"If you like to be in a sulk and be sour, that's your business. I'll do my best to behave the way you want, but only for a matter of hours!"

I didn't reply, but, for a change, terrorised by the same burdensome guilt, I treated her as if she were an unknown woman from whom I wanted to take my distance as soon as possible, without any special reason, except one of clarifying to myself whether I had done something wrong and how I might compensate for the possible error. This was because in the bed, near Mara, I had been accompanied by all the women I'd known, Daria above all, and, obviously, Teodora – to whom I needed to explain what was inexplicable to myself, for the time being.

I left home and we didn't see each other for almost two days, a time during which I aimed great reproaches at myself. I repented, I was ashamed, but I also felt very happy, as I had understood that, at least now, at the end of my life, I too had the right to a little egotism. For all my life I had paid attention only to other people, ignoring myself, forgetting I existed.

"What an interesting experience to reach the years of senescence. I think of what has been less than I feared, with the exception of the moments when the will dealing with what you are supposed to do today and tomorrow gets weaker. The past is a giant book of drawings, but its subject is not shown to us in a clear manner, being in continuous, ever-changing movement, impossible to catch and, because of this, coy. Meditation soothes by the courage of losses and acquisitions – as we are not just losing; with the passage of years we gain the architectonic sense, and the clarity of the lines, like in a crystal, is like a reward for the insufficiency of warm colours. In the same time, we learn how to be resigned, since it is known that the distance between a name and any utterance cannot be defeated, even if once I entertained such

hopes. It is to see yourself, as you once were, like in an old portrait made by somebody else."
Czesław Miłosz – *The Land of Ulro*

I would have never returned to Pădureni if I hadn't taken part in this dinner given by a colleague from the University Department who had just gained his doctoral degree. It is pointless saying how much talent he had and how much scholarship he'd acquired, but nobody doubted the fact that he was perfect in the cultivation and maintenance of relations in the most unexpected milieus, and with persons who were apparently incompatible. Highly-placed party activists, churchmen, scientists and former political prisoners got along pretty well with the Securitate officers who passed themselves off as professors or directors for various factories.

At this dinner, I had been seated near a confrere who, in a short while, was going to be appointed chief medical officer for the county. Because we had to talk about something, I confined myself to the most special cases I'd had in the clinic, and he told me about his visits in the company of the Party first-secretary of the county, who had stopped in this mountain locality called Pădureni, where there had been great success in developing rabbit and pheasant farms, along with a trout farm. Because I had drunk a little, I found myself making some notes about the locality that had aroused his enthusiasm, a locality in which, some years previously, I had cursed my days. In the end, I was forced to admit the truth, and this encouraged him to exclaim happily: "Bravo, sir, you are my man!"

He didn't want to tell me what the undercurrent behind this exclamation was, so, after some weeks, I woke up to an invitation to his office at the county administration.

"My dear fellow," he told me in a conspiratorial tone, "they say that, in a while, it might be possible that even the big boss, the Comrade,[42] will come on a short working visit. He wants to convince himself in person whether it is possible to build a hydroelectric plant on the Repedea river, a fact which, of course, would change people's lives for the better. Until the time when the visit will be announced officially, which is not our business, we shall have to keep the secret," he emphasised, sketching with both hands gestures from which I was to understand that we were listened to and watched.

"Unfortunately," I said to him feeling confused, "I do not see what my role would be in such an event. I am just an ordinary lecturer for the Department of Psychiatry and nothing more. I think," I whispered in my turn, "he does not need my services."

"This is not good to say, not even in your thoughts," he addressed me in a whisper, repeating with even more conviction the gestures he'd made previously. "You have been checked, you correspond, what will follow is that you are going to be notified whether you will be accepted in the team responsible for the good running of the visit. This is decided only by those with the proper powers. Don't ask me any questions, as I don't know any more myself. In any case, it is not a simple job."

He then enquired after my family, if I had anything in the works or whether I still was a solitary hunter of skirts? This would have seemed to be a joke. The truth was that

---

42 The Comrade – in Romanian, *Tovarăşu'* – was a name which meant, in certain contexts, Nicolae Ceauşescu, General Secretary of the Romanian Communist Party (from 1965) and President of Romania (from 1977), de facto ruler (or rather dictator) of the country. His only courtesy title, as in all communist countries, was "Comrade".

I hadn't hunted anything. I had not been preoccupied by the idea. I had a commonplace relationship with a female colleague, in which both of us were involved only by our hormones, but not by too much soul. She was dissatisfied with the husband's services, but she didn't want to divorce, or to attract attention to their drama. I had got lost in science, information was procured with great difficulty, and the possibilities to truly conduct research were much reduced. We saw each other periodically and these meetings were very convenient to us, especially because we could find sufficient time for them. As for marriage, I had reconciled myself to the thought that the woman who was destined for me had not yet appeared. The chief medical officer didn't seem to know this story, he had asked casually, in order to fill the time until we would both reach the street.

"The news of this visit must not be spread," he whispered. "You know how things are: some lunatic might crop up and, Lord forbid! In a provisional programme, there's mention of a hunt in Pădureni. Pheasants, rabbits, and especially bears, and that's without mentioning the boars which exist even in the peasant households. Ceaușescu is a great lover of hunting, but before he fires the first shot, things are damned complicated. Even the children who bring him flowers are not chosen haphazardly, they must be carefully selected, because they are going to be kissed, and for this one, we need very serious sanitary control, so that they won't have any diseases or, Lord forbid, more special microbes. Then, it is well understood, he will shake hands with the villagers, but not just at anytime, and not with just anyone. The specific people have to be known by the state organs, they must not have psychiatric issues, so that they won't cause any incident. Everybody asks for all sort of weird things that might upset

415

the Comrade. Moreover, the road must be properly laid, tarmacked, trees need to be brought and placed on one side and the other, the fences need painting, ditches need digging, so he can be happy with the country he's leading. We must have a country worthy of the *Conducător*.[43] From the experience of other visits, the Comrade will want to go into a house, this is why, for this eventuality, it is mandatory we prevent any discontent. Wherever he's gone, it has been ascertained that there would be a few well conditioned houses like that, with fine animals in the paddocks. The cows over here look like hell, it's mandatory to bring others, from serious farms, so that the people who make recommendations have something to choose from. Your role? As a man who knows the locality very well, if it comes to it, you will feel when something would not be airtight, and you will be able to prevent anything that seems unusual to you. It is a mission one cannot refuse. The responsibility is overwhelming and, as a consequence, you will go with the team that prepares the welcoming, the hunt, everything. Because the rabbits and the bears must also understand who has the honour to be shooting them," he was trying to joke. "And after such an adventure you either go very high, or you definitely set your own trunk on fire,[44] but I do hope we'll come well out of it. If he is content, he'll come again, and he will come because I don't think he can find bears or boars as wild as in Pădureni, or at least that's what people say. The doctors over there have been warned of your arrival. Their chief is Daria Pop, the daughter of a church painter who is very talented but whose mind is away from home. All the saints have the faces of the people in the village,

---

43 *Conducător* - literally meaning "The Leader," another name for Nicolae Ceaușescu.

44 In Romanian, *a da foc la valiză* – to be finished, done, dead and buried.

and the devils – I can't tell you who they resemble. It's very lucky that the Securitate men and the party activists don't enter the church, otherwise even they would be afraid to say what they've seen. He is silent all the time, but if he smells drink, nobody can stop him. It is said that he was left by his wife, the doctor's mother, immediately after she gave birth to her. In fact, she is very free with her mouth as well, she doesn't spare anyone. People say she's never seen her mother, a frustration which is hard to repair. You will have to deal with her in a special manner so she won't possibly let her mouth get the better of her good sense. Explain to her the 'what about' and 'how' of it all. She is unmarried, beautiful, and you might have just the right needle to stick in her sheepskin coat."[45]

From this long discussion it was not hard to understand that there was no way to turn back. I was forced to see the village again. Only one issue made me wonder about it all, more than anything. Of the thousands of localities in the country, fate had tied me with indestructible bonds to Pădureni. This seemed to be the village from which, bizarrely, I could in no way separate myself. It is probable that in another life I had been a bear, a boar, or a rabbit and I had haunted the wastelands from over there. In any case, the fear or returning was, step by step, replaced by curiosity. I was thinking that there was a certain thing I had not taken to its conclusion in that place, or that over there, in that wretched village, something was starting, a rupture taking place in my life. I didn't exclude the fact, however, that I'd already been punished. In the end, I had run away from there. I had separated from the village as if cutting myself off from a great illness I'd had, and I didn't want to

---

45 In Romanian, *a avea ac de cojocul ei* – to find the appropriate solution for somebody's failings or misdemeanours.

know what happened to the people to whom I'd been close. I'd run away in order to protect myself, to save my life and profession, because I felt myself to be more useful outside prison than inside it. That was what I told myself back then, and, in some moments, I even believed it. The honest truth is that I had a terrible fear of being tortured. The peasants from the village who had returned from prison described directly, without nuances, the life inside. It was clear to me. I had entered the star sign of the brutes, of the illiterates, but history could in no way stop with them, and remain in that state, turned into stone in a state of ignorance and shamelessness. It was just that, until the unavoidable change, there might be a long time to go, even a lifetime. Those who fought with weapons in their hands had lost. Nobody helped them. What support could only a single man count on? Fortunately, I escaped only with the fear while waiting for the misfortune. Now that I was forced to see the village again, the series of coincidences seemed strange. I had to go to that party, where I was to meet that particular doctor, who had to be promoted in order to reach the company of the initiated at the head of the county. Even more, a visit by Ceaușescu was also necessary, so that I won't be able to refuse this trip into memory unless I took enormous risks. I had to stay there, in Pădureni, at least one week and at the most one month.

"The Comrade is unpredictable," the chief medical officer assured me, "so we must be prepared at all times. These villages where the army fought the partisans are under a special regime, controls are tougher. In his own country, he is convinced he can go wherever he wants and when he wants to, but those who organise such visits – pity their dicks as they might lose them![46] There is always an idiot

---

46   In Romanian, *vai de puța lor* – literally meaning woe is their willy.

to upset him! So your role is very complex: eyes in all four directions and be careful nothing escapes your attention! A psychiatrist discovers – feels, maybe – everything which is inaccessible to a regular policeman or Securitate man. You've lived there in the harshest years, when there were skirmishes, so you have an advantage above anyone else. Plus, the specialist's expert eyes."

By the manner in which he'd finished his discourse, I was waiting for him to hand me a statement of cooperation I had to sign, or something of the sort, but he was content to draw my attention to the fact that he also knew something more about me. And that was it. The rest, I had to deduce for myself. We left as friends or, to be more exact, as accomplices, and the following day I was visited by a plain-clothes officer who gave me the necessary documents, the travel sheet and the per diem. I had been treated like one of them, which rather disturbed me, but I didn't have the courage to ask for specific details, not even later on, when he invited me to a restaurant, where he wanted to put on a show of force by telling the waiters to bring the wine and food from the places they'd hidden them. During that terrible food crisis, he was eating normally, since he knew where the quality foodstuffs of a restaurant were stored, but he didn't want us just to eat properly, like ordinary people do. He had worked hard to suggest that he knew everything about me, and starting with that time, I felt liberated from my old obsessions. There was no point in asking myself why nobody had informed against me, as it was known I had helped the partisans. There were no rules. The slogans about the enemies of the people worked perfectly well, it was just that anyone, and at any time, could be considered one of those. The important thing was fear. Everybody should be afraid that they might become an enemy. Exactly as I feared.

In Pădureni I was accommodated in the house of a peasant who, because he worked in the forest, used to come home every two weeks, and one of the rooms had been transformed in a guesthouse by the village hall. The first visit, even before I got to the dispensary, was to Father Calistrat Goga. I had great trust in him, not only because we were connected by the numerous trips to the mountains we had taken together, by the fears and the events that had haunted me ceaselessly, but also because I had a feeling of admiration for the inner force given to him by his faith.

"Who can you fear when you feel God is with you?" he used to say to me with a conviction that admitted no trace of doubt or hesitation. I was interested to discover what had happened in the years when I had not visited the village, and, at the same time, I wanted to free myself from a brutal feeling of guilt. In fact, I had run away from the village, and I had not been capable of looking back. He was the only man I should not have avoided. Or Florica. Furthermore, as I had just entered the locality, like by miracle, there came to my mind, with unsettling clarity, not just Florica's face – it was as if I could feel her very fingers which had caressed my body feverishly and especially my face. In any case, it was only here that I realised how profoundly I had kept her in my feelings and how powerless I had proved to be in the confrontation with my own past. This was a past which fate had now forced me to live again. Not one sentence uttered by Florica had stayed in my mind – we had been united by our senses, our silences, and the joy beyond them – but she existed in another manner, and it was precisely this thing that unsettled me. My reckoning with the past was not over, it was simply that the fear I felt from before, tended to be transformed into shame as I got closer to the village. As it is, the first sensation I had was that the mountains were smaller, maybe also because part of the forest had been cut down – under the pretext of maintenance, as I was going to learn. The same sensation was true with regard to the houses, more numerous than I'd left them, but somehow smaller, in proportion to the scale of the mountains.

Only Father Goga's dimensions had increased a little. He had a big, white beard, and long, rebel hair. He seemed not to care about how he looked anymore. He welcomed me with a puzzlement which was more simulated than real:

"Such a surprise! How come you've still remembered our village? It seemed to me you didn't want to look back. And I don't think it was fear that stopped you, as we have climbed the mountain together tens, or even hundreds of times."

His reaction confused me: he had, all of a sudden, entered the subject that preoccupied me. In reality, he was not surprised at all, he gave the impression we'd separated some days previously and that we still had some argument to resolve. He wasn't even talking in a whisper, as in the times when I was a doctor in this village.

"I ask your forgiveness," I said to him, "but I looked behind me too often and I don't know what weighed heavier: the courage of climbing the mountain together so many times, or the permanent fear of being arrested once I got home. I was happy I could help, as a doctor, and even happier than nobody denounced me, although I lived with fear in my chest waiting for the Securitate. I am not cut from the cloth of a hero. I remembered our trips thousands of times, I think, but I was afraid to return to the village in case anybody might perhaps remember me. Maybe even one of the people I helped, somebody freshly out of prison, and beyond all this, I laid myself belly down on the books – working hard, since I had been dropping behind in my studies. The reasons are more or less these. Can you forgive me?"

"As a priest and a simple Christian I cannot ignore the commands of the Redeemer. As a former friend, a brother in suffering in those ugly years, I am tempted to say no," he said firmly, as if he'd been prepared for this dialogue for a long time.

"Nooo?" I was surprised by the distance which, step by step, he was putting between us. "It is impossible to understand. But I thank you for your sincerity. Maybe you can help me learn how you think, and what upset you the most in my way of being. What did I do wrong? What can you not forgive?" I insisted, and the priest didn't let me wait for too long.

"The fact that you haven't been arrested, interrogated, that you haven't experienced those investigations. And with this, I hope, you've understood that I know all and that our discussion has become useless," he said, standing up, as a sign that he was inviting me to leave.

"It's only now that I intend to stay, and, furthermore, I'd like a glass of water," I replied with a strange fury, in which curiosity was also mixed, because I actually didn't understand anything. "You know I am religious and I would like this discussion to continue in the church. None of us can lie in there. It is an explanation that I truly desire."

"There are people, unfortunately, who lie wherever they are. People without faith... but if this frees your conscience from the weight of sins, we'll go," he agreed, getting ready to leave.

I stood up in a hurry, possessed by the conviction that there was no way to get back into our relationship, although, in any case, the road had to be trod to the end. We didn't talk and didn't look at each other until we got to the church. It was only there, after he lingered a long time behind the altar, that he returned dressed in vestments and, with the Bible in his hand, he gestured that I should come closer to him. I then swore, with my hand on the Bible, as he asked me to, that I would tell the truth and only the truth, and after I did it without hesitation I saw his face relaxed, at peace, and I felt that the misunderstanding, the brutal coldness that had descended upon us might reach an end.

"It seems absurd to me for you to be upset that I haven't been arrested," I said, starting the attack. "And unfair. Especially for a priest."

"Yes, but this priest was investigated for months on end, held in the basements on Traian Street, beaten up and starved, and the Securitate men told me how you saved the doctor with whose wife you'd had certain relations. Who could have talked about that which only the two of us knew? About saving the doctor."

"The man we saved, for example," I hurried to answer. "Even the doctor, the husband of my colleague with whom – it is true – I had a short love affair. No matter how strange it might seem to you, I was never tested by the feeling of guilt after it. Back then, more than now, I had a scientific vision of sex, in which the idea of sin had no room. But beyond this, we both had a need to free ourselves of an ancient, irrepressible desire, something hard to explain, a kind of beautiful blindness – noble, if I may say so. And then, were it not for that episode, it is probable that I would not have risked my freedom or even my life. If I maintained that it was a reward received in advance, I would be descending very low, but I'll go with my sincerity to the end. I took risks only for Dana, for her sake. I can understand and explain her husband's madness to myself, but this doesn't mean that I automatically think he was right. Then, I think the doctor had learned about my relationship with Dana from the Securitate men. It seems strange to me that back then, at an advisory meeting, where we met some time after finishing university, we were both convinced that nobody knew or even suspected what we did in a dark room."

"Those were terrifying days," said Father Goga. "They would come on a Sunday night and put me inside a black Volga car, they'd release me on Friday so I could do mass in church and on Monday they picked me up again. They threatened me that if I said anything to anyone, I was finished. I haven't told the details not even to Madame, my wife, although she saw the wounds on my soles and on my back and I often found her crying. At the Securitate, they would bring me in front of various people I'd never seen before, they enquired about situations or confrontations of which I had no idea, they would beat me up until I lost consciousness, I would be thrown on a pile of straw in a basement, and they would start all over, shouting at me that they knew everything from the doctor. That it was no use hiding."

"Curiously, nobody ever asked me about the things that happened in the village, in the mountains, or about any specific person," I hurried to assure him, convinced that this time he would believe me. "It is true, I was terribly afraid that I might be taken to the Securitate. I was especially terrified by the thought I could be tortured. I am not cut from the cloth of a martyr. I am afraid of dogs, of rats. I have claustrophobia."

"It's only when you are in such circumstances that you

get the true image of your physical and mental endurance," Father Goga remarked. "The first beatings, of bestial cruelty, I felt them for a long time, like deep wounds in my soul. I then got used to it. I would lose consciousness after the first blows with the rubber truncheon and I would wake up to the clanging of water buckets. Seeing I did not react as they wanted, they would strip me to my skin and mock my manhood and they insisted that I should deny the Creator, Jesus and the Virgin Mother of God. I would have perhaps crumbled, I would have lost my strength to resist if they hadn't asked such a thing of me. I assured the torturers, a number of times that the God who didn't exist saw the way they mocked me, and that there would come a moment of judgment. You should be afraid of His punishment because I have no power, myself, I told them. Probably, without a connection to what was happening to me, one of the officers who investigated me had a car accident. He'd hit, head on, a cart that was driving at night without a cat's eye. The car was gravely damaged, the horses had to be killed, as they had many fractured bones and they thrashed about horribly, the man was taken to the hospital as an emergency case. I still got beatings for some two weeks, but they didn't ask me to foreswear the One who gave us life, and they didn't give me any explanation when they released me. I waited for a trial which didn't take place."

"I, too, have lived waiting for the same thing," I said to the priest. "If I look back, I think that the subject turned to us, as well, during the trial. It is probable that Dana covered up for us. She blamed herself for the trip from the mountains to the hospital. Probably. Why they didn't call me as a witness or why I wasn't accused – I don't know, and I don't even suspect. I thought many times about asking

Professor Albu whether he had any connection to my salvation, for the second time. Due to his scientific authority, he was frequently called in to make some diagnoses and he preferred to keep the so-called enemies of the people in the clinic, rather than letting them die in the prisons. Those people had diagnoses that forced the Securitate men to intern them on the religious feastdays, but in any case one could live in the clinic. I always postponed this discussion and, one day, a heart attack shortened his days. I don't know, what is going on, Father, why it is that I can't manage to take too many things to a good conclusion, although I strive to, with all my might. In an absurd world, normal things have no future. In any case, I am waiting for any other question. I would like us to come out of here with our souls at peace."

"How is it that you've come back to the village, though, after such a long time?" enquired the priest. "What feelings brought you here? You told me that you've been afraid in the past."

"I still am," I replied. "I was, this time as well, forced."

I then told him about my dialogue with the county chief medical officer and, of course, about the potential visit by Ceaușescu.

"If the Securitate accepted you in this moment of national madness, that means you are, in their eyes, as clean as a tear. I wouldn't feel honoured to receive such duties," Father Goga said in a grave voice, which annulled the reconciliation I thought we had reached.

"If I swear again that I did not and do not have any understanding with the Securitate men or the party men, will you believe me?" I asked him again, placing my hand on the Bible.

"You don't have to swear, I am trying to believe you,"

said the priest. "They either converted you to atheism, or there is nothing normal is this world anymore. I cannot explain many things to myself, but I believe you, that is – I am striving to. From now on, we can discuss in my home as well. If I didn't know in what world we live and that everything is at the mercy of chance, I'd probably have other questions..."

I waited until he took off the surplice and said a prayer, and then he invited me to dinner. I thanked him sincerely, although I was feeling terribly tired and especially unhappy due to the fact that I wasn't certain that I had convinced him. I thought of the years during which he'd kept the pain that I had deceived him in his soul, of the physical hurts which the Securitate people had caused him for in reality, because, look – he treated me as if the wounds on his back still bled. I also felt his pain and revolt in the reactions of his wife, who looked at us confusedly when she saw us entering the house. She had not expected us to come together, but she didn't ask anything, she was content to improvise something to eat so that we wouldn't drink on an empty stomach the red wine she'd brought.

"Wine on an empty stomach doesn't do any good to the Father," she excused herself, and he hurried to add:

"Especially when he doesn't have it!"

"I am not a courageous man," I tried explaining myself to him after we'd gone past the first glass. "In fact, I have never tested my courage. I also know there is a threshold of physical suffering, passing which, a man is no longer responsible for his deeds and words. But I do know that the road to that limit is long, and I would not declare the things I don't believe and the things I didn't do. And, on top of that, I uphold a cult of friendship. It's probably why I don't have friends," I said, trying to joke about it.

"Until we get to our first beating we don't know our limits. It's only afterwards that you start to suspect how much and how far you can endure. I asked myself many times what sense does so much suffering have. In the end, what did I do? I gave a Christian burial to some poor innocents who had been promised help if they fought against the communists with weapons in their hands. I encouraged others to bear their crosses to the end. This is my profession, which very much resembles yours. You ask the man what is his pain, not what is his ethnicity or what party he's joined. But they didn't want to accept this truth. I was many times, I admit it, on the verge of giving up. The resistance had been annihilated, the villagers who had helped them languished in prisons. I would not have admitted to anything besides what they already knew. But they made a mistake when they asked me to deny my faith. How could I approach the altar after such a sin? They always mentioned your name. Sometimes I doubted you could have done such a thing, but I thought that after some beatings you might have. I felt it was not true, but logic contradicted me. Nobody knows better than a priest what lies in the souls of men, how much darkness and fear, how much thirst for sin and how much repentance. I asked Florica, the drawing teacher, whether she knew anything, whether you had contacted her, since people talked about your relationship. She said she had realised even from the moment you two separated that you would never see each other again. And in this case, what was I to believe?"

"Lord, what is she doing now? If you only knew how many times I thought of her!" I admitted sincerely. "She asked nothing of me, ever, and I did not promise anything to her either. But she became more important for me only after I had left the village."

"She stayed for some two years after you left, then she simply vanished. Meaning that she went to her parents, somewhere in Moldavia, and didn't come back. I have never talked to her at length. I knew her and nothing more. She didn't come to the church. She was afraid, she probably wanted to hold on to her teaching position. Back then, after I returned from the Securitate, I asked about what she knew and where she thought you could be. She said that one time only a girl came around here and asked about you, but around our parts nobody replies to this kind of question. The fear of being called as witnesses to something later on, or being made to sign a statement taught the people well. They know everything, because they are curious; and, don't forget they have always been put in the situation to defend themselves, but they don't say anything and they don't admit anything."

As we expected, we didn't stop after the first glass. Nor after the second. We both felt guilty for the coldness that had fallen between us, for the years in which we did not meet.

"It had to be that, after all these years, Ceauşescu would come to reconcile us, to rebuild the trust," I joked, to which the priest made the sign of the cross over himself three times, as if scared that somebody might hear me saying something that could be misinterpreted.

"After the political prisoners were released, they brought new people to the village, as it had been raised to the status of a commune. Two new sawmills were built, the logging of the forest began, two party activists were appointed from the commune and, in order to feed the multitude of people working in the woods, they built a trout farm

429

and some pheasant and rabbit farms. The boars and bears, that multiplied and became cheeky, started to attack the people, and to devastate the scarce crops. And where there is game, there will appear hunters as well. The party activists I was talking about decided to make a surprise for Ceauşescu, a great hunter, and an easier route to the Capital for themselves. The forest and the clearings are filled with hunting platforms waiting for the man who might come by. But because you appeared as well, I am starting to understand why they are cobbling and tarmacking the streets with so much enthusiasm, why they are moving trees to the edges of the road and why they are digging ditches and constructing culverts. Furthermore, they painted the village hall, the school, and even the fence of the church. Numerous cars with people who seem to be looking for something have started to appear, too. Now that you have confirmed my suppositions, the madness will start. Cows brought in from who knows where, herded forcefully in the people's yards, pure breed horses and pigs who've met Ceauşescu in some other places as well."

"And people will applaud enthusiastically," I intervened, "will shout the slogans they are given, after which they will retake their positions in queues, with the hope they will be rewarded with some merchandise in the stores because they've behaved with discipline. The bowed head will not be cut off by the sword, but it will not get any respect either! Look, I don't have the right to condemn them, as I didn't have the strength to refuse them either. For me it is a show from which I feel that I don't have the right to be absent."

"My good fortune is that my presence is excused," the priest intervened, "the only thing is that for those days the church will be full of strange people. You recognise the

Securitate men quickly: they either cross themselves too fast and too widely, or they don't cross themselves at all, and they don't look at the priest, merely to the left and to the right."

We then talked about me, about my journey in psychiatry and especially about my new passion: mountain climbing. As for marriage, it still didn't preoccupy me at all, maybe because the person I waited for, my pair, the necessary other half, had not yet appeared. I promised him that, whosoever would be my future wife, the marriage would take place there, in the village, and he, Father Calistrat Goga, would give us his blessing and place the spousal crowns on our heads, as is the custom.

"Do I have permission to ask you one question?" I enquired after I'd seen his face lighten up, a sign that the bitterness and distrust had softened. "If I were to ask you a thing or two about the doctors in the village, but also about the people I should avoid while I am in these parts, would you mind? I mean, you would not believe that I came here to pull words from your tongue? I know the suspicions are generalised: nobody trusts anybody. *Shut up so they won't hear you!* This is the advice or warning you always hear."

"It's not because you've sworn on the Bible that you've impressed me, but your serenity and the haste with which you've accepted the idea," Father Goga told me, a sign that he'd forgiven me. He then talked about the teachers in the village and only in the end about the doctors. "I wouldn't want to influence you," he said. "There are three women who work as hard as slaves. The heavy load is born by the paediatrician, Lina Lupu. I have plenty of baptisms here. The people, in the majority, work in the woods, so they pull hard at it for a week or two, they come home for food, they

431

get drunk until they forget about their own heads, they leave their wives pregnant, they return to the forest and then start again from the beginning. The laws are harsh. For a child who died out of its mother's stupidity or because of too much poverty you will pay as if you've killed it yourself. The laws are draconian. The dentist earns the most by capping the Gypsies' teeth with gold. Nobody knows where they bring the gold from, people say they have agreements with the border police and that they give them a share of the loot, and then come here and sell it.

This dentist is not married either, the same as their chief, Daria Pop. She is smart, but rather free with her mouth. 'I'll be a doctor even in the prison,' she maintains. 'Otherwise, in a small room, in a cell, sorrow is easier to take than in the greater cell, which is the country.' When you say this kind of things, you don't know whether it's provocation or courage. In any case, people shut up and are afraid. Otherwise she is very skilled. They say that all three waited to choose for so long that all three stayed unmarried. I don't know her too well, she doesn't come to the church, and I've been pretty healthy, despite the beatings I took."

From what I could understand, Father Goga did not really feel inclined to answer my questions. He'd become tired, that day had had many emotions in it, and the wine had started to take effect. I left promising that I would look him up again, which is what also happened.

I was introduced to the female doctors the following day, presented as an inspector, by the mayor. An inspector, in general, was all he said. He didn't really understand what my occupation was, but he knew that anyone who came for an inspection from the county office had to be well received, so as a consequence he had called all the chiefs from the institutions in the village to the village hall, as a sign of his authority. I didn't have anything to tell them, but I assured them that I would try to meet each and every one of them, so that I could build an opinion on my own. In these kinds of circumstances, you usually need to be as evasive as possible, to leave the impression that you know everything and that you've only come in order to confirm the data you already hold. As for me, I completely disliked playing the inspector, especially since I had already learnt the reason for my presence in Pădureni, but I understood that I should play my role until the moment I would be notified that the visit was a certainty. At that moment, probably, they expected me to say: I did my duty, we have so many schizophrenics, so many sufferers from delusions, so many depressives and so on. From what I got to hear from the people involved in these visits, *"those who might pose problems,"* if I may use the consecrated phrase, were taken away from the locality, taken for health checks in various hospitals or, if they were younger, were expected to be drafted into the army. It was well understood that I was going to be asked to do the same things, but I was told this in stages, in instalments, out of fear that I might find a solution which could prevent me from participating in this "historic" visit. Everything that the head of the party and of the state did back then came under the aegis of the "historic". Of course, I was very aware that any incident, no matter how petty, an unsuitable word bandied around by anyone, some letter of a person which had managed to pass the "protective wall" around the "most beloved leader" could cost me enormously. As a consequence, I had no choice. I had to be more careful, and, to cover any eventuality, I decided to start my "inspections" with the general medical practice of Doctor Daria Pop. I had seen her at the already mentioned meeting, I noticed her demeanour and her beauty immediately, but I did not look at her with too much attention, fearing people might say I was not up to the importance of my position, in line with the mayor's introduction. I was also in a period of anxiety, a time when I didn't really know what I should cling to. As I entered the village, the fear from which I believed I was free, had been brought back to life; and then, the discussion with the priest, in the church, had stayed very vivid in my memory, but a pathetic feeling of humility had been added to it.

Daria Pop did not welcome me with too much amiability. "In case you are interested in the truth, it would help to know that we do wartime medicine here, without equipment, laboratories, hygienic conditions and all that. The only essential thing is the will of the Heavens. People live because God wills it, not because we help them. The state talks, but it does not do much."

I was content not to reply, but I looked at her with attention: big, black eyes, curly, rebellious hair, impossible to appease even with the aid of hair gel, plump lips, very well drawn, a strong chin and a nose which was slightly aquiline.

"Did you come with a special purpose?" she asked with an undertone of ulterior meaning. "People say that it might be possible for our eyes to be gladdened by *Our-esteem-and-pride*[47] himself and everybody is up and out of their minds. It is just *possible* and they just *suspect* and there are plenty of inspections. People are looking for something, but nobody says or knows what precisely. You have the impression that, after such a visit, the rains will stay put, there will be more

47   A reference to Ceaușescu, as this is part of a slogan praising the leader: *Stima-noastră-și-mândria / Ceaușescu-România*, Our esteem and pride are in Ceaușescu and Romania.

sun, and each strand of wheat will automatically yield five crowns of grains!"

I felt the need to gloss over the irony and to hand her the notice with which the chief medical officer had sent me. At the same moment, the assistants entered to let her know she had two serious cases. They seemed very anxious and, in the end, aware that the inspectors would leave but the patients would remain, they whispered to her that the woman brought in on the stretcher was the wife of the director of the logging plant. I asked her agreement to continue the discussion after we'd dealt with the patients, and she agreed gladly.

"Maybe you still remember what it's like to be a country doctor, without means but with great responsibilities."

"From the time I left this consulting room, it's only the cupboards and the gynaecology table that have changed," I replied, and she was more than surprised.

"This can't be. Here? In Pădureni?"

"Yes, here, but we'll talk about this after your medical consultations!" I assured her.

"One single question you still have to answer to me," she said: "How did you manage to escape from here? By what miracle?"

"I was lucky," I replied. "But my connection to this village seems not to be over yet. I never believed I would return here, but I was sent precisely when I had managed to separate myself from it, to forget it."

"It is probable that, after the success of this visit, you will take a new step forward," she said.

Her irony, although justified, was not to my liking, and it pushed me away from her. I didn't answer. Instead, I pointed to the patient brought on the stretcher by two strong men, two lumberjacks. Daria looked at her somewhat confused, a sign that my presence made her feel uncomfortable. With all this, I didn't leave and I didn't express my opinion either, I waited to see her at work and, after a short hesitation, she proceeded to asking questions, but the workers had no idea what had happened. One of them simply tried to joke.

"Maybe she's argued again with her man. She wanted to give him a beating for a long time now, but he's having none of it!"

For me, the diagnosis was clear, but I was curious to see Daria's reactions. This was the known hysteria arc, nape, heels, eyes rolled up, normal breathing. The usual treatment was with a couple of slaps and pressure on the ovaries. But she read the blood pressure, after which she extracted from a small bottle a syringe with distilled water which she injected subcutaneously. She had seen the diagnosis with plenty of certainty, for which fact I hurried to congratulate her, in a whisper.

"I felt like slapping her, meaning to apply the traditional treatment, but the two companions would have spread the news in the village that I beat my patients up," she explained to me. "No matter if they are needed or not, the syringe and Roentgen machine are fundamental in these places! They ensure your prestige," she informed me later on, "and magisterial prescriptions are very well observed. A colleague advised me to add a drop of opium tincture in a prescription because people need to feel an improvement immediately. Otherwise, the medicine is not good and, there's no doubt about it, the doctor's not good either! This unfortunate woman, the director's wife, was not having her first fit of the hysterics. Unfortunately the husband no longer has time for her. He is busy with fulfilling the planned quota, with a female engineer. How it all came to this, is not hard to suspect. Unfortunately, since there's a great confusion going around – here as much as in the whole of the country – we no longer have time for our souls."

I didn't say she was right, but I didn't contradict her either. I felt happy to gloss over her conclusions, which were true and full of common sense, but which rather intrigued me. She seemed very free in voicing her opinions in front of a stranger who had nevertheless come on an inspection. So I involuntarily asked myself whether she was provoking me. We lived in a world where you could expect anything from anyone, especially since we'd got used to suspecting each other and to seeing a possible informer in each one of our fellow human beings, a person with no qualms about hurting you. But my instinct told me that, this time, I had no reason to doubt her sincerity. She spoke looking you in the eye, as if she were certain you thought the same way.

"How did you end up in this particular place?" I enquired more out of a desire to maintain a dialogue than anything else, and she looked at me with irony:

"Is this part of the inspection as well?"

"Everything is part of the inspection!" I answered in the same tone.

"Should I have been somewhere else? What makes you keep on with this?" she asked, with the air that she was disposed to chat on that subject.

"I don't know," I replied. "I feel you are not from around here. Don't ask me for evidence, as I have none."

"Am I carrying out a punishment? That would be the first question in a long series which might be followed by many others. How is it that I am unmarried, in this place, where I have no chance of finding a husband who might be to

437

some extent honourable? How do I put up with the routine wretchedness in a corner of the world where everybody believes themselves to be exiled, or deserted by fate?"

"I don't deny it, the questions are interesting, but I would not have asked all of them," I answered. "Especially about your private life."

"Of course, when I chose medicine, I thought about all that might await me. I didn't think I would get special conditions. If I'm able, I'll leave this place, if not – I deserve my fate. This would be the answer, in general," she told me. "In reality, I ended up in Pădureni almost by chance. Being engaged with a colleague in the same graduate series at the university, we planned to go to some locality where they had open positions for both of us. Since we were together, we were not really interested about where we ended up, especially as we didn't know the country in detail. As I had a higher average grade, I was first to choose when it came to the distribution of workplaces and, of course, I asked for Pădureni, because there were two places here and we wouldn't be far from home either. When Sergiu's turn to choose came – that was his name, Sergiu Medan – he suddenly opted for a Securitate hospital. In fact, a prison doctor. He hadn't asked for my opinion, although I was there, he only explained the advantages to me: it was in a town, a salary according to rank, little responsibility and many others. We'd have a foothold in the city, a very important fact for our future. What he didn't tell me was that the papers for this option had been filled in a long time in advance, as these people check the past of your parents, the social origins and many other things. Did he think I was not going to find out a detail like that? Was he afraid about my parents' origins, of their past? From that moment onwards, I no longer wanted to know anything about him. He cried, he seemed as desperate as in the hour of his death, but I told him that when it came to our separation, there was a single concept that weighed the heaviest: few responsibilities! How come? Are those people not human? Aren't they people who pay for their mistakes? Do they have to be treated without responsibility? Unfortunately, I didn't know him, but he didn't know me either and he could not believe I was going to give him up without shedding a tear. After a while, he wanted to resign, to come with me, but our connections, such as they were, were definitively broken. Of course, it hurt horribly. In such moments, you feel that the world is crumbling. Fate turns its back on you, abandons you. On this great and patient earth, there is no place for you anymore, no point of support. As if you don't any longer have air and light. But I didn't accuse him, not for one moment. Instead, I accused myself – for allowing myself to be ruled by my good faith. I had judged him according to what I felt for him, and here I am, with the risk of becoming an old maid, but at peace, because I was as I had to be, stronger that I could have imagined. I know I take after my father. I am not made for compromises, but such structures don't end up being happy, and they don't succeed. It's hard to tell you this, and I don't know why I am doing it, but sometimes it's as if the whole loneliness of the world comes crushing down on me."

In the space between us, which had been cold enough and deserted up that point, Daria had introduced a wave of warmth and humanity. I suddenly felt that from that point onwards we could discuss absolutely anything, without a trace of reservation.

"Were it not for my father, I would have probably wanted

to try my luck differently. I am a very good swimmer and it's more than a few times that I thought of taking a risk and crossing the Danube to Yugoslavia and, from there, to Austria. Others have managed it, the majority of them, so I had my chance too, but I gave up. Father would not have come with me, nor my grandmother. I could not abandon them. Grandfather died of cancer and, with him, grandmother seriously lost her balance. A horrible depression. She sits in the cemetery all day, cares for his grave, cries and maintains that she talks to him. She exists more in the beyond, than among us. Every time I think about them, I reproach myself that we haven't talked enough, that, in fact, I don't know them. I've always postponed it, always convinced we had the time, that the spare day will come, that day set apart for them. But it did not come. And they stayed somewhere in my memory as a symbol of sorrow and lack of achievement. I would not have had anything special to say to them, not even that I loved them, because they knew that, they raised me – father behaved with great awkwardness with me, and he was home rather seldom. In any case, I feel pangs of conscience because of my past, because of my memory of them. I don't know how this life is ordered, because we do everything with difficulty. But why am I telling you all these stories?" Daria asked herself, somewhat surprised that she found herself talking about strictly personal facts and feelings. Her sincerity moved me, especially because, after the first sentences, I had stopped being a psychiatrist and even less the inspector whose role I had to play.

"Crossing the Danube would have been an extremely risky adventure," I said to her, out of a desire to keep the conversation going. "There have been many people killed by border guards. Others have been sent back and surrendered to the Romanian border guards, who sent them to prison. Is it really worth dying in order to reach across to over there, to a world where you are a stranger? What use is freedom in a country which is not yours and where, whatever you'd think, you are not well regarded? We dream of freedom, they dream of workplaces. You still meet hatred, either here or over there, and then, there is a bad fortune: that of waking up earlier than the others. I don't want you to believe that I am trying to convince you not to leave. Because, in the end, I would be an ordinary opportunist. These are questions I often ask of myself: what's better? We have a single life: in what conditions do you have to risk it? How much would you value it? And, asking things of ourselves, life passes by and we find that we haven't done much. If you pass on the side of the power, it's immoral, it's abject, but you can realise at least a part of your aspirations. Opposing power, you are free, even in prison, but you have no chance of making a career as a professional. A world smeared by politics. What is the road? I don't know! It is, in any case, the beginning of a new discussion, which we can't continue during the hours of the medical consultation schedule," I said. I then asked whether there was a canteen or restaurant nearby.

"Yes," she replied, "at the lumberjacks'. There is another restaurant which I don't recommend, too many drunks. They fine them, but if they go for drastic punishments they would leave a lot of people without their income. There is also the 'Daria Pop and associates' B&B, but we would need to cook and get provisions here. The two of us and the girls: the paediatrician and the dentist. Cleanliness is guaranteed, but the imagination and the qualifications of the cooks are lacking. The advantage is that you are not alone and that evenings have no surprises in store for you. What you had

441

for lunch, so you shall consume in the evenings. Omelettes, potatoes baked in the stove, beans, as much as you like, and, instead of sophisticated soups, tea! That's it, more or less."

I thanked her for her good thoughts, but without saying whether I would go. I had simply forgotten to discuss such an important detail with the mayor, who didn't have any idea, either, whether he'd have a particular guest or not. But there had been a detail that moved me: the communication established with Daria, beyond words, and beyond our rather hurried dialogue. She had won my trust and, apart from the priest, I had not felt for many, many years that I could talk openly with anyone without feeling afraid, without controlling my words.

Unfortunately, I only had two days to get as close to my new friends as I would have done during my student days, which were distant enough, because everything suddenly went mad. The whole place was filled with Securitate men, and at the same time as their arrival, there started the digging of ditches, the painting of fences, the transplantation of beeches from the forest in order to situate them along the sides of the road, and, of course, the building of viewing platforms in the mountains, together with a grand stand, on a plateau at the edge of the village. In the centre, not far from the village hall, a madly feverish building process started, of ultra-modern stables for the cows that were going to be brought over, for the duration of the visit, from southern Transylvania. People said these were the official duty animals, the presidential cows that welcomed him on any visit, irrespective of what part of the country he went to. They could not decide with regard to the sheep. The local sheep, and there was no doubt about it, had ticks on them which could reach the distinguished guest, with catastrophic consequences; but they didn't have the time to bring others from alternative sheepfolds, and the main worry of the people dealing with the animals was justified.

"What do we do if the Comrade asks us about sheep? He has to see with his own eyes that the people have everything, that socialism is victorious everywhere!"

In the end, between making him gravely ill, which would have cost them time in prison, or even their lives, and a tough session of criticism, they opted for the latter. The medical personnel was summoned to the town hall by a team of doctors in civilian dress who asked for answers to some questions. What houses will be prepared in the hypothetical case that the Comrade wanted to visit the home of a villager? If so, they needed to change the interiors, the furniture, the carpets, while the poor wretches' houses needed to be provided with fridges and TV sets, and the health of the owners had to be severely monitored. The same went for the health of the school children who were going to be embraced and kissed by the Comrade and the Madame Comrade, his wife. Daria had to deliver a report on the psychiatric state of the people in the village, whether there were any madmen, how many and what kind of psychiatric diseases they suffered – the mission to check them falling onto me; while they, the doctors who came to prepare the visit, would isolate them for that specific period of time. After the preparatory meeting, I was asked to stay a little longer for a separate discussion, in the mayor's office. A colonel dressed in uniform was waiting for me. This was a man whom – maybe because of the emotions swirling around– I had not noticed during the session.

"I am colonel Onaca," he said to me, "and I would like to ask you to walk around the village, maybe you will find something special. We are all interested in the visit running well, like others before it. We count on you, a man who knows the village and who still remembers, I am sure, some one or another who once fought in the mountains. If the Party freed them from prison, as a sign of generosity, it doesn't mean that our vigilance has weakened! We know accurately who fought, who went to prison, how specific people behaved in prison, but also who helped them."

The colonel looked me in the eyes and laughed under the narrow moustache, like that of a barber's.

"Should I continue?" he enquired slyly, holding my gaze.

"Yes," I replied coolly. "That would be the right thing. I want you to take your ideas to their conclusions."

"No problem," he replied, seeming to feel very certain of himself. "I thought it was sufficient only to suggest some specific things, but, if need be, we have details as well. You shouldn't believe, doctor, that we don't know how many times you climbed into the mountains to see the bandits. We were up to date with any movement."

"Then why didn't you arrest me?" I asked, suddenly free of any fear or restraint.

"It's never too late," the officer assured me, with the air of unveiling a great secret. "Reasons can always be found. In the end, we don't really need reasons. We gather witness statements, we investigate, we verify, and, due to an oversight, old age can catch up with you in our underground cells, while you're waiting for a sentence. Waiting for a sentence which will not be pronounced! The world is nasty. Hunger and fear can make you corruptible. You have no idea how many people can accuse you of anything!"

"This particular thing – I am really not afraid of," I replied. "I only did my duty as a doctor. For me, the sick, the healthy, believers or atheists: they are all human."

"Leave wisdom out of it," said the colonel, annoyed. "People are sinners, and doctors are people as well. Don't complicate things. You know what they say: if you didn't do anything, you get five years. What about if you did something? And not just any thing! Let's not talk about it, we know even the colour of the knickers on that female doctor who took you to the mountains. So, what seems important to me is for you to do your job, and in such a manner that the visit and the hunting party will run smoothly. We've closed our eyes for such a long time, we can continue to keep them closed."

"Your understanding doesn't satisfy me," I replied. "I don't need mercy, and I can't bear that somebody should tell me how I need to do my duty, with the exception of those who have more scholarship than me. I assure you that, from this point forward, I will not live with fear in my bosom. I do not defy you, but I don't want to co-operate with you either."

"Doctor, doctor, you don't even know what you are talking about," said the colonel with much gravity. "If it comes to it, I would not have any remorse. Where there is an obligation, no morals exist. Or morals have no importance. I forgive you because you actually do not know what you are saying. But if your eyes don't stick out of their sockets looking around, when you walk through the village, and if it happens that a madman pops up when the comrade arrives, you are finished. I will make it through, in the end, but *Giuseppe è morto definitivo!*"[48]

I knew I had to leave the last word to him, the certainty that he had intimidated me; as a result, I said goodbye in a hurry and left without asking his approval to go. He shouted

---

48 *Giuseppe è morto definitivo,* in Italian in the original: Giuseppe is dead for good.

something after me I didn't understand. I wanted to take my distance, as soon as possible, from the village hall and, without stopping to think about it, stimulated by the noise of my own steps, I almost broke into a run getting to the medical practice where Daria was waiting for me.

"You don't seem to be much at peace," she said to me, intrigued. "Do you feel unwell? Can I help you with anything?"

Some time needed to pass before I regained mastery of my own words. I had to replay the discussion in my head in order to understand truly what had happened. Did I do well in answering back to threats? Wouldn't it have been better to say he was right, and then to go about my business? In any case, I had not behaved like a psychiatrist, but rather like a threatened man who was trying to be dignified; and all this at a time when people had got used to listening silently to this kind of authority and then, when they took their leave, to consign them to the devil. In the end, I managed to recount everything to Daria, not because I wanted to free myself from the fright, but in order to have a witness in case they did something bad to me. That is, so that she should know exactly what happened to me.

"You don't have to worry," Daria said to me. "People have been very closely looked at for a while. If you have a hunt, there will be weapons, too. There is a record of those weapons and specific people need licences in order to have them in their houses. The officers do this with everybody. They threaten, and they do their best to give you the impression that they know everything. If they really had known something, they would have been calmer, they wouldn't have set on people with so many threats."

"The fear they cultivate is part of their arsenal," I replied.

"And we are in an area where people fought with weapons in their hands. But the villagers also, in particular, helped the people who fought. I think Ceauşescu knows only about rabbits, pheasants and bears, not about the partisans!"

"Truth is that we'll need to be careful, as well," said Daria. "If they killed him, that would still be something, but, in the best case, a potential assassin would only scare him, and then it would be woe on our heads. I don't even want to think about the investigations and especially about prison. Because, since I came here, to Pădureni, I've only heard talk about prisons and beatings!"

"For myself, I confess that their threats have really got my knees weaker," I said. "I've been asking myself for a while now where there are more mentally ill people, in the hospitals or outside them? In this place, I'm beginning to have the data for a possible answer."

"I'll say that we should now go to dinner. Surprisingly, I haven't yet been called to a birth or to some political instruction. Maybe there will be no accident this evening and I'll manage to cook something," Daria said, suddenly getting up from her chair. I immediately followed her, with the feeling that I hadn't achieved anything. I hadn't managed to take the discussion to its proper end, and the colonel's threats had begun to obsess me so that, strangely, in that deserted village, lit only by the moon and terrorised by the agitation of the dogs, I felt fragile, more uncertain than even during the times of the fights in the mountains. Daria had taken a large, black umbrella with her, and a rather strong flashlight:

"Self-defence," she said. "I don't leave them behind, no matter the season or the weather. You don't know how many things you can learn about life in such an area."

"I've passed through these places too," I answered, "and unfortunately I did not draw those conclusions at the right time. There are many questions with whose answers, even now, after such a long time, I am unhappy."

"Can you tell me one of these questions?" she asked. "We can't exclude the possibility they coincide with mine."

"Maybe in a moment of peace, if, as long as we still have the threat of that visit, we can benefit from such a thing around here. Look, in a world led by the stupid and the illiterate, where everything is mixed up and everyone does things according to their own ideas, is it good to be a doctor until you reach the white sails on the horizon, to the bitter end? That is, to perform your profession at the cost of life or freedom?" I answered, somehow set off by our proximity to the main highway, from where there came intense noises of machines and human voices. "In a world where the prison camp mentality has gained ground, meaning that each person saves themselves in whatever way they can, does it seem fair for you to make exceptions, to risk everything for the sake of some people you didn't encourage to risk their lives in the first place?"

Of course, I was talking just for the sake of talking, since professional ethics demanded sacrifice, but reality and the instinct for self-preservation compel you to a different reaction. I had to say what I believed, however, to preserve the feeling established between us, a kind of sincerity and trust which was impossible to deny. Unfortunately, as I had suspected, we didn't have the time to continue with our discussion because we had reached the main road, where they were working intensely at laying the tarmac. On both sides of the road, people fixed large light bulbs on the lamp posts they had just stuck in the ground, hurrying to bring trees from the forest in order to plant them in the deep holes on which tens of people worked. Numerous civilians and individuals in military uniforms agitatedly supervised everything that was happening, so that the honoured guest would find them prepared.

"It will be very hard for us to sneak through these industrious people," said Daria. "My good fortune is that I live close-by. The cleaning woman and the coach driver told me about something that's even more of a hoo-ha. Apparently, in the clearing where they have built the main stand, that of the Comrade, they are working at back-breaking speed to dig deep ditches where they will bring the cages holding pheasants and rabbits. Very well trained people will release the birds and animals from those cages, in a special sequence which will allow the Comrade to reload his weapon – if necessary, the animals will come straight into his line of fire! Is he a dupe? Or does he allow himself to be duped? Can the thirst for blood be pushing him to such arrangements?"

"It could be all this in one," I replied, exasperated by the dust raised by the giant trees pulled by the tractors.

"And after the visit is over, what is going to happen to all the stage props?"

"I don't know, this is the first and probably the last visit in which I take part," I hurried to assure her. "From what I heard, the cows return to their real owners and wait for another visit; the trees, if they catch root, that's their good fortune – if not, they'll become firewood. The light bulbs are taken away – we're saving electricity. The ditches will be filled with leaves and wild things that fall in by chance and won't be able to get out. The boozer will be filled to suffocation by drunks, and life will be like it was. It's just that the disappointment will be greater. Maybe not even that."

At Daria's home, Colonel Onaca was waiting for us on the veranda with three soldiers.

"I hope I haven't scared you," said the officer, with the air of having given us a pleasant surprise. "This is what happens when you are in a hurry to finish off a conversation."

"And what if we didn't come home, what would you have done then?" Daria said, trying to joke.

"We would have opened the door and I'd have taken a nap," said the colonel with great seriousness. "These are hard days in which you do thousands of things without having the time for rest."

"Was it somehow open?" Daria asked, scared.

"I worked for some years in a prison and I learnt from the inmates all the techniques for opening padlocks, complicated locks and many others. We, the officers, have only prison doctors or the inmates as our competitors," he said, addressing me in a complicit tone.

"If you are so sleepy, we can return to the dispensary," said Daria. "We wish to add our contribution, even in this manner, to the success of the visit!"

"Tomorrow morning, I'll be waiting for you at the village hall. I have summoned there, at eight o'clock, the former prison inmates, the survivors of the bandits in the mountains and those who are more or less off their heads, people who are in the sights of the militia. I want to hold an instruction session for them. You will be doing your professional duty: eyes on all four corners and reporting everything which seems suspicious. It is also in your interest for the Comrade to be happy. And if he should be," he emphasised, looking at me, "we won't see each other again. If not, life has many clouded facets."

"We shall be there too," Daria hurried to assure him. "We know the benefits the village might get, and ourselves too, in case of a success!"

"That's how I want you," he said, starting to cheer up. "I am trying to grab a little bone to chew on from an animal the mayor managed to hunt down. Under the pretext that he needs to see whether the animals and birds were diseased, he has caused ravages. I warned him I knew what he was busying himself with, and that it would be good for him if I didn't have my eyes on him. 'What's yours is set aside. On ice!' he promised me. 'You find ice here only in people's souls, because they haven't really heard of fridges!' I said, in my turn, so that he wouldn't believe I will let myself be duped. In the end, he swore to me that I need not worry."

"In any case, we would have come too," Daria insisted. "I talked today at great length with the doctor and, rest assured, we are at your orders."

It was pointless contradicting her, or asking supplementary questions, although Daria's hurry in assuring him of our support rather upset me. Yet another additional disappointment, I said to myself. To my surprise, the colonel seemed very content, shook our hands hurriedly and, followed by the soldiers, left the room without explaining to us why he insisted on informing us of a routine meeting in person. How was it that they didn't arrest me, since they knew everything about my meetings with the fighters in the mountains, why do they continue to follow me, why was I sent here if I don't represent a reliable element? Maybe it was because fear makes you execute whatever is asked of you without grumbling, and that is what they needed. In the end, all these circumstances help us to know ourselves better, to discover who we are in reality and how much we still need to polish until we manage to have feelings that won't betray us from the very beginning. Daria closed the door hurriedly, and, for a while, she leant on it, holding her head in her hands. Thinking something had happened to her, I hurried to help, but she, with eyes full of tears, looked at me, revolted:

"Would our national madman just come already! I can't take it anymore. From morning till evening, only instructions, only rabid people like this one, who come and threaten me. Don't be angry with me, but I wanted to get rid of him, otherwise I would have become notorious for what might have happened. Onaca is just a tool and any discussion with him seemed useless. Either start wrestling with the big man or give up!"

She placed her head on my shoulder, defeated; but I don't think that it was me from whom she was asking support. Instead, she was appealing to a creature who was stronger than herself, willing to protect her at any moment. She didn't stay there for too long. Wiping her eyes and, somehow ashamed of the moment of weakness she had gone through, she tried an explanation:

"If you were not here I would have been different. I would not have let a tear escape, and I really think I'd have told him off, too. But as it is, irrespective how funny this might seem to you, I was trying to protect you from the fool's vanity. The stars on his shoulder insignia drag him down. He is not talking to us, but to the stars on his shoulders." She went into the kitchen. "I like to cook, if I have what I need to cook. My grandmother taught me everything I know from an age when other girls were not allowed to play with the knives so that they wouldn't cut their fingers."

"I would not have believed it," I replied, trying to imitate her ease. "When the time comes for me to marry, I will take this specialisation into account!"

"But are you not married already?" she was surprised.

"Although I may seem so, I am not," I replied. "Nobody's taken me, because, it's well known, women are the conquerors! And I couldn't tempt anyone, except for short distances. And I wasn't tempted by any woman in particular, so much so that I'd be dying without!"

"I think it's understandable: it is hard to live near a psychiatrist or a gynaecologist. Every day with their noses up somebody's fanny, so that…but I'd take you. If you are patient, I can draw up a list with what I know how to cook and what other things at which I am skilled: I wash, I iron, I watch football matches and I learn anything quickly. I don't have a very linear biography, on the contrary, so I also have defects worth the attention of a psychiatrist!"

"In that case, I am disposed to risk it!" I replied with relative seriousness. "Let's say it's love at first sight."

"It is not the first, but the second sight," she specified. "I was very attentive and I saw how you looked at me when you came into my consulting room. And I was charmed when I noticed with how much appetite you looked at my breasts. And my bottom!"

"Yes, I have to admit that you have a spirit of observation. And after all this excess of sincerity, what would be the next move?"

"Let's get to the first test: the kitchen! You've confessed that it is part of the mandatory requirements. In fact, I am dying of hunger myself. And then I also have some things left to clarify. The answer? Optional."

"I am waiting for the questions, even if I am also hungry. I can think of them like that, in between one drop and another," I assured her.

"Agreed. Look, I feel you are a good person, although reason urges me to be prudent. What are you doing with these people? Were you afraid to refuse them? As a consequence: you're a coward or a trustworthy man. There might be another version: as a psychiatrist, you've turned the proposal of the Securitate men round and round for so long, that you ended up choosing the solution that torments you the most."

"If, let's say, you should learn the whole truth, would you be inclined to understand me?" I enquired, in quite a hurry. "After all, at the most insignificant hesitation the possibility of marriage is suspended."

"We'll see," she laughed, probably annoyed by the seriousness with which I had engaged in the discussion.

"Gossiping with a colleague," I said, "it didn't even cross my mind that he would turn out to be the chief medical officer and that Ceaușescu would make a visit to Pădureni itself, a visit to which I would be summoned to make my contribution. I was a coward, too, and I admit it, especially since they rather blackmailed me, and I thought that such a working visit would have to be a success, since all the men and women breathing in the area would contribute to it. Furthermore, we are not under the star sign of courageous people, but under the sign of toadies. You oppose it all and, it's indisputable that, in the end, they will manage to destroy you as a man, slowly and certainly, in a context where nobody will jump in to help you – on the contrary, the majority will say you're an idiot or lacking in common sense for showing your fangs, to them of all people! I also have a rather idiotic principle. Instead of seeking out the evil in others, it is better that I should try to do good myself. The truth is that all these explanations became clear only after I got here. So you can judge me as seems fit to you."

"Yes, that's more or less what I believed, too," she concluded. "In your turn, you are allowed to ask a single question this evening."

"Proposal approved," I said, "although I would have asked anyway: where are the girls, your colleagues?"

"You have noticed that although we had talked of a meal cooked by eight hands, four of them are missing at this time. Bravo! I didn't call them. I saw the confrontation behind the words you had with Onaca and I wanted to be the only one here with you. You are not an accomplished psychiatrist: one can still read the feelings on your face. Even without that confrontation, we would have still been alone. That's what I felt. It is not a debate, but it's the holy reality."

I assured her that I was glad of it, but I didn't have the strength to continue the discussion which was located at all times on the thin line between truth and mockery. I did not suspect what would be the next move. Mine and hers. Should I get closer to her? Should I elaborate my growing feeling for her? Should I be content for the moment with this warmth that united us, beyond the words? I was convinced she was asking herself almost the same questions because she was deep in her cooking, but I could perceive her gaze looking for me, from time to time, trying to steal a reaction from me, a sign which could betray my intentions, my moves, or at least my next words. After she had finished frying the schnitzel, in a deafening silence where both of us gave the impression there would be nothing to discuss before the meal, she poured for me, in a big, deep earthenware plate, some chicken noodle soup, lit a candle and uncorked a large bottle of *țuică* plum brandy.

455

"Around these places of ours, in the former Valea Boului, you begin every meal with this, only to finish it all in a heap under the table, without remembering if you've eaten or not," she said, trying to explain. "However, we'll stop after the first glass because, according to the customs of the region, the Securitate guys might call us or, why not? some sick person."

"Speaking frankly," I confessed after I finished the soup, "you've passed the exam with a very, very good mark."

"Fortunately, it is the only exam possible until the visit of the Most Beloved[49] is over. My hosts are paying attention to all the noises. Furthermore, I can bet you that Onaca's boys are swarming outside," she said with a casualness that paralysed me.

"Frankly, I am glad you don't give me any chance to conquer you, a chance to get muscle spasms chasing you or only thinking about you," I replied, although I was not too proud of my attempt to defend myself against what had seemed to be irony.

"I would not want you to believe me to be very easy prey. I am not a woman who desires a man because she hadn't had one for some thousands of years," she said with the most serious air possible. "Matches and mismatches are decided much later. After the body, there comes a very long time of the soul and of the mind. Even until death."

"Did it seem to you that I am rather unripe, without experience and lacking a sense of the ridiculous? Is that how it is?" I enquired as naturally as I could.

"Not really. Lusty and a bit too sophisticated, and I thought I might be the bandage you need. Even if for a

---

49   *Cel mai iubit*, in the original. A contraction of the full formula *"Cel mai iubit fiu al poporului"* - the Most Beloved Son of the People, used for Ceaușescu in some propaganda materials.

shorter term. When you walked in the house, before meeting my eyes, you looked at the books, at the records and at these posters with which, in the absence of holy icons, I cover my walls. This, too, is a kind of test. For me, this mattered a lot."

Our talk, which was very strange, seemed to be more of a bargaining negotiation in which we were not talking about ourselves, not even by chance. How much of it was a joke stretched beyond the limits, and how much of it was a simple transaction – I could not grasp at that moment. I had reached a dead end over which I could not cross without consequences which were hard to foresee. In any case, I did not feel the master of myself. I had started as wrongly as I could, so that the only thing left for me to do was to leave the initiative to her, but I felt that she was more or less in the same state of expectation, of lying in wait. I felt the air between us had a special property, it was different. Even if words and logic hindered us, above all that, we were united by that air, by the need for affection, for reciprocal protection, and another indefinite state of spirit which refused to be stated in words. Something had to happen which would be strong enough to transfer us to another state of being, without disturbing this particular one, and, unexpectedly, Daria mentioned the wine she was going to offer me: a red liquid, without a name, which came from the grapes cultivated in the area. We wished each other all the best, and, strangely, she asked me to tell her, hand on heart, what I was thinking about when I spoke these wishes. I hurried to assure her that she could not be missing from my thoughts.

"Now, that's better," Daria confessed. "Tomorrow, when we meet, I shall be very happy, even if Onaca is also standing there with us."

I understood that I had to go, but my mind was at peace because she had found the solution which could maintain that clean air between us: without conclusions, without promises, and without gestures that could be misinterpreted in some way. I left there feeling calm, waiting impatiently for the following morning, when I was going to see her again, and I saw her, lost among the tens of scared people brought by force to the yard of the village hall without being told why they'd been invited there. They were scared because the presence of people in military uniforms and their shouts, as well as their diligence in making the villagers stand in columns, reminded everyone of the prisons, of the canal,[50] or of the cellars of the Securitate in which they had been investigated. Most of them huddled near Daria, in whom they seemed to have trust, and she assured them that absolutely nothing was going to happen to them. From behind a desk, I watched, together with Daria and Onaca, the bizarre parade of the people scared by the presence of the officer, who had not considered it proper to give them any explanation. He asked them for their surnames and names, looked them up on a list, enquired whether they had been in prison, and for what reasons, and then dropped some threat now and then, knowing it would be transmitted from one man to the other:

"If anyone of you dares to come out of their houses tomorrow, they won't get to see it again for the next ten years! Tomorrow is a celebration day!"

Every now and then a soldier would appear, reporting on how the operations were going. The cows had arrived

---

50 The canal referred to is the Danube-Black Sea Canal, a project started by the communist government in the 1950s where political prisoners were sent in labour camp. The canal was inaugurated by Nicolae Ceaușescu in 1987.

outside, the grand stand had been painted, but they prayed to heavens it wouldn't rain. Some other people had brought pumps for spraying paint, in case the firs and beeches would fade faster than foreseen. The ditches from where they were going to throw pheasants had been well camouflaged so that nothing may be seen from the stand where the Comrade would be. The refrigerated crates with the game, and his favourite tomatoes and cheese, had finally arrived, and so had the *Galbena de Odobești* wine, as well as with the other dainties which were consumed in such circumstances – a sign that the visit was very near. The unforeseen appearance of the Party first secretary forced Onaca to leave to us the checking of the people that were still there. The next thing, later on, when he considered the time was right, was that the newly arrived personage should hold the final instruction for all of us who were engaged in the "great event". We contented ourselves to continuing what we had started, we asked some passing questions or shared some smiles, in an attempt to make people relax. Unfortunately, we did not make great advances as, a little later, Colonel Onaca came back, irritated to the maximum:

"*Băi*, brothers, why didn't you say one word about the samples? What if he comes today? Why didn't you collect them?"

Furious, all set for scandal, he kept his eyes on Daria, but she did not seem alarmed at all.

"I am sorry, I am not the person coordinating the preparations. And we haven't even talked about any samples... what samples?"

"What do you mean – what samples?" shouted the colonel, in surprise. "The children who give them flowers and will be kissed, and held in their arms, don't they need to be checked? What if they have a haemolytic streptococcus and they pass it on to the Comrade or the Madame Comrade? Haven't you thought of this? What about the peasants in whose houses the Comrade might go? What if they have some grave illness? Should we be happy with whatever the militiaman or the mayor tells us? If I survive this one, it's either prison or the noose that awaits you!"

He felt guilty. I had no doubts about that, but he had probably forgotten to tell us, and he threw the blame on us; or, even more certainly, the arrival of the first secretary showed the imminence of the visit, but the local authorities were not ready yet, and the Securitate did not yet seem to be masters of the situation.

"You should know that, if we're talking about pharyngeal secretions, I don't have the means to collect them," said Daria. "What bases for the viral culture do I have? These things are found only in town, and even if we collected them today, it would be too late! Around here, people are living badly, woe is their heads, so it's better that nobody gives him any flowers! Or we can go ahead and take the risk.

"Lady," Onaca shouted angrily, "if anyone dreams – you hear, if anyone, a person from around the big boss, simply only dreams that we exposed him to a disease, none of us sees the sun again, not even in our future lives! Do the collection whichever way you know and with whatever you have, but I want the samples!"

"Why don't you make an appeal to your doctors?" Daria enquired, feeling very hard done by. "I heard there might be some of them around here, dealing with the hunt beaters."

"How do you know what we have and what we don't?" the colonel barked, going out of the room angrily. For a fraction of a second I had managed to discover surprise on his face, or a feeling of relief. It seemed that this detail provided by Daria, had eluded him: "Well, I am going to cut off the bollocks of the cretins who failed to draw this to my attention!"

Because he had called us to accompany him, we continued to deal with the people gathered there, but without any enthusiasm for it. By the way he reacted, the colonel needed victims, and we had no time at our disposal in order to conduct a serious monitoring exercise with the people gathered in front of the village hall. We were not interested in it, either. In that atmosphere of tension stretched to paroxysm, from the moment of the first-secretary's arrival, it was impossible to take anything to its conclusion. Everybody was irritated, everybody was giving orders, everybody felt, and even knew, what the Comrade would like to see, everybody had learned what he was thinking in a certain situation, even the stable boys ended up being tougher with the cows so that the animals wouldn't release any dung in front of him. After two hours, we were gathered in the village hall, where I was destined to discover a multitude of unknowns who presented their reports.

"Main stand?" the first secretary asked and, automatically, two men – the site manager and the Securitate man responsible for the solidity of the construction and guaranteeing that not one nail would jiggle in it – jumped as if burnt with something: "Objective is finalised!"

"Stables?"

"In good order, *să trăiți*, the animals brought here are sated, but we have not milked them, awaiting your orders!"

"Don't milk them yet, so that *they* can see their udders full! The pigs?"

"In good order!"

461

"No-one should sense any trace of smell for an area of ten thousand square meters! Understood? The trees?"

"With the exception of two beeches and a pine, all in good order. We have painted the beeches, we've replaced the pine as we've had another one nearby."

"What of the gusts of wind?"

"We have solutions against it, too!"

"What about the game? How are we with the pheasants? How about the rabbits?" the first secretary enquired in a slightly calmer voice.

"The pheasants are in their places, in the areas reserved for them; they are rather crammed but they've been well fed, so they won't be too lively when it comes to it!"

"The rabbits?"

"The rabbits are rabbits: rather stupid, but fit for the gun!"

"How about the tents for the meal and recreation for after the hunt?"

"In their places! In their places! The comrades will eat the things brought from Bucharest, the others from their own bags and from whatever will be allowed to cook from the hunted game!"

"Did the doctors finish their investigations?"

"Finished," reported an officer standing near Onaca. "Analyses conducted, the mad and suspicious people under observation!"

"In that case, comrades, I will ask you to return to your objectives, but with increased vigilance. Nobody makes any move without it being reported. Any questionable or suspicious fact to be immediately brought to my attention. For your own good, I hope that the comrades will be satisfied!"

With this last word, over all present, but also over the

village and even over our side of the world, a funereal silence descended. Everything was frozen: the air, the sky, the earth, the mountains and the sun which was fighting hard to come through the white clouds coming from behind the mountain. A sensation of powerlessness, of absurdity, possessed everything: you had no one to talk to, no one to ask an explanation from, it was impossible to hear a word uttered with calm, with kindness; only yells, threats and disjointed sentences. In the hallway of *Căminul Cultural*, the House of Culture, or rather the Command Centre, as it was now called, Onaca approached Daria and whispered to her between his teeth:

"You've forced me to lie about that business with the samples. If anything happens, I'll put it in you, I'll pull it back, and then put it back up to your throat."

Daria pretended she didn't hear, turned her back elegantly to him, then suddenly changed her mind:

"Did I ask this of you? What if I report you to your boss?" she enquired, to which the colonel burst into laughter:

"Try. I am very curious who he will give credence to. If I want, I can shaft him too. Take note, nobody knows who fears the other most!"

"Until you learn how to deal with me," Daria added, "continue the apprenticeship with your mother-in-law for a while."

Onaca had not expected such rudeness, so he was content to make a discreet gesture with his hand, a sort of: we'll see! In the street, we parted with the other people and left for the dispensary in a hurry, trying to separate ourselves from the nightmare. As we went farther and farther from the Command Centre, Daria started to lose her patience:

"A country of madmen. I am no longer staying here,

irrespective of the risks. Even if the Serbian border guards shoot me, or send me back in exchange for a train container of salt, as they do, I have to try it."

"Such a decision may be taken later on, only after the madness ends," I said, trying to calm her.

"In our country, madness is eternal," she said through the tears and, by the time we reached the dispensary, she didn't let one word out, maybe also because I didn't know what to ask her, nothing came into my head, and any encouragement was pathetic. Once there, she shut the door and, huddled in a ball on the chair, with her head in her fists, she burst into peals of crying and she cried like this until despair changed into fury:

"Should I cry because of a cretin? Should I feel guilty? What for? Should a wretch, an illiterate, talk to me like that? Don't be scared, the crying is waking me up. When you throw me into the water, I'll be afraid, but I know how to swim, how to face the facts, I don't surrender easily, but I start very hard. I only wonder at one thing: that they haven't brought Sergiu here! He was probably afraid of my mouth, or, for the first time in his life, he managed to be a gentleman. The truth is that I accord too much importance to myself," she restarted the monologue after a long break during which she wiped her tears away. "That citizen isn't coming to visit me, nor even the village, but to visit some pheasants, bears or whatever he feels like killing. In fact, I should not cry, but the fears and the suffering of the people who worked themselves up close to madness were transmitted to me as well. We have what we deserve."

"Of course we cannot stay indifferent to these people's threats, but think of the fear there must be in their souls," I said to her, more to maintain the dialogue. "I think Onaca crossed the line in annoying you."

"Him, too," Daria admitted. "The moment he said those scabrous things to me, I could have killed him immediately, without a trace of regret. At that point, but only at that point, I grasped the dimensions of my own powerlessness. I do not know another world, but I am convinced that this one in which we live was planned by imbeciles, for the imbeciles!"

As her voice became increasingly calm, I started to be more intrigued by Daria's face, on which a warm, generous light had settled, welling up somehow from within her. Back then, in those moments, I felt a complete certainty of her exceptional beauty, despite the fury and aggression which she had successfully exercised. I also felt certain that she possessed a kind of frailty. I felt, finally, as if I was in the vicinity of a revelation, but one which, after the episode with Onaca, I could no longer confess to her, although I was convinced she would have understood me. At the same time as this full, almost overwhelming feeling, I realised that words could no longer express the new situation. Although I felt the need for it, I didn't know how to transmit to her the things I was living through. I was in an unsuitable moment, in an unsuitable place and in a situation where it was impossible for me to foresee her reactions.

I was also terrified by the fact that, from one moment to the next, the grand guest might appear, and that the agitation of the welcoming team might provoke thoughtless reactions in her. I didn't know, also, what I could say to her in such a situation, even if the circumstances would have allowed me the time for it. It was impossible for me to describe the impression that we could manage to communicate without the use of words; the impression that she, just as she was, was transmitting other things to me, despite the tears and the feeling of revolt that possessed her, and that the closeness to her, her nearness, was giving me joy and a feeling of trust. We stayed in the same room waiting for something to happen, to be summoned, and, until that time, I was glad we were together and that we had discovered this thing. In the end, Daria felt the need to break the silence.

"I was thinking what might have happened if they'd sent Sergiu here to me; a doctor, a Securitate officer, of a pretty high rank and good, even very good, professional status. It seems horrifying to be near a man you once loved, who is now a person who doesn't mean anything anymore, not one thing, to you. You look at him as if he were a display in a museum. Lord, how could I have loved him? How could I have caressed, kissed him, how could I have shared with him my bread, my every thought, and even my bed? When we separated, I remembered the *Sânziene*[51] nights. I would run in the fields with my grandmother and she would teach me how to know the plants and how to pick those from which I had to collect the dew during that night when the heavens open and you can communicate with other entities from parallel worlds. The black nightshade, lunaria – the love-herb, wild marjoram, salvia, camomile, verbena, lavender, rosemary, marsh-mallow, mugwort, or rue: these carried as many chances to stay healthy, protected from evil spirits or illnesses. We would braid crowns from them and throw them over the house. I would place the lady's bedstraw flower under the pillow, convinced that my chosen one would appear in my dreams. Strange, but even when I was certain this would be Sergiu, when I had no more doubts that I would marry him, I never dreamt about

---

51   *Sânziene* is a folk celebration occurring on 24 June, mixing pre-Christian and Christian practices into a summer festival when fairies (the *sânziene*) become powerful and women are able to pick magic plants.

him. Grandmother would wake me up at dawn so we could collect the dew off the lady's bedstraw plants, so we could wash our faces in star-water and be protected from evil for the whole year. I'll never forget, in my entire life, the solemnity with which we picked the flowers, early in the morning, at the crack of dawn, and the zeal with which I washed myself in the evening so that the dream bridegroom would take me as clean as the dew. Grandmother knew Sergiu and, at dawn, when she woke me up, she would ask if I'd dreamed of him. I had no other option but to tell her the truth, and she would become sad, assuring me that he was not destined for me, and this is how it turned out to be."

"But have you dreamed of anyone else?" I asked, entering the game.

"Yes," she replied with sadness, "I did dream, but I don't remember the features of the face. Maybe because I no longer wished to marry. The story with Sergiu cured me for a long time."

"What a pity that you no longer remember the face," I said almost without wanting to, and she, feeling revived, burst into laughter:

"I know those plants very well, and, on the *Sânziene* night, I am up to sleeping with the flowers under my head. What will you do if I dream of you?"

"Simple: you come and tell me about it, then you ask me to marry, and I will say yes without thinking too long about it," I said in one breath, with most the relaxed air possible. "And then I'll see how you patch this one up! I think we've talked about the distress of marrying a psychiatrist. Difficult, sophisticated people who say yes even when they should not, and follow you minute by minute without you knowing what they really want from you. They never raise their voices and they won't allow you to deduce what exactly they are thinking of and how they have categorised you."

"For me, this would not be at all complicated: since you accept me as your wife that means you haven't found too many defects in me. Who would willingly marry a stupid woman? I know how to cook, I speak English, since I planned to run away from this country, I can walk on very high heels, so I am not a clumsy woman, and I earn the money I need by myself. In bed, there's not much merit to me, but I learn quickly. Defects. I do not allow myself to be trampled over. I often react too violently, after which I am sorry. I sometimes cry without a reason. I am like caged animals: I have the nostalgia of freedom, of endless space. I feel a kind of strange air that comes from another world, maybe from an unearthly one. I wouldn't want to seem too smart to you. I don't know how psychiatrists think, if they prefer intelligent women or only those who wear skirts, but if I have managed to survive even in Valea Boului, it is a sign that I am not too rigid and I am not an egotist either."

We had both spoken the truth, but in the most uncomfortable manner: with a smile on our lips, performing a balancing act on the narrow wire that separated truth from mockery, leaving each other the opportunity of an elegant retreat at the moment when, for some unforeseeable reason, the discussion might reach a point of no return, when the conclusion could no longer be avoided. In those moments, I was visited by a sad memory of my childhood when, one winter, I was coming from school, and the bridge on which I was walking fell, struck by a massive ice floe. Without realising, I found myself violently carried away by the water current. Following me, there came a great tree stump, a remnant of the bridge, and very close to me, at a distance of two or three widths of my palm, I could see the shore, thick with bushes of crack willow and alder. It was handy to touch them, to hang off them, but I don't know why I didn't do it, why I didn't have the strength to save myself. It was inexplicable, but I didn't feel unwell in that madness of water, ice and runaway logs, I was only afraid that the branches which I could hang on to with relative ease might break. I was saved by a huge chunk of ice that pushed me to the shore. Father thought that was my guardian angel. He forced me to understand that, in this life, I had a specific job to finish. The fear of things which had happened that day penetrated me with all their brutality only in the following days, after the fever had passed. I could now see with immense clarity the distance between my hand and the branches on the shore and, involuntarily, in the most unexpected moments, awake or in my sleep, I found myself desperately jerking an arm towards the imaginary bushes which I had once refused.

Daria was close, very close even, I felt that she too wanted us to surpass that confused moment of apprehension and expectation. I could see her lips trembling and her eyes, somewhat larger, fixing on the hand that refused to move; in fact, my entire body found itself in a different time, a quicker one, while the mind doubted, got caught up in arguments, and even started to live with increased intensity a defeat that had not taken place. Then came the patients, who didn't care about the visit that had driven everybody mad, but Daria sent me, wordlessly, the same stable, living call, maybe because she also had felt my hesitations, my weakness. In the afternoon, when everybody's impatience had reached the point of spasm, we received the news that the Comrade would no longer come; he had simply changed his mind, again for some very important reason, but one which nobody knew.

"There is other business more important than this, state business," the mayor said with disappointment, contemplating the empty main stand, the trees with leaves smeared in paint and trunks painted with lime wash, as required by the regulations. "All this bloody load of paint's gone to mother cunt![52] From now on, we'll see a hydroelectric plant only when the poplar trees bear pears and the willow blooms in wallflowers!"[53]

The news of the visit's cancellation hadn't come merely through the telephones or the mobile radio comms. It had been brought by a team of comrades, very important party activists and Securitate men, sent by the people "from above" to thank the local organs, as well as all who had ensured that the preparations were of "the highest level of competence and patriotic wholehearted generosity."

"I've called you here," Onaca addressed us, "so you can go among the people and defuse the tension. I have lived through events of this kind before. An important visit is only cancelled for reasons which are even more important. I will not hold my hand over the fire for it, but the Russians or the Hungarians should not be left out of our sights. They either move the northern frontier for a good few metres, or they send trucks carrying weapons. I, myself, have found numerous crates with weapons in the basement of a

---

52 In the Romanian (and Latinate) tradition, swearing makes use of metaphors, often centred around the idea of abusing one's mother. Simply to mention someone's mother, or their mother's genitals, is to launch a deadly insult.

53 In Romanian – *când o face plopul pere și răchita micșunele*. An expression denoting the impossibility of something happening. It was famously used by Nicolae Ceaușescu in a speech in July 1989, referring to a time when Romania would switch to capitalism. The revolution that deposed the regime came on 22 December.

Hungarian church. I now invite you to the stands so we can see how the boys with the barbecues are. Those who know the Romanian people also know they don't miss the chance of getting rid of some bullets, just by chance, in a poor wild boar. It was not fated to live for more days, they will excuse themselves, it came at us and what could we do? And since it's dead, we're not just going to throw it to the dogs!"

People had given up all safety measures, nobody took care of anything, except some more fearful officers who still shouted at the animals' grooms: "Careful with the cows so they don't stay without being milked, otherwise their udders will burst! They need to return home healthy, because there's other working visits awaiting them!"

In the clearing in the woods where the stands were, the hunters and the foresters had lit fires; some dealt with the freshly-shot wild boars, others specialised in plucking the pheasants, people laughed with gusto, without any restraint, as the guards had lost sight of the crates with *Galbenă de Odobești*, wine that had been brought for the high-up guests, and the people who had trembled with nerves wished to know in their turn the taste of the real wine drunk by their representatives in the leadership of the country. The locals, in their own good tradition, managed things with the *țuica* plum brandy produced in the clandestine alcohol stills in the nearby forests. Onaca was relaxed as well, smiling, and once he discovered the people responsible for the Comrade's food, he tried to make jokes at the expense of the hungry, among whom unfortunately we could also count ourselves:

"This is a sport at which nobody beats us," he said. "As long as there is a little beer, a wee bit of *țuică* and *mici* spicy sausages, this country won't die!"

People were attentive to Daria, and invited her to stay for

471

"their pig," but she assured them she would come back, and there was no trace of duplicity in her voice. She wanted us to somehow wander away from Onaca, which was almost impossible, as none of the people he seemed to be looking for approached. Having reached a tent where the provisional occupants had started singing, Onaca tried to make room for us: "The first to have arrived, leave the area," he ordered, and, unexpectedly, some of the people there straightened their backs and welcomed him. One of them, hard to see because of the weak light, set three plastic plates in front of us, and as many glasses, and Onaca showed himself satisfied when he felt the taste of wine: "It's that kind..." After three other glasses, which he had drunk without even breathing, the colonel became sentimental.

"He works more than us, but he eats very modestly, not as he's entitled to. Cheese, tomatoes, onions, macaroni, a little meat. Whatever you can still find in this little country of ours. Radio Șanț[54] says that 'errr..., umm...' – people love him and know that he is not to blame for the hardships we are going through." After another glass, Onaca winked at us: "Let me tell you a joke which is full of meanings. An American journalist – who was resolved to get information straight from the source about what the Romanian people believes about the Comrade, went to the house of this average man and asked him directly about the issues that riled him. Look, old man, he said, I am from Washington, from Radio Șanț, and I would like to know what you personally think about Comrade Ceaușescu. You know, the man replied in a whisper, I can't speak in the house, you might have perhaps

---

54 *Radio Șanț*, in Romanian. In English, Radio Ditch. One of the many names Romanians used to refer to Radio Free Europe, a US-sponsored, Munich-based radio service broadcasting for the countries behind the Iron Curtain.

heard of microphones, and words get punished like deeds. That's fine, replied the American, we'll go outside. Well, we can't do it outside either, because there's electricity pylons and you can't exclude the possibility there are microphones in the pylons. People sit around in their courtyards, they talk about all you want and all you don't. Fine, the American caved in, then let's go to the forest. I don't think there can be any microphones there. Yes, the man accepted, that wouldn't be a bad idea. Once in the forest, the American asks straight away. So, you have nothing to fear here, you can give me a direct answer, with all sincerity: what do you think about Ceauşescu? Yes, the man replied in a whisper, I see no reason to lie to you. I, for one, like the man!"

The colonel laughed a lot, noisily: "I know jokes worth five years in prison, some worth tens of years, and some others worth even full life sentence. If I were convinced you could keep the secret, I'd tell you a few."

We did not assure him of our discretion and we didn't want to maintain this conversation that rather scared us either, so we tried to get up – the back, tiredness, difficult positions – and Onaca agreed with the idea of continuing our walk.

"Look, because you seem a little sad, here's a ten-years-worth joke. At school, the teacher offers up a prize worth 100 Lei to the pupil who knows the main characteristic of socialism. Bulă,[55] who was one of the pupils, hurries to answer. In a socialist society everything is done for the good of man, but if you give me another hundred, I'll tell you who that man is!" Onaca laughed, looking very pleased. "The people who are merely listening get five years only!"

---

55 Bulă is a character who is the butt of many Romanian jokes. He is presented as a sometimes shrewd character, but normally it's a synonym for being dim. An equivalent could be Simple Simon.

We both came up with a forced laugh, and this satisfied him. We were walking onwards with difficulty in the tall, fat grasses and among the hunt beaters who had rather abused the alcohol – so it was that people sang, told jokes without too much reserve, while the sun was getting closer to setting. Daria was walking in front, and the colonel didn't let her out of his sight:

"Doctor," he said to me finally, "speaking just among us men: are you going to do something to this creature or will you let me try my luck?"

"Comrade Colonel, Doctor Daria Pop is nothing but my future wife," I replied with all conviction, "so you can take the most appropriate decision. If this connection was not visible, there are explanations for this: we are both at work."

"Old boy, forgive me," said the colonel without a trace of regret in his voice, "you have chosen well. I hope you won't betray me, but the legs are nice legs, the hips – nice hips, and the lips are just as if nature had asked me to draw them myself. This is the situation: the eyes see, the heart desires, man is sinful, whatever you do. Time passes by, old age comes and finds you with your allotted work quota unaccomplished. Well, how would humanity multiply if people just sat around looking at each other? Even with the strictest Muslims, if you sin or steal, they will cut your hand off, but they leave your dick alone!"

When we reached the edge of the clearing, people started to get agitated and scared:

"The Comrade's changed his mind. He's coming! He's comiiiing! We're done for!" another officer, who had the mission to call Onaca to the Command Centre, shouted in despair.

"Let's not lose our cool," Onaca said, smoothing his

attire which was full of leaves and grass. "Soup is never eaten as hot as it's served. Let us penetrate to the crux of the problem calmly."

Saying this, he took the arm of the man who had brought the news and left in a hurry, leaving us there as if we didn't exist, but after a few steps he turned his head: probably remembering we'd been left without any tasks:

"You two go to the dispensary, the Lord on High will eat you alive if anyone gets sick! No, you'd better stay at tent number 5, where you will place yourselves under the command of Colonel Oprea!"

At the same time, as if there'd been a signal, from the middle of the forest, there appeared tens of soldiers with pitchforks and shovels who started to cover with dust the fires, which the water – very little of it, and poured in a hurry – caused to burn even more intensely. The men who were going to throw pheasants into the crosshairs of the Comrade's gun or chase the wild boars moved with immense difficulty. Some had tumbled down into the well masked ditches, and some could not find their bird cages, while from the main tents you could hear short, desperate orders:

"The Comrade's wine! What about the tomatoes? What about the mineral water? Our good fortune is that the refrigerated crates were left intact! Run off to the main stand! See whether some idiot's fallen asleep up there and ends up giving a fright to the Comrade! Search for the drunks and take them quickly out of the forest!"

The noise of footsteps, the short, desperate orders, and the clouds of smoke that settled solidly over the village accompanied us everywhere. We asked about Colonel Oprea, but he, feeling irritated, was in no mood for us and sent us back to the village, or wherever we wanted, anywhere but there where we would be in the way.

"Each man to the positions already checked. Nobody gets to walk aimlessly in this country!"

Checked and re-checked, we managed to pass through the guards with difficulty. They all advised us to walk "in plain sight," so that we wouldn't find ourselves pierced like a sieve by the bullets of the more vigilant, or even the bullets of some of the foresters who'd got drunk early. In the village, there had appeared, as if sprouting from the earth itself, new people who cared for the animals' carers, for the verticality of the trees, for the solidity of the dais, for the flags and for the giant portrait of the beloved leader, set between the crests of the country and of the party. A few women distributed mint and parsley leaves discreetly, so that the smell of alcohol and roast meats would disappear from the breath of local – and not just local – officials. In the end, there began to arrive the cars heading the procession, and, at a later point, the Beloved Leader himself, in a jeep of native, Romanian fabrication, the Aro. Tens of soldiers dressed in folk costume started to shout: "Ceaușescu-PCR".[56] The trumpets of the pioneer children[57] who had been brought in special cars, as an emergency measure, from all surrounding localities, sounded chaotically. The Pioneer who had been brought from the town, with his samples already officially tested, handed him the bouquet, and a young woman officer dressed in the folk costume characteristic of our folkloric area, also brought in for increased safety, offered him the traditional welcoming dish of bread and salt. The Comrade shook the officials' hands on the run, kissed the previously

---

56   One of the most common slogans at the time, with PCR standing for Partidul Comunist Român, the Romanian Communist Party.

57   The pioneers were a Scouts-like organisation under the aegis of the Communist Party, present in almost all communist states.

chosen children who had all their vaccinations up to date, after which he thanked everybody for the beautiful welcome, wished everyone present to reach the highest peaks of socialism and communism, threw a hurried eye around the stables, and, once back up in the Aro, started out for the clearing where there were the hunting stands and the birds and animals in cages, which were going to be sacrificed in exchange for the hydroelectric plant with a rock field dam – of which not a word was any longer spoken, as I was going to learn later on.

The hunt was a great success, said the first secretary, but each person who was engaged in organising it had an opinion which they confessed later on, in a whisper, to their families and close friends. The village midwife, whose husband was the chief of the Militia station, told me that once the Comrade had left, many arrests were made, since not everything worked as it should have. The people responsible for the pheasants had gotten dead drunk and, instead of the birds, they threw from the ditches, into the crosshairs of the Comrade's gun, a load of rabbits – something which had the effect of confusing him. Of course, he had noticed himself that something was not right, but since the animals jumped two or three metres away from the ditch straight into the gun's range, he did not hold back from shooting vigorously towards the bush from which the rabbits were flying. The pheasants, also found in the same ditches, had started running to the valley, as the guards had forgotten the direction in which they had to be thrown. The Comrade heard the noises made by the birds, but he did not understand why none of them came into the crosshairs of his gun, while instead of the noises characteristic of the hunt, people had started singing – a gesture which was interpreted to him as an expression of the great joy of having him in their midst, after preparing to receive him for such a long time. The hunt was almost compromised because of the wild boars and bears which, since they were given everything necessary in their cages, had become lazy and no longer wanted to leave them. Even more, since they had waited for the presidential bullet for a long time, they had grown accustomed to people and gave no sign that the agitation of the beaters scared them very much. In the end, a bear, which was a very rare specimen, satisfied the huntsman's pride of the Comrade fully, especially since the boars were equally distinguished, and hunger helped him forget the strangeness of the rabbits and the rather exaggerated jollity of the people who had organised the hunt. The boar cutlets, brought in absolute safety from Bucharest, satisfied his most pressing needs, but after the meal he said nothing, and didn't utter any "appreciation" of the events. He stood up suddenly and started for the nearby jeep, leaving the mission of cleaning up the battlefield to the locals. In his wake, nobody dared to drink or even to speak. Hunters, beaters, pheasants and the rabbits forgotten in that particular ditch were discovered together, at the dawn of a "historic day" for the commune of Pădureni, formerly known as Valea Boului. Nobody knew whether the Comrade was satisfied or not, and in the absence of this judgement, the dominant feeling was that of guilt. That was that for the hydroelectric plant!

Daria and I stayed at the dispensary for the entire night, and I slept with my head on the table. I didn't know what was happening, and how the hunt was going, but considering the things we had been fated to see in the forest, it seemed impossible not to have a difficult night waiting for us, with wounded, drunk and despairing people. But, luckily, it was only Colonel Onaca who came to see us. In fact, considering the way he looked at Daria, with undisguised animal lust, he would have preferred it if I were not there. However, he threatened us that we would meet again, and sooner than we imagined, as there were many things to clarify for the better and for... the less better! We assured him of our wish to see him anytime, and he was happy to laugh with the mouth wide open, and to slap my shoulder with his hand:

"Doctor, during my childhood, in the places where I'm from, in the countryside, there was a priest who, because I took what was not due to me, meaning apples from his orchard, threatened he would cut my dick off! I don't know why this event came to my mind especially now."

"Experience shows that a dick is cut off quicker from people who make threats," Daria intervened unexpectedly. "Did anything happen to that priest?"

"I don't have time for discussions now," the colonel said, annoyed, before closing the door, "but I promise not to forget about this subject."

Because the hunt was over, I deduced that my role in Pădureni was also over. It was time for me to leave, but I could not admit that immediately. During these days – in which we had been more or less silent, or, forced by the circumstances, we had to listen to other people – I felt very connected to Daria. I don't know how it happened, what exactly made her so necessary to me that I had the certainty that we'd actually known each other since forever. I don't know the source of our gestures, our reactions in the most unusual circumstances. I could master her and she could master me in just the way I desired; but nothing helped me tell her what I felt. I was afraid that it might be precisely my words, no matter how well chosen, that could destroy the strong structure which I believed we were building. As a doctor, I tried to penetrate the states of feeling of so many people, even the most desperate ones; and I managed many times to discover a sense and an aim in them, to find the trace of light which is so necessary before they could continue their paths. But, as it happens, I did not have in me the necessary energy and self-belief that would make me certain of not failing, because this is what I feared: potential defeat. In the end, I bet everything on the moment of our separation, because my mission in Pădureni was over. I was expected by the university department, the clinic and the hundreds of sick people whose appointments had been postponed or entrusted to other colleagues. I didn't know what to say to them, because the truth was hard to believe. Who had sent me to Pădureni and why? Why was I chosen particularly? All the confusion led in a single direction, one I didn't want, but which was in the control of people who had no love for me. I was going to be avoided, suspected of something, blamed by everyone who had chosen the most advantageous road of professional ascent: sweeping away the competition by any means.

I was not preoccupied, however, with all this in any way. Instead, I feared Daria's possible reactions. In the end, trying to control my voice and gestures, I told her that, to my regret, I was forced to leave.

"I don't have the smallest idea why I came, but I know for certain that I have to leave. In any case, I am happy about the chance of meeting you," I said to her with conviction, to which she replied ironically:

"And the chance to go away again."

"If I were convinced that you regret my departure, I'd come back. Or I would wait you at my place."

"You are really not joking?" she asked in all seriousness. "What if you find me there one day?"

"I say you should not hesitate," I insisted. "I am starting to become superstitious, and to believe that Ceaușescu's visit had to happen so that I could have the good luck of meeting you, etc, and I'm stopping at this point."

"The Party is in everything," Daria laughed, only to become uncertain afterwards. "I would dearly love to understand something in connection with us two. Doesn't it seem to you there might be other details worthy of discussion, unconnected to the Comrade's hunt? There are circumstances where feelings run quicker than logical thinking and words. They might even win in any such confrontation. Am I wrong?"

"You are not," I replied with relief.

"And if you are not wrong, why don't you kiss me?" she asked in a voice which was totally altered, uncertain.

"Because men are left only with the impression that they can conquer a woman," I hurried to say. "In reality, all men are conquered!"

"It was not like this with us. We walked, both of us, from the first moment, at the same pace, although I was afraid when I was notified you'd come here. In fact, it wasn't fear, but hatred! I realised afterwards that you too are lost in this world, that you too are feeling your way around, that you too are haunted by loneliness like a terrible disease."

We got closer to each other without realising it, with the feeling that we were not doing what we were doing. In any case, we were breaking, with closed eyes, the last barrier that still separated us, and the second I felt her lips I had the certainty that I was being given an undeserved gift, and that, precisely in that same moment, another creature within me, locked in the depth of memory by numerous preconceptions and fears, had been liberated forever. It seemed very strange that we hadn't talked a great deal about her. I had learned only one event from her life, and even this one was told in passing, about the lover who had betrayed her, but I relied on my senses, and on the few reactions of hers that I had noticed in the days when we waited together for the arrival of the Great Huntsman. Above all, I relied on that special feeling that announces failure or victory before they are realised.

"You have two weeks to meditate," Daria said to me, since she was the first to come back to herself from that embrace. "If you don't give me any sign, I will understand what needs understanding and my life will remain, if not sadder, at least the same as it was before."

"I think that it should be you to give me signs, because you have been braver than me, and you've taken all the necessary steps first."

"If you were not a psychiatrist, I would never dare to take this extra step. You were talking about characteristic hesitations. I shall take the next step only if it is truly fated for us to meet, the way I feel you want in this moment."

With tears in her eyes she then led me to the bus that made the connection with the town, a pathetic piece of machinery, ancient and overloaded, stopping every now and then because its engine overheated. Strangely, I no longer desired now, as in the olden days, to put as much distance, as soon as possible, from Pădureni. I was no longer chased by fear and threats, although they had not been absent. From all that had happened down there, I was haunted only by Daria's face. After a few days, my secretary stepped into the classroom pretty anxiously, which was unusual for her, and announced that a beautiful lady from Valea Boului was desperately looking for me because she had to resolve a very serious problem which could not be postponed. A story of life and death! It was, of course, Daria, who was carrying a giant suitcase.

"I've run away from the village," she explained to me hurriedly. "Onaca appeared unexpectedly and told me that I had a beautiful bottom. It could be that this is a reasonable opinion, in the end, and I can't hide it. I put him where he should be,[58] but I didn't wait for his next visit. Help me to construct a leaving note. Write whatever you want or don't want about how I am, anything just not to be forced to go back."

"To suit any eventuality, I will also write a medical observation sheet," I said to her, "and I promise to keep you under observation for as long as you want."

"I see you have very prompt reactions when you are in your own environment," Daria said, satisfied.

"Until we clarify things, I am very grateful to Onaca," I said, but she intervened quickly:

"You should be grateful only to me, because I had a mind to come anyway."

To my immense joy, she didn't leave my side, until that morning on 21 December 1989, when – believing that they would shoot at the crowd that had flooded the streets in revolt – she also went out, as a doctor, together with Iulia, Dan's wife, so that they could administer first aid to the protesters, if needed. Fate decided, however, that the first bullets shot by the so-called terrorists would be for them. I am convinced that the bullets had been fired a long time

---

58 An indirect manner of saying you've sworn horribly at someone, as it refers to a popular Romanian profanity threatening to send somebody back into their mother's womb.

before, in Pădureni, and I am certain that it was only in that moment that they hit me terribly in my soul, in everything that I was. I will never understand if I need to be grateful to Destiny for giving me Daria in a moment of sorrow and loneliness, or to rebel with all my being because it took her away in another moment, equally painful, of anxiety and confusion. I have not yet understood exactly what I had to learn from this question: that we belong to each other only to a small extent? Is, perhaps, somebody playing with us, just as we, in our turn, play with the animals and plants which we have in our dominion? Is this my karma? Should I rail against the ancestors, who might have committed sins I don't know about, or should I look in my inner depths for the suffering I caused, out of ignorance, carelessness, or from other reasons as yet unclear?

"How strange it is to live no more on earth;
To make no further use of customs learnt;
No longer to attribute to the rose
Or anything of fair especial promise
A metaphor of human destiny;
To be no longer that which once we were,
In over fearful hands; to throw aside
Even our personal name, a broken toy!
Strange, to desire no more the consummation
Of our desires! How strange to see all things
Related to this earth, float free in space!
And death's a weariness so overcharged
with incompletion, that we slowly come
To the conception of eternity,
Yet all the living fall into the error
Of over-sharp distinction. I have heard

That angels may themselves be unaware
Whether they move amongst the quick or dead,
The eternal current sweeps all ages on
Through both these realms, and dominates in both.
Those who were called away in early youth
Have no more need of us: detachment comes
As we outgrow the mother's gentle breast..."
Reiner Maria Rilke, *First Duino Elegy* [59]

I profoundly dislike loneliness, but even so I wanted to stay a little longer near my papers and, especially, near the questions that tormented me. Yet, unfortunately, I was not capable of formulating even one of them. Words had engaged in a sort of random zig zagging, a Brownian movement which was impossible to control. They somehow existed outside of me, refusing to yield to logic and will power, while my gaze slid over objects, trees and stars, over the white paper. Nothing had a name as in the first day of Creation. It was just that I, the insignificant man, knew my sorrow and my incapacity to name them. I was. I simply was.

Mara appeared exactly when she was supposed to. "Old man," she said to me very anxiously, "I feel there is something going on with you, that something is not right, in the end. How can I be calm when half of the population of this mountain is suffering?" she said, taking my head in her hands and trying to joke.

"Do you blame yourself for what you imagine was a great mistake? In the beginning, I thought it would be better to leave you on your own, so you can remonstrate with yourself and then

---

59 From *Duineser Elegien - Elegies from the castle of Duino*, translated by Vita and Edward Sackville-West, London: Hogarth Press, 1931. Available online at https://archive.org/details/duineserelegiene00rilk

make peace, but I realise that, for you, sorrows and anxieties are catastrophic. Did you do this each time after you've slept with a woman – I mean, did you have pangs of remorse which are so idiotic? Or, could it be that I am so special?"

"It is hard for me to say what I feel," I trying to calm her down.

"If I know you are going to be so sad, we'd better not do it at all and that's that! If I won't be brought down by some bear or I don't break my neck in some chasm when running after those stupid goats, I might find a madman who is willing to free me from here, from this crap life. Unfortunately, I am also a woman. Maybe, in the end, my monk may come himself. I am afraid here; but in the city I am even more afraid."

"I thought many times of how things might be better for you," I said to her in all seriousness. "In the first version, I decided to take you to my house and ask my son to hire you in his clinic. Any position, until you managed to get accustomed to the world and you learnt some trade. Back home, I liked nothing – but absolutely nothing at all – from the moment Daria died. Everything reminded me of her. It was as if even her soul refused to leave the house. I had always lived with the impression that I had my life ahead, that we would have had the possibility of discussing everything that had remained up in the air, that we would sit together and the two of us would look at the past. Suddenly, one day she is no more, and the time I had banked on doesn't exist. I am alone in the world, as if abandoned in a desert. Sand behind me, sand in front of me and a confused sky above, without stars. Alone, nobody knows about you any more, and none of the people you might need is going to answer, because they have left before you for the world beyond. You are forced to understand that your time has run out and that the only inquisitiveness left is to speculate about what it would be like when the time comes. With you, things will probably be pretty simple. Dan will not question anything. I think he's already found my diagnosis: senile vagabondage. As a consequence, he will behave as nicely as he knows how. One single question will torment him for a while: whether you are somehow his sister! And I kind of feel like lying to him. He would probably behave more nicely to you after I am no more. But we'll find out about this when it happens."

"What about the animals?"

"You leave them in the care of Dogaru," I said to her. "If you don't return for a while – two weeks, one month – it will be his right to sell them or to do whatever he thinks fit with them."

"And my parents?"

"They stay there. You don't have to worry. I think that even in heaven or wherever they might be they are blaming themselves, and I don't have any doubts about this, for leaving you on your own."

"And your mountain?" she asked, possessed by a painful feeling of guilt that, look – she's destroyed my dream, the dream for which I had come there.

"You don't have to worry," I replied resignedly. "Each thing has its time, a specific moment when it can be accomplished. I think I have missed that moment. But I realised this only here. Maybe up there, at the top of the mountain – if I'd have gotten there – I would have discovered what other people could not, but now I think that I will discover through my death what I haven't managed to in life. Unfortunately, we never reach the place we planned to reach. The strongest, and the luckiest, end up somewhere close to it, but this is no consolation. In any case, this mountain exists inside me and, in the end, at any risk, I'll try to climb it. Probably, again, with your help," I said, although my assurances did not seem to change her state of spirit. "I have the feeling you're hesitating more than normal. You can leave the address for the monk with Dogaru. I am saying this in all sincerity. Fear? I don't see why you should be afraid. Especially since you lived in this town while you were at school."

"Yes, I am rather afraid," she admitted. "And there might be some things to tell. But I am not up to it now. At the exit from the town there are, on each side of the motorway, some giant panels with adverts for bras. After you've seen them, I'll tell you more."

"Are you perhaps the woman wearing them?" I asked, surprised at the new discovery.

"I didn't say this," she said, retreating. "There are too few people who can face changes, without fear."

Despite my curiosity and the surprise she had caused me, I gave up asking more. I saw her in front of me, tall, beautiful, with a strong chest, and I tried to reconstruct her, inside me, from everything I knew about her and especially from the things I hadn't felt. I could ask her everything that passed through my head, I was free to place my hand on any part of her body, so I that had more than imagination could offer me, but my arms didn't help, they stayed inert, as if they didn't belong to me; only my soul continued to wrap her in the light and warmth I had in me. But, as always, the moments of intense happiness were followed by panic: I could not imagine they would last, and I, especially, didn't believe that I deserved them. It was as if I had entered into a total unreality, and the terrors of these last years, which had censored any explosion of joy, now were convincing me that, after this moment, the only thing that could follow was the end. It seemed logical to me, but the face of the woman and the violent light around her urged me not to surrender, to chase this thought away.

"I will do exactly as you want; if you want, I'll go to Dogaru to hand the animals over to him. I'll close my eyes and throw myself in the water, although I am very afraid," she said, interrupting the silence.

"We'll think for another night and then we'll decide," I said, knowing that everything we lived and felt at that moment would never be repeated. Also knowing that we were at the beginning or at the end of a road on which, I for one, at least, went forward but with the uncertainty of a blind man.

I shed tears every time the sun sets. Will there be another day for me? Will another night come again? Will I look again at another sky and other clouds? Or will the night that comes lose me in the great night, the final, definitive one? I write, I suffer, and I try to understand something of the confusion that surrounds me. I don't know how to do anything else, but I build illusions for myself that, among the words entrusted to the paper, there will also sneak in the miracle which can lend some sense, or at least an explanation, to my search. I am waiting. This word covers everything I do and everything I desire.

I breathe, I shed tears, I mechanically feel my pulse and I concentrate on a ray of sun flooding the room. I open the window. Far away, enveloped in a restless, bizarre light, there is my mountain, the Margin of Life, and beyond it there is a puny cloud, an insignificant one, an agent of the coming storm, and the inevitable feeling of death. However, the fact that not even the cloud will be no more doesn't console me. A long time ago, a friend sent me a photograph of the Milky Way taken by the Hubble telescope. White and greenish lights, red swirls of dimensions which are impossible to imagine and utter, without a feeling of horror. Incandescent celestial bodies, trillions of worlds that are born only to disappear swallowed up by the unimaginable agitation of matter and celestial energies. Worlds that appeared, worlds that have been destroyed in a chaos without time. Death and Life entwined in an endless vortex. In their astounding succession, the Word will always be eternal. Alone and confused, maybe, contemplating a dead world. Alone, twisting, unimaginable energies, thinking, the matter waiting for its consciousness and for the chance to see its own face. But will He want to repeat that which he did wrong? Will He ever give another chance to life as it once was, shameless, with endless failures, misses? Or will He perhaps become embodied in something else He's never been before? Logically enough, it will probably be something else, since it is pointless to repeat a failure or a missed phase, but it's mistaken and also without mistake as my much limited understanding sees it. The little cloud grew appreciably, so a great storm will be born. I am waiting for it with fear and I think of the second stolen by the Hubble telescope from the giant struggle of the worlds that have been and will be born, and I ask myself what meaning can still exist, from this perspective, in fear, morals, sorrow, love, life and death. What else can I be now, and what meaning do I have, what meaning is there in my blind fumbling for things, since there is a world beyond us, a world beyond the giant struggle of worlds?

For the moment, I won't see the sunset, since my mountain is burning and its bizarre flames make it through the dark mists that start to threaten everything: trees, earth and sky. Maybe the irrepressible and violent wind will accompany the last evening of my faith. Maybe tomorrow I shall be over there, beyond. If not, just as up to this moment, I will be in a sort of here-ness, trying to lie to myself that dying doesn't really mean to die, but, perhaps, to return, just as living doesn't mean... I think the most pathetic moment will be the one when I start to surrender.

Tomorrow is the day we should leave. We decided suddenly. In fact, I decided it. Mara is moving things meaninglessly, from one place to another, and cries without hearing my questions. The fear in us? Who doesn't have that? But I am convinced she is much more complicated than she appears, and this makes me believe she will be able to resist the confusion to which I am about to entrust her. That's why I let her cry, to get some release or to solve her conflict with herself. I feel that she is still hiding many things from me. Her way of thinking, her somewhat surprising maturity have at their root – and I have no doubts about this – numerous events which I will probably never learn. Or maybe I'll learn about them later on, if this later should be prolonged. I close my eyes and I try to detach myself from her, from the sin which follows me ceaselessly, and I try to place her among the countless patients who had asked me to restore the light of their eyes, their calmness, their lucidity, their dead or aborted children, their failed loves, the women with whom they could not make love, the parents lost by negligence, or the men chased away by their stupidity, and their youth. At the end of this giant row of unfortunates, I also place myself with all my fears, because my profession has sorrow, existential sorrow, as its object. Mine can only be shouted out to the Heavens, and as much as I pray to it, Heaven cannot exempt me from death. This is why I pray that I should at least not die before my time, that I won't disappear before lucidity...that I won't be embarrassing, that I won't think all the time of the world *beyond the beyond*, about which I create illusions which would open even the more accessible gate, not only to me, but to the natural things near to us.

I often recalled the words of my professor of microbiology: "I must have been a whore in another life, because I don't know how to refuse anyone!"

Dan and Claudia, and especially Claudia, a great lover of receptions and meetings with the high-life of the town, insisted that I should get out of the house, because it would not be bad for me to roam around the world in order to feel the atmosphere of the times and to get properly informed about people who, so maintained Claudia, I always regarded with contempt.

"Good, bad – these people lead us, and they must be met," was also Dan's opinion. "Here you will find future and former ministers and presidents. In fact, everything that is still left from the reserves of Ceauşescu's reserves of political cadres. Part of the cream of the country. Enemies on the surface, firm friends underneath. A party with several faces, in order to confuse the naïve and the stupid. We can't find others who are better than them, and it makes no sense to find someone just like them! Here, in our country, at the Gates of the Orient, centuries will pass before people abandon petty agreements, baksheesh, influencing and reciprocal help as it's understood locally."

Although I had several reasons to refuse, I didn't, even if at my age there are plenty of things to do, and especially plenty to avoid, because it is unseemly to be among people who shamelessly ask themselves whether you are still alive. As I wanted, however, to form an opinion about the people who will be leading our poor country for the next twenty years, I intended not to refuse Dan any longer, as he seemed very desirous to be present for the birthday of a candidate to the country's presidency – or at least to a very important office of state. I did not expect to meet a great luminary, but I didn't set out without any hope either. I would have been glad to like him, for him to be a good man, and for me to find as few defects as possible and, on returning home, to tell Dan my opinion – even if I suspected he wouldn't take it into account. In our relationship, although he had reached the age of maturity for a long time now, Dan always situated himself on the position of the son who must not necessarily share his father's opinion. After the first *no*, uttered with a categorical air, not suffering contradictions, we could discuss things very naturally, and this was what I expected to do at the end of the reception.

"The man is terribly vengeful," Dan explained. "His wife has a very precise list of friends and enemies, which she updates almost daily. The courtiers he keeps around him, because of their love for the positions he's promised, only need a simple signal in order to start to battle, as they all have a terrifying thirst for destruction, and moral nonentities attack in packs, by preference, and then, only by making a noise can one be taken into consideration any sooner."

"If you know beforehand how this individual is, why do you want me to come as well? Usually, almost everybody who cropped up after the Revolution, almost the entire fauna, is part of the category of: *I didn't expect it to be quite like this!*" I replied. "What business can you have with him?"

"I have a project which I haven't yet had the chance to confess to you," Dan explained himself, feeling a little embarrassed. "I am visited by the thought of taking refuge in an embassy in Latin America. My obsession is Costa Rica! Two oceans: if you grow bored of the Atlantic, you move to the Pacific. A country without an army, with tropical climate, palm trees, coconut trees, real monkeys – not like ours from the political world, very beautiful women and, more important than all that, our officials do not haunt the place, nor do our journalists. Plus it has a very active volcano. Of course, I am not competent to speak, but many specialists are of the opinion that Romania would do much better without diplomats, rather than with those we have now. Of course, I wouldn't just sit around over there. I want to finish my treatise on psychiatry, to finalise a book of my scientific research and, I'll admit it, to do a bit of tourism in the neighbouring countries. If I should manage to organise a working visit for the president, it will ensure the next posting for me, somewhere in Uruguay, Paraguay or the Philippines, since Asia is not something to dump in the bin, either. Without his help, nobody will discover me and they won't understand what I want. I know I am not rising in your esteem for it, but it's good to think of our customary practices, before you condemn me."

It made no sense to confess what I believed. In fact, he'd replied indirectly to what he suspected I was going to say, and I was happy to divert the discussion to the direction in which I was interested:

"So what does this Matei Goarnă look like?"

"You'll see when you get there, so you won't blame me of trying to influence you," he replied in a voice which contained some perfidiousness. "Stick around with me and you will get acquainted with the most noble and renown'd flowers.[60]"

Claudia, feeling I might alter Dan's projects, came closer and started to work on me, like an embroiderer, in her particular style: "I promise to hold the umbrella for you even on Copacabana, because we won't leave you here, alone and restless. Have mercy on us and condemn us only for the errors which are exclusively our own, that is, only if we have sins which others don't commit!"

I promised her, of course, that I wouldn't ruin their relationships and that their projects would enjoy all my support, a promise for which Claudia showed herself very grateful, although it was well understood that I would not have been able to ruin their plans anyway. He had bought himself a villa which used to belong, before the Revolution, to *Gospodăria de partid*, the Communist Party's Assets Department. In that house the Party's first secretary had lived, a man Goarnă imitated in many ways: dress, drinks, the accent used for some words, and even the way in which he held his cigarette in his fingers. Again like the former first secretary, on special occasions, he too would smoke Cuban cigars procured from a special supplier in Florida. As this was an entirely special moment, Goarnă welcomed us with the inevitable Cuban cigar, but in home attire, jeans and white, short-sleeved shirt, so that his muscles, well worked on in various fitness clubs, would show. Mrs Goarnă, on the other hand, was wearing a long, black dress, with a red rose above the right breast and, as a welcoming sign, she started to praise Claudia's dress and beauty:

"I don't think such an attractive creature lets you sleep

---

60 Commonly used paraphrase from the poem *Scrisoarea a III-a* (The Third Epistle), by Mihai Eminescu, widely considered Romania's national poet. It is used to refer the cream of society.

too peacefully. If you're not paying attention, you'll be left without her. Has your brother come out of prison?" she then enquired with a conspiratorial air, to which Claudia replied very drily:

"I think you're confused. This problem never even came up."

"Apologies. You probably don't even have any brothers. I was misinformed," she said, moving her eyes to the guests coming behind us, while Dan chatted with Goarnă.

"Doctor, we'll have to see each other again in a smaller circle. In a discreet poll, the president's popularity is under 35% and the numbers need to be driven up. But now it is important for you to feel good. You'll find here all political orientations: Lenin, Trotsky, Ceaușescu, Guevara, Marx, Antonescu, Brătianu and Maniu,[61] but especially those who are waiting to finance an electoral campaign for us, the like of which has never been seen before."

To me, he offered only two fingers by way of handshake, because, it was well understood, I did not matter for the future fights. But I didn't expect more either. An attendant appeared as if he'd sprung from the ground, and he led us to the table reserved for us, a table very close to that of the chief of the festivities. Near us were seated Professor Ghika-Șorecani, rector of a freshly established university, and Savu Boulescu, a prosperous businessman who, if the Social-Liberals won, was going to be given the Ministry

---

61 Marshall Ion Antonescu, de facto ruler of Romania between 1940-1944, during World War 2, an ally of Nazi Germany. The Brătianu family founded the Romanian Liberal Party at the end of the 19th Century. Iuliu Maniu was an important politician in Austro-Hungarian Transylvania and then in Greater Romania, after World War 1, founder of the Romanian National Peasant Party. Various members of the Brătianu family, as well as Maniu, remained prominent in successive governments until the advent of the communist state in 1947. Maniu and several Brătianu scions were then condemned to hard labour, and died in the communist prisons.

of Economics, or Finances, although – as he declared – he would be content with Internal Affairs as well. Until that time, he had to open his purse, because visibility is expensive, and you don't enter parliament without financial sacrifices. Their wives, corpulent and laden with jewels, had just returned from the distant Islands of Fiji and were unhappy with the conditions offered by the touring agency.

"I proposed to Puricel," said Mrs Boulescu, "that we should go to the Bahamas, and rent an island: the Isle of Happiness, for example. We could do such a thing once in our lives. Given that when we're home at he doesn't want us to get off the bed. I called him Puricel – my little flea – because he doesn't give me peace for one moment. He liked this nickname, so it stayed: Puricel! Like any tool, while it works, you'd better use it!"

Dan's forced laughter convinced me to imitate him. I knew these people pretty well, just as I knew many others: senators, deputies in parliament, prominent figures in all the fields of activity, and I was exercised by a painful feeling of being mismatched. What was I looking for here, among people I no longer fitted in with? Many falsified biographies, hidden pasts, social and political positions bought for heavy loads of money, professors with many books printed at their own expense with pocket-sized publishing houses, journalists of all kinds, apparent enemies who negotiated their prices periodically, and true enemies whom Goarnă had invited only in order to demonstrate his inclusivity. A motley world dominated by excess and flattery. The place of the previous party activists, who were arrogant and tastelessly dressed, was now taken over by small merchants, political and labour union activists, owners of businesses with sonorous names, dressed in expensive clothes bought from grand fashion houses. They were much more impertinent than their predecessors. They were racketeers and businessmen without anything sacred or non-negotiable. Ghika-Șorecani, who was extremely attentive, looked at the people coming to kiss Goarnă, or looking for their seats, and, seeing that I tracked his gaze, he whispered for each one of them:

"Mossad, F.S.B., C.I.A., D.S.T., belongs to the Hungarians, belongs to the Germans, this one belongs to anyone who wants him, this one's under cover, this one is a little chamber pot boy of the Democrat-Progressives."

I would have liked to ask him whether there was anyone who was one of ours, but, for a long time now, this *ours* no longer had any trace of meaning in real life. The country's men? But who, among the persons present, truly cared for the country? Especially since there was not much to steal from it anymore. I was looking at them, in my turn, with great pity, terrorised by the feeling that all my life up to that point had been an undisputable failure. To my mind there came, involuntarily, all the deeds in the mountains and, especially, the death of Moise, which had transformed many nights into harrowing nightmares. I also remembered the hopes desperately invested in each man or text that spoke differently or stepped out from the ranks. I was terribly hurt by the seconds, days, years, in which none of the hopes, invested with such candour and generosity in some person or other, could find any point of support. It was as if the entire body of expectations from those long and pressuring years had been brought back, alive and unchanged in my memory, precisely by the present company.

"Just look what I've waited for, and what's come instead! Did so many people die for this lot?"

That December morning, a warm, snowless and rainless

December, Daria had looked at me and kissed me *differently* than up to then. I felt the need to convince her not to leave home, but I didn't have the courage to follow up the thought, knowing I would be harshly refused. I too was going to the clinic, but my patients, protected by walls and medication, often led daily revolutions in worlds inaccessible to me, and, furthermore, while I felt that nothing would happen to me, I felt that she had to be protected. As in many other circumstances, my feelings, my premonition and my exaggerated care for her were rebuffed by her logic. Of the two of us, it was Daria who followed up her ideas to their logical conclusion. I knew it would be impossible for me to change her decision and it was as if I was sending her to her death myself, but, unfortunately, I was incapable of confessing this thought to her. Logic told me that anything could happen. Everything had the flavour of waiting and of dying. Each person was something else than what I knew, hiding something grave, decisive, unforeseeable. Not even I could any longer understand what I was, and what was the best way to react: the waiting had confused me. Should I safeguard myself, meaning that I should hide, knowing that after the fighters left, the cowards would come, along with the imposters and the sycophants? Should I go out in the streets, to liberate myself from the past, from fear, from cowardice, from my own self? Should I ask help from Death?

I left the clinic and, lost in the crowd shouting its fears and desires, I too had become a simple pawn, but I never felt more clearly than in those moments that I was free, that I simply existed. I didn't want to tell Daria that I would be there, in the square, although I would have liked to confess to her what I felt, but I suspected that she was somewhere else, trying to organise the crowds. Were I there with her, she would have probably been missed by that bullet. I had already lived through, in some way, this kind of moment and I had an absurd trust in my own luck.

I've been haunted by a painful and inexplicable feeling of guilt ever since. I've also been tormented by a feeling of uselessness. I was not capable of saving the human being who was closest to me. Everything that has happened to me from that time onwards, even that evening when Goarnă celebrated his half-centenary, were punishments which I considered to be deserved. Obsessed by memories, I wasn't paying attention at the moment when they asked for people to be silent, and when everyone present rose to their feet, as they sang the Anthem of Romania, and everyone felt obliged to mumble, as well as they could, and as much as they knew, the lyrics by Andrei Mureşanu. Then followed applause and, suddenly, the lights went off. They demanded silence again, a large screen appeared on the wall of the building, and, against the background of a fragment from *The Second Rhapsody* by Enescu, there appeared the golden effigy of Goarnă, under which was written in capital letters, also golden: A DIGNIFIED PAST, A BRILLIANT FUTURE: ROMANIA HAS FOUND HER PRESIDENT!

Immediately, on the screen, images of Cozia Monastery and the gentle waters of River Olt were followed by other images – easy to recognise – from the same historic province. The scythe-wielders on a very wide field of wheat were accompanied in silent tones by *Mă făcu muica oltean, măiiii – My mother's brought up a man of Olt*, the celebrated local "anthem," sung by an unknown with a rather unpractised voice, which made Puricel wonder whether it was sung by the birthday boy himself.

"It's not impossible," Sava Bobulescu agreed with the premise. "I heard that he does everything by himself in that party. Or, well, almost everything, because he is married."

"Well, I do know some married men who do not ignore, if I may say so, the practices of their childhood," said Mrs Boulescu, without any apparent connection to the reference made by her husband, after which she asked us to be silent since the story of an exemplary career had begun to play, a career which, without any doubt, would have a great impact on the history of the country.

"A very important year for the history of mankind," the announcer's baritone voice said. "The Soviet Union, the former communist empire, launched the first cosmonaut in the world, Yuri Gagarin, a success hard to deny, which, back in those days, won serious advances in the competition later won by the Americans. The same year, the French president Charles de Gaulle would visit Romania with the capital city of our province, Craiova, also being part of his itinerary. We find ourselves in a moment where the history of relations with France and the world sees a major step forward. Eternal France, our elder sister nation of the Latins, remembered us and drew our attention, by means of her most official representative, the legendary General de Gaulle, to the fact that we have a common future, that history would step in front of us on our predestined road. This year is beneficial for the history of Romania, especially because of the fact that, in Moțăței-Haltă, a person who is known and respected by the whole world was born: Matei Goarnă. His ancestor trumpeted, in the most ancient Oltenian locality of Moțăței, on this musical instrument, which accompanied him during his whole life, the victory of the *dorobanți* soldiers in Pleven, in the 1877 Independence War. Who doesn't know that the great painter, Nicolae Grigorescu, immortalised a trumpeter who was sounding the attack signal in the unforgettable War of Independence? Well, the trumpeters of that time were the same who announced the dawn that, look! has come after years of suffering, blind fumblings, and communist terror. History knows how to select her chosen ones and to watch over their path through time."

Then, naturally, followed the steps of history and, of course, the steps of the future great politician. What was he doing during the Cuban rockets crisis? In what segment of his personal journey was young Goarnă the year that the American president John Fitzgerald Kennedy was killed? In what way did he understand the 'Prague Spring', and where was Unit-Leader Pioneer Matei Goarnă when Prague was invaded, at a time when a little something of his great potential feeling to love and for understanding history overflowed, for a moment, to also include Ceaușescu. Even back then, despite his young years, he was stepping in the same rhythm, as that country, and the entire country of Romania opposed the invasion of another brotherly nation. He had lived through one of the propitious moments of history, the moment when every Romanian was ready to sacrifice himself in the name of the hope of a better future symbolised by the 'Prague Spring'. Young Goarnă had felt, in the few days when the dictator changed masks, not the death of hope – but the value of freedom. The speech in the seaside resort of Mangalia, in 1971, the debut of the mini-cultural revolution, showed Ceaușescu's true colours. His fear of change and freedom convinced the young man of those days about the fact that men who are afraid are men who lose, and that it is important to reach a position – as high as possible – in the political hierarchy, in order to convince the masses of your value.

I watched, without any sense of involvement, the images – family photos – that populated the screen: Goarnă as a schoolboy pioneer, Goarnă on parade, Goarnă visiting a building site with his pioneer unit, Goarnă Senior, the Communist Party activist, throwing a ball at a basketball hoop, followed by his son's admiring gaze, then Goarnă Junior, now a teenager, receiving a diploma from the hands of a female teacher. And on and on: Goarnă as a student at the school of Electro-technics, and, after many other images in which he was partying with his young girlfriend – the wife of later years, both members of the central leadership of the student body, there came Goarnă as a student in Paris, which is where the Romanian Revolution found him. The ideals for which he had fought were almost ready to be accomplished. He quit the university in a hurry, immediately after Ceauşescu got shot, and, in January of the following year, in front of the Government's building, where the crowds demanded the death of communism, young Goarnă jumped on "that particular tank, the tank which was a symbol of the fight for freedom and democracy, so that today he could be in a situation where he is able to fight for the foremost position of state, and where he might be the person with the most right to earn that position."

Running in parallel with the historic events that changed the fate of important human communities, and even that of the world, there came, on the screen, important moments from the biography of the future candidate for the presidency. I hope that I haven't missed out any idea from the panegyric to Goarnă, but the film was far from being over, and I had really lost my patience. Daria somehow materialised, I felt her by my side, and, in her unfailingly kind, and protective voice, she asked what was I doing there. Of course, I was not in a place and among people with whom I was compatible. She – poor woman – could not know that the people who had not fought were the winners; that, in the name of freedom, the amoral and the faithless had imposed their rules. I was not among my own, but where… oh where… is my world?

It's probable that, without realising it, I had started to get agitated, because Dan came closer and enquired whether I had some physical discomfort – but not if there was an intellectual problem.

"You must not lose your sense of humour. I don't think there is long to go. I didn't know and I didn't even suspect there would be screenings from the well-known soap opera: the Catastrophes of Freedom!"

"If the film bores you, look at the legs of some women," Claudia also whispered to me. "There's a lot to see. Not one of them goes to bed free of charge. The offer starts from a jeep upwards! And with the gold and diamonds on each one of these madams you could live for at least one long summer in the most pretentious foreign resort. They say those fat women have diamonds pierced not only in their bellybuttons but also further down. But I ask myself who the hell is sleeping with them."

"They would not have placed the piercings if they didn't have spectators," I answered. "The spectators are able to pay for them."

But such a possibility had not yet passed through Claudia's mind, and it was ridiculous to discuss it now, at the moment when there came to the screen the opinions of colleagues and friends, and especially, the opinions of the voters from the most distant corners of the country. Naturally, they had started with the neighbours in Moțăței-Halță.

"He was an admirable child," said the former schoolmistress, a respectable old lady; and from the hesitation in her voice one could deduce that she didn't remember him at all. "He was the first to do his homework, the first to raise his hand in class. Maybe too lively, but all children that age are the same. He was at the head of the Pioneers back then. In any case, his father could not even conceive of anything less."

After the schoolmistress, again naturally, the village priest followed: "Despite the times of sad memory when attending church and baptising children constituted, in the eyes of the rulers of the times, grave failings and obscurantist practices, his parents insisted on baptising him in secret. They wished to call him Gheorghe, the most common name back then, but I suggested they should call him Matei – Matthew, like the Apostle of Our Lord Jesus Christ, so that the sign of the lion would be with him for his entire life! Gheorghe Gheorghiu-Dej, the old communist leader, will die one day and be forgotten, but Matei stays; that's what I counselled them, and they listened to me. I remember that, at the contact with the water, the child cried a lot, but I liked the fact that he was opposing it, that he had personality. But I did not suspect the value I had in front of me, and what a brilliant career awaited him. His father helped me in the fight with the neo-protestant sects, and his son, the great politician of today, as a Pioneer – the way things were back then – would gather the children who were his underlings in the Pioneer unit, and, led by an instructor, they would go and blow their trumpets as the religious sects were holding their meetings!"

Then came the turn of the people from Moțăței-Village

and Moțăței-Station, who gave way to people at the forefront of the political party, and then it was the turn of the numerous cultural figureheads who had joined this particular party.

"He is a brilliant militant," said Andrei Covurlui, the former leader of the party, "rallying around him, our international politics and the country will have much to gain. Mr Matei Goarnă has qualities which separate him categorically from the rest of the competitors. To his intelligence, to his know-how and his political culture, we have to add the charisma which nobody can deny. With him at the forefront, and with a new Constitution in which the role of the head of state would be different, with greater powers of decision, the country will gain the thing which all Romanians have been waiting for since the Revolution: a leading role in the assembly of nations."

Over the effigy of Goarnă was then superimposed, unexpectedly, the face of "the great scientist Raoul Ghika-Șorecani, one of the exports of Romanian science," and, suddenly, the entire hall moved their eyes to our table. "Great men from any field of activity, from sciences, the arts or even from politics, are rare, they appear in crucial moments, in order to clarify, or often, stir up the stagnant waters of history. Mr Goarnă is, and everybody knows this, an emissary of destiny, a torch in a moment of historical confusion, a hope in an era of sorrow and misunderstanding, a light in the night created by the current incompetent powers-that-be."

"Would that I had sent him back inside his mother's belly, the impostor," Ghika-Șorecani whispered, annoyed, and scratching his intensely dyed black beard. "He asked me for this statement for his personal archives, and look how he's taking advantage of it! In fact, I didn't have too much wrong: he could an agent of destiny. If the old woman had an arsehole she'd be a minister for war! I gave him a chance, it very much depends what he'll do with it. I can't see why these idiots are ogling me, since everyone present are his friends or admirers, and absolutely all of them are waiting for a crumb if this boy wins."

In the end, the film ended with the effigy of Goarnă superimposed on a tricoloured Romania. The music: the Hymn of Europe. *Joyful, joyful, we adore Thee.*[62] There followed, of course, prolonged applause and ovations, during which Goarnă, with eyes bathed in tears, climbed the stage in order to thank us all for the way in which we had understood and appreciated the surprise presented by his family. But he had to wipe his tears away immediately, as his father – who'd had rather too much to drink – also climbed on the stage, and started to sing an old revolutionary song of the communists:

> *From the prison of Doftana I gaze through iron bars,*
> *And far away, in the distance, I see a patch of sky...*

Unfortunately he could not go beyond the first two lyrics because the bodyguards, at the son's signal, took him away but without being able to put a stop to the flow of his curses: "*Băi*, poofters, is this your freedom of speech?"

So that the laughter would not prolong in any way the state of confusion created by the old man, Goarnă's daughter put in an appearance on the stage. She was a student at Cambridge, a fragile creature, with the face of a teenager. She dedicated to her father, and not quite by accident, a

---

62   The Romanian lyrics to the Ode begin with *Slavă ție, stea curată* – Glory to you, O pure star.

poem by William Blake, *My Pretty Rose Tree*:

> *A flower was offered to me:*
> *Such a flower as May never bore;*
> *But I said "I've a pretty rose tree"*
> *And I passed the sweet flower o'er.*

The applause, which was actually well deserved, was interrupted by the appearance on the stage of Goarnă and his friend, Cătălin Vâslaşu, a well-known singer of romantic songs, excessively popularised by the local television channels; and, without warning us, they started singing, together with the entire audience, *Pe lângă plopii fără soţ... – Down where the lonely poplars grow*. Goarnă's father, stimulated by the melody, tried to come out from behind the stage. This time around, Miss Spring, confidante of Mrs Goarnă, who had come accompanied by 30 bodyguards, saw him and she gestured discreetly to her people to keep the old man in his place until the singers finished the recital. By my side, Mrs Boulescu could not restrain her antipathy for Cristina Bobu, Miss Spring:

"Puricel darling, what is this stinking tramp doing with so many bodyguards? What does she need them for? Why should they guard her? Can't you see she looks like a hat stand?"

"Why do you need to ask?" said Puricel a little louder, so that we could hear him as well. "Well, ten people are riding her, ten are waiting for their turn, and the other ten keep watch so that they won't be caught by the pimp, the man with the custom built Mercedes."

Hearing them speak, Dan looked at me, convinced that I had lost my sense of humour for good: he's always known the moment that I couldn't take things anymore and he would try, each time, to prevent my boiling over.

"Nobody forces me to see any more cretins. I have enough of those as my in-patients," I explained, and Dan felt the need to justify himself:

"We live in an environment created by them, and for themselves. Should I climb on the stage and explain to these people who're applauding him that they are making a great mistake? In a matter of minutes, I would be kicked out to the general applause of everybody here, although the immense majority of those present despise the birthday boy. Stupidity is not, was not, and will never be discreet. It cannot live without being courted, without having enthusiastic supporters, without scoundrels."

"My dear boy," I said to him, "it's around this age that Ceaușescu also went off the rails. All the suckers believed they could master him, whereas the truth....but now I realise that Nicolae Ceaușescu was assassinated for nothing!"

"Are you suggesting this man should also be liquidated, nipped in the bud?" asked Dan.

"No," I replied, "I'm suggesting we should find out why this type of malformation appears. They can't come into being just like that, out of the blue, without the support of some idiotic courtiers who they will eliminate the moment they've reached their goal."

The people at the table rose to their feet in order to chase the numbness away and, of course, in order to express, in clear voices, their unmediated admiration for the quality of the film.

"A new redeemer of the nation. This is what we deserve. You stay here, you are young," I said to Dan and Claudia, deciding to leave. "I've lived through this kind of moment before. I'll take advantage of this circumstance in order to sneak away gently towards the exit. Nobody will notice me, because I only have the past left to me. I belong to another world, but I don't know which world, and I still haven't answered an old question of mine. What kind of people are we if we have got to the point of tolerating, for such a long time, all the nonsense of impostors?"

> *It is impossible to say what kind of shout*
> *is my shout: it is true it's horrifying –*
> *so much so that it disfigures my features,*
> *making them resemble the snout of a beast –,*
> *but, in some way, it also is happy,*
> *so that it reduces me to being a child.*
> *It is a shout meant to invoke somebody's attention;*
> *or their aid, but, maybe, also to curse him.*
> *It is a shout that means to announce,*
> *in this uninhabited place, that I exist.*
> *Or maybe not just that I exist, but that I know. It is a shout*
> *in which, in the depths of my disquiet,*
> *one feels humble accents of hope;*
> *or a shout of certainty, an absolutely absurd hope,*
> *inside which resounds, in all its purity, despair.*
> *In any case, one thing is certain: anything*
> *this shout of mine might want to mean,*
> *it is destined to endure beyond any possible*
> *end.*
> Pier Paolo Pasolini – *Teorema*

"Old man," Mara said to me through her tears, "promise you won't leave me." I assured her of that I wouldn't. I swore to that, but I still didn't manage to convince her. Her entire being expressed a refusal which she had not, as yet, the courage to utter.

"We'll stay for a while, and we'll see if you can adapt. If you don't want to settle in town, we'll return, and, it's well understood, I'll stay with you for as long as the Lord on High will suffer me," I replied to her, somewhat dissatisfied that she had abandoned herself to me, just like the thousands of patients who saw in me their eyes and a walking stick, in a world which they feared.

I sat on the stairs, gazing, maybe for the last time, at the way the mists in the valley rose towards us, isolating us, giving the sensation that we belonged to the cold, shining sky that spread itself out, above us, unfeeling like an unaccomplished promise, and I strove in vain to write down in some way the feelings that visited me at the moment when we had only a few hours left before leaving.

Unfortunately, I lost myself among the words like a blind man in a desert of questions. A terrible feeling of dissatisfaction increased with each attempt to describe what I feel, but I tried to console myself with the thought that perhaps the answers are waiting for us in the world beyond, from which we came and to which we shall return.

Lord, I said to myself, powerlessness and ignorance are transferring all the anxieties and questions from over here, to that supposed world. Answers? For the moment, what do I know as definite, as incontestable? What could I say to this girl? What was I looking for? What must she truly learn about this life? How can I explain, I wonder, that the secret probably resides in the Word that moves the energies and the billions of worlds revealed by the Hubble telescope? The Word that creates them in order to destroy them, and then destroys them in order to cause them to be born again.

In the thousandth part of a second which has splintered away from eternity for us, we love, we hate, we toil and we die with the hope that we are going to be born again with a different face, without a part of the sorrows and fears which huddle together in our wretched bodies, without the anxieties that direct our thoughts away from the true questions. In the same thousandth part of a second, that unseen hand took me everywhere, and threw me wherever it pleased, even here, in the mountains.

Most of the time it would only be after I got to a specific place that I would discover the profound significance of being there. Now, and this is more than certain, I would be obliged to save a creature who confuses me, who gives me life but also death, in equal proportions. A reward or a punishment? We'll see, I say to myself. If I should have the time. In any case, Mara will be left with this massive notebook from which she will only learn that I have lived, and that I have looked for myself, for my whole life, in everything that happened to me, and in everything with which I came into contact. For me, clear thinking moments also meant, at a different level, failed attempts to free myself from the loneliness which, especially after Daria's departure, followed me everywhere I went.

As if almost obsessed, I also looked for *something else* as yet not uttered or conceived, a space that might be capable of satisfying me, and, not just a few times, I felt extremely close to it, like being in front of a miracle or a philosophy, which could save us from all our fumbling for meaning. Unfortunately, I never managed to pass *beyond*, and knowledge – however complex it might be – cannot defend you from the brutality of time, our merciless executioner.

I would also like to leave Mara a letter through which I will ask her to destroy this notebook, which, in any case, will not be of use to anyone. We always make the same errors because we do not truly learn anything. In particular, we ask those questions whose answers we know in advance. With all this, I persist in the same error of looking closely at myself with fury and despair. I will probably destroy it myself after I have taken the story to its conclusion. I am writing and I don't know what I hope to discover, but I have to admit that, for the time being, I feel incapable of taking the next step. I am bizarrely impeded by my faith in a miracle, by Mara, by the mists that isolate us from the rest of the world, by the grass, by the leaves of trees, by the violent storms and frozen skies, by the ants and the beasts of the woods, by the still very good rhythm of my heart, by the unconquered mountain, and even by the existence of this first notebook, which, as you see, ends now.

> *"There is enough time to begin to live just when one has to stop!"*
> Seneca – *Dialogues*

> Madame du Barry, on the scaffold: *"One minute more, monsieur executioner."*
> Albert Camus – *Notebooks*

I am leaving, but one thing is repugnant to me: someone's pity. On the other hand, Mr Executioner, things have been and will always be the way you wanted, I know this. I am ready, but until that time, until *that moment*, you have no power over me. You cannot stop me from rebelling, from loving and detesting, from believing stubbornly that, by dying, I will discover something which I never managed to discover while I was alive.